Surya

Scarlet Darkwood

DARK BOOKS
PRESS

Text and Cover Design: Simply Defined Art

Artistic Image: Jay Aheer

Formatting: Will Armstrong

Chapter One

The world of Atlantis lay within Surya's grasp. The fact that it rested on a planet over thirty thousand light years away from his own didn't matter. There was something about this place one couldn't fully understand by merely reading about it or viewing it through a lens. The island of Poseidia must be felt, breathed, lived.

"You really want to go through with this?" Del-El squared off, facing Surya. A leather bag swung from his hand.

Together they stood on a patch of barren land known as the "orbital edge" of Ontarus 9, a planet in the Lyra Constellation. At the proper time, a portal would appear.

"You didn't see what I did. Humans have tendencies with each other. The way they touch, the way they look when they're together. They're feeling something we don't. I have to do this. I want to feel what it's like to be human."

Surya remembered the view from the lens in his father's royal observatory. He had watched with heightened curiosity as a young woman's unclothed body moved in perfect synchronicity with the man on top. He clearly viewed the man's back and the way his muscles tightened on delivering the last thrust from the lower part of his body. The movement sent the woman in a heady shudder of pure ecstasy. Surya knew it by the look on her face and the way her fingers raked over the man's back, leaving stripes of throbbing red. The vision would never leave his mind. The color of her hair, the hues of her skin, the tips of her breasts, all lit up in vivid colors from the darkest black to the most curious shade of pink.

"I hope we've covered our tracks well enough with you planning this. At least I'll have a good head start before my father finds out." Surya cast a worried glance at his friend. "Make sure you have your story ready, if anybody asks."

Den-El shook his head. "You are really taking a chance going there. Alone. You have no idea what to expect. Being royalty, a prince, makes this project especially dangerous."

"You're my best friend. Thank you for sticking your neck out for me. It means everything."

The two men had decided earlier that it would be best for Den-El to work on the particulars of this voyage to Atlantis. Living in a fourth-dimension world, both knew that detailed deep thinking not only created thought forms, but also led to their manifestation. Reality. The last thing Surya wanted was his father Mal-Ek to tap into a thread of ideas where Atlantis, on a forbidden planet, was concerned. His father most likely would not think of Den-El as quickly. With any luck, never.

"I still can't believe you're going to Atlantis for a girl. A human. Substandard. You know nothing about her or humans."

Surya answered, "She won't let me go. She haunts my dreams, intrudes on my thoughts during the day. And I can't get any new information from the Infinite Hall of Records. They've shut down tighter than an animal trap on unwary prey."

"Agree. It's locked down tight. I barely got information that led us here. Whatever it is, the powers that be don't want us finding out more about Atlantis." Den-El frowned.

Surya nodded. "Blame that on Father. He will not discuss the records I read on his desk."

"You had no business reading records that didn't belong to you, and I can't believe you admitted it to him. It was forbidden knowledge, and you know it." Den-El's eyes flashed with emotion.

"Can't help it. He caught me red-handed. Serves him right for being so careless."

Den-El opened his mouth to rebuttal his friend's statement, but Surya cut him off.

"Besides, I just turned twenty. That's the age I start learning how to rule our country. He was bound to discuss it sooner or later."

"Surya, you don't know that he would have ever discussed it with you."

"Look, we can argue all day, but there's no other choice. If I don't find this girl, I'll be doomed forever. Locked in her spell."

"You're so dramatic." Den-El laughed. "You have more power than she does. More than any of them on Earth, really." He sobered a minute. "But maybe you need to go and get that place and her out of your system."

Surya nodded. "I'll find her. I'm not totally without information, Den-El. I remember the bits I've read and the visions I saw through the lens. Maybe all I have is all I need. It looked advanced enough for my satisfaction."

Bits of information didn't begin to describe how little he had. From his father's records the following words glowed in his mind:

Project: Earth Experiments

Operation: Human Genesis

Status: Failed

Task: Abort

Other words he had briefly read popped into his mind: genetic programming, humanoid vessels, great race, disconnection, "Things."

Before shutting out the light of knowledge, The Infinite Hall of Records grudgingly showed him the following:

Law of One, Sons of Belial, heart-centered.

Much to his dismay, he always saw two additional words light up and move in line next to the other words at the end: failed, abort.

Surya stared at his friend. "I'm telling you something. It is a waste for the Galactic Federation of Planets to abandon their darlings, Earth and humans. It's irresponsible. You do not abandon a beloved creation you worked so hard to manifest. Especially when it lives and breathes."

"And you don't go after a strange woman just because lust grabbed you where it counts most. That, too, is irresponsible." Den-El cocked an eyebrow.

"Says you." Surya folded his arms over his chest.

"Your optimism will serve you well." Den-El patted his friend's shoulder and glanced at the sun blazing in the sky. "We only have a little time left before you go. I've brought some things you can use while you're there. Or at least get you started."

With gratitude, Surya took the leather bag from Den-EL. "Thank you. Something to remember you by?" He grinned.

"Think of me when you use them." The young man's eyes clouded. "You will come back, won't you, Surya? Don't be like the others who became smitten with that place."

"You worry way too much. I won't get that sucked in."

"Until you do. I just get a bad feeling about this." Den-El's gaze fixed on Surya. "I got a quick peek at all the coordinates, frequencies, and timing before the Hall of Records locked me out. In five minutes, our planet, Earth, and the sun will line up. The current rotation aligns Ontarus 9 and Atlantis with an old portal of theirs. Our people used it thousands of years ago, before the second destruction. You leave then."

Surya nodded, clutching the bag tighter. "You think anybody will be guarding it?"

"Don't know. We can hope for the best. Oh, by the way. I made you a human vessel, a body of skin you will slip into when you cross over. I've programmed it to your soul frequency so there's a seamless union between you and it. I've also added a language capacitor, so you can speak to the people." Den-El's lips pulled into a wide smile. "I gave you every advantage I could. Not bad. If I were a woman, I might be okay with you." He laughed, smacking his friend on the back.

"You think I'll be as helpless as a baby, don't you?"

"I'm not taking any chances. You're my best friend." Den-El's expression went blank. His body stilled. Without a word, he turned Surya in a direction that didn't face anything in particular. "Get ready."

Before Surya eyes, a wall of shimmering waves formed. They reminded him of heat radiating from something hot. As the seconds ticked by, the waves became denser. He quickly glanced around. Everything else looked the way it did when he and Den-El arrived, except for this band of waves that stretched out enough to accommodate a human body.

"When I say 'now,' you jump through." Den-El stood behind Surya.

Surya's neurons fired off with such frantic energy, he feared passing into the fifth dimension. He could back out if he wanted. Surely he could force the strange woman out of his mind, block her like he'd been blocked from the Hall of Records.

"Three. Two. One. Now!" Den-El pushed. Surya jumped through the radiating waves. Den-El tossed the human skin through the portal at the same time.

The experience was like none Surya had ever felt before. His mind whirled in time. Visions of him and Mal-Ek in the observation room, his own bedroom, the meditation room he'd created, Den-El's smiling face, flashes of light switching to darkness. All and more passed by faster than scenes and realities moved on Ontarus 9. His body took on a strange sensation, a weightiness he had never felt before. Sometimes if he slipped into lower vibrations on Ontarus 9, he sensed more of a heaviness in his being. His skin would thicken slightly and turn a pale pink grayish hue, as opposed to the normal thin white texture.

But this time, there was no snapping himself out of whatever mood had lowered his frequency at home. The third dimension contained its own frequency and set of natural laws, and the gravitational pull shocked him in countless ways. His soul locked onto the body Den-El had created. In a nanosecond, body and soul became one living unit. The physical joining fired up every nerve, leaving Surya with the sensation of having crashed to the ground. A blast of pain radiated all over him. He barely breathed.

"Take deep breaths. Inhale. Exhale."

The voice in Surya's head belonged to none other than Den-El. His friend had lingered by the portal, making sure everything went well.

"Yes . . . Okay." Surya's eyes slowly opened. The blast of sunshine nearly blinded him. Pain shot through his eyes. "Ahh, that hurts." Did he just talk in a human voice, even if it came out as a hoarse whisper? This was encouraging. He could speak. He followed Den-El's commands. Breathing took a level of concentration much higher than where he came from. He ached all over.

"You're okay. You didn't crash. Just keep breathing. In. Out."

Surya took some deeper breaths, acclimating to his new body and mind by degrees. He touched the grass beneath him. Soft, rustling, with a smell that could only be described as coming from Earth source itself. A warm breeze blew over him. He wiggled his fingers, his toes. Little by little, the nerves in his body computed in synchronicity with his brain. Through squinted eyes, he quickly noted the afternoon sun high in the sky.

"Get dressed fast. Someone may see you."

"Okay, okay." The stronger sound of his own voice grated in his ears.

Rolling over took a concerted effort. His brain commands and muscular coordination were sluggish at best. Surya blinked several times, desperately focusing his eyes so he didn't see double. He looked around for the leather bag and found it beside him. With shaky hands, he opened it and peeked inside. He located some clothes. Undergarments, two pairs of trousers, and coordinating shirts.

Colors of black, gray, yellow, and blue met his eyes. He rubbed his fingers in wonder over the softness of cotton material. So this is what clothing felt like. His five senses kicked in with increasing comfort and speed. The clothing resembled what he remembered when he viewed the people of Atlantis through the lens, right before seeing the couple. He'd viewed the whole island of Poseidia, including the gorgeous lands of concentric rings.

His lips pulled into a wide smile. How unusual feeling the body respond to such an intense degree. Back home, scenes passed swiftly with a dream-like quality. Emotions brightened and faded in an instant. Sometimes he knew things without direct logic behind it. The slowly fading memory of his former life ratcheted up a certain nervousness. Forgetting where he came from would be a huge mistake. Dangerous.

The fact that his fear didn't result in an automatic shift in his environment to one of darkness with frightening creatures relieved him. He liked this third-dimensional stability. He wiggled into a set of undergarments, trousers and a shirt. Muscle coordination became easier the more he moved. There were a few other dress items in the bag.

Surya quickly pulled out a soft thin black leather belt and wrapped it around his waist, tying it off in a clumsy knot. Last but not least, he fished out a fine pair of leather sandals. After sliding those on his feet, he worked his way into a standing position, lifting slowly. His head spun while his heart raced with the exertion. He stopped, stretched out his arms for balance, and steadied himself.

"I'm leaving you, now. You can always call if you need us" Den-El's voice faded.

Without a word, Surya waved his hand toward the sky. His friend was gone. He knew it. For the first time, solitude hit him. He was alone in a strange land.

For several minutes, he stood on the clear grassy area near the portal. Apparently, he was on a remote, rural side of the island. Lots of woods, trees, green grass dotted with rocks peeking out. Not a city remotely in sight. The sun blazed down hot and strong. He pulled back one sleeve of his tunic, fearing his skin might combust with the heat. He viewed solid, smooth, pale skin with pink undertones, slender hands and fingers.

He swiped his hair with his hand. The tickling sensation from the slow drip of sweat set him on edge. It was time to walk. Find the City of The Golden Gates, do something. Find the woman.

Turning left out of the small clearing, he reached a dry dirt, rocky road. He walked onward, taking in the view around him. The countryside lit up with colors of deep greens, gray, and the soft blue of the sky. Small stone homes dotted the landscape. Cows, sheep, and goats grazed. Occasionally a farmer smiled and waved at him. Surya returned the gesture. Humans seemed friendly enough.

In the distance, he saw the first sign. It read, Air Lift Taxi 2 miles ahead. How long had he been walking? Would he make it? The sun had already singed his cheeks. A couple of toes stung with blisters. His legs ached. His desire for a quick way to the City of The Golden Gates burned strong. He imagined himself farther down the road, moving toward his concept of what an air lift taxi looked like.

"Need a ride?" A man's voice called out.

Surya whirled around. He'd been so engrossed in reaching the City, he hadn't heard anyone or anything from behind. His eyes widened. A man sat inside a slender vehicle. "Sure. I'm going to the Air Taxi."

"I'll take you. Go around to the other side." The man smiled.

***

Hidden in the distance several yards away, a lone man watched Surya ride off with the stranger. Khaluj had seen the extra-terrestrial come through the portal and hidden himself just in time. Did his mind play a trick on him? He stayed and watched everything to make sure the vision wasn't a dream. How strange for a star creature to use that portal now, especially since nothing had come through it for at least several thousand years. Why did the young man come? Were others like him following?

Dropping his immediate plans for the afternoon, he tracked Surya with the stealth of a tiger on the hunt, keeping his distance and staying well out of sight. If this young man were indeed from another galaxy more advanced than Earth, this could be a game-changer—if he could manipulate events in his favor. In his mind, he'd do it or die trying. Khaluj glanced at the ornate golden time piece dangling from his belt.

The secret meeting he had originally planned on the neighboring island of Aryan would have to wait. He must find out more about this new visitor. Khaluj turned his eyes toward the whistling sound in a nearby tree. He spied a bird ruffling its feather on one of the branches. Concentrating his thoughts, he sent out waves of benevolence and love, requesting that the animal come to him for a favor. The bird flew in his direction, landing on his shoulder.

Khaluj psychically tuned into the bird's frequency. "Dear friend, would you be kind enough to follow the gray vehicle that just passed and give me details on the young man inside?" Twittering, the bird inched closer to Khaluj's ear. "I will meet you in three hours in front of Orubis Way Apartments." The bird blinked and dipped its head up and down in acknowledgement. With a quick chirp, it flew off down the road.

Khaluj chuckled. Like his ancestor, the great King Belial, he had the gift of telepathy with animals. People of Atlantis this day and age, regardless of the island on which they lived, didn't use many divine gifts anymore. Not like they did before the first and second destructions.

Their connection with spirit sank along with everything else, it seemed. They'd become mundane, earthbound. Though many of the priests could still practice their gifts at fifth dimensions or higher, even they were losing their abilities fast.

No matter. Khaluj had decided a long time ago that he owned the ideals that his ancestor started thousands of years ago. Along with the strength of his organization, he would show people the error of their ways and lead them to another truth—the realization that they were gods. In his heart and soul, Sons of Belial would prevail.

***

Mal-Ek found himself in a dark place on Ontarus 9. Blackness dripped all around him. Thousands of gray faces loomed. Through their wide open misshapen mouths, they cried out with mournful wails that ripped through his soul. His heart seemed in tatters, each beat painful at best.

He wouldn't have believed it if he hadn't looked through the lens himself. The sight of his son, a royal prince, walking among strangers—humans, of all things—on another planet in another galaxy was too much to bear. Where had he gone wrong as a father? Where had he failed? Mal-Ek chastised himself for not acting sooner after Surya and he talked that fateful day in the observation room. Closing off certain subject matter from the Hall of Records and locking down information in the books on his desk had been futile.

How had Surya obtained the knowledge to get on planet Earth without any transportation? His eyes narrowed. Someone or something had helped. Worse, how would he explain this chain of events to the Galactic Federation of Planets? Mal-Ek closed his eyes and wept.

Chapter Two

"Where are you from?" The man driving glanced over at Surya. He narrowed his eyes briefly before turning his attention back to the road.

Surya's mind whirled. He had no idea what to say. "I—"

The man snapped his fingers, smiling. "Now I know. You look like the ones from Scandinavia. The light skin, golden hair. That's it." He nodded in Surya's direction. "We don't get many of them here, but there are a few like you."

"Yes, that's exactly where I'm from." Surya let out a soft breath. Other than basic human surface characteristics, he was pretty sure that there wasn't a soul like him on Atlantis.

"What do you plan on doing here? Any family? Friends?"

"I'm alone. Came on a small ship with some nice people who let me ride with them." Good thing Surya knew a little geography of Earth.

The driver smiled. "Sometimes a man must make it on his own, seek his fortune in the world."

"True," said Surya. In his mind, a nice beautiful woman would go well with that fortune too. Where would he even begin to look for this mysterious lady he'd seen through the lens?

The man turned the wheel around a curve. In the distance, Surya saw the Air Lift Taxi port. A simple white wooden building sat next to a large dark square patch of land. Nothing sat within the square's boundaries but an enormous elongated fat balloon carrying what resembled some kind of metal cargo container a little smaller and much narrower in size.

"This is it," said the man. He pulled up next to the building and stopped.

"Thank you very much, Sir." Surya gathered up his bag and got out of the car.

"Best of luck to you, young man. Welcome to Atlantis." The man backed away and turned his vehicle onto the open road.

Shading his eyes from the sun, Surya stared up at the balloon. The body of the craft appeared to have been designed with an inner framework covered by either linen or leather. He couldn't tell. The bigger question, was it safe?

He slipped into the building. The moment he did, several people glanced up at him and stared several seconds, puzzled. There must not be many Scandinavians in the rural parts of the island. Perhaps the city would be different. Turning his head, he quickly discovered the ticket counter. Three staff members sold passes to customers waiting in line. A large sign hung on the wall behind them. The itinerary for the day glowed in bright blue letters. When would the next taxi go to the City of The Golden Gates?

Surya found a vacant chair in a deserted corner and sat down. He had no idea what Den-El had packed in the leather bag. Would he even have money to buy his way on a balloon taxi? One thing he knew, the leather bag had grown heavier the longer he carried it. If it hadn't been for the man's generosity, he would have been supine on the side of the road until he built up energy to move again.

He rummaged through his belongings, happy at once to see his full collection of crystals and stones that he used in his meditation temple back home. Searching for the right stone and energy level all over again would have been a monumental task, especially in a strange land. In the pile of items lay a journal and two pillar candles. Something gleamed at the bottom. Surya plucked up a gold disc resting on top of several others and smiled.

It was like the orichalcum coin he'd taken from his father's desk. He ran his finger over the surface, feeling the indentations with his fingertips. The coin flashed. Brilliant. Seductive. Tempting. Residue of energy from every human who'd touched it hit his senses in a dizzying array of vignettes. Faces, emotions, snatches of their lives sped by him.

Sitting back in the chair, he gazed at the coin, quickly recalling the day in the observation room when his father caught him viewing Atlantis through the lens.

"What are you doing in here?" Dismay from his parent flowed all over him.

Mal-Ek scowled. "And what are you looking at?" He tapped gently on the lens. "You've been in here a lot lately."

"I'm viewing Atlantis." Surya wished he could have kept his secret a while longer.

"See anything interesting down there? Anything strike your fancy?" Mal-Ek paused, grimacing. "On second thought, don't answer that."

Surya's cheeks warmed. Mal-Ek had barely tapped into his last view of the woman and her lover.

"Tell me what you saw on my desk. Those were top secret papers." Mal-Ek stared at his son.

"I'm sorry, Father. You didn't block the coordinates of this room or the work on your desk, so I just came in, that's all."

Mal-Ek shook his head. "I step away a second, and here you come." The older man narrowed his eyes. "And curiosity got the better of you, yes?"

"You know we're a curious people by nature." Surya grinned. He had hoped that a little levity would make his father open up more. "When I saw the books on the desk . . . and those coins . . ." He quickly reverted his mind away from the spare one resting deep in his pocket, lest his father catch on.

The older man stared straight ahead with a thoughtful expression in his eyes. "Those coins are from Atlantis. Orichalcum, a metal forged of copper and gold. A metal like no other. It won't be easily replicated or found anywhere else on Earth, either. That much I foresee."

"You foresee a lot more, Father." Surya smiled at his parent. For a much older man, Mal-Ek still looked youthful and quite attractive at his age by any standard. He also admired his father's great skill of being able to accurately tap into likely future events based on present time-space circumstances. "Why do you want to end the human project on Earth? By the way, I didn't read everything on your desk."

"You'd be spending numerous hours reading everything in those books and records. There's way more than that hidden away. They must be kept safe. We must never forget."

"Forget what? What happened that was so bad that you have to keep it hidden? We learn from what we do. There should be no shame in that." Surya insisted on this discussion. He would get to the bottom of this mysterious, beautiful Atlantis and the questionable Human Genesis project. Clearly, both held a sordid past. He wanted to learn more.

Mal-Ek reached for his son's arm and placed his hand lightly on it. "It's not so much shame as caution. Here's the long and short of it. We of the Lyra Constellation are great beings, with divine powers reflecting the Logos Creator. Earth was uninhabited when we discovered it. We thought populating such a place with beings much like us would be a wonderful idea."

"But third-dimensional, right?" Surya tried keeping his thoughts away from his view of Atlantis as Mal-Ek spoke.

"Yes. Earth is a third-dimensional world. As experiments go, we tried and failed at creating humanoid vessels until we came up with the perfect one. One our souls could inhabit and control and use for the glory of the great Creator."

Surya grinned. "Looks like you succeeded, to me."

Scowling, Mal-Ek delivered a quick pop of his hand against the side of Surya's head. "No, not success. And quick thinking about her. She's just like the rest of them." He looked briefly away in disgust.

"Sorry, Father. I'm not making light of this, but is it wise to abandon this project forever? Everyone was excited about it at one time. You worked so hard perfecting everything. What a waste to walk away."

"No, not a waste, son." Mal-Ek's hazel eyes blazed with passion. "Sometimes noble intentions go awry. There comes a time when you must walk away. There's nothing more to it than that."

"There's more to it than that. It's lazy and irresponsible to walk away from your created beings just because you've grown tired of them." Surya's face turned sullen.

"You're letting ignorance rule your thoughts—and your mouth, son. I'll not have it." Mal-Ek wagged his finger at the young man beside him. The words bit at Surya's ears. His father's energy whipped at his with a rush, chilling his body. He knew he must also guard his tongue and cockiness.

Mal-Ek continued, "Let me tell you something. There's an outcome that scientists of the Federation hadn't bargained for. There's something inherently powerful in the human way once it's created and allowed to take root, the whole experience and feel of it."

Intrigued, Surya sat up straight and leaned toward his father, not wanting to miss a single word. "Like what?" he asked.

"Atlantis has already suffered two cataclysms, son. Did you read that part? All due to their recklessness. Human emotions and behaviors are wily at times, and it's getting the better of them. Don't think we haven't tried remedying their situation and their odd notions."

Surya, nodded. "Yes, go on."

"What we also discovered in the process was a formation of an inherent judgment—or should I say lack of judgment—that these souls and their bodies have apparently encapsulated. Humans with free will are unpredictable and capricious." Mal-Ek tapped his fingers on the table for emphasis. "They are substandard compared to us and the others in our star constellation—and don't you ever forget that."

The realization of his father's words left Surya with the sensation of an empty space in his heart. Anyone who could look and possibly feel the way that couple did on Poseidia couldn't be all bad. Just because other beings had their own ideas didn't make them necessarily wrong, either. He had one more question for his parent.

"Father, will any of our people ever go back there to help? You must have been considering this. Otherwise, why did you have the records on your desk?"

"This issue has come up again in meetings lately. Trying to decide if it's even worth it or not." He gazed at his son. "We're almost sure it would be best to leave the humans to their own ways. Whatever the outcome, it's their own doing. I'll be making a motion to not return."

Surya immediately snapped back to reality. A man had come up beside him.

"Sir, can we help you? You've been sitting here several minutes. Wouldn't want you to miss a flight."

Through the smile, his eyes held a look of intense curiosity as he gazed at Surya.

"When is the taxi going to the City Of The Golden Gates?"

The man turned in the direction of the sign. "It's leaving now. You better decide. Or you can wait for another one, which won't be here again for another couple of hours. Your choice."

"I'll go now." Surya would soon find out exactly how much or how little money he really had. He followed the man to the counter.

Surya handed him the coin he'd been holding. "I'm new, so I haven't quite learned the currency exchange on the island."

"I see," said the man, still scrutinizing him. "We'll help you figure it out." He whisked up a small speaker device and mumbled a few words into it.

The other two clerks tried looking casual as they watched passengers boarding. Surya's curiosity heightened. Did he look that strange?

"Um, Sir, did you mean to give me this coin?"

The man's colleagues glanced over, no longer hiding their curiosity.

"Do you need another? I'll check." Surya opened his bag and pulled out another coin, pushing it toward the clerk. "Is it not enough?"

The man shifted from one foot to the other. His lips twitched. "Where did you get those? They are thousands of years old. They belong in a museum, actually."

"Then I can purchase a trip to the City?" Surya remained hopeful, but from the look on the clerks' faces, that wasn't likely. The coins being too old would have never entered into his mind. Obviously not in Den-El's, either. He must have replicated the ones in his bag from the pile on his father's desk. Or worse, he stole all the originals. A chill shot down his spine. Stealing from the King could end up in death.

"Are these the only two you have?" The man's brows wrinkled.

On instinct, Surya answered, "Yes, it's the only two. I'm sorry." His instinct told him to keep quiet about the others at the bottom of his bag. He'd have to deal with the currency dilemma another way.

One of the other men spoke up. "Sir, if you'll put those away please, I'll give you a token so you can reach the City. Our way of saying welcome." He handed Surya a small metal token with an emblem on it resembling the craft outside. "Deposit that into the receptacle at the gate. This shows you are allowed on the flight."

The first man spoke again. "Let me give you some money for the ferry. You'll need it to enter the land rings. You can't use what you brought." He reached into a pocket of his trousers and pulled out a small leather drawstring bag. "This should be more than enough." He smiled and dumped five coins into Surya's hand. "And," he said in a low voice, "I'd advise you to not flash those old coins around. They are quite valuable."

Surya nodded. "Thank you. And you." He acknowledged the other man. Without another word, he trotted to the gate, deposited the token for the flight and disappeared into a long narrow walkway.

***

An hour and a half later, Surya stepped off the ferry and made his way up the sidewalk until he reached an intersection that struck his fancy. From the advice he'd gathered on the way in, he chose the last ring next to the land core, which held the great Temple of Poseidon. This last ring, he was told, was where the wealthiest important people on Poseidia lived.

Being a prince, he believed such a place applied to him, even if no one else knew his real status. His stomach lurched. Surya crossed over and sat down on the next available sidewalk bench. The motions of the air taxi and ferry during travel had wreaked havoc on his new system.

This sensation of wanting to open his mouth and force out everything from the depths of his body frightened him. He closed his eyes and inhaled deeply, moving his mind into a place of blankness. For all the discomfort he felt at the moment, Surya wouldn't have traded the experience so far for any reality created on Ontarus 9.

He would never forget viewing the entrance to the concentric land rings, watching with awe as two enormous golden statues came into view. Sunlight glinted off the metal, shooting garish golden flashes as the taxi moved with smooth swift speed through the air. Constructed in the likeness of warriors, they stood as sentinels on either side of the main entrance. Ships lined up for miles across the ocean, waiting for entrance into the city.

The ride through the canals on the ferry showed him a solid view of the different architecture. Round stone houses stood in neat rows around exquisite courtyards for several blocks. Temples with their spiraling steps and various geometric shapes had been placed in various locations. He'd seen a large pyramid in the distance on one of the rings.

On another, a gargantuan sphere. Buildings several stories high presented in all kinds of shapes and sizes. Streets held businesses of every variety. Landscaping and structure placement seemed based on a type of sacred geometry or spiritual configuration. Layout and planning had not only physical meaning, but spiritual. He sensed it with an inner knowing.

Sitting on the bench, he watched people come and go. Clothing ranged in all styles and colors. Men wore sleek trousers and shirts. Women wore dresses or skirts fitted with belts. What also struck Surya's attention was body decor.

Women didn't hold back, wearing multiple gold bracelets on their wrists or up their arms, rings on their fingers, earrings. Several had added bright beaded necklaces. Many men and women wore a type of head covering or decoration. A few women wore elegant hats laced with beads or shells. Others wore headbands of silver and gold.

That he had defied everything his father and the Federation stood for and come to this planet would have consequences. He needed not only to find the woman, but needed to make himself useful during his visit. If he could convince those in his constellation to reconsider their stance regarding Earth, the trip wouldn't be totally in vain.

Time to start walking again, but where? Closing his eyes, he centered himself, letting his intuitive guide kick in. He would only go where he felt led, where the energy pulled him most. It was the only way. Maps were meaningless right now. He got up and didn't stop walking until he came to a sign in front of an attractive stucco apartment complex. Vardhase stood out from all the rest of the buildings he'd passed.

The whole complex contained a powerful energy that pulled him in. This was the right place. The odd fountain in the courtyard didn't diminish his impression. Surya didn't know whether to laugh or be embarrassed. The fountain consisted of two shiny silver life-size statues of a male and female. Stone shells, starfish, and dolphins playing in a sea scene surrounded them. Jet streams of water flowed from the male's genital region and from the nipples on the female. Surya grinned. If only Den-El could see this.

A neat walkway with large round stones led the way to a wooden door with the image of a trident carved deep into the surface. Surya stepped up to the door and ran his finger over the impression. His excitement built.

The area of his solar plexus ached. Carefully, he opened the door and stepped into a tiled entrance hall. A spiral stone staircase led up to a second floor. He saw a doorway down the hall on the left and moved toward it, hoping someone could help him. The energy he sensed earlier grew stronger than ever.

Surya stood in the office doorway and gazed inside. When the young woman looked up from the desk, their eyes locked. Her face wore a stunned expression with a brief flicker of questioning recognition. His mind whirled, shooting him back in time when he first saw her through the lens in his father's observation room. The very same girl who had captured his attention and not let go. He knew her, the color of her hair, the lines of her face. He knew what she looked like in a moment of ecstasy. She had led him here.

"May I help you?" For such a large open office with high ceilings, the girl's voice filled the room with the crispness and clarity of a well-toned tinkling tea bell. Her eyes had not moved from his.

"Excuse me. I'm new in town. I need a place of my own." Surya swallowed hard. His mouth seemed sticky and dry, making conversation difficult.

The girl stepped away from her desk and came toward him. His heart pounded with excitement. He calmed his breathing so he could talk.

"Did you have a particular size in mind? We have up to three bedrooms."

"That sounds good." He smiled. Not really. Back home, he created countless rooms if he needed it. Three sounded awfully small and limited in a third-dimension world.

"I'll get a key. We have a unit I can show you." She smiled and turned toward a large wooden cabinet against a far wall.

The movement of her body fascinated him. As her footsteps glided over the floor, he viewed with interest the sleek gentle curve of her buttocks under a bright pink silk dress she wore. The polished silver headband glinted on her head. He admired the bright blue enamel butterfly resting in the hollow of her throat. Her delicate frame reminded him of a fairy, the mysterious elusive spirit divas he saw in dreams when his vibration lifted higher.

She returned holding a key with the apartment number dangling from the top. "It's on the first floor. Will that be a problem for you?"

"Why would it be?" He hadn't considered a reason for wanting a particular floor.

"Some people like being higher up. Others, not so much."

"I'm fine with what you have. I'd like to see it."

"My name is Martaam, by the way. I didn't catch yours when you came in." The girl smiled wider now. Her whole face lit up.

"My name is Surya."

"Where are you from?"

"Scandinavia." Answering became a bit easier each time a person asked.

"Oh." Martaam turned around, surprised. "How strange. Your name doesn't sound like one from there."

"It means sun. My parents wanted something different, rather than the usual." Surya hoped she'd believe that explanation. He wanted so much to tell her where he came from, what he really knew.

"If you'll follow me, I show you where your new unit will be."

Surya followed Martaam out of the office and out the front door. They crossed through a breeze way, rounded a courtyard, and at the end of the row, she stopped. "This is it." She inserted the key and opened the door.

The smell of fresh paint met his nostrils. The unit hit his senses as quite cramped, just as he'd imagined. He wandered from room to room. When he viewed himself in the bathroom mirror for the first time, Surya stood in shock. His complexion glowed with a rich creamy hue, complete with the softest pink undertones. The surface of his skin bore no blemishes or flaws. The eyes in his head beamed a rich golden brown. No wonder others had stared at him. He was shockingly handsome.

Did he possess a streak of vanity on Ontarus 9? He didn't exactly remember. Though he was considered nice-looking, the skin he wore now varied from the way he looked at home.

Martaam slipped up beside him. "Are you okay?" Her gaze focused on his face. She moved her lips like she wanted to say something, maybe an acknowledgement of what he knew. But no words came out.

"I must look worn from traveling," Surya chuckled.

"Not at all," she answered. "As a matter of fact, you look . . ." Her gaze lowered. "You look fine." A smile crept on her lips.

Surya stepped away from the mirror, quickly reviewing the other rooms. There was no other choice. He'd have to make do with the space during his stay.

"Do you work here every day?" Surya asked.

"I do when I'm not in school. My father owns these apartments. I help him during my free time."

He turned around and faced Martaam. She'd stayed close to him. He viewed the contours of her face, the deep dark brown in her eyes, the brilliant sheen of her coal black hair. A flash of sunlight shone through the window, showing off her soft red-brown skin, the color of most Atlanteans he'd seen so far.

His gaze had lowered to the soft red lips, down to her breasts, and back up again.

Martaam lifted a slender hand to her forehead, swiping it across. "If you want the space, we can sign a contract in the office, and the key is yours."

With eyes still fixed on her, Surya replied, "I'll take it, but there is something we have to discuss."

Her eyes narrowed briefly. Silently she turned away and led the way back to the office.

"I don't know what to do with these." Surya laid two coins from his bag on Martaam's desk. "I'm told they are very old and quite valuable."

She picked one up and studied it, turning it over from front to back.

"I don't know who to trust, but you seem nice." He smiled.

"Is this all you brought with you?"

This time Surya decided he needed to come clean. "Martaam, I have quite a few of these in my bag." He reached in and placed the remainder with the first two.

"I'm not a coin expert, but I know these are from before the first and second destructions. I've seen them in books and records. How did you get these?"

Surya grinned. "How come I knew you were going to ask me that?"

"It's not like people are walking around with them." Her face showed a sober expression.

"I had an ancestor who came here thousands of years ago, and these have been in the family for ages. I finally inherited them." His lies amazed himself. Thousands of years was a long time, but he couldn't think of another excuse.

"That's a long time to be in a family. Why would you ever want to part with them?" Martaam looked a little skeptical.

"What good are they in a museum? I need them now." This excuse may not go as well, but he hoped so.

Martaam sat up straight in her chair and fluffed her hair lightly with her fingers. Surya watched her face tense a little.

"Surya . . ." She smiled and licked her lower lip. "I really want to rent the unit to you. More than anything. Have you thought about what you'll be doing here? I'm assuming you don't have work lined up, being new and coming from as far as you have. You will need an income to rent here."

Surya stared back at her. She would never believe just how far he'd really come. "You're right. Nothing set up right now." He tapped on the coins. "How much do you think all these are worth, and where can I cash them in?"

Chapter Three

Two priests sat at the table in their apartment, gazing down in amazement.

"Do you know who would want these?" said Martaam. She turned toward Aleemirin, her uncle. "That's why we came. If anyone could help, I knew you two would be able."

"My dear, who wouldn't want these?" Aleemirin's eyes gleamed as he perused the small pile of coins. He held one of the discs between his fingers, flipping it back and forth as he studied each detail.

Tujuk spoke up. "How interesting that your ancestors would have collected so many to take home. And to still have them survive, passed from one generation to the next for thousands of years? Quite remarkable, really." He eyed Surya with interest. A look on his face indicated a twinge of disbelief.

"I'm not sentimental. I want the money for their worth." Surya sat back in his chair. Would these two either say nay or yay and be done with it? He rather liked the priests' apartment. Cozy and neatly decorated. Somewhat bigger than his, they had chosen sleek and simple furnishings. On the wall hung various stone glyphs. No doubt these reflected ancient writings and people. How would he make his unit like home?

Aleemirin placed his hand on top of Tujuk's. "Do we purchase these or not?"

The younger priest nodded his head, thinking. "These coins would be a wonderful addition to our collection of antiquities." He glanced up at the older man next to him and smiled. "We'd always have the value, which would increase over time. I see it as an investment, honestly."

"What were you thinking, son?" Aleemirin looked over at Surya.

Surya stared intently at the two men, and back at Martaam. "I'm trusting that you'll be honest and give me an appropriate value." When he tapped into the vibrational frequency of others, his psychic skills knew no bounds. He'd know in a second if either of the two men were out to cheat.

Tujuk said, "These are difficult to price. Everything was destroyed in the first two destructions. Again, not many people, if any, would have these." He raised an eyebrow. "But here we are. They are authentic."

"And you'll give me—"

"Over a year's worth of earnings. This will cover all your living expenses and then some," Aleemirin said.

Surya turned his face toward Martaam's.

"My uncle is knowledgeable on these issues. He's trustworthy," she said, nodding.

"Son, said Aleemirin, "Tujuk and I are the highest-level priests in our order, Law of One. Honesty is a cornerstone in how we conduct ourselves in daily and personal affairs.

"I'll take it." In Surya's mind, he would take their declaration of honesty with a grain of salt. For the moment, he sensed the price was fair. Such an arbitrary choice. One they made based on little to nothing. A number he would accept because they had something they thought of as valuable, and a year would be sufficient to find out what Atlantis was all about. He would have information to share with his father.

***

Standing outside the gate of his apartment complex on Orubis Way, Khaluj waited for the bird. It should land any minute, by his watch. He'd tried meditating a few minutes earlier in his apartment before coming outside. Whether he was too tired or he knew he'd receive his information soon enough, the visions were not happening for him. No clue, except that the newcomer had been searching for a place to stay.

Unfortunately, it wasn't in his building, so he'd have to work harder in keeping tabs on the young man. Today he had originally planned on slipping away from Poseidia in his custom-crafted Ultra Marine Pod all the way back to his beloved Aryan island for an important meeting. Maintaining a dual life wore him down at times. He tolerated living on Poseidia, but cohabitation with like minds and being true to his ideals happened on Aryan.

He lifted his gaze to the sky. A bird flew his direction, landing on his shoulder. Khaluj's eyes darted around. Only an occasional person passing by. This would be a quick gathering of information, and he'd figure out what to do next.

"Yes, my friend. What did you see?" He reached up, taking the liberty of stroking the bird lightly. Khaluj closed his eyes briefly, tuning in to the bird's frequency. In a flash, he saw the visions. Surya staring at Vardhase Apartments. Martaam showing him the vacant unit. The next vision sent him into a pit of dismay. Simply bad luck in timing for him, as far as he was concerned.

The last thing he ever would have guessed is that the woman would take a prospective renter to see Aleemirin and Tujuk. Those priests gained an advantage befriending the young man first. Exactly to what level, he didn't know. He still didn't like it.

The fact that they now owned rare coins was not a good start in his favor. Sons of Belial would never have a shot at those valuable pieces. They would have enhanced the coffers greatly.

The emotional spark between the star creature and Martaam nearly sent him over the edge. An incredibly strong energy ran between the two. Khaluj's gut clenched. He knew about instant chemistry all too well. Deep inside his psychic centers, he sensed a knowledge gap existed. The young man knew a little too much about this woman before having arrived. What he loathed worse was the great possibility of Martaam falling into the man's spell.

"Well done, beautiful creature." Khalug reached in his pocket and pulled out a small piece of bread. The bird chirped with approval, snatched up the tiny bite, and flew off.

***

Through a set of gleaming copper gates, Aleemirin and Tujuk sat at one of the outdoor tables inside The Atlan, a maze of small cozy shops and dining establishments. A glorious fountain stood behind them in the middle of the courtyard. From a large orichalcum jug, water flowed, infusing the ambient air with a light exotic spicy scent.

They waited while Martaam and Surya walked winding stone paths into the world of merchants. Atlantean funds in hand, Surya shopped for items he needed.

Tujuk, reached for Aleemirin's hand, holding it in his own. "What do you think about your niece's new tenant?"

Aleemirin drummed his fingers on the table. "I find it odd that he's alone with no friends or connections here. Didn't seem to have a specific plan in mind. Young. The money was highly unusual."

"Family that kept those for ages." Tujuk stared off in thought. "I don't think I believe a word he said." He looked directly at Aleemirin.

"Those coins were real, Tujuk. I probably would have believed his situation more if he came with absolutely nothing."

"So you feel the same as I do?"

The older man nodded.

"There's something unusual about his looks," added Tujuk. "He's too beautiful. Too perfect. It's almost unnatural."

"Won't disagree with you there." Aleemirin brushed his cheek quickly against Tujuk's. "We both agree that there's something different about him. He's like no one we've seen before. I feel it. I sense it in my bones."

Both men sat in silence for several minutes, each one sipping on tea with honey.

"I also think Surya is deeply attracted to Martaam." Aleemirin placed his clay mug on the table. "The attraction is so strong between the two you can slice it with a knife."

Tujuk's eyes widened. "I say we come right out and ask him about his origins. You know, find the right time. Because if there is something special about him, we might be able to use it to our advantage." He squeezed Aleemirin's hand. "And we need every advantage we can get."

"And," added Aleemirin, "my niece being involved with him would make the bargain sweeter."

"But what about—?" Tujuk asked.

Aleemirin held up his hand. "Don't say anything. Let's set our desires on the newcomer. I don't think much effort will be needed."

Khaluj crossed the street. He'd been hiding near the Sadarma Apartments, where Tujuk and Aleemirin resided, when he caught all four leaving and heading toward The Atlan. He rolled up his newspaper into a manageable parcel, keeping a distance away to avoid detection. When he reached the table where the men sat, he placed a hand lightly on Tujuk's shoulder.

"Khaluj, how are you? Enjoying this lovely day?"

The two men smiled at Khaluj.

"Ah, Tujuk, all is well. The same with you, I hope. Are you two shopping or merely enjoying the sun?" Without waiting for an invitation, Khaluj pulled out an empty chair and sat down.

Tujuk gave Aleemirin a personal signal to do the talking.

"Just waiting on my niece and her friend."

All three turned in the direction of two voices in the distance. Tujuk kicked his partner lightly under the table.

Khaluj bowed his head in acknowledgment toward Martaam and Surya as they arrived at the table. "And who do we have here?"

Aleemirin said, "This is Surya. He's just migrated from Scandinavia."

"Oh, is that right?" Khaluj said, feigning surprise. He offered his hand to the young man. "You've come a mighty long way."

Surya stood staring, not sure of what to do at first. At last, he held out his hand, and Khaluj completed the gesture by shaking it firmly. He didn't know what to expect from touching an extra-terrestrial. Maybe a bolt of energy, a shock, or tingling sensation of some kind. Disappointment set in when none of that happened.

This creature from the heavens had fully amalgamated his soul into the earthly skin he wore. What struck Khaluj most was the radiant beauty, from his flawless creamy complexion to the mesmerizing dark soulful eyes. He looked human, but almost not. Just enough to keep under the radar of most discerning people. Kudos to him or the one who created such magnificence. No wonder a woman may be instantly smitten.

Tujuk continued with the introductions. "Surya, this is Khaluj. He's our colleague, another esteemed high-level priest in Law of One.

Khaluj cringed inside, but forced a smile at the young man. "A most honorable group. You'll find no better people in all of Atlantis."

"Do you live on this ring or another?" asked Surya, surveying the man up and down.

"I live on this ring so I can be closer to my brothers." Khaluj bowed his head lightly toward Aleemirin and Tujuk. "Where are you staying?"

"He just took one of my last units," said Martaam.

"Too bad he didn't find our complex first. I can tell we'll be great friends." Aleemirin smiled toward Surya, who simply stared back with no emotion.

"I hope we'll all be good friends. You can never have too many fine people around." Khaluj sat back in his seat, eyeing the two priests across from him. He didn't care for Aleemirin and Tujuk's lifestyle. But the men still had free choice. After all humans could make choices. Like the great Creator, but apart. No wonder they wanted Surya in closer proximity. A beautiful play toy he would have made for them.

He shunned the intrusive thoughts of the two indulging in physical pleasure with a celestial humanoid. The idea sickened him. Obviously, this creature wanted no part of it, his heart and mind being bent toward someone else. Like it or not, he sensed the energy full force between Surya and Martaam.

Khaluj watched as the newcomer considered Martaam out of the corner of his eye while the girl wore a stoical expression. Again, the clenching in his gut unnerved him. "Surya, you now have friends within walking distance. You can always call one of us if you need anything."

"Sir, thank you for your offer. Nice to know."

Khaluj forced a light smile on his face as he listened to the young man next to Martaam. Deep inside, his displeasure grew. This man would have to show more emotion and animation to win over anyone in Atlantis. Perhaps Martaam may not care for such an aloof disposition. Interacting with such a strange creature reminded him of an ice-cold bath.

"Son, if you'd like to meet with Tujuk and myself, we can help point you in some direction regarding work. Perhaps in the temple or something else entirely," said Aleemirin. "You know, something to occupy your time so you don't grow bored."

"I'd be delighted to assist as well," added Khaluj. "I have many connections."

"Honestly, I think I'm capable of looking after myself. If I need input, I'll surely let you know." Surya cocked his head, gazing at the men.

Khaluj's eyebrows raised. His disappointment knew no bounds. Hopes of having the young visitor willing and amenable to suggestions had just been severely challenged. How dare such a young man, a mere boy as far as he was concerned, just blow him and his colleagues off as unimportant?

Surya said, "I'm going home. A pleasure meeting everyone." He picked up his bags and turned toward Martaam. "Thank you for your help." For the first time he smiled. Without another word, he turned and left.

Martaam remained seated. Her gaze followed Surya for a few seconds before she turned her attention back to the men. "Don't know about you gentlemen, but I'm starved."

***

Surya stood looking around in his apartment, relieved at finally being alone. A place of his own at last. Furniture would arrive the next day. Tonight he would tough it out on the floor until then. As far as his first true meeting with humans, he liked Aleemirin and Tujuk well enough so far. It was Khaluj he had instantly disliked. A black aura shrouded the man, and Surya couldn't quite put his new human finger on the reason why.

The aroma of hot food from one of his shopping bags sent his stomach in a rumbling fury. For the first time, weakness hit him, and he detected a bit of light-headedness. Sitting down on the floor, Surya tore into the wrappings holding a large piece of flat bread filled with hot spiced beef, onions, and green pepper. When he bit down for his first bite, the taste sent his neurons into a wild frenzy. For a moment he experienced a brief disconnection of mind and body. Pulling out a thick waxed cup, he swallowed down warm tea.

If this was what eating would be like as a human on Earth, no wonder there were souls who preferred finishing out their lives here. Consumption of food had to be equally as pleasing as what Martaam felt when she and her lover engaged in hot passionate love-making that day in the field. Thoughts of her sent a shot of longing through him. She'd been friendly enough while shopping, but still formal and reserved.

A strong spark of interest burned between them. He saw it in her eyes, the way she sidled in close to him, brushing against his skin. Mostly he sensed it in her vibrational energy when they were together. Strong. Palpable. They would break through the barriers. She and the man broke through it.

When he finished his meal, Surya picked one of the bedrooms and immediately assigned the intent to it as his meditation room, his temple where he would continue working on his vibration levels and divine gifts just as he did back home on Ontarus 9.

The first thing he needed to do was determine exactly how much power he had here on Atlantis. Would there be certain things he could do on Ontarus 9 only? Surya sat on the floor and carefully removed everything out of his leather bag.

Setting the stones in a large circle, Surya prepared his sacred room with an affirmation. "May all I do in this space work for the higher and greater good of the universe, humanity, and myself. May all glory be for the Logos." Holding his thumb and forefinger together, he made a sacred sign in the air.

The two pillar candles had been placed at each front corner of the room. Surya sat in the middle of the stones, closed his eyes, and visioned blazing wicks. He murmured the ancient protected word for calling on fire. With deep concentration, he sank slower and deeper into his vision, remembering how his candles glowed along the walls of his temple room back in another galaxy.

Within a minute, a tiny cracking sound came from the candles. Surya opened his eyes and smiled. Both wicks glowed with a dancing hearty flame. Satisfied, he picked up one of his new coins. He etched the look and feel of the metal and design in his mind.

Closing his eyes, he concentrated and visualized that one coin replicating itself into a large amount of like coins. The harder he concentrated, the more intense his psychic third eye, the pineal gland in his brain, vibrated. An intense pulsing and tingling sensation erupted in the space between his eyes.

He broke the exercise after a few minutes, bringing his vibratory level slowly back down to his level of consciousness. His disappointment knew no bounds. Nothing had happened. No additional coins on the floor. He still held the one in his hand even though psychic connection had been strong. Not a good sign at all. His heart pounded. He didn't like the fact of owning a limited amount of funds. In his world, there were few limits.

Perhaps if he tried materializing something else he might have better success? He closed his eyes, envisioning a bed for his master bed room. In his mind, he picked out the color of the coverings, what it looked like, envisioned the details. The space between his eyes throbbed with greater intensity than the first time. When he determined the creative exercise had reached its limit, he opened his eyes and headed to the bedroom.

Empty. Discouraged, he returned to the circle of stones. He'd created fire. On impulse, he decided to try something else. Centering himself again inside the circle, Surya closed his eyes, focused on his breathing a few seconds, and called up another ancient secret word. He concentrated, seeing the vision of his intent clearly as if it were real.

His body tensed. Something was about to happen. He felt it. The air changed inside the room, thickening, growing denser, slightly cooler, damp. Droplets of water condensed, raining down, growing stronger and heavier by the second. He held out his arms and smiled. This was exactly what he wanted.

"Surya?"

A female voice called out from the front door. The sound of shoes echoed across the floor.

This was not what he wanted. Surya uttered the sacred word to stop the rain, finishing with another for drying out the room. He looked up, heart nearly beating out of his throat. Martaam stood in the door way with a perplexed expression on her face. She rubbed her eyes, cocking her head as she gazed into the room.

"Did you need me for something?" Surya sat up straight, struggling for some semblance of composure. He hoped his casual demeanor passed muster under her scrutinizing eye. He'd never considered someone walking in on him unannounced.

She stepped cautiously inside the room, glancing around, eyes narrowed. "You obviously weren't in the shower. Because you're here. Dry." Her face showed disbelief and confusion, no matter how much she tried smiling. "I could have sworn I heard it actually . . ." She stifled a laugh, clapping a hand over her mouth. "Raining in here. This room. The one you're sitting in now. Dry." She rested a hand against her cheek. Martaam walked over to a candle, staring at the flame. "Your candles are still lit."

Surya sat motionless, staring straight ahead, avoiding her gaze when she turned and faced him. "Um, no. Why would you think it would be raining? Inside as opposed to outside?" He chuckled. He thanked his good fortune that the sacred words for fire, water, and heat still worked on Earth like it did back home.

"At the very worst, I thought a pipe burst, and we'd have to repair the damage." Martaam glanced up at the ceiling.

"No. No pipe problems or water issues. We're fine right now." Surya smiled. "Do pipes burst on a regular basis?" His whole body relaxed more.

"No. We take good care of our property. Sometimes things happen."

"Again, was there a reason you came? Though you're welcome any time."

She shook her head a little and smiled. "I've arranged for the furniture store to at least deliver your bed today."

"Oh?" Surya quirked an eyebrow. "How nice of you." Sleeping on the floor had not appealed to him at all. He slept on a mattress filled with air at home in his old bedroom.

"You'll get the rest of your things tomorrow, though. They did this one favor for me because I send them lots of business." She nodded.

"I appreciate it, Martaam." Surya stood up from the circle and walked toward her. He gently touched her shoulder. His hand tingled. She jumped a little, startled.

They both stood facing each other in a few moments of silence. Surya liked the way he felt around her. Her energy with him surged with strength mixed with kindness. He determined she wasn't a push-over type of person, as if he knew about humans with their associated personalities in the first place.

As a prince, he'd grown accustomed to different personalities and energies on Ontarus 9. In a fourth-dimension world, realities flowed and shifted with a person's simple emotion, will or desire. The stability of a third-world dimension required acclimation. Outcomes resulted slower, it seemed.

Martaam looked at her watch. "They're coming in an hour or so. Also, here is your personal communication device number." She stepped into the tiny hall and pointed to a box on the wall by the kitchen. "I added the office number if you have questions." Her face pinked as she handed him a piece of paper with the information. "I also added my personal number if you need me for anything like emergencies. I live on the second floor where the main office is, so I'm not far away."

Surya took the paper. Her body heat warmed him. From her skin, he breathed in the rich spicy scent of an exotic perfume. He hadn't smelled that when they first met. Did humans ask for the company of another after a first meeting? He wanted to.

Martaam walked toward the door. "Some simple advice. Lock your door if you want to keep people out." Smiling, she disappeared through the threshold into the evening sun.

When dusk turned to darkness, Surya slipped away from his apartment carrying his key in the pocket of his tunic. He wandered across the street and up a sidewalk until he came to a small park near the edge of the canal separating his land ring from the center land core of Poseidia. He turned his face toward the sky, staring up at the stars. A pang of homesickness hit him so hard tears burned his eyes.

He longed for his father and mother. Even his younger brother and sister, who plagued him at times. What were they doing now? What about Den-El? Martaam may have consumed his thoughts, but a best friend was always there. Surya gazed across the water. In the distance he viewed the crystalline domes over the temples. With their glowing lights, the vision appeared as though the land core wore a protective glistening shield over it.

From the tallest tower in the center, an emerald green light showered an angelic glow over the land below. Surya gazed at the light for a long time, mesmerized by its beauty. Deep in his veins he knew that this source from where the light shone held the life blood of all Atlantis. A source that sustained itself and never died. A source that came from deep within the earth and the heavens on high. If he concentrated enough, he noted a mild tingling in his whole body. The sheer power of the source both frightened and awed him.

Later that night, Surya lay in bed consisting of a soft thick pad resting on a low heavy dark wood box. Soft pillows under his head, he listened to the sounds of the night through the open window of his room. At times, he heard the occasional roar of a vehicle passing on a nearby street. People chatted as they entered their units. In the distance, the water let out a low rumble from the canal he visited earlier.

A soft cool breeze blew, lulling him into a state of calm. Home became a dim foggy image, almost a distant memory. The realization frightened him somewhat. Forgetting home, forgetting his mission for coming here—other than Martaam—would be bad. Would his father come looking for him? Would he be missed? Would Den-El keep the secret between them?

Martaam. In a somewhat hazy brain riddled with fatigue, he thought about her. What was she doing in her apartment on the second floor above the office right now? Surya thought back to the day he first saw her unclothed. He struggled to block the memory whenever he saw her. Tonight, there was no reason for blocking anything. His mind, near the brink of sleep, snapped wide awake. Deep inside his body, what started as a dull ache grew more intense. With the intensity came strong longing, a great desire for connection.

His muscles tensed. With gentle fingers, he reached down and touched himself in his most sensitive area. What had been a flaccid bundle of flesh earlier now raged with thick, hard determination. When he worked certain parts of himself, Surya writhed with an indescribable pleasure. What would Martaam do if he touched her?

Tenderly, he rubbed himself with slow rhythmic up and down motions. His thumb instinctively knew where to add pressure, sending him into heady bliss.

His body tingled. All the nerves throbbed with growing power. Urgency filled his being. The throbbing grew stronger. Surya imagined her stroking him with soft, gentle fingers. His mind called out to her, though he tamped down this thought wave so it remained only with him. The urgency and internal pain consumed him. He wanted relief, but not too soon. His fingers worked with greater speed. When the pleasure pain became unbearable, he gasped and shuddered.

An explosion of heat washed over him in one deft wave. Every circuit inside himself vibrated. Neurons fired all over. Energy shot up through the center of his body, starting at the place where his fingers moved, exiting through the top of his head. He lifted his hand, covered with his own passion, and opened his eyes.

The room glowed with soft white light. Desire and ultimate release did that, especially if the sensations consumed him to the degree it had moments ago. Surya chuckled. It was good to be human.

***

Khaluj engrossed himself in watching Martaam undress. With each part of her body exposed as she shed her clothing, his own flesh thickened. A hazy glow of lamplight enveloped the room.

From an open window, a crisp night breeze infused the air with the scent of freshly mowed grass and blooming flowers. Tonight should have been like any other since they met. One filled with reckless abandon and passion. But tonight didn't reflect the others. Embedded in her current mood, hints of disconnect and distraction flashed. The discovery nearly sent his erect member on an unhappy deflating decline.

His original goal, use her as an entrance into Law of One, played out according to plan. The outcome he didn't bargain for, genuine attraction and fondness for the girl. He was old enough to be her father, but difference in age didn't stop either of them.

He admired the way Martaam carried herself with confidence, grace, and a sharp wit. As long as they didn't interfere with plans he created or anything he wanted to do, the more he supported her. Complement, not contradiction or contrariness. If she walked, lived, breathed his favorite mantra, he swore he'd make her his wife.

Martaam turned away from the mirror, casting her dress in a chair next to her vanity table. Her firm breasts swayed when she walked toward the bed. Khaluj salivated at the sight of her plump nipples. The mere thought of her coming into bed sent him raging again into full stiff attention.

Khaluj smiled, pulling back the golden silk covers. Martaam slid in with ease beside him. With nimble fingers, she teased and caressed the most sensitive parts of him. The only element missing, her full mind and concentration. Her motions, almost rote, robotic, hit him full force. Tapping into her thoughts yielded nothing. She had locked this part of herself off for the first time.

He wanted to ask about him, the newcomer, the creature of the stars whose boundless beauty had captivated her. But he desisted. Such conflict. Wanting to know, yet wanting to know nothing. Not having Martaam would be a loss for him in many ways. Beside the bed on a small table sat a long black box. Khaluj came prepared.

No woman resisted his charms or jewelry. He reached over and pulled out a glittering diamond necklace. "Allow me," he whispered. "You're every bit as bright and beautiful." Martaam sat up from the bed. Khaluj clasped the necklace around her throat. "There. It looks much nicer with you wearing it."

With a polite smile, Martaam lay back down on the pillow, her black hair spread across. "You spoil me." Her voice came out in a soft whisper. Khaluj wanted to ravage her. The gems flashed in the light. She trailed a finger from the tip of his nose all the way down to the space between his legs. He landed his lips on hers and closed his eyes, tasting her.

Obedient, Martaam gave herself over to him. Khaluj indulged in her invitation. Somewhere in the darkest recesses of his mind and spirit, he sensed these nights were numbered. He wouldn't go down without a fight.

Chapter Four

Within the capital city of Meruvia, Khaluj gathered with twenty of his top council advisors. After a night with Martaam, he slipped away as the sun peeked from the horizon, making the four-hour trip in record time back to Aryan Island. Sons of Belial sat around a glass table in an ornate meeting room, their writing tools poised for taking notes. Khaluj rapped his gavel against the wooden block, calling the meeting to order.

"My sincere apologies for canceling our meeting yesterday, but there is a most interesting reason for it." Khaluj viewed the members staring at him with great interest. "I witnessed a strange occurrence, and I need to share it with you." As he recounted his experience of seeing Surya come through the portal, men scribbled quick notes. "Any thoughts on how to approach this man, if you can call him that?"

Rhaneen, Khaluj's vice commander, spoke up. "Were you not able to get any information from your girlfriend who rented him the apartment?"

Khaluj's face colored. "It's a rather delicate situation. Martaam usually makes it her policy to never discuss her tenants or their business. A privacy issue she has imposed on herself. Of course, I can ask her uncle and his partner. Maybe give it another few days."

The vice commander grinned. "They still have no idea about you, do they?"

"I've played it to the best of my ability. Acting like I'm fully into Law of One nonsense." Khaluj shook his head. "Keeping up appearances is so wearing, but it must be done if we want everything under our control."

A council advisor asked, "Do you think this star creature knows about the crystals and how their power controls everything in Atlantis? The technology is Arcturian, but that doesn't mean he doesn't know about it and how it works."

"Again, I have no additional information about where he comes from, let alone his knowledge base. He's Martaam's age, actually."

All eyes widened.

"Any risk of competition?" Rhaneen asked with a sober face.

Scowling, Khaluj answered, "Why would you even ask such a thing?"

"It's a worthy question, Khaluj. Some of these celestial beings have irresistible traits. Beauty, which includes the males. They can engage in persuasive talk with the best of us. They have other skills that almost seem like pure magic." Rhaneen tapped his writing implement against the paper in front of him. "And their knowledge of technology surpasses ours."

"Rhaneen, seriously?" Khaluj's lips rumpled with frustration. "Where does our Human DNA originate? And why do you think they finally left us thousands of years ago?" Khaluj's gaze met all eyes around the table. "We don't need extra-terrestrial help anymore. They launched us, so to speak, and now we take responsibility for our own destinies. Besides, galaxy man has no personality. He's not only insipid, he's a snob through and through."

"Then why are we worried about this one?" The advisor who spoke up earlier focused on Khaluj. "If we can come up with a plan to gain control of the main crystal powerhouse on Poseidia, then why does the presence of an outer space creature bother us?"

Rhaneen looked at his leader.

Khaluj sat back in his chair. "Having an extra advantage never hurts. We don't know what this gentleman brings to the table. We don't know how he thinks, what he thinks, or what gets him out of bed in the morning."

"Do they even have beds or sleep where they come from?" Someone else from the group spoke out.

Everyone chuckled. A smile crept on Khaluj's face. "We don't know that, either. If I could find a way to cut down on wasted time sleeping, I'd definitely be up for a chat on that subject."

Another round of laughs.

"Like I was saying. If he has any new ideas, or can help speed up the process regarding us controlling the crystals, it can't hurt to engage him."

"And I guess you will do that? Be the one who engages him?" Rhaneen's expression turned thoughtful.

"How would you like it if I could convince him to come here and talk with us directly?"

Everyone let out a sound of approval.

"Yes? I thought you might like a shot at that." Khaluj smiled.

"And just how do you plan to do this without blowing our—your—cover? Would be a huge shame for one slip or transgression to undo the work you've already done, Khaluj." Rhaneen cocked an eyebrow.

"You are always such a party pooper." Khaluj chastised his second in command.

Rhaneen laughed. "That's why you put me in this position. Remember?"

"Let me give it some thought. We'll find a way to pick space man's brains." Khaluj sat up straighter, looking at everyone around the table. "We must remember that having total control of the firecrystals on Poseidia means controlling the lifeblood that makes all of Atlantis tick. When you have a land's power grid in the palm of your hand, it's winner take all."

"Shut down the conveniences that make life easy, the machines, vehicles, and tools that people take for granted every day. Stop all means for distributing food and halting other technology people they think they can't live without. Do all that, and I'll show you a society begging for mercy. Once Sons of Belial have total power control, it's our game." Khaluj smiled. "Anyone who can help us win the game is worth talking to. What's the worst that can happen?"

**

In the Sadarma Apartment complex, Surya visited Aleemirin and Tujuk for lunch in their unit. On the same table where they had first viewed the coins, modest meals steamed on plates.

Curious, Surya asked, "Will Martaam be joining us? I wondered, with you being her uncle." He viewed Aleemirin with mild interest.

The two priests glanced at each other and back to Surya.

Aleemirin answered. "We chose not to invite her today. You see, we had some questions we wanted to ask, and thought it would be better to do it privately." He smiled politely at the young man across the table.

"I see." Surya's brow furrowed. He took a quick bite of salad, briefly closing his eyes while savoring the mix of greens, balsamic vinegar, and goat cheese.

"But speaking of Martaam," said Aleemirin, "she says you've settled in nicely. Got everything you had requested from your shopping excursion the day you came."

"She said that?" asked Surya, eyeing the two men.

"Have you?" Tujuk said. "Is there anything you need from us to help make you more comfortable?"

"You can start by asking whatever it is that you want to know." Surya smiled and sipped some wine from a sterling silver goblet. "By the way, this meal is wonderful. Sends me out into at least the sixth focus."

Both priests smiled.

"We'll get right to the point, then," said Aleemirin. He watched as Surya loaded up his fork for another bite. "Tujuk and I both have a sense about you."

Surya's eyes narrowed.

Tujuk added, "We don't think you're from Scandinavia. Nice try, though." He smiled.

"Mmm," Surya mumbled.

"You see, priests at the highest level like us have gifts. Of the psychic sense, if you will," said Aleemirin.

"Oh? What kind of psychic gifts?" Surya truly wanted to know the extent of power in humans. Were they able to do what he could? Did they do more?

"We can telepath. To those who are truly receptive. Natural and spiritual laws still apply to all situations. If someone is closed, there is nothing else that can be done. We can heal others." Tujuk nodded. "That's the start of it."

Aleemirin said, "We can also tap into someone's energy level, their vibration, and get a sense of their character, their personality."

Cocking an eyebrow, Surya said nothing. No matter how much he had wished to hide the truth a while longer, it wasn't happening. These priests were too inquisitive, not giving up.

"We think you've come from somewhere else entirely, a place not anywhere on Earth," said Tujuk.

Both men stared at Surya, waiting for an answer.

"Son, who are you, and where did you come from?" Aleemirin's eyes gleamed.

The young man looked from one priest to the other and said, "I'm the son of a king."

As they ate, Surya spent several minutes explaining what he found on Mal-Ek's desk in the observation room and shared in detail the conversation between him and his father. He described his experience consulting the Infinite Hall of Records and how it shut him out entirely about Atlantis.

"I've basically come here with little to no information, other than what I was shown before everything went dark. I used the portal on the other side of the island to get here. My best friend helped me."

Aleemirin dropped back in his chair, shaking his head. "I still can't believe this." He eyed Surya, astonished.

"You came against your father's will. Do you know the danger you have put yourself in? The danger we're in? A king will be coming after his son. Unlike you, he won't be alone."

Tujuk shook his head. "I don't know about that, Aleemirin. You heard what Surya said. I think they've given up on us."

"Given up on humans, yes. Him, no." Aleemirin pointed at the young man across the table. "I don't care if he's wearing a human third dimension skin. He still belongs with them." Eyes flashing with emotion, he turned his attention directly at Surya.

The young man blinked, trying not to think too hard about his father. He still didn't want to leave any kind of deep akashic imprint with his thoughts. The Hall of Records may have shut down with him, but that most likely wouldn't happen with his father. And what about Den-El? Once the discovery occurred that he played a role in this venture, who knew what the consequences would be.

"You are aware your friend will probably be in big trouble for helping you do this." Tujuk wore a worried expression on his face.

Surya nodded. The fact that these two priests were adept enough to tap into his thoughts on any level annoyed him somewhat. This was like being back in the fourth dimension.

Tujuk asked, "Then why did you come? To risk retribution must mean you had a solid reason for coming through that portal—at least I hope so."

"I had to find out for myself why such a large group would go great extremes to create humans like you and then just throw up their hands and walk away. Or fly away. I don't know the details, as we have discussed." Surya looked at each man. He wasn't about to tell them the real reason he came is because he had his eye on Aleemirin's niece. He'd look like a bigger fool. "I needed to be discreet, and the portal was the best way."

Aleemirin said, "Has there been any discussion of your people coming back, or any beings from other star systems?"

Surya hated answering. "My father says if there were, he'd vote no. I have no idea about others in the galactic system."

Both men stared down at the table in silence.

"Dreadful." Aleemirin spoke up after several seconds of silence. The corners of Tujuk's mouth turned down in sadness.

"What do you mean by that, Aleemirin?" Surya said.

Tujuk spoke up. "We have been lighting candles of intent, sending prayers to the Creator to please bring you back. We need the wisdom of our extra-terrestrial mothers and fathers again. We need a lamp in the darkness, someone or something to help light our way."

Aleemirin said, "What we want to say is that highly advanced beings from the stars taught us all the technology that has helped us be a great human race to this very day. Atlantis was once a glorious empire. Now it has hit a downward spiral. Connection with the Creator and advanced beings from other star systems has all but gone."

Surya nodded, encouraging the man to continue.

"Over thousands of years, humans have become conceited, greedy, corrupt. We're fighting each other at every turn." Aleemirin took a quick sip of water from his cup. "Nobody is winning here."

Surya rubbed his lower lip in thought. With the priests' stories and the words he received on Ontarus 9, the puzzle of Atlantis, its beginnings, and current state fell into place. He gazed back and forth at the two men. Did everyone else on Atlantis feel the same as these two priests? If he wanted to make a difference and help, his time on Atlantis would be a good chance to do it.

"If I could grant you one wish in the world, what would it be?" Surya asked.

Tujuk answered, "We want Atlantis the way it was thousands of years ago when we all behaved and practiced within divine law and for the greater good. It's a simple request, really."

"Is it really that simple?" Surya wrinkled his brow. Somehow, he didn't think so. Today's discussion highlighted the brazen truth about simplicity. Whatever the politics swirling in Atlantis, it most likely contained nothing simple. From what his friends suggested, nothing leaning on the honorable side, either.

Aleemirin grasped Tujuk's hand. "Nothing is ever simple, especially when there is an opposing side."

Surya asked, "In your mind, who or what is the opposing side?"

"It's not a matter of anything being in our mind. It's the truth," said Tujuk. "Law of One rule the people on Poseidia. The problem is with Sons of Belial, those who rule the isle of Aryan and the other small remaining islands of Atlantis. Our differing ideas of how things should be keep us at odds."

A light throbbing sensation perked up in the top of Surya's head. He closed his eyes. How uncomfortable. Taking a deep breath, he placed his hand on the area where the pain resided and repeated a healing mantra he learned years ago. The pain disappeared. "Mmm, better." He smiled.

Tujuk held Aleemirin's hand. "What powers do you have?" he asked.

Surya grinned. "You really don't want to know that."

"Of course we do. And you want to show us. Your aura is bright red just thinking about it."

"If you say so. Get ready," said Surya.

In an instant, he called on his soul knowledge for assistance like he did the first time inside his apartment. He closed his eyes, willing himself into a deep meditative state.

The air in the apartment thickened, condensing into palpable dampness. Heavy droplets of rain dripped over the men where they sat. With a last touch for effect, he held out his hand toward Aleemirin's. Another sacred word, and a thin streak of lightning sparked from Surya.

The man cried out, jerking back his hand. "Stop. You'll ruin our apartment." He looked around, frightened. Tujuk sat stunned, only his eyes glancing around.

Surya called on the other sacred word. The rain stopped. A quick flash of heat consumed the room, leaving everything and the men dry like before. His eyes narrowed. "Powerful enough for you?"

Tujuk burst out laughing. "Well, I must say. That was pretty impressive."

Aleemirin shook his head, letting out a loud breath.

"You're lucky he didn't zap you into oblivion. No doubt he could do that." Tujuk punched his partner's arm, acknowledging Surya with a sober nod.

Aleemirin sat, rubbing his hand, which pulsed dark red.

"Allow me, please." Surya reached for the man's hand and held it. Closing his eyes, he uttered the healing mantra. He envisioned Aleemirin's hand in its normal state, the soft red-brown skin like his friend's. Though the lightning spark was small, it still held enough energy to make one feel its effects. The redness disappeared, along with the tingling and light twitching movements.

Surya sat back in his chair, drained.

"Have you discovered anything that you can't do here on Earth that you used to do on Ontarus 9?" asked Aleemirin. "I'm sure switching dimensions must have had some effect on you."

"I can work with forces of nature, it seems. I can't materialize objects or change my reality like I could back home. It's much slower here on Earth." Surya sipped from his goblet. "I have to put out the desire and the thoughts behind it to get what I want, and really focus on it, like an obsession. Sometimes, even that doesn't always work. Especially if I'm tired or not in the emotional frame of mind."

"What else is different?" asked Tujuk.

Surya answered, "Even in an advanced state such as yours, you still would have a difficult time believing how different my world is. It's as if you are in a constant dream state. Reality shifts on a person's whim. Scenes morph and change in an instant. Whatever you believe, want, or fear becomes real. Inner knowing is another feature where I come from. You may not see a person or an object, but you know it's there. You have to be extremely conscious of your thoughts. Changes occur in almost an instant. You'll either get what you want, or not. It's getting what you don't want that will bring trouble."

The priests sat still, listening to every word.

At last Aleemirin said, "Does Martaam know any of this?"

Tujuk kicked his partner lightly under the table.

Aleemirin continued, "I mean, did the subject come up when you two were at The Atlan?"

"No." Surya, shook his head. He didn't dare tell them about the near-miss, when she walked in on him. From his read on Aleemirin, the niece had not said anything.

Tujuk added, "Not the normal subject of small talk, I would imagine." He admonished Aleemirin with a light frown.

Surya looked straight on at the two men. "Do you think we could keep this just our secret right now? I don't want everyone knowing about me. I don't even want your highest leader knowing about me. It's tricky to keep up pretenses as it is."

"Oh, I don't doubt it," said Tujuk, chuckling. "I'm sure you've seen yourself in a mirror by now." He grinned. "And we promise to keep your secret to ourselves."

"I do have a question for the two of you," said Surya. "I see you two reaching for each other's hand or mentioning yourselves as 'us.' I'm curious about that."

Aleemirin glanced at Tujuk, who motioned for him to explain. "Surya, I don't know exactly how society works on Ontarus 9, but here on Earth, there are people who prefer being with those of their own gender."

Surya remained silent.

"Tujuk and I are lovers, and this particular apartment supports those who choose that lifestyle, both for men and women."

"Isn't that a problem with your position. You know, as priests?" Surya asked. "On Ontarus 9, we don't have issues with gender preferences and partnering, but I know it's different with races on other planets."

"We live our lives in a matter-of-fact manner. When we perform our duties as priests, we simply focus on the task at hand and make sure our sincerity and intent is pure. You don't have to be heterosexual to do that."

"True," said Surya.

Aleemirin added, "It's not like we try to keep everything a big secret, but we use a little discretion as much as possible."

Surya said, "Well, that's about par for the course, isn't it? We all have secrets. I shouldn't be here, and one of you should be a woman."

The men chuckled.

Tujuk said, "Surya, just know that we'd like to help in any way we can. Maybe you can help us on certain things, provide input. You know, kind of like sharing ideas or different viewpoints. Would that be okay with you?"

"I wouldn't mind at all. My father had planned on teaching me how to rule. Perfect timing, I'd say." Surya smiled at the two men.

"Lovely," said Tujuk. "We are the class rulers on Poseidia. Maybe we could be sort of like your Earth parents." Tujuk nodded at his partner.

The older man grinned and briefly lowered his gaze. "I know there's a father in the universe who must be absolutely heartbroken. And the sad thing is we can't get you back to him."

***

From the observation room on Ontarus 9, Mal-Ek, peered through the GalXR90. With the aid of the satellite x-ray telescope and its recording capacities, he viewed the inside of the priests' apartment and heard everything discussed. His gratitude went out to Aleemirin and Tujuk for helping his son, but not without a huge pang of disappointment. Unlike what Aleemirin had said, the priests had the divine ability to send Surya home. Their powers were more than sufficient to contact the fourth dimension and higher. If they wished him there on Atlantis, they could wish him back to Ontarus 9.

"The problem is they're so enamored with having one of us on Atlantis again, they'll never consider sending him home. Or maybe they simply got lucky and everything was a coincidence." He shook his head. "But there are no coincidences. Their desire and my son's lined up. Too perfectly." Mal-Ek clenched his fists and swore.

"And you . . ." The king whirled around facing a sullen, scared young man cuffed to a confinement chair. "You helped him. Whatever possessed you to do such a thing?" He turned Den-El's face up to his. "Do you know that meddling like this has grave consequences?"

Den-El averted his gaze. The fear building in those eyes of his sent a brief flash of compassion through Mal-Ek before anger rushed in again. "Can you give me one good answer?"

"Your Majesty, that's all he talked about. Atlantis was in his heart and soul. I tried to talk him out of it." Den-El blinked back the first drops of tears.

"So much so that you discovered the coordinates to the portal, packed his bags, and took him there?" Mal-Ek clenched his teeth.

"Sir, may I suggest something?"

"It better be good."

"Do you think it's possible that Surya has a sacred contract to see Atlantis, gain a feel for humans and where they are in their current evolution? Perhaps he's assigned to elevate their consciousness. Why else would he have been so attracted to it?"

Mal-Ek cocked his head from side to side, studying Den-El with interest. He grinned. The grin turned into a smile. The smile morphed from a chuckle into pure maniacal laughter. "And maybe that's why he was determined to go there or explode." Mal-El laughed some more. "Oh, you're good!" He patted Den-El on the back. "That's a very worthy question, I must say."

He moved his face close to Den-El's. "You believe in sacred contracts, Den-El?"

The young man looked timidly up at the king. He barely nodded.

"Now that I consider this, Den-El, I like the idea of a sacred contract." Mal-Ek placed both hands on the arms of the chair and continued staring Den-El in the face. "I haven't looked into your sacred contract, but I have a sneaking suspicion that whatever it is, it's about to take an unexpected turn."

The skin on Den-El's face paled to near translucent.

"What you've done has interrupted a course of events that had been set in motion. You have defied the Federation's agreement to end all matters Earth-related. Helping my son onto that planet has put him in danger and maybe others. We won't fully know the impact for probably a long time."

Den-El lowered his face. Tears streamed down his cheeks. "I'm so sorry."

"Not anywhere near as sorry as I am. We must right this transgression, and I have a way to do it. In the meantime, I'll have to find a way to break this information to the Federation.

Chapter Five

Surya stood, entranced. A long silver wall shimmered before him. An occasional tower loomed above, topped in gleaming gold. The Temple of Poseidon blazed in all its magnificent glory under a scorching sun. Along with others, he and Martaam had already walked through the massive golden walls surrounding the temple and adjoining grounds. Several yards away, a small group of men pounded out a relentless rhythm on primitive-style drums while accompanied by three flute players.

Today Surya dressed in a new black silk tunic and slacks. A cerulean blue belt hung from his waist. On each lapel of his collar gleamed two silver tabs studded with onyx, outlined with labradorite gemstones. Since he failed in materializing what he wanted, he had sought the expertise of an artisan in metalsmithing. The artist fashioned a copper headband based on Surya's personal design. On top of the band, four eye-catching oval labradorite stones flashed with iridescent colors of blue, green, and gold.

"You look like a prince," Martaam murmured in his ear.

The words startled Surya. He turned his gaze away from the temple walls and stared at her. She reached up, gently rubbing a finger over one of the stones in the headband. "A truly remarkable piece. I like it." Her words trailed out in a whisper.

"Tell me again what the occasion is." He smiled, lightly touching her shoulder.

"Today is the traditional Meeting of The Kings. It's an age-old tradition that started with Atlantis itself." Her focus shifted to one of his silver lapel tabs. She brushed a fingertip over the surface of the metal and stones.

Surya considered her explanation. "I thought you didn't have kings anymore. Was I mistaken?"

"We don't, now. It's the current leaders of the districts on Poseidia who carry out the tradition. Every six years we have a problem with sun spots interfering with our crystal power grid. We offer a sacrifice and prayers to the spirits, hoping they will be gentle with us. Losing power is a horrible inconvenience."

"You use crystal power here on Atlantis?" Surya gazed at Martaam, surprised.

She nodded and turned her attention in the direction of a man dressed in bright maroon robes coming toward them. Her face clouded with a scowl. Surya grimaced when he knew the identity.

"My dear, I see you brought our friend." Acknowledging Surya with a cold quick nod, Khaluj ended up beside Martaam, wrapping an eager arm around her. An attempt at a kiss on the lips ended with a light peck on her cheek. The fact she'd turned her face away didn't go unnoticed by Surya. He looked on with concealed amusement.

"What? You're not wearing the diamond necklace I gave you the other night. Did you not like it?" said Khaluj, brushing back Martaam's hair. His words came out in a gentle scolding tone, but his expression showed pure dismay.

Martaam ignored the question. "I was telling Surya about our crystal power source and why we're here today."

Khaluj perked up. "Ah, getting an education, are you?" He grinned a little at Surya. "Every few years energy from the sun is temporarily decreased because of those confounding sun spots. They also affect the magnetism in the earth by altering the strength of the ley lines. Such an event doesn't play nicely with our crystals. No sun, poor magnetic strength, poof goes your power."

Surya stared at the priest. "Arcturian, yes?"

"Excuse me?" Khaluj stepped away from Martaam. He licked his lips.

"Your power system is based on Arcturian technology. Perhaps they taught this to your people?"

A smile broke out on Khaluj's face. "Why, yes. How did you know this? Have you studied it somewhere? Back in Scandinavia?" His eyes brightened.

An inner alarm went off inside Surya. He didn't care for the man's tone nor his unsettling questions. They reeked with a certain insincerity.

"I guess your ancestors had their lore about the great extra-terrestrials who came and taught us Atlanteans a thing or two. I really wish you had given me a chance to offer you more money for those coins you brought. They must have been quite magnificent."

"Uncle Aleemirin told you about those?" asked Martaam. She shook her head. "I thought he would have kept such personal information quiet."

A strained smile covered Khaluj's face. "Shh, dear. It's okay. I forgive him, and I still adore you as always. But you could have been my angel and told me first." He grinned in Surya's direction.

"Blood's thicker than water, you know." Martaam patted his cheek.

"Yes, I see." Khaluj frowned and turned his sights on the temple door. "I must go inside and prepare for the ceremonies." He turned to Surya. "I'd be delighted to talk more with you about our crystal power, if you're interested. Perhaps I can take you to the tower where we keep ours."

"It would be a great honor, Sir." Surya bowed lightly toward Khaluj. He may have been used to people bowing to him on Ontarus 9, but tables had turned. If bowing to Khaluj meant learning about Atlantis's ancient technology, he'd bow a hundred times. Through all the ingratiating gestures, he sensed something deeper at stake, more powerful.

Surya watched as Khaluj disappeared into the crowd. He turned back to Martaam. "So why didn't you wear the diamond necklace? Khaluj must think highly of you." Surya knew he asked a baited question. "I think you hurt his feelings," he whispered in her ear.

"I didn't ask for such a fancy trinket." Martaam cupped the back side of Surya's arm and delivered a gentle squeeze. "He goes overboard at times in his attention."

Surya recalled the man in Martaam's arms the day he watched through the lens. The outline of his body, the waves in his hair. If he viewed Khaluj from the back, he fit the vision with perfection. The mere realization sent his stomach in knots.

"What do you see in him?" he asked. His faced colored. "It's none of my business. Just curious, that's all."

"Let's go inside the courtyard." Martaam tugged on Surya's sleeve.

The beauty awed him at once. They walked over a blue tile floor, a near illusion of walking on water. Fountains met the eye at every turn. Some trickled water. Others shot water from one point to another in a delightful giddy little dance. One fountain exhibited motion art, with a pendulum swinging through a cutout piece that moved when water poured over an activation point.

Around the walls, exotic plants and brilliant colorful flowers surrounded several pairs of golden statues. "And these represent whom?" Surya gestured toward a pair tucked away in a corner.

"All these statues are the previous kings and their queens," said Martaam.

"Pure gold? Surely not."

"Gold leaf. Same as the statues at the entrance to the rings." She smiled, leading him around in orderly fashion like a well-versed tour guide. At times she stopped and shared bits of history, how each ruler made Atlantis greater through the ages.

As the crowd grew, voices rose to a mid-level drone. Several yards away from the entrance into the interior of the temple, Martaam spied an empty spot for the two them. She took Surya's hand, pulling him closer.

"Do you ever get tired of the usual and find yourself wanting more? Like there's something out there greater and more magnificent?" Martaam stared him straight in the eye.

The question took Surya completely by surprise. What surprised him more, Martaam still held his hand. He answered, "Is living here on an island with everything you could possibly want and more not perfect enough for you?"

"Anything lived day in and day out eventually loses its luster, no matter how perfect. Don't you think?" Her eyes searched his.

"Most likely you're right." Surya grinned. In a dimension where he came from, where everything was possible, he also fell into a trap of searching for the next sensation.

"You asked me earlier what I saw in Khaluj." Martaam glanced around before continuing. "He's different. Older. More experienced. He can be quite charming."

Surya added, "Can give you anything you want?"

Martaam's cheeks flushed. "He can. Does it on his own free will. I make no demands. I walk his path with him, serving."

"Why? What would happen if you changed course?"

She fell silent, thinking a moment. "I don't know."

"Try it and see what happens. Or are you afraid?" Surya gazed into her face.

"I'm not sure of that, either. I'll admit liking the attention, the lifestyle I could have with him, but I fear losing myself."

"Then you've answered your own question. Go against him, you'll either earn his wrath, or you'll simply go back to being what you were before he charmed his way into your life. Alone. Uncertain." Surya angled his head, staring at her.

Her headband gleamed under the sunlight creeping through the windows. Today she wore a soft dusty orange long dress with a purple belt tied around her waist. Surya averted his eyes from the light rise and fall of her breasts.

He focused on the enamel blue butterfly resting neatly in the hollow of her throat. At once he wanted to touch her, kiss the ruby lips tempting him every time he saw them.

"What are you looking for, Martaam?" He touched the smooth surface of the butterfly pendant.

A bell sounded. People headed to the main doors leading inside the temple. "Let's go." Martaam pulled Surya along, not letting go at the risk of losing him in the crowd.

The interior of the temple nearly took Surya's breath away. Orichalcum covered the floors and pillars. Ivory with gold and silver inlay shone from the ceiling. Gemstones of jade, beryl, and amethyst lay in geometric designs on the columns.

In the middle of the room, dolphins carrying sea nymphs surrounded a monstrous golden statue of Poseidon driving a chariot of six horses.

"Nothing is simple, on Atlantis, is it? Everything seems more—"

"Pretentious. Outlandish. Pompous."

Surya turned, facing Martaam in surprise. "That's how you see all this? I was going to say magnificent, stunning, and bold."

"You're still in the honeymoon phase of being here." She placed her hand in the small of his back, gently leading him toward another set of doors separating the ceremonial altar room from the main one. "We are entering the holiest part of the temple, the kirtana. Uncle Aleemirin has special seating for personal guests and family. He knows you're with me."

The inside of the kirtana held an atmosphere in stark contrast to the courtyard and the main gathering room of the temple. Benches sat in tidy rows. In the front stood a marble altar flanked by glowing blue crystals five feet tall and three feet in diameter.

Tall quartz crystals in the four corners emitted a white light. The floor consisted of red jasper and the walls, orichalcum with tiles of red banded agate. Copal resin with its rich clean scent permeated the air.

Martaam ushered Surya to an ornate carved wooden bench where Tujuk sat waiting.

"I'm so glad Martaam invited you today," said Tujuk, clasping Surya's hand. "This is a public affair. New people who don't know about it often feel alone and don't come."

"Are you not part of the ceremony?" Surya tilted his head toward the altar.

"Not this one. I do others, though." Tujuk reached behind Surya and patted a smiling Martaam on the shoulder in greeting.

A chorus of twelve people stepped through a wooden door to the right of the altar. They divided up into threes and situated themselves in each corner in front of the crystals. Everyone quickly seated themselves and sat up straight. On cue, the singers let out a monotone sound and held the note for several seconds.

They switched to another sound with a different pronunciation and pitch. After several of these vocalizations, the space between Surya's eyes tingled. He used sacred sounds all the time in his personal spiritual work. Apparently, humans on Atlantis knew how to use them too.

Aleemirin and Khaluj filed in together, each one taking a seat on a high throne-like chair behind each side of the altar. When the last note floated through the air, everyone became silent. Khaluj stood up and walked to the altar.

"Greetings my brothers and sisters on this special day of The Meeting of the Kings. May your days be filled with love and prosperity. Let's close our eyes and send positive thoughts of good will and light to the earth and sun. May our conscience be infused with purity so that we can attune in divine perfection."

Surya closed his eyes, following Khaluj's lead. The warmth from Martaam as her arm rested solidly against his created a brief distraction. He took in a deep breath, holding it several seconds and exhaling in measured breaths. Between his eyes the vibration and tingling started over again.

In his mind, he visualized the earth surrounded by white light and the bright orange sun radiating pure fiery heat with no interruptions, no blemishes. What he didn't count on, a dark image. It flashed through out of nowhere, unbidden. In the depths of his soul, he saw a lone figure in a pit of darkness. Human? Animal? Howls of misery seared into his consciousness.

Chills shot down Surya's spine. He involuntarily jumped as if waking suddenly from a nightmare. The squeeze from Martaam's hand kept him grounded and from bolting from the kirtana, out of the temple.

"You okay?" she mouthed without a sound.

He didn't answer but looked straight at the altar. The sight of Khaluj watching him and Martaam set his nerves on edge. Why wasn't the priest participating in the meditation exercise? Aleemirin sat in his chair, eyes closed. Khaluj lowered his head and closed his eyes. Several seconds passed before he spoke again.

"My brothers and sisters, may the cosmic intelligence bless our vibrations of attunement and worthiness."

Aleemirin stepped up to the altar as Khaluj seated himself in his chair. His voice rang out loud and clear.

"We gather today as our ancestors and forefathers did in days past. Though they met willingly and with love in their hearts, a thread of fear wove itself in the fabric of their noble intentions. Cosmic law rules above all. Rules of nature follow.

"The law of cycles must be respected. Seasons come and go in perfect order. The tides of the sea swell and retract. We are born. We die. The universe goes on in its quiet way without interruption."

Surya stifled a grin. The universe did everything but move in silence. Wars cropped up on other planets. Alien races sought power over others. The universe created its own noise. Planets themselves, orbs of land and water or those entirely constructed of gas, moved without ceasing. Their sounds spilled out so high in pitch the human ear would never hear. He'd heard the sounds in their purity with no interference. Angelic, tinkling, thrilling to the soul.

He glanced over at Khaluj, whose intent gaze burned hot in his direction. Surya at once shut down, scattering his thoughts until nothingness inhabited his mind. He listened to Aleemirin's words without reaction, making a conscious choice to block his emotions. Khaluj's frown didn't extract a sense of satisfaction, though he noted it.

Aleemirin quickly turned around and gazed at Khaluj. Surya knew without error the frown passing over the priest's face. Khaluj's gaze fell on his hands. Aleemirin continued his speech.

"In the beginning, our ancestors didn't understand these laws. They hoped their offerings and sacrifices would please the spirits, whatever their conception of what this force actually was. Today, we understand the law of cycles. In routine order, occurrences happen in our environment, in our solar system.

"Our blessed sun, a major energy source for us, accepts the insults to it. We can only request a lessening of the blows, weakening of the outcomes when occurrences come to pass. We solicit the powers of higher spirits, using their ability for action in conjunction with our own. It is today where the leaders of Poseidia come together once again.

"Like their counterparts of yesterday, they will judge each other's deeds and hold each other accountable in the way they rule their allotted section of the island. The laws for governing are etched on the pillars of this temple. For it is with kindness, benevolence, and for the highest and greatest good that all are uplifted for the glory of the Cosmic Creator."

Surya watch Khaluj, observing an instant expression of exasperation covering his face. The man lightly drummed his fingers against the arm of the chair as if he were bored. Everyone else in the room wore faces of piousness, hanging on every word coming from Aleemirin's mouth.

He viewed Martaam. She wore the look too. At once she turned and smiled at him, placing her hand quickly on his. Surya didn't move. He wanted to savor the warmth of her as long as she allowed it.

Aleemirin spoke again. "Our leaders are following this tradition now in another room of this great temple. They are reviewing their deeds, their hearts, their intents. In open council amongst themselves they judge, chastise, or applaud. Their leadership is questioned or approved. They pledge to serve at the will of the people, for the good and greater glory of the people as a collective oneness that is and will be for all eternity.

"In the glory of oneness filled with love and purity, we reflect the perfection, love, and boundless energy that is our Logos Creator."

Khaluj's fingers drummed quicker. His lips twitched. He stifled a yawn. Surya's eyes narrowed. Why the behavior? Was he not a Law of One highest-level priest like Aleemirin and Tujuk? He of all people should be nodding at his colleague's words. His eyes met Martaam's. She darted her gaze from Khaluj to Surya.

Her brow furrowed. Again, her gaze pricked Surya's awareness. He closed his eyes, centering himself into the moment, focusing on Aleemirin's words and his ending comments.

"As we continue the ceremonies, let your hearts be glad. Full power comes when all walk in wisdom and understanding. Truth and concern for each other is truth and concern for yourself. Knowledge and enlightenment will make universal change for the better of all. Go in peace."

Aleemirin held out his hand and made a gesture in the air with his fingers. Surya look on, surprised. He knew the sign. It was an ancient symbol signifying a blessing for all souls.

"We go now for the sacrifice of the bull," said Tujuk, standing up and whispering in Surya's ear.

Surya shrank back, appalled. "A real animal?"

"Of course. You surely don't think we'd offer a false sacrifice, do you?"

"I would surely think people as advanced as yourself would never consider offering the life of a sentient creature when it's not necessary." Surya scowled.

Tujuk stared in shock, speechless.

"Excuse me, but I'm leaving." Surya pushed past Tujuk, rounded the bench, and rushed out of the kirtana.

"Where is he going in such a rush?" asked Aleemirin. He hugged Martaam, kissing her on the cheek.

"What did you say, Tujuk?" Khaluj stepped up to the three. He pulled Martaam into his arm, holding her close.

"I . . . I didn't say anything except mentioning it was time to sacrifice the bull. He didn't like it at all. Seemed almost angry."

"Mmm," said Khaluj, looking in the direction where Surya left. "Perhaps where he comes from, they don't make sacrifices."

Tujuk and Aleemirin glanced at each other.

"I'm sure the Scandinavian people have their own rituals. Blood sacrifices are quite common in many cultures," said Tujuk.

"Ah, yes. The Scandinavians. Yes, you're right about that," said Khaluj, chuckling. "Then he shouldn't be so surprised." He kissed Martaam on the lips. "Come, my child. Let's go watch. I'll make sure you have a bite of the roasted meat from the bull. Not everyone has such a chance."

Martaam gently pushed away. "I'm going after him. He seemed extremely upset."

"Shh, dear one. He'll be fine." Khaluj tried pulling her back, but she tugged herself free and scurried to the door. "A little headstrong today, isn't she?" He raised his eyebrows.

Aleemirin grinned at Tujuk. "I wouldn't worry about it, Khaluj. My niece will be fine. Perhaps her school studies in the healing arts have increased her level of compassion."

"Never a truer consideration, my friend. For now, I think we move on to the remaining ceremonies. People will be looking for us." Khaluj led the way out of the temple.

***

Surya sat on a stone bench overlooking a garden outside the golden walls of the temple. On a sunny day like today, he didn't want to be indoors. Spending time with Martaam occupied his thoughts all week, once she invited him. He'd longed for this day, dressed for the occasion. Witnessing a poor innocent creature being cruelly slaughtered didn't set well with him.

Eating meat had been no problem. Killing a creature for a needless sacrifice bothered him. The Creator didn't show special favors for sacrifices, and the Atlanteans continuing such a tradition disappointed him.

"Here you are." Martaam slipped up beside Surya. "Mind if I sit with you?"

"Don't you have a sacrifice to watch? Or a lover who wants you with him?"

Martaam placed her hand lightly over Surya's thigh. "I'll let you in on a little secret. I don't enjoy watching a bull get clubbed to death. The leaders eat the meat after it's roasted and wash it down with a wine and blood mix. They toss some of the blood on the fire where they roasted the poor animal. The public eat what's left of the remaining meat until it's gone."

"With such a description, I could have just stayed and watched myself." Surya frowned.

"I'm sorry. I only watched one time when I was a little girl. The other times, I looked away or distracted myself somehow. No matter what I did, I couldn't block the cries from the poor creature."

Surya held up his hand. "Okay. You've enlightened me." He grinned. "What other buildings are on this land core? I see more than just the temple."

"All the healing centers and other temples are here."

The heat from Martaam's hand soothed him. He wanted to walk, have a drink, go somewhere with her. The farther away he stayed from Khaluj, the better.

"Do you want to see where I go to school?"

"You go to one of these buildings?" Surya looked at her surprised.

"I'm learning to be a healer." Martaam gazed out across the garden. "I made the decision last year. My father supported me. He likes the idea of having a healer in the family. Everyone else helps run or maintain the apartments."

She plucked at the sleeve of his tunic. "What about you? You've never told me about your family."

Surya pressed his lips together a second. "I have a brother and sister, and my parents."

Martaam nodded, waiting for him to tell more. "Any pets?"

"Nooo. None for us."

"What did your family do back home?" Martaam continued.

Surya tapped his foot. Scandinavia. What would Scandinavians do? "My family were protectors. They helped guard the village where we lived. Along with some others who were also chosen, of course." He placed his hand on Martaam's "I'd really like to see the healing centers. Show me where you learn."

Holding hands, they followed a sidewalk toward a collection of buildings farther away from the temple. The architecture amazed the eyes. Several of the buildings had been constructed of white stucco and bore geometric shapes. Others were glass covered with metal or stone lattice designs.

Two buildings resembled a cluster hematite crystal points with a zig zag lightning-style ledge splitting through the middle. The exterior shone sleek and shiny, reflecting the sky. One building consisted of a large stone square balanced on a round cylinder comprising the lower half of the structure.

"Everything is so beautiful. Creative," murmured Surya. "Humans are full of artistry."

Martaam grinned. "We have some of the best architects on the planet."

"We're not that fancy in Scandinavia."

"Mmm, I see." Martaam eyed Surya with interest. She pulled him faster. "That's my building over there."

Surya stared at the structure, taking in the view of an enormous sphere.

"The panes aren't glass. They're made from quartz crystal. It serves two purposes. The building itself and healing."

From the outside looking in, Surya detected a spiral staircase wrapping around from bottom to top. The rooms made up the interior.

"If you like, I can show you my healing room. Every student has one for practice."

"I would love nothing better than to see it." Surya smiled.

When they reached the front door to the building, Martaam pressed some numbers on a metal pad. A beeping sound emitted. "After you," she said, waving Surya inside. She led the way first to rooms on the main floor. "These are the classrooms. They make up the first two levels. The remaining four are for students."

"Truly remarkable." Surya peeked from the doorways into large open amphitheater-style rooms with seats going up multilevel around the room. In the centers, the platform for the teachers.

Martaam walked up the spiral to the third level, picked out one of the metal bridges to the center, and headed inward. Taking a left, she kept walking until she and Surya ended up at one of the doors in the middle of the hallway.

"I'm lucky mine is on the third floor. Usually the better students are given the privilege of rooms closer to where the professors teach," she said.

"Good at what you do, yes?"

She smiled, blushing. "I'm pretty good." After tapping out a series of numbers on another keypad by the door, the two stepped into a small cozy room. "Like you, Surya, I also have my collection of crystals." She turned on the light and walked over to a small shelf and picked up a ruby red point. "I had to search high and low for these, holding each one to make sure they aligned with my vibratory level."

"What do you have in here?" Surya pointed to a large wooden box with an ankh carved into the top.

"Those are the healing stones I use on my clients. They can also be used with light for different types of therapy." Martaam opened the box, exposing an array of crystals and gemstones. "And in this box," she said, picking up another, "is where I keep my divination cards and pendulums. I also have my scrying ball over there."

Surya turned his attention to a large clear quartz crystal ball sitting on a metal scroll stand in the far corner of the room. "I'm guessing this is your treatment table." He ran his hand over a thick layer of leather padding.

"You're correct. I would ask if you wanted some brief energy work, but it looks like you know how to re-energize and rejuvenate yourself with your own stones." She dropped her gaze.

"I do it on a regular basis. But I've been using stones since I was a young child. I've had years of practice." Surya touched Martaam's arm. "You can practice on me if you like. Letting someone else do the work every now and then offers another energy perspective. That's a good thing."

"We can do it now, if you like. Something simple, easy. Maybe a clearing of the mind and re-balancing of the chakras."

"Perfect idea." Surya nodded with approval. "Did you need to place anything over the table?"

Martaam opened a cabinet and pulled out a cotton sheet. "Let me open this before we start." She walked across the room and slid back a panel in the wall.

"What is that?" Surya asked.

"All the rooms have access to crystal light or rain, depending on the weather."

"I don't understand." He walked over and joined her.

"Long pipes from the roof run through the center of the building and connect to the rooms. Each pipe has a moveable crystal cap on top."

Surya reached through the opening in the wall, touching the back.

"As you see," said Martaam, "the insides are lined with faceted crystals. The light is so strong when it shines down, it refracts off the stones and into the room. If it rains, the crystal at the top is moved away. Water falls all the way down to the earth below the building. It's soothing no matter what the weather."

Surya grinned. "Pretty clever." At Martaam's request, he reclined on the table after she placed the sheet.

She opened her box of stones, selecting seven of different colors. In a straight line she arranged certain stones on select areas of Surya's body. When finished, she turned off the main light to the room. The soft glow from the panel emitted enough light for creating a meditative atmosphere.

"Close your eyes, Surya, and concentrate on nothing but your breathing. In. Out. Nice and easy." Martaam placed her hands around his head without directly touching him. At once she became silent.

On her command, Surya closed his mind and centered himself with his breaths. A void of blackness filled his mind. He absorbed the energy from the crystals radiating from the opened panels.

He detected the faintest heat from them. The crystals sent a slight tingle throughout his body. Martaam's body heat hit him with a constant pressure, strong, solid, grounding.

Sinking deeper into meditation, Surya focused on his breathing and the images floating through his head. Martaam's words, "in" and "out" repeated over and over in his mind. Her words, His breath. The portal. Den-El's commands. Crashing. Breathing.

A light wind whistled through the open panels in the room, creating a small moan as air passed through the pipe. The moan grew louder in Surya's head. Blackness closed in, more persistent than before. An image of a beast flitted in the darkness, its contorted face raised to the sky as it let out a mournful wail.

In. Out. Breathe. Crash. Pain. The image of the beast came in full focus, so clear the fibers of hair on its body shone as if someone had switched on a light. The face, pitiful and hideous held a connection to something. Somehow. Some way. A piercing wail filled his ears. Surya jumped, startled.

The stones on his body rolled off and onto the floor. Martaam cried out and stepped away. Surya sat up straight, gazing at the crystals flashing out white light from the opening in the wall.

"I saw something," she whispered, inching back to Surya.

Swallowing hard, Surya nodded. "Yes. I did too."

"Do you know what it means?"

"I would have to do more in-depth meditation alone." He looked at her. If she saw the exact images, he risked discovery. An impromptu session should never have been considered right now. The folly of his own eagerness filled him with regret. Martaam's face showed grave concern.

Surya grinned. "Don't take the exercise we did as a bad experience. That's the whole purpose, you know. Letting out the negative, restoring the positive."

Martaam gazed across the room toward the crystal light. "I wanted to restore chakra balance. Nothing more." She moved closer to Surya, rubbing his arm. "Whatever it is, there is darkness near you. Something or someone is in danger or in a hostile place." Her eyes moved upward toward his, staring him head on. "There were other sensations, and a doorway. You've locked in some emotions within yourself. There may be consequences to something that's recently happened."

Surya grasped both Martaam's shoulders, inching his face close to hers. He spoke in a low voice. "Nothing I can't handle. Travel and a new land is stressful. You know that good and well. It's nothing more."

She placed a hand lightly on his chest. "I can help you through it. If we've unlocked something, we can deal with it." She whispered in his ear, "You're not alone."

"I think we're done for now." Surya knelt and gathered up the scattered stones. Martaam quietly returned them to the box. She closed the panel in the wall.

"Can I buy you lunch and some drink? I don't know about you, but The Atlan sounds good right now."

Smiling, Martaam led the way out of the room and out of the building.

***

The solar plexus area of Khaluj's body tensed. An uneasiness settled in his gut. Watching the sacrifice of the bull had not taken his mind away from Martaam and Surya.

When he thought about them, a strong emotion of jealousy and sadness rocked inside him. The two had gone somewhere together. Every minute they spent in each other's company meant the same minutes his relationship with her stood in jeopardy.

Something had been unleashed. He had seen a fleeting vision. Martaam and Surya had unlocked it together. A wave of isolation gripped him, but he shook the emotions off. He'd charmed her the first time. No reason he couldn't do it again.

In the distance, standing beneath a tree, Aleemirin and Tujuk watched their friend with interest.

"I think things are looking good for us," said Tujuk. "I liked Khaluj, and so did Martaam."

"We need Surya on our side. There's conflict brewing among the islands. We'll have to face it, like it or not. I'd like to stall, wait everything out. I don't think we can." Aleemirin hugged Tujuk. "Please tell me all will be okay."

***

Infernal heat wrapped around the beast with a tenacious grip. It would surely suffocate and kill in due time. Scorching temperature was a monster in its own right. A cracking sound of a whip followed by teeth-gritting pain. Screams wouldn't stay locked inside an injured body and a broken soul. Despair and heartbreak stung no differently than throbbing wounds inflicted by a relentless sadistic master.

Another roar, this one louder. Pain racked the animal's body, and it couldn't help but cry out at the injustice of it all. Was the animal not human too? Did it not have a soul? It did once. Where had it gone? The beast held up and gazed at what looked like a human hand. It looked down at its feet. Was something else there in place of what should have been toes?

"Back to work!" A gruff voice commanded

Inside the depths of the earth, rocks burned, branded skin, and bit into flesh. Holding a pic and swinging it became impossible at times. Moving around didn't work like it used to. The body had shifted, changed. Nothing made sense anymore.

Sweat and blood dripped down matted, stinking fur. Bare flesh itched until madness set it. If the beast tried scratching against the stones, sharp points cut and singed.

There had to be a way out. The beast would find it or die trying. Could it die? Or did it simply remain in limbo? It must get out. Find sanctuary. Surely someone held a a little love or compassion in their heart.

Chapter Six

"And this, my good friend," is the powerhouse that protects our beautiful fire crystal." Khaluj pointed to a tower several yards away.

Surya followed the length of the monstrosity with his gaze, shielding his eyes away from the sun. "You're telling me the main source of your power is shielded in the building over there?"

"It is." Khaluj walked several steps toward the tower, Surya following. "Inside is the wondrous crystal. So powerful and mighty, its source is like no other. It gets its energy from the sun, stars, moon, anything in the heavens that's a fire source. We open the top for charging and release of energy." Khaluj pointed to the top of the tower.

"How does one source power everything else?" Surya asked.

"We have posers, mini power receptors made of crystals bound together by a gold and copper wire mix. Vehicles and other appliances powered by this energy all have crystal receptors too. They merely lock on to a relay source."

Khaluj took out a key and unlocked a door at the bottom of the tower. The two men stepped inside. He led the way to a stone bridge wrapping around the giant crystal.

"Here we are. Please do not touch anything. The energy is powerful. Your auric field will be fractured in an instant if you handle the stone directly. The recovery could be weeks, maybe several months to fully heal."

Surya grinned. "I'll keep my hands to myself." He knew about the aura, energy fields surrounding humans and animals. He also knew the sluggishness, fatigue, and general ill feeling accompanying the fractures to which Khaluj alluded. Would Martaam be proficient in healing fractured auras?

Khaluj whirled around facing Surya with a frown. "Um, there are healers on Atlantis who can help with all kinds of rejuvenation and restoration to the human body and its energy fields. Only go to seasoned practitioners, never students."

"I'll keep that in mind, Khaluj. Sometimes it's okay to practice, other times it's not."

"Good. I see you recognize this." The man's smile faded as he returned his focus on the crystal. "Do you see the top of the tower?"

"I do."

"It's moveable. The stone can receive and release energy as needed. Careful and deliberate faceting helped enhance these two actions. Atlanteans enjoy power at full capacity almost non-stop."

"Except when environmental factors disturb the fields. I see how it works, now." Surya studied the six-sided crystal, which stood about fifty feet high and several feet in diameter.

Khaluj continued his explanation. "The bridge around the stone allows workers to move about without making contact, but still perform maintenance or tuning when needed." Surya followed him until they completed an entire circle around the crystal.

"It's beautiful, really," said Surya. "The mechanics of the entire system amazes the mind."

"Arcturian," said Khaluj, grinning. "You and I briefly mentioned that a couple of weeks ago at the Meeting of The Kings." He stood closer, his lips near Surya's ear. "I'm sure you know Arcturians have some of the best technology in the universe."

Surya backed away. "I've heard that in history lessons. Did you know that our sailors used crystals to navigate seas, to locate the sun on cloudy days?"

"Is that right?" Khaluj snapped his fingers. "Now that you mention it, I think I've been told such a thing before." He nodded. "May I show you something else? Arcturian and extra-terrestrial technology too?"

"Absolutely." Surya followed Khaluj out of the tower. While they walked, he determined thoughts were best left scattered. No focusing on any one person or subject matter too long when Khaluj came near. The priest knew too much, and he suspected a much greater power in him than Aleemirin and Tujuk. Or did the two other priests choose passivity when dealing with challenges?

Khaluj opened the passenger door to his roadway transport vehicle, a slender bullet-shaped craft. Surya immediately liked the way it sped swiftly down the roadways. When free from traffic, Khaluj pressed a button. The vehicle shot straight at nearly max speed.

The sheer thrill of zipping down the road with no obstacles launched his spirit into high gear. The sensation left him as one who had taken a mind-altering drug without the cloudy effects.

Instead of driving to a ferry port, Khaluj navigated the roadways until they arrived at a bridge.

"We're going onto the mainland of Poseidia." He glanced at Surya and back on the road again. "Where we're going is quite special, because this adds to our power source as well. I think you'll find it all very interesting." Khaluj turned a knob on his control panel. Music piped into the car, soothing and uplifting at the same time.

Sitting in the padded seat, Surya rested his head back. He allowed himself a brief moment of not worrying about Khaluj or his non-stop chattering on the subject of crystal energy.

The priest turned down a road and arrived at a long wide stretch of highway. At once, the vehicle blasted forward, leaving a light trail of smoke behind. Wherever Khaluj planned on taking him, Surya knew they would arrive in no time.

***

No dwelling stood for miles on the surrounding desolate land, except the structure where Surya found himself with Khaluj.

"In this building we manage and operate our crystal mines. We can grow them ourselves when we need to." Khaluj walked over to a screen with writing on it. "We catalog everything we've mined from the earth or grew in the labs."

Surya's eyes widened. "Are earth-grown different from lab-created?"

"Crystals from the earth have a vibration inherent within them. It's naturally born and bred, you might say. Lab-grown crystals are placed next to earth-parent forms so the energy can be shared from the one in nature to the new one just getting accustomed to vibration."

"You make them almost sound like children," said Surya, chuckling.

Khaluj chuckled back. "We love our crystals. Sometimes we almost think of them as our children, so you're not far off in your thinking." He stepped away from the screen, allowing Surya a closer look at the information.

Names of each crystal along with identifying numbers had been entered as line items. Notations included physical characteristics, whether the crystal had been mined or lab-grown, and the function it served. Khaluj scrolled through the information by rotating a dial. Both he and Surya reviewed several pages of information.

"I'm sure it's no surprise to you that we have temple crystals and industrial ones," said Khaluj.

"It makes perfect sense. Ones for healing. Others for generating power so everyone can enjoy creations that make their jobs and lives easier." Surya continued staring at the screen.

"I want you to see the mines." Khaluj motioned for Surya to follow him. "It can be very hot, so be warned."

The entrance to the mine lay several yards away from the office. Rocks and dirt cracked under Surya's shoes as he and Khaluj walked. Seeing a mine and its operations thrilled him. He wanted to touch and view the crystals in their own environment and in the lab.

"We're here," said Khaluj, pointing to a wooden framework that looked more like an entrance to a boardwalk. "Just stay close to me, and you should be fine. I'll let you know what you can touch or not." He turned and smiled at Surya. "Perhaps you can select one of the small crystals for your own use. We'll help you pick out the right one."

Surya grinned. "I like the idea already. One can never have too many crystals."

"Indeed." Khaluj bowed lightly and passed inside the mine entrance.

The wooden planks soon ended, and a dirt path continued in measured descent deep into the earth. When they had landed several yards down the path, a mechanical lift came into sight.

"Ah, we've reached the transport lift. When we get inside, it will take us down to the mine." Khaluj slid the door aside, and both men stepped into a small box-like unit with a ten-person capacity.

Grabbing on to the handrail, Surya held his breath as the lift hummed, lowering deeper into the earth. His stomach held the same flip flop sensation as the first time he traveled to the land rings.

"Takes a little getting used to," said Khaluj, patting Surya's back. "A few deep breaths, and you'll be fine." A quick shudder of the compartment, and everything stilled. A small bell rang. "We're here. Be careful stepping out. Sometimes it's a little slippery."

The hot blast of air took Surya off guard. He shielded himself with his hands as if he could fight off the oppressive blanket of heat. The sound of picks and other machinery clicked and hummed in the distance. As he stepped into an enormous chamber, he recoiled in an instant.

Instead of humans, he saw numerous creatures. Human. Animal. They all were both at once. Faces looked more human, but bodies reminded Surya of goats or horses. Some had the makings of a third eye in the middle of their forehead. On further scrutiny, the extra eye didn't function.

Some of the creatures held an extra appendage or ear. Hands resembled a blend of hooves and fingers. They moved like living, breathing machines, screaming out in pain when a foreman cracked a whip, or if a rock burned or cut.

Khaluj studied Surya's face. "I'm sure you've never seen these before, have you? Quite honestly, I don't think you'll see them anywhere else but here on Atlantis.

"What are they? Who are they?" asked Surya, horrified.

"We call them 'Things.'" Khaluj brushed past one of the beasts without acknowledging its presence, moving on into the center of the room.

Surya nodded in greeting at the same beast. At once the Thing's eyes lit up briefly at the kind gesture. "Do all these . . . what did you call them? Things?"

"Yes, that's correct." Khaluj turned around, waiting for Surya to catch up.

"Do all these beings work in here? In this heat?"

"Of course. What else would they do?" Khaluj kicked at another Thing that stepped in his way.

The half man, half horse jumped back in pain. Surya briefly tried consoling it, rubbing the lower half of its leg.

Khaluj stifled a look of irritation. "No need to worry about them. That's what they're bred to do. Work. They're our workers. Our help, if you will." He tried smiling again.

"You mean to say these creatures are literally bred to do hard manual labor? Why would you create these when their bodies don't seem the most ideal for moving the way a human would?"

"Surya, another thing I'll add is that we use genetic engineering for creating ways to make our lives a little easier. Any way we can work nature or a system for human advantage, that's what we do."

Surya looked up, stunned. "Do humans breed with animals to create these Things?"

"How else would you do it?" Khaluj asked. "Of course."

Whether it was the heat or shock of hearing the priest's confirmation, the struggle to keep from fainting overwhelmed Surya. He nearly stumbled with the next step.

"Whoa. Easy there, young man." Khaluj grabbed Surya's arm before he dropped completely to the ground. "I see the heat is really getting to you. Let's look quickly at some crystals, and then we'll leave."

For the next few minutes, Khaluj showed a rather ill Surya the giant crystals spiking up from the ground or dangling from overhead. At times the crystals intertwined, creating chaotic gridwork of rock. Heat made everything sweat. The rocks looked like they were almost pliable.

Off to one side of the room, an area had been sectioned off. Khaluj led the way there. "This is our lab. We seed and grow crystals here. As you can see, we keep all of the work as close to nature as possible."

A sharp roar filled the air. Both Khaluj and Surya looked up.

"Is something wrong? That was loud," said Surya.

"Hmm, probably a Thing got hurt, or received a good thrashing for not working like it should." He turned back to one of the crystals. "As I told you earlier, we have temple crystals and ones we use for industry. When we extract them, we determine how the form will be used."

"And how do you make that judgement call?" Surya asked. The roar in the distance still cried out, echoing off the walls. He barely heard Khaluj's answer.

Khaluj raised his voice. "We have some high initiates in the order who can read energies quite well. From the stone's vibration, they know for what purpose the stone will be used."

"I see." Surya nodded. At once, his gut clenched. A wave of anxiety gripped him. He licked his lips and swiped his hair back. Sweat rolled down his fingers.

"I think it's time to go up." Khaluj grasped Surya's arm. "You look really ill."

"I want to know more about the horrid noise. There's something about it that bothers me. I don't know why." Surya took in a deep breath. "I don't see how these poor creatures stand it down here." He stumbled up to the elevator and rested his head against the side. "Can't you at least ask about it?"

"My dear Surya, you worry too much. Does your kind . . . I mean, do you concern yourself with animals? Not that we don't have some responsibility for their care."

"These aren't mere animals, Khaluj. They're part human. Do you not see that? And yes, I care deeply for them. For most sentient creatures, if you want to know the truth."

The priest's face clouded with impatience. "I see. Well, in our culture, we don't concern ourselves with the Things."

"Perhaps you should," Surya retorted in anger.

The lift arrived, and the two men entered. Surya sulked in silence as he and Khaluj rode upward.

When they reached the top, Surya strode out, heading back to Khaluj's vehicle. His face tensed. A noise came from several yards away from a small red dirt hill. A loud wail followed by one last attempt at a bellowing roar. It sounded a lot like the one he'd heard in the mine. What was it doing behind a hill? Had someone dragged it from the mine to the open elements and no protection?

He turned toward Khaluj, a questioning expression covering his face. Khaluj stared off in the distance toward the hill, eyes squinted against the sun.

"Are you not going to see about it?" Surya asked. "Whatever it is, it sounds like it's hurt."

"I really think it will be okay. If it can't do the job, it needs to go. That's the way of it, I'm afraid." Khaluj opened the driver's side door.

"No, it's not the way of it. And I'm not afraid." Without another word, Surya ran in the direction of the hill, stopping briefly as the beast limped out from behind.

It tried moving on its four legs before collapsing to the ground. From what Surya surmised, it appeared injured or perhaps simply exhausted. The creature's rib cage rose and fell with each labored breath. Surya ran faster. Khaluj called out, frantic.

No matter what, Surya knew he must reach the human animal struggling alone, scared, maybe hurt or near death. When he reached it, he viewed the being with horror. The lower half was definitely a goat, with back legs like the actual animal. The legs, bearing cloven hooves, twisted inward.

The front legs confounded Surya more. Between the cleft in the hooves, he saw three human toes. Two of them on one foot overlapped. Three toes on the other foot were severely bent at the joint, giving them a claw-like appearance. Human heels made up the rear of the hooves, stopping where the toes started.

The upper body looked human in every way, except for an unsightly third nipple between two natural ones. On top of the head, Surya detected beginning formations of human ears. A pair of goat ears stood out as they would have with a real animal. A flat goat-like nose and definite human mouth made up the face, as did human cheeks and jawline.

Surya wrinkled his nose. The fur and body held a stench so strong, he nearly vomited. Lash marks and dried blood peeked through dark brown fur. The creatures back showed scars from previous beatings and oozed blood from new wounds. Hands and arms seemed flawless, fully human. Other than dirt and grime, the hands were almost attractive.

"Young man, can we dispense with such waste of good time, and leave him alone?" Khaluj, a little breathless, had reached Surya.

"Him?" Surya glanced up at Khaluj. As the being rolled slightly, he saw what resembled human male genitalia peeking out from a sheath of soft fine fur.

"No, we will not leave him alone. He's been beaten; he's bleeding, frightened. Have you seen his legs? No wonder he can't do hard labor. It's wearing on his body." Surya scowled. "Where can we take him for help?"

Khaluj blanched at the question. "Excuse me? Take him for help?" He shook his head. "I'm sorry, you're asking too much. Again, we don't concern ourselves with Things."

The Thing let out a wail. Surya chilled at the sound. His memory shot back to his session with Martaam and the vision they both saw. He cleared the thought out of his mind. Khaluj didn't need to know what happened in lover's work room. The vision came to him for a reason, more prophetic in nature. He knew that now with more certainty.

"Will you let me take him to an animal healer? I'm sure you must have those on Poseidia."

"Surya, I'm not trying to be unreasonable. I promise on that statement. But I can't place such a vile creature in my transportation craft. It's not done."

"Really, Khaluj? Is it truly not done, or is it you who are being callous? Shame on you. A priest of all people should have compassion for all the Creator's created."

"But, Surya, these creatures have no souls. They are . . ." Khaluj scratched his head and looked out over the landscape. "They are soulless. They don't return to the ether or cosmic intelligence when they die—which can be three or four hundred years, you know."

"Three of four hundred years? Suffering a life of pure misery?" In anger, Surya leaned in close to Khaluj's face. "I'm not trying to be difficult, either. You've been pleasant up until this point. However, if you don't help, I'll call Martaam. She's compassionate enough."

"No, you don't need to do that." Khaluj's brows furrowed.

"Or I can call Aleemirin and Tujuk. Maybe they have some heart." Surya turned his face toward the office. "I saw a communication box in there. Maybe a quick call will do the trick. I have three people I can contact."

"I have an idea," said Khaluj, brightening a little. "If I take Thing with us and leave him with you at your apartment, will you be willing to meet some of my other friends, those outside Law of One? I'm wanting them to become acquainted with you."

Surya looked at Khaluj, confused. "Sure. I'll be glad to meet some of your friends. Why is that the subject of an offer?"

"Well, you seem always occupied with other tasks. I just wanted a stronger agreement. My friends mean a lot to me, just like this Thing apparently means a lot to you," said Khaluj, smiling.

"I hope you treat your friends much better than you treat this poor creature."

Khaluj's faint smile disappeared in an instant. "I'll help you get this odorous Thing into the holding area of my vehicle. It's where I store my luggage when I make longer trips overnight, but it should hold him."

"You'd put him in a dark closed-in box? You have a passenger area behind where we sit." Surya raised is voice in indignation.

Holding out his hand, Khaluj answered, "Now, now. It won't hurt him. He'll be fine."

"He won't be able to breathe, Khaluj. You put my poor friend in a forsaken compartment, any meeting with your friends is off."

"I'll run back to the mine office and see if they have some protective covering. For you, I'll place him in the back seat. He's a mess. And I advise you to refrain from calling Thing your friend. It's frowned upon here in Atlantis."

"I personally don't care what is frowned upon in Atlantis. Maybe you humans need to learn some common compassion and decency."

Khaluj tilted his head. "'You humans?' A wide smile covered his face. "Yes, I see what you mean."

Surya fell silent, averting his eyes toward the Thing. Khaluj skipped off toward the office. He had slipped, and Khaluj knew it. That priest held a secret, knew something, and it concerned him on many levels. For a priest functioning under Law of One, the behavior didn't seem to fit. The man's energy still didn't feel right.

The Thing whimpered and tried to sit up.

"No, Thing. Just lay back down," said Surya in a soothing voice. "We're going to get you some help. Don't mind what that bad man said. He's just mean." Leaning in close to Thing's ears, he whispered, "I'll never let anyone hurt you again."

The poor beast let out a light sigh and lay his head on Surya's open hand.

***

Surya watched Khaluj drive off from Vardhase, thankful to be rid of the priest's company. Getting the poor Thing out of the car with little to no help had been tricky.

"Easy does it, fellow. We'll take it nice and slow." Surya wrapped an arm around the poor Thing for added support. Khaluj had gladly given him the large sheet used for covering the back seats of his vehicle. Wrapped up and mostly hidden, the beast limped its way to the apartment, stopping and resting a couple of times when it grew tired.

"Let's get you cleaned up," said Surya, unlocking the door. "I'll run a bath for you. You'll like that, won't you?" He hugged the Thing, who rested its head on Surya's shoulder. "Did you say something?" The creature made some noises, moving its mouth as if wanting to talk.

"Can you speak at all?" Surya moved his head away for a better look at Thing's face. Deep in the eyes, he thought a spark of animation lurked there, a desire for freedom, to be heard, to have a voice.

Thing only burbled out a few unintelligible sounds. Whatever they were, this being meant them sincerely, from what Surya could tell. He made it to the guest bathroom that also had a doorway into the guest bedroom. These rooms would be Thing's.

"We've got to give you a name. Calling you Thing is disgraceful and humiliating. You're part human, which means something."

Once the tub held enough water, Surya helped the Thing inside, making sure it landed easily without harm. He'd wanted to add some essential oils for aromatherapy and healing, but with open wounds, decided against it.

The creature whimpered as water engulfed its body. Surya carefully wiped a cloth with soap lightly over the upper parts. Though tanned by heat and sun, the skin clearly showed Caucasian features, similar to his own. Maybe there had been some Caucasian humans who bred with animals? How strange. Most of the Things had red-brown skin tones like the Atlantean people.

Surya held his hands out, getting a read on Thing's vibrations. He closed his eyes. A vision of him and Den-El at the portal. The feeling of Den-El pushing him. Den-El's voice, which sounded far away, dream-like. These memories made no sense in the present context. But they meant something. What?

"I miss my friend back home," Surya said to Thing. "It's a little lonely being by myself all the time." He moved his fingers over the rest of the beast's body, lathering hide and fur with cleansing soap. "I'm glad I found you." Thing opened his eyes briefly, lips pulled into a soft smile. Another round of sounds came out, each one as unintelligible as the first. Surya shook his head, chuckling.

Chapter Seven

The Thing lay on its new bed, dark luminous eyes darting around the room. Six appendages splayed wide open as the beast rested on its back. It seemed mostly comfortable, but Surya didn't like the legs turning inward because he suspected some pain as a result. He didn't like unsightly deformities. Not only were they unpleasant to see, they were worse for the Thing. It limped, wincing if its body moved a certain way.

Calluses covered the bottoms of the toes; they bled and cracked. A third nipple needed to be removed. Had Thing's ears formed enough to function, or did the goat ears collect all the sounds? Soulless. What did Khaluj mean when he made such a remark?

Surya knew every aspect of creation contained a soul on some level, from beings with astral bodies down to the rocks and minerals themselves. The only characteristic separating them was level of mobility and creative thinking. He knew the progression from rock and mineral kingdom, to plant, animal, human, and astral body existed.

Progression had been this way since the Logos Creator formed the universe and mechanics behind it. Things had souls. How could they not? No matter how perverse, these beings had been born from the union of sentient creations. They felt pain, bled, mated, gave birth, got sick, died.

Surya wanted total comfort for the human animal. He lightly rubbed one of the legs. Closing his eyes, he centered himself. His mind found nothingness, calming on command. Sacred sounds echoed in his head as he called on certain ones for healing. Associated chakras in his system vibrated. The space between his eyes vibrated like it always did when he meditated or prepared for a spiritual action.

Ambient white noise in the room stopped. Thing barely breathed, it seemed. Surya placed his hand on Thing's right hip, finding bone ends and joint spaces he needed. An etheric set of hands emanated from Surya's, transcending all human limits of Earth. He reached into the body of fur, slipping fingers around the bones, pulling, pushing, manipulating, until ligaments, tissue, and muscle shifted.

Gently, he moved the hip back into alignment, twisting the femur into the desired location. The tibia and bones of the ankle followed. The ancient healing mantra auto played in his head. When the look and feel of the leg met his approval, he slowly brought his consciousness back to the present.

The Thing breathed with measured breaths, as if coaching itself into a state of calmness. Had the maneuvers been painful? Surya didn't recall any sounds, which would have disrupted the procedure immediately. An expression of increased comfort covered Thing's face. The action had been a positive one and ended well.

Time to heal the other leg. Surya readied himself. Just as he closed his eyes, a knock at the door reverberated through the apartment. The Thing jumped, startled.

"Shh, it's okay. Wait here." Frustrated, Surya raced to the door. A most inopportune moment for disruptions. He swore under his breath, jerking the door open.

"Have I come at a bad time?

"Martaam." Surya stuck his head outside, checking around for other people. She came alone. "Are you okay?"

"Fine. I wanted to see if you wanted to go out, maybe have some drinks, food?" She craned her neck slightly, looking over his shoulder.

Surya turned his head back in the direction of the spare room. If he'd been alone, an afternoon out with Martaam would have met with an immediate yes. He rubbed the side of his face and blinked a few times.

Disappointment washed over her face. "Sorry I interrupted you. I'll let you get back to whatever you were doing."

"No. Wait." Surya grabbed her arm, pulling her back. "Don't go. I'm sorry." He sucked in his breath. "Come on in."

"Is something bothering you? Khaluj said you two spent some time together today. Did you enjoy yourself?"

"If you want to call seeing poor beaten down hybrids breaking their backs in ungodly hot mines, no I didn't enjoy myself. I'll have nightmares for a long time. Seeing the power crystal in all its glory, yes. It was beautiful."

Martaam placed her hand lightly on Surya's shoulder. "You look really upset. You saw the Things, didn't you?"

Surya sensed his anger building. "I can't believe you people allow this. It defies any laws of human decency. It's despicable." He stepped away from Martaam, shaking a finger at her. "And for you to approve of humans and animals breeding? So you can create a work force? Humans can do that work. Others in the universe could teach more."

A light wail sounded from the bedroom. Martaam's eyes grew wide. Surya clenched his fists. He wanted to scream, but he ignored the noise like it didn't exist.

"I know you're terribly unhappy about what you saw." She took one of his hands in hers. "But let me just say that Law of One people are fighting this. We don't agree with it at all."

She tried maintaining a calm voice while keeping direct eye contact with Surya. "It's the Aryans who are perpetuating this horrid practice. They like the idea of having a slave force to do their bidding."

"Aryan? Law of One?" Surya wore a look of confusion. "Your dear Khaluj showed no care for those in the mines. He said people weren't concerned about them, and that they were basically made for work. Did you know that he thinks creating Things is okay as long as it makes life for humans better? As a matter of fact, I threatened to call you when he wouldn't . . ."

"What?" Martaam turned her gaze toward the back of the apartment, in the direction of the rooms. "What are you talking about, Surya? Khaluj would never say that. He's a Law of One priest. Highest level, mind you. Right up there with my uncle and Tujuk. They don't approve of breeding and keeping Things."

"You sure about that? About Khaluj, I mean. Aleemirin and Tujuk were my next people to call." Surya grimaced.

"Call for what?" Martaam squeezed his hand.

The wail from the spare room came louder, along with a shuffling noise. Surya turned his head in the direction of the sound.

"What's back there?" Without waiting for an explanation, Martaam charged past Surya and headed straight for the noise source.

He squeezed his eyes closed as he heard Martaam cry out in surprise. "Wait. I'll explain."

Martaam met him in the hall. "You brought one home? Why?"

"Because he was tossed outside, left to die. I heard him when Khaluj and I were in the mine. I know it was him beyond a shadow of a doubt." Surya grasped Martaam's shoulders and pulled her close, whispering in her ear. "He was in the vision I saw that day in your healing room. You saw it too."

She paled at the comments. "Are you going to keep him?"

"He stays, or I'll take him and move somewhere else, if you don't allow Things."

"No need to move. Many people have Things in their homes. They help with chores or whatever you need them for. They're everywhere." Martaam turned back and entered the room. "It looks like you got him cleaned up. He doesn't smell. Have you fed him?"

"Not yet. Anything special they eat?"

"Mainly grains, vegetables, and fruits. There are some that have an appetite for meat, but it's not the norm." Martaam, walked over to the bed. "Thing, would you like something to eat?"

Thing sat up, nodding. He uttered one word. "Food?"

"That's the first sense he's made since I brought him here. So he can talk?" Surya stood beside Martaam, resting his hand lightly in the small of her back.

"I'm thinking he's calming down, trusting you. When they trust someone, they communicate okay." She whispered in Surya's ear. "But they are not the brightest creatures. Very simple in their thinking."

"Not true," Thing cried out, indignant. The words dragged as the creature spoke in a higher-pitched tone.

"Are you smarter than the others, Thing?" Martaam stroked one of the ears. "Are you glad this sweet man brought you home with him?"

"Home. Glad." Thing clapped his hands and lay back down. "Hungry. Food."

Martaam looked at Surya. "If you have something in your kitchen, I'll put a meal together for him."

"Be my guest," said Surya, smiling.

Sitting on the edge of the bed, Thing ate the salad Martaam brought him, swallowing it down like its life depended on it.

"Easy, fellow. Nobody's going to take it away from you." Surya ran his fingers through the fur. He scratched a little deeper into the hide, laughing when Thing's ears waggled back and forth.

"He needs some healing." Martaam cocked her head, studying the creature. "I can help with that."

Surya considered her words. How much should he tell? He wanted to say so much. "I've already healed one of his hips. Straightened it up. I was about to start the other when you knocked."

She turned, staring at him. "You heal?"

"If I could turn him into a human, I would do it."

"I want to see you heal the other hip." Martaam's eyes sparkled. "Some of our healers can reach into the body and work without making one mark on the skin. They're the most advanced of all."

Surya rubbed his lower lip. "As you can see, that's the method I used on Thing."

"Not a single mark." Martaam rubbed her finger over Thing's leg, inspecting the joints. "Do the other one, Surya."

"Thing, are you finished?"

"Yes." Thing handed the bowl to Surya.

"I want to fix the other hip, Thing. Maybe work on your feet so you can walk better. Would you like that?"

"Fix." Thing swiveled himself back on the bed, digging his head into the pillow.

Martaam stepped to the foot of the bed. "I'll tune in and help, but I won't interfere with your work directly."

"Sounds good." Surya blinked and took several neutral breaths. He closed his eyes in preparation, going through the steps he completed earlier. The room quietened. An energetic charge filled the air. He placed his hands in position on Thing's body. Through will and visualization, an etheric set of hands carefully moved inside toward the hip joint.

A flash of light streaked across the room, ending with a sharp snap. Surya shut down his mind at once. The disruption created a sharp burst of pain through his head. His eyes opened. Martaam gasped. Joining them near the bed, a figure surrounded by glowing light.

Surya knew such astral bodies belonged in the higher dimensions, nowhere near the fourth or fifth focus. They only appeared as humans so real humans could relate to and communicate with them. The face beamed with benevolence. Long golden hair fell to the shoulders. Light emanating from the figure had bent and angled in such a way, it looked as if it wore robes.

"Beloveds, I am Zedekiel. Do you not know that you are interfering in what has already been determined?"

Martaam shrank back in fear.

"In what has been determined? What do you mean?" Surya contained no fear of Zedekiel. These higher astral beings didn't contain anything but truth, light, and love, regardless of how a human may interpret a situation. Law of the cosmos and universe were funny that way. True illumination made the difference between full understanding or confusion.

"There has been a transgression. To change or alter shifts the journey toward redemption."

"I'm afraid I don't understand." Surya shook his head. "I'm trying to heal this poor creature. How can that possibly be wrong? It has been wronged by being perversely created in the first place."

Martaam flashed a look of admonishment in Surya's direction. She lightly shook her head.

Zedekiel smiled with compassion and understanding. "Dear Surya. Your great love serves you well. Never lose sight of it. But always be aware, still, that you are not to judge what is righteous or perverse. Such judgement belongs to the Creator. The receiver of your beneficence is of noble blood. He dwells among those with honor and power."

"I still don't know what you mean. How could this genetic anomaly be of noble blood? Whomever helped in its making would never be considered noble. Not on this planet or another, for that matter."

"Beloved, folly of youth has just as dire consequences as folly of the elder ones. It is hoped they think and reason more clearly. But youth is puffed up, inexperienced in reason, lacking in knowledge. This leads one astray."

"What did this creature to do deserve its fate?" Surya squared his shoulders, locking his gaze on Zedekiel.

The archangel tilted his head. "Can you say you do not know, when it is you who led it to transgress?"

Surya's mind whirled. The question sickened him. He wanted to shut out everything, run, leave. His secret lay in tatters. Martaam would demand answers.

Khaluj most likely already suspected something unusual. He hadn't asked Tujuk and Aleemirin if they told their fellow priest what he'd shared with them. The pit of his stomach tightened with dread.

Zedekiel continued, "Your cherished friend has called out from the depths of darkness. He trusted. You heard his cry. Thus, you two were led to each other. What has been done cannot be totally undone. I will allow some softening. The ones in power will determine the outcome, for they started the process. Continue in love and peace, Beloveds."

The archangel vanished. Nothing but silence filled the room. Martaam stood, hands on her cheeks, dumbstruck. Thing lay on the bed, wild-eyed. Surya didn't know what to say, where to start.

"What was that?" Martaam spoke up.

"You've never seen a heavenly being?" Surya asked.

"There was a time long ago when Atlanteans walked in the company of gods. We mingled with aliens from the stars." Martaam ventured away from the bed and stepped in close next to Surya. "They were not only advanced in technology, but they carried light, love, and enlightenment within them."

"And then it all went horribly wrong," whispered Surya.

"What did the angel mean when he said you led Thing to transgress? Who are you, and why is he called your friend?"

Martaam gazed at Surya. He couldn't keep his identity from her any longer. When would there ever be a good time to tell?

"Can we please take care of Thing first? We can talk later."

She nodded.

No matter how unsettling the angel's appearance, taking care of the helpless creature on the bed remained Surya's priority. By his selfishness, he'd created an unspeakable horror for someone he cared about.

He'd do everything in his power to right the wrong. Surya struggled a few moments with clearing his mind and dismissing what just happened long enough to complete what he needed to do. Taking in several deep neutral breaths, he started all over again.

Etheric hands completed the work on the second hip, like the first. Surya visualized with great concentration, sincerity, and accuracy. He called out in his mind the ancient healing mantras and sacred sounds. Now for the feet.

He had a choice. Human or animal. Surya chose animal, much to his chagrin. Human feet would make the body more unsightly and unnatural than ever. Animals had their own balance. Choosing hooves kept the animal part of the body consistent. Within minutes, the troublesome toes had been removed and the hooves moved back to their natural position. Removing the third nipple was the last and easiest task of all.

"You okay?" Surya briefly glanced at his friend. "I have one last thing I want to do." He closed his eyes and tried finding the grid of coordinates and pathways in the ether, the limitless circuitry connecting all. He tapped into the coordinates he wanted. It meshed with his immediately.

In the depths, he locked on to his friend's true vibrational frequency and pulled. He saw the dark layers peeling away, giving way to light. The fog lifted. A dulled and blunted frequency grew brighter, stronger. Simplicity of mind blossomed into a complex network of neurons exploding into high power, taking in every sensation the five human senses could handle.

Clarity set in, swift and true. The creature on the bed grabbed Surya's hand. "I thought I'd never find you. I tried. I prayed hard." Tears slid out in a stream. His cheeks flushed, and his lips quivered. "I don't know how much longer I would have lasted."

"Den-El, I'm so sorry." Surya wrapped his arms around Den-El's neck and kissed his forehead. "I don't think I can change you any more than what I've done. It's all I'll be allowed."

"Your father was so angry. I tried everything to keep my word and not say anything. The more I kept quiet and tried avoiding him, the worse it got. He found out. I had to tell him the truth." Den-El let out a loud sob. "Just look at me. I'm ugly."

"Shh. Stop. Don't think about that right now." Surya sat on the edge of the bed. For the first time he noted Martaam's absence. She had slipped out of the room without a sound. "Why would Father do something like this? Your father is his top advisor. How would he support such a decision?"

"Your father's the king. Mine isn't. Simple." Den-El grimaced and wiped his eyes.

"What did they do, Den-El, to put you inside this body? Surely they didn't use the portal to get you here."

"They placed me in the vaporization chamber, and that's the last I remember. I woke up in the mine. The rest is history. Until you found me."

Surya's blood nearly chilled at his friend's words. His father had disconnected Den-El's body and soul. The unhoused soul had been placed in the shell of a Thing.

"Was she worth it, Surya? Was that her standing beside you?" Den-El scowled.

"So far, she's worth it. She's smart, kind. Seems to have a good head on her shoulders. Her father owns these apartments. She's learning to be a healer. She'll be a good one by the time her studies are over."

Den-El turned his head away. A bitter expression covered his face. A stroke from Surya's hand and a kiss on the ear didn't console him in the least.

"We'll get back home. I'll see to that," Surya whispered.

***

Martaam sat alone in her kitchen, sipping a glass of the best wine she owned. If her mind dulled enough, would she discover the experience of the last hour as nothing more than a bizarre dream? She and Surya shared a connection, and no matter how hard she tried, she couldn't figure out why. The moment he stepped into her office, a spark ignited. Not a day since did she go without thinking of him.

When she and Khaluj made love, she closed her eyes and tried blocking out images of Surya, lest Khaluj tap into her thoughts. At nights alone, she pleasured herself, pretending Surya touched her.

The mysterious images she saw when working on him started to make some sense, based on what happened in his apartment. A strange doorway, sensations of dizziness and disorientation. The other voice must have belonged to his friend.

Once Surya's friend spoke after the final healing, she didn't stay. Staying meant intruding on a moment meant for the two of them alone. She had no place in it. How long had Surya planned on keeping his identity a secret? Where had he come from? Gripped by an urge to call her uncle, she squelched the desire with another swallow of wine. She'd get to the bottom of this mystery at some point herself. Surya's words about Khaluj disappointed her greatly. Through all his charm and seeming congeniality, a thread of insincerity always lurked in the background. Putting away the suspicion had become harder lately.

Surya's arrival challenged it even more. A breaking point had arrived. Intoxication loosened inhibition and brought out a certain honesty. If she were honest with herself, staying with Khaluj probably meant heartache at some point. He thought he hid himself well, but arrogance and narcissism never kept low.

The dark traits peeked out from behind every corner of his psyche, leaking into the heart of his personality. Tonight, it all ended. She'd have no part of the charade any longer. Martaam got up from the chair and headed to her bedroom. Retrieving a bag, she placed in it every piece of jewelry given to her by Khaluj.

The next time he knocked on her door, he'd be answered by tokens of his own shallowness. Never again would she allow flattery to win her over. Nor would she fall into the trap of thinking high living and fine possessions made a fulfilled life. Exemplary living is what she wanted now, to help those in need and enjoy the simple pleasures in life.

If you weren't a kind, honorable person, what good would come of anything you did? She carried the bag back to the kitchen. For the remainder of the evening, she sipped wine and buried her sorrows. Tonight, she may weep for her own loss, but tomorrow she'd find new joy.

***

The bird had watched with great intent. Through a slit in the curtains, it witnessed everything. The angel, the healing. The same bird that had spied on Surya when he first arrived on Poseidia also followed Martaam from her apartment to his.

It heard most of the conversation too. Filled with information, the bird flew back to the man who waited impatiently in his home. Food had been earned for the night, and he'd promised extra. The man didn't seem happy asking for help. Would this information anger or please?

***

Mal-Ek breathed a sigh of relief. The moment Surya found Den-El, he cheered inside. Delivering a horrendous punishment saddened him beyond words. He had guarded his emotions with utmost care, avoiding inevitable darkness waiting to swallow him whole.

Ahtan-Mir, Den-El's father, sat watching along with his king. He quickly wiped a few tears trickling down his face.

"They've found each other," said Mal-Ek. He turned and wrapped an arm around his advisor. "We'll both rest a little easier at nights."

"I'm sure we'll both rest easier when our children return home, Your Majesty."

"That will, indeed, be a joyous day. To celebrate, did you want to add a healing touch of your own? According to Federation guidelines, we have some flexibility in this punishment."

"You're too kind, Your Majesty. You can't imagine how my son's role in this whole affair has pained me to the core. He's blemished our family's good name and honor."

Mal-Ek placed his hand gently on Ahtan-Mir's shoulder. "We're forgiving people, and so are many on this planet. So are most of the members in the Federation. We know mistakes are made all the time. The consequences can be a devil. That's the bad part we may have to swallow."

"Your Majesty, if it's okay with you, may I please restore my son's face? Just the face, get rid of the goat-like nose. I know I can't change anything else regarding his body. Your son has done so much already. He wanted nothing more than to reverse everything in an instant."

"I must admit, Ahtan, I'm rather impressed with Surya. He's able to hold his own pretty well in a strange place, not knowing much information."

"He's strong, Your Majesty. How could he be less? You're his father." Ahtan-Mir managed a faint smile.

"Tonight, when Den-El is asleep, we'll perform the last of the healing. At least when he awakens, he'll be a little more like himself." Mal-Ek nodded to Ahtan-Mir in affirmation.

***

Surya thought about his decision, weighing the pros and cons. After convincing Den-El to close his eyes and rest, he quietly stepped out of the apartment. He picked his way in the dark, glancing up at the flash of green reaching to the sky. One night, he wanted to visit the central land core and see the Temple of Poseidon at night—with Martaam.

Opening the lock to the main office took a few seconds with sharp visualization. Surya moved over the hallway and up the steps with lightning speed. When Martaam opened the door, she nearly dropped her glass of wine.

"Do you mind if I come in, or are we going to talk out here?" He glanced up and down the hallway, detecting other rooms. She had never told him if she lived alone upstairs above the office, or if others live there too.

Martaam said nothing as she opened the door. "Would you like a glass of wine? I can open another bottle."

Surya arched an eyebrow. "Another bottle?"

"Don't ask." She moved toward the wine cabinet.

When Surya seated himself at the kitchen table, he first took a long sip from his glass. "I guess you want to know why I'm here."

"I do. But you don't have to say anything you're not comfortable with. You haven't broken any apartment rules, and you're entitled to your privacy."

He smiled, grateful for her words. "I owe you an explanation. I wanted to wait a while longer, but it looks like nothing is working out in my favor in that arena."

Martaam sat silently, fighting against the fog from drinking too much. She didn't want to miss or forget anything he had to say and chided herself for being so weak in the first place.

"I'm not what you think I am. I don't come from anywhere near Scandinavia." He watched closely, gauging her reaction. Surya continued. "I don't come from this planet, and neither does my friend Den-El."

She licked her lips, shifting in her chair. "I'm listening."

Surya said, "I'm the son of a king."

Chapter Eight

Khaluj and Surya walked the trail toward the coastline. Their destination, the island of Aryan. Surya carried a small bag holding a few toiletries and the tunic and headband he wore to The Meeting of The Kings celebration. He and the priest had retraced the transportation choices and routes Surya had chosen when he first entered through the portal.

Much to Surya's dismay, the priest had invited him to a cocktail party and dinner. Worse, they would be spending the night and returning to Poseidia the next day. Khaluj hadn't gone into detail about their lodgings, merely stating that he took care of everything.

"I want you to meet some of my closest friends, and you'll get to see more of Atlantis. Aryan is a beautiful island too," Khaluj told him. Surya knew he still had a bargain to uphold.

He couldn't fathom why someone would create a bargaining chip by helping him with a Thing. Khaluj didn't measure high on his friend radar, but when he made the decision to explore Atlantis, taking the good with the bad was part of the deal. Learning the dark side of human nature held equal weight to learning and appreciating the good.

"Why do you store it so far away from everything?" Surya couldn't wait to see the Ultra Marine Pod Khaluj told him about.

"I like keeping it safe. Most of all, I like keeping my life as private as possible," said Khaluj. "This is not a craft most Atlanteans have at their disposal. I'm a humble priest, so seeing me with my own underwater vehicle would raise a few eyebrows."

"If I may ask, Khaluj, how do you manage the nice possessions you have? I can't imagine a priest's salary allowing lots of luxuries." Surya had taken the public transport to Orubis Way, where he met Khaluj at his lavish apartment. From there Khaluj drove them to the ferry and air taxi port.

"I must admit that I have a prosperous family." Khaluj hesitated a moment. "And I have certain private business endeavors, which help my funds immensely." He glanced over at Surya as they came closer to the dock. "I might add that your friends Aleemirin and Tujuk don't do so badly themselves. We are ruling class priests, not the lowly humble kind who manage a place of worship."

Surya looked at Khaluj in surprise, dismayed at the arrogance of such a comment.

"I mean that in the most matter-of-fact way I can, young Surya. It's not said out of malice or ill will. The church priests are kind and well-meaning people. They care very much for uplifting their congregation and creating good in the world."

Unlike Khaluj and others of his ilk, thought Surya. He knew for every Aleemirin and Tujuk, there was a Khaluj and legion more like him who only cared for their own interests. This much he had surmised.

The priest looked over at Surya, scowling. "Like it or not, there are hierarchies on Poseidia."

"Of course there are, Khaluj. Did I say anything to dispute your education on the religious community and how it fits into the social construct of Poseidia?"

Khaluj chuckled. "You are the most high-spirited being I think I've ever met. Have you always been like this?"

"Probably," Surya retorted.

At times, he disliked guarding his emotions and thoughts on Ontarus 9. The mental exercise of it grew wearing at times. He'd hoped being in a third-dimension world would have lessened the need. He hadn't banked on powerful priests tapping into thought waves whenever they felt like it.

The two reached the land's edge, where water lapped at the shoreline. Several yards away, Surya viewed the whitewashed building where Khaluj's prized pod lay docked.

They walked over the dock toward the building. Salt and fish scented the air as the breeze grew boisterous at intervals. Surya scanned the ocean, not seeing anything looking like land or an island.

"In case you're wondering," said Khaluj, "this will be about a four-hour trip."

"Oh?" Surya whirled around, staring at Khaluj. "Four hours?" Thoughts of spending an inordinate amount of time in cramped quarters with someone he didn't especially like stirred up a flash of panic.

"By the way, Surya, we will be traveling under water. My Marine Pod is a tiny underwater sea vehicle, not an ordinary boat."

"Should be a fascinating trip." Surya took a deep breath, mentally preparing himself. The only thing holding his sanity together was the excitement of traveling in such a craft at all.

Khaluj pulled out a key and unlocked the door to the building, which didn't amount to much more than a covered slip.

A large round orb lay tucked inside, bobbing gently on the water. Surya stood on the small loading platform, studying the craft with curiosity. He had to admit, Martaam had made a good point on the merits of associating with the priest. Never a dull moment, he suspected.

"Surya, my good friend," said Khaluj, turning quickly, "I know we have our differences, which you've expressed and shown quite well. I would like, however, for us to be more . . . how do you say it? Simpatico. We may have more in common than not, if you just give it a chance."

He seemed so sincere. Surya almost believed him. He kept his thoughts strictly on Khaluj's words and the Pod he was about to experience. "Absolutely. No reason why we can't make that happen, despite our rocky moments." Surya forced a grin.

On a tiny remote-control fob Khaluj pulled from his pocket, he pressed a button. The top half of the Pod lifted up. Four people could ride in comfort. A small storage compartment rested behind the passenger seats. Off to the side, he viewed an enclosed area resembling a small tiny room.

"Did you have schooling for managing such a vehicle?" asked Surya.

"Most definitely." Khaluj carefully stepped inside, motioning Surya to do the same. "The nice part is how it locks onto the nearest power source from one of the crystal grids. It will do this on any of the Atlantean islands."

Surya sat down in the passenger seat while Khaluj readied the Pod for travel. On the same fob, Khaluj pressed another button, which opened the door of the building. The top of the Pod closed into place and glided over the water. Strapping himself in his seat, Surya prayed the motion wouldn't make him ill.

Khaluj shifted a gear. The Pod let out a hissing noise, descending slowly into the ocean water. Surya gripped the sides of his seat. What was this suffocating sensation humans felt? He resisted the urge to call the whole trip off.

"It's okay, Surya. We go about three hundred feet down. No worries, though. The Pod has strong seals and can withstand the pressure. If there's a problem, my alarms will come on."

Khaluj gazed at his control panel. The screen lit up with sonar graphs, maps, and dials. "Oh, if you need to go, we have a place for that." He turned briefly, pointing to the enclosed area Surya saw earlier.

"So that's what the big cabinet is." Surya grinned. "Nice to know. Four hours is a long trip."

Gazing through the front windows, Surya settled in his seat, mesmerized with an otherwise hidden ecosystem. A whole world around them pulsed with a life of its own. The craft moved with amazing swiftness through the water, dodging large coral formations and adjusting for changes in the environment. Fish scattered in all directions. One larger fish sliced through the water, the tip of its tail tapping the window lightly as it passed.

"Have you ever hit anything big?" Surya asked.

"I've had some near misses. The windows are several inches thick." Khaluj chuckled. "The fish usually see me first and swim around."

With a flick of a button, Khaluj sent a stream of soft music flowing into the Pod. "I love listening to something nice when I'm traveling. Don't you?" He glanced at Surya.

"Me too. Nothing better." Surya couldn't remember a time on Ontarus 9 when he'd created a reality under water, listening to music at the same time.

"Do you miss Scandinavia? I hear it's a lovely place," said Khaluj. With a quick shift of a gear, he shot the craft to the right several feet, avoiding a couple of large whales.

"I'm liking Atlantis a lot."

"Good." Khaluj's face clouded. He shifted in his seat, letting out a light breath.

Out of the corner of his eye, Surya watched the priest tap his foot, drum his fingers on the gear controls. For a few moments, Khaluj hummed lightly to the music, maintaining the tones with a rich resonant voice.

Surya had tried tapping into the priest's thoughts, but the man also avoided concentrating his mind on one subject. The priest knew something about him. He'd sensed it early on, though he tried continually putting the notion out of his mind.

"You have wanted to ask me something for a while, Khaluj, so let's just get everything out in the open and be done with it."

For a moment Khaluj said nothing, staring straight ahead. Surya almost viewed the virtual wheels turning in the priest's head.

"Young Surya, I'll not mince words. I was there the day you came through the portal. I watched it all."

Both sat in silence for several minutes.

"I see," said Surya, forcing his gaze briefly toward Khaluj. He turned his face away, staring out the side window of the Pod. Learning that the priest had known about him before Aleemirin and Tujuk unsettled his nerves. He didn't dare tell them about his current trip to Aryan Island. They already possessed a certain disdain for it, but had never gone into great detail as to why.

"My dear friend, can we now dispense with the Scandinavia charade and discuss everything out in the open?" Khaluj asked.

"There's nothing else to do. I had hoped to keep my secret much longer."

"Buy why? There's really no harm in someone like you coming to Atlantis. Before the second destruction—and definitely before the first—Atlanteans walked among beings such as yourself all the time. It was the norm." Khaluj smiled.

"From what I'm gathering, that hasn't been the norm for quite a while. I didn't tell Aleemirin and Tujuk I was coming with you this weekend. They don't seem very fond of Aryan. Why?"

"I take it you've told them about yourself?" Khaluj asked.

"Yes, as a matter of fact I have." Surya's discomfort grew. "They came right out and asked me about it."

"Oh." The priest frowned. "They always seem to be a step ahead of me." He glanced at Surya, a hardened expression on his face. "How long were you going to wait before telling me?"

"Am I supposed to tell all of you everything?" Surya's voice raised.

"Aleemirin, Tujuk, and I are part of Law of One. We work together. Why would you not, since we know each other?"

"Since we're being so honest, I'll come right out and tell you." Surya scowled at Khaluj. "I think there's more to you than meets the eye. You're up to something, and you want me to be part of it because you think I can help you on some level."

"Touché, my friend." Khaluj nodded, a faint smile crossing his lips. "I'm so glad we're having this conversation, because I would have most likely brought it up at the party. At least you're prepared and not caught off guard."

"And you didn't think discussing this earlier would have been better?" Frustration broiled inside Surya. He was more irritated at himself for not pushing questions harder.

"It all would have worked out the same. Not to worry." Khaluj lightly tapped Surya's thigh.

"So what else do you know?"

"Only that you came through the portal. I have no idea from what star system, or why you even came to begin with." The priest's eyes lit up. "I'll add this. I know who the Thing is and why he's here with you." Khaluj looked at Surya. "Your turn."

Surya's anger ignited. "How would you know such information?"

"Dear Surya, I have ways of finding out what I want to know. I'll leave it at that."

"Really?" Surya stretched out his hand toward Khaluj, shooting out a few powerful veins of lightning. The priest cried out, taking all hands off the controls. The Pod continued moving, propelled by crystal power. Closing his eyes, Surya called on the ancient word for turbulence, which worked for both water and wind.

In an instant, the Pod possessed a mind of its own, spinning and rollicking around like a toy top in a choppy sea. Lights on the control panel flickered.

Surya's joy knew no bounds as he viewed terror and the look of pain brewing in Khaluj's eyes. One more ancient sacred word, and the Pod resumed its normal course. Lights on the control panel blinked on, brighter than ever.

"And I'll leave it at that," Surya smirked back at Khaluj.

The man's hands trembled as he reached for the controls. Though he loathed the idea, Surya touched the priest, healing him from the effects of the lightning shock.

"What you did could have gotten us killed or at least in very big trouble. We're under water, you know." Khaluj's voice rang out with extreme annoyance, topped with a hint of remaining fear.

"Nothing I can't handle, old man. So don't worry about it." Surya stared straight ahead. "Now tell me why you have friends on an island that's disliked by two other Law of One priests."

"Because I'm not only a Law of One Priest. I'm also the leader of Sons of Belial. Belial is my ancestor."

"And why would Tujuk and Aleemirin allude to your Aryan group as being problematic? They did that, you know." Surya gazed at Khaluj with suspicion. "They feel like there's conflict going on, and that people have lost their way."

"Oh, for goodness sakes, Surya. Don't you think I and my brethren can say exactly the same thing?"

"What do Sons of Belial stand for?"

"Let me tell you something my friend. Sons of Belial promote the attainment of all the wonderful things life has to offer. Possessions, the right to pursue creative endeavors. To live a hedonistic life filled with beauty and pleasure, the way we were designed to do."

"And why is your order so against Law of One? It sounds noble to me," said Surya.

"It's limiting. Everything has to be weighed and determined that the outcome benefits all. If it's not for the greater good of all, an idea is tossed aside. There is no encouragement to pursue personal desires. There's no individuation."

Khaluj's words rang out with a tone of desperation. The look on his face matched his emotions. "You see, young Surya, one can only be concerned with oneself. You have no control over another. It's as simple as that."

The priest sat back in his seat, eyes concentrated on the control panel. He twisted a knob until the desired speed came into view, and the Pod sailed faster. "You still haven't told me from what star system you came from and why you're really here."

"Maybe that's something that should wait until we're with your friends." Surya sulked, arms crossed.

"Sounds good to me. We'll be delighted to hear. Perhaps we can make your trip to Atlantis worthwhile." Khaluj smiled.

Or maybe not, Surya thought. If he wasn't careful, getting tangled up in the crosshairs of politics could spell trouble. And he didn't like the fact Khaluj lived a dual life. Nothing good could surely come from it.

***

The Ultra Marine Pod ascended to the surface by degrees, leaving the underworld of marine life far behind. If the conversation hadn't been so revealing and intense, Surya would have enjoyed the trip much better. The experience of riding in such a craft as the Pod didn't come to most people.

On Poseidia, people used underwater carriers for transportation between the land rings, instead of taking an air taxi or ferry. From what he'd heard, the marine carriers didn't go down very far, but only enough to cover the craft with a few feet of water.

Khaluj docked the craft in a similar covered slip like the one on Poseidia. The coastline of Aryan looked completely different. In Surya's opinion, it lacked spiritual design and care for all things sacred. The architecture displayed more linear designs, stark and more functional rather than bearing cosmic appeal.

As he gazed at the skyline, he sensed a coldness there. People who lived on this island must have already embraced what Khaluj described during the trip.

Steely cold analytical thinking pervaded the environment of this place. It affected the way people conducted business and their personal lives. Surya didn't know this directly, but felt it in every fiber of his being. At once, he missed Poseidia. Aryan would likely offer nothing or very little of comfort on a higher level.

"Surya, we're in the capital city of Meruvia. We'll go to my home first, rest a bit. We still have some time before dressing for the evening. You've come prepared. Whatever else you need, I'll see to it that you want for nothing." Khaluj escorted Surya off the dock and led the way to a plot of land holding vehicles similar to what he used for travel on Poseidia. "My vehicle is just a few more rows over. I don't live far from here."

Energy from Khaluj emanated with an intensity Surya had not experienced before. A heightened level of excitement bubbled from within the priest, and he wore an air of contentment and happiness. Aryan was Khaluj's real home. Poseidia served as a makeshift surrogate, an evil necessity.

"Is Aryan not a beautiful place?" Khaluj said. He strapped himself into the driver's seat of the vehicle.

"I suppose it's a matter of one's taste," Surya answered.

Khaluj waved him off. "Trust me, you'll love it here."

Within minutes, the two men sped down the streets toward Khaluj's home.

Surya watched as they passed business complexes, shops, eateries, and homes. Aryans built their structures a little higher than those on Poseidia. Merchandise in the windows appeared ostentatious in decor, costly, catering to customers with bold tastes.

Restaurants seemed more upscale, formal. As he watched people along the sidewalk, Surya found the color-scheme and clothing of inhabitants more basic in color, black, grey, earth tones. Darker, muted, like the impression he had of this island.

The priest guided his vehicle through a few turns, leading through a neighborhood of tall buildings. Some of them contained golden and silver tinted windows that flashed when the sun struck the surfaces at certain angles. Making one last turn, Khaluj pulled up to a complex called Anantara.

"These are not apartments for rent, Surya. I own my own space in this building."

Anantara held a more attractive architecture style than other homes Surya had seen since his arrival. Stonework and iron fencing around the complex had been keenly thought out by the creators of this property. The edifice had been constructed of neatly chiseled sandstone.

Khaluj parked in a designated area built for only the owners who lived here and their guests. "We're home at last."

"You miss this place when you're not here, don't you?" Surya looked over at his companion.

"My dear friend, you can't even imagine how much I miss Aryan when I'm gone. My heart cries."

"Has Martaam been here? Does she know about what you really are?"

"Shhh, dear Surya." Khaluj shook his head, frowning. "No, she's never been here, and she doesn't know what I've told you."

The two men got out and headed toward the building. A lobby with marble floors, richly upholstered chairs and table had been placed in select areas.

On one side of the room, a large fire area held some logs, but due to the season, were not burning. Khaluj led the way to the carrier lift, where they traveled to the twelfth floor.

"I've purchased a unit on the very top. At night, the view is breathtaking. You see the lights twinkling. The air is fresh. It all perks up your disposition quite nicely." Khaluj smiled as he opened the door.

Surya's eyes widened. This area looked richer and more lavish than his rented unit on Poseidia. Soft cushions lined a large brown leather sofa. Throne chairs with ornate carved legs and arms sat at either side of a fireplace. Rich paintings covered the walls. At the far end of the room, a small tiled bar sat in front of the wet bar. Shelves held various wines. Glittering crystal goblets hung from racks.

"You've purchased yourself quite a place, Khaluj. You really like the fine life, don't you?" Surya turned toward the priest, facing him head on.

"You'll find that most of the elites on this island and the remaining ones prefer a more voluptuous lifestyle. We're not ashamed of it at all."

Khaluj motioned for Surya to follow him. The two walked down a hallway lined with four bedrooms. "Your room is here. I do hope you find it comfortable."

He wouldn't let on in front of the priest, but Surya liked the room immediately. It looked like a style fit for royalty. Plush bed with a small table and lamp beside it, a divan for reclining and reading, if he wanted. A bookshelf contained several leather-bound tomes.

"Your private bath is beyond that door." Khaluj pointed to a modest, carved door. If you wish, I can bring you in a decanter of wine and a glass so you can partake when you wish."

Whether it was fatigue or the unabashed display of wealth, Surya found the priest's energy humorous. Stifling a laugh, he merely nodded. "Thank you. That does sound nice."

Without another word, Khaluj left, retracing his steps back to the main living area. Surya placed his travel bag on the bed and pulled out his clothing for the evening. He placed his headband neatly on the table with the lamp. On Ontarus 9, he wore a crown when attending special public events. He at once missed those times. Mal-Ek always wore his king's crown, complete with royal cloak.

Khaluj returned promptly, wine decanter and glass in hand. "This should hold you until we leave."

"Thank you." Surya grinned. "Would you mind if I lay down and rest for a while?"

"Be my guest." Khaluj bowed lightly and closed the door behind him.

***

Rhaneen, glanced up from small group of men standing in front of him when Khaluj entered the room. Surya, decked out in his formal tunic and headband, garnered a head-turn from every guest.

Khaluj's smile whipped across his face, wide and bright. Surya followed at his side. "Good evening Rhaneen. I have brought our esteemed guest with me."

The vice commander stood speechless a few seconds, before recovering himself. He extended a hand toward Surya. "A great pleasure to meet you. Did our friend Khaluj have to twist your arm, or did he charm you like he does everyone else?" Rhaneen chuckled.

"I was more than eager to come. He's spoken so highly about all of you." Surya's expression remained sober. He didn't know which man's energy hit him the worst. Khaluj or Rhaneen. Both struck his senses as two devils in cahoots, surrounded by their minions. More than ever he wanted to be back on Poseidia and have dinner with Den-El—or Martaam.

He banished those thoughts faster than they'd come. If Khaluj's colleagues contained half as much divine skills as the priest's, they would still present a formidable force.

"Did he enjoy the ride over from Poseidia? I've yet to take a ride with you in that fine Pod you own, Khaluj. I'm envious." Rhaneen grinned.

"We had an interesting time." The priest frowned briefly. "We were able to get much better acquainted. Being cramped in close quarters for several hours kind of allows for that." The priest laughed.

"How do you like Aryan so far?" One of the council members spoke up. "Much different than Poseidia."

"It is much different, but quite eye-catching just the same." A faint obliging smile crossed Surya's face.

Rhaneen and Khaluj exchanged glances. Rhaneen arched an eyebrow.

"I take it you have your own place there?" asked the council member.

"I rent. Not ready to own right now." Surya answered.

"When you do, you might consider a place here. It's a faster pace. Much more excitement, especially for someone your age." The council member smiled.

Surya licked his lower lip, averting an expression of exasperation. "A slower pace and gentler lifestyle suits me well, but I don't doubt that Meruvia has wonderful things to see and do."

The chattering in the room had dimmed substantially from the time Khaluj and Surya entered the room.

"Surya—that is your name, right?" said Rhaneen.

"Yes."

"I understand you're not from here. Khaluj has told us a little, but we'd be interested in hearing more about you."

Khaluj and Surya gazed at each other. The priest tilted his head, raising his eyebrows. "Go on. Tell them what you told me. It's okay, Surya. You're among friends. You really are."

Surya sucked in his breath, looking at everyone in the room, making eye contact with each member. He didn't know if these men were truly friends or foes. In fact, he couldn't necessarily determine one hundred percent the same for Aleemirin and Tujuk, either.

The group around him contained an air of assertiveness. All were impeccably dressed. Their conversations seemed intimate, but intense nonetheless. The energy of it all swallowed him whole the moment he stepped through the door.

A waiter offered a golden tray of drinks. Surya took a glass of wine and swallowed a quick sip. All secrets would completely come to an end, right here, right now. With a full strong voice, he made his announcement.

"I'm from the Lyra Constellation. I'm the son of a king."

Chapter Nine

On a large platform in the middle of an amphitheater, Rhaneen and Khaluj sat on either side of Surya. Members of Sons of Belial filled the vacant seats, waiting with excitement. Word had been received, and the crowd joined together. An alien sat in their midst, and they wanted a good look. When all the seats contained an occupant, the doors closed. The room grew quiet.

Khaluj picked up his speaking device and spoke. His voice filled the room, loud and clear. "I want to welcome everyone today. This meeting is important because we have a special guest who is not even from this star constellation. His name is Surya. He comes from the constellation of Lyra. He's the son of a king."

The room filled with sounds of approval. Many members pulled out paper and writing implements for taking notes.

"As you are aware," continued Khaluj, "we have been discussing for quite a while how Sons of Belial can become partners in guarding and caring for the main power crystal that is housed on Poseidia. Control of the crystal means total power over all. How we live, how we function.

"Those who control the crystal not only give power, but they can also take the power away at will. This puts many of us in danger, should there be differences in social views and ideas. Crystal power becomes a bargaining tool on a whim, in the worst scenario. In the best scenario, there is harmony between all the islands and everyone lives in peace.

"Law of One have had the privilege of guarding and caring for the main power crystal since its installation. Sometimes a neutral party is the best used in situations requiring delicacy and diplomacy. We are asking our extra-terrestrial brother to play the part of neutrality so there is a discussion with Law of One about shared responsibility for controlling the crystal.

"We want to open up the floor for questions and dialogue. Anyone who wishes to ask a question or make a comment, please do so. Keep in mind that we want this meeting to end on a productive note.

"No question is forbidden. Please know that anything said to us will not be taken as a slight or insult. What happens in this room stays in it at all cost."

A hand went up in the audience. One of the technicians walked down the aisle and aimed a speaking device attached to an extender toward the man. He was none other than the same council member who met Surya the night before.

"Not meaning this as an insult, but you seem extremely young to be on a quest so far from your home. Why did you come to Atlantis?"

Surya sat still, quickly thinking how to answer. He spoke into his microphone. "I came here with little information. It's a long story that I won't go into at the moment, but I decided on a trip to Earth so I could try and see what humans were like and how I could help them."

Another member held up their hand. "What do you mean by help us? We would like help in gaining shared control of the crystal on Poseidia, but did you have another reason for thinking we needed help? Something we're not aware of?"

The room grew quiet. Surya glanced around at the audience. How much should he reveal of his conversation with Mal-Ek? Did Atlanteans remember their history? Did they care?

"Let me ask you this," answered Surya. "Your leaders, Khaluj and Rhaneen, felt my presence was so important that they have this meeting we're in now. Other than playing a neutral part—which could really be done by anyone—why do you feel that a being from another star system stands a better chance in you getting your wish? What do you find significant in someone like me?"

The room exploded in a chorus of murmuring voices. Some people shook their heads.

Rhaneen held up his hand and spoke. "Let's calm down a moment. Since no one is eagerly jumping up to answer the question, I'll share my take on this."

Silence filled the room.

"What many don't appreciate or even know about is the power and knowledge that aliens have. Much more than we do as humans. With their perspective, they can offer suggestions on persuasion, or perhaps share how to create something more powerful and better than what's currently used. Surya, would you agree with that?"

Surya thought a moment, considering his words carefully. Conversation at dinner last night had been light, a getting-to-know-you phase. But the looks, questions, and congenial smiles all held a deeper undertone today.

"I would agree that there is a lot of remaining untapped knowledge owned by others like myself. Some of the races are far more advanced than others. It's not like all are equal in that arena."

"What specifically do you know about advanced technology? Anything different than what we already have?" Another member had held up his hand for the technician.

The question threw Surya a little off guard. He knew about some different technologies, but wasn't sure if any of it would necessarily apply to Atlanteans or their current needs. "I'm not prepared to review everything I know. Of course, I don't know it all, either." Tired of sitting and feeling a little claustrophobic, he stood up and moved toward the front seats. His eyes maintained their focus toward the person who asked the question. "There's something that I've come to question about humans since I've been in Atlantis. That question is worthiness."

Silence in the room became so intense, Surya almost heard his own heartbeat. "To learn specialized technology from distant beings, there is one requirement that must be met. The requirement is worthiness. Aliens require the attribute. Are you worthy of gaining the knowledge?"

"What would we have to do to show worthiness?" asked the person, who had remained standing.

Surya paced the floor, glancing up at the speaker and the entire audience. "Anytime an extra-terrestrial race wishes to share information, it's usually decided by a higher council. Not just by one. Also, the knowledge must be beneficial, for the highest and greatest good of all." He turned around briefly facing Khaluj and Rhaneen. "From what I've been told, these are not necessarily the same views this group holds. Am I wrong on that fact?"

The speaker who asked the question sat down immediately. A burst of low murmurs filled the room. Surya spoke louder. "Am I wrong in thinking that this group has a different goal than gaining knowledge for the benefit of all? Who, other than these two gentlemen behind me, can answer the question?"

Rhaneen and Khaluj whispered in hushed tones to each other.

"He knows how to take control of an audience. I'll give him that," said Rhaneen.

"Trust me, I've experienced a little of his power. Makes you think." Khaluj nodded in agreement.

One member of the audience motioned to speak. "I'll answer your question, Sir."

Squaring up his shoulders, Surya watched the man.

"If you have been told anything about Sons of Belial, you'll learn that we don't go around blathering on about highest and greatest good and everyone benefitting from something. That doesn't mean we don't care about it.

"We believe that each one is responsible for their own success in this world. When someone creates a new technique or new device that everyone can enjoy, how is that not benefitting all?

"When someone creates a business and makes money, many people benefit from that as well, such as the workers who earn a living. There are customers who will enjoy and reap the benefits of what is offered. How is that not benefitting people?"

Surya quickly turned around and faced Khaluj and Rhaneen, viewing the animated nods of their heads and smiles across their lips. He returned his gaze to the man speaking from the audience.

"People," the man continued, "may be allowed an equal chance to go far in this world, but most are okay following, maintaining the status quo, and not worrying themselves with high ambitions. They simply want to live an unencumbered life and leave the big decision-making to those who want to do it."

"And for those who aren't ambitious," said Surya, "what happens to them? Are they any less because they prefer a simple life, and may not see an inherent value in greed and high living? Do they receive less and suffer more because of it?" Surya paced the floor a few times.

"Are those who believe that all you need is just enough penalized for being who they are? Who says they don't have the right idea or the smartest intentions?" Surya turned around again, facing the two men behind him and back to the audience once again.

Everyone in the room grew still, faces solemn. The two leaders behind Surya sat with grim expressions. Surya knew he'd hit a chord, but he still had questions.

"If Law of One have been caring for the power crystal all this time, and their mantra is 'for the highest and greatest good,' then what does it matter if they continue as they've always done? How have they interfered with you living the life that you want?"

From behind, Surya heard Khaluj and Rhaneen shifting in their seats. He viewed many in the audience doing the same. Some wore indignant looks on their faces, especially the men he met at Rhaneen's party the night before.

One last member spoke. "Assuming we take fine enough care of everyone to your liking, will you help us talk to Law of One? If needed, would you help us fight for our right to at least share control of the power crystal on Poseidia?"

"Fight?" asked Surya. He gazed around the audience. "Why would there ever be a need for that, even if they refused? They don't interfere with you. Their philosophy would never allow it."

The ugly truth had been spoken. Sons of Belial wanted control of the great crystal on Poseidia so they could have their rule over others. Period.

Surya felt this truth the moment he laid eyes on the Aryan coastline for the first time. He knew the truth as he viewed the garish, formidable shops with their merchandise of gold, silver, and fine threads in the clothing shown in the windows. He knew the truth when he viewed all Khaluj's glorious possessions.

Khaluj's attitude toward the mutant Things drove the point home for good. Sons of Belial believed in oppressor versus oppressed. If one lived and believed their way, prosperity lay within reach. Woe to those who didn't share similar values.

The worst realization, Khaluj had tricked his way into Law of One to try and do what he was being asked in this meeting. It all sickened him. As much as he looked forward to the day he'd rule on Ontarus 9, he had no stomach to get deep into the heart of a human political war brewing between Sons of Belial and Law of One.

His only desire had been to taste life as a human, find the girl, and return home—hopefully with the girl. He had not banked on being used as a pawn for one side of a faction to out-best and overthrow another.

"You didn't answer our question," said the man who asked about fighting.

Khaluj stood up and said, "I think we'll end this meeting now. Unfortunately, we've run out of time for using this space." He nodded toward the gentleman who still stood behind the tech's speaking device. "Thank you for bringing up your question, good Sir. We'll most assuredly get an answer."

"Do you know when?" asked the man.

"Let's let our friend Surya think on this a little more. The verbiage of some of our questions and conversation may have come across a little strong or confusing. Understandable, since he's truly not from this planet and familiar with our customs." Khaluj smiled, motioning toward the tech.

Just as the gentleman opened his mouth in rebuttal, the tech walked away.

Khaluj sidled up to Surya, placing a hand lightly on his shoulder. "Thank you for speaking with our group. That was an interesting conversation. We needed it."

Rhaneen stepped up alongside Khaluj, smiling. "Surya, don't let some of our people bother you with their approach. They tend to get a little excited when they're passionate about something."

Surya said nothing, but returned his equipment to its stand. Rhaneen frowned lightly in question at Khaluj, who shook his head, indicating for his friend to say nothing more.

"I don't know about you two, but I could surely enjoy some good food and drink right now." Khaluj grinned.

Later that evening, Surya slipped out Khaluj's condo and onto the streets of Meruvia.

***

The night air of Poseidia invigorated Surya's spirit as he stepped out of the air craft and headed for the ferry. Arriving home a day earlier than planned improved his mood tremendously. He wouldn't bear another ride in cramped quarters with Khaluj. For four hours.

He had penned a quick note goodbye, leaving it on the bed where he had slept. Much to his relief, Khaluj didn't press too hard when he politely declined an invitation to join him for another party. The whole departure presented itself in a perfect flow of circumstances.

"You're home!" Den-El belted out when Surya walked through the door. He threw his arms around his friend.

"You can't live one day without me here? You did it on Ontarus 9." Surya grinned, hugging his friend back.

"Don't be mean." Den-El frowned briefly. His ears twitched with excitement. The tail on his rump flicked in all directions.

Surya laughed watching it all. "I still don't know what happened to your nose, but I'm glad it's gone." He walked to his master bedroom, Den-El following.

One morning, the goat-like nose had disappeared, and in its place, a human nose had formed. Den-El's face resembled the one he possessed on Ontarus 9. A grotesque creature that he had once been had morphed into a more oddly bewitching one.

His face, undeniably handsome, blended well with an upper body that would have rivaled a god. The eyes, deep brown and soulful, entrancing. The horns on his head lent him a certain diabolic beauty. A proper ability to speak did wonders. Den-El was no ordinary Thing. The remaining goat-like body merely added to the mystique.

"Looks like you kept everything in order." Surya unpacked, and placed his empty travel bag in the closet.

"I'm a very organized person." Den-El's smile faded when he turned and caught sight of his lower half. "You know what I mean."

"Of course you are. You're also one of the smartest people I know." Surya wrapped an arm around his friend's shoulder and led him down the hall. "I'm starved. Have you made anything for dinner?"

"I know my place." Den-El's face wore an exasperated expression. "I'll have a plate ready for you in a few minutes. Would you like for me to fetch your slippers too?" His eyebrows wiggled up and down.

Laughing, Surya seated himself at the table. "No. If you haven't eaten, fix something for yourself and come sit with me."

"I just finished right before you came. I'll have some wine, though." Den-El headed for the kitchen.

"You need to go easy on my good wine. That costs money, you know."

"Sorry, but I need something to drown my sorrows. If I'm going to suffer, can't I at least suffer in comfort?"

"Den-El, I'll see to it that you're the most comfortable Thing on Atlantis. By the time I'm done, people won't know who commands whom."

Den-El popped his head around the kitchen entrance and answered, "I'm holding you to that."

Surya stared at his plate when Den-El returned. "I'm simply amazed at how pretty you make the meals. Did you do this back home?"

"It was one of my secrets," said Den-El, swirling his wine. He held the glass closer to his eyes, watching the wine stream down the sides.

"You never invited me." Surya dipped his fork in a medley of chopped vegetables and meat. He knew his friend only added the meat for his pleasure. Den-El had lost his appetite for it since being transformed into a Thing.

"I'll make up for lost time. How does that sound?" Den-El sipped from his glass. "And why are you so agitated? I can feel it over here. Felt it when you walked through the door."

"Can I talk to you about something?" Surya swirled the sterling fork in his food.

Den-El narrowed his eyes. "Sure."

For the next hour, Surya told his friend everything that had happened on Aryan Island, including the ride over.

"Since you've been here, have you not read a news bulletin? While we're discussing this, it's a good time to ask. Can we please get a picture communicator? You know, like the ones I've seen in the windows of some device shops. I think having one will keep you informed."

"And you're more informed than I am?" Surya stared at his friend. "How is that, exactly? For your information, I do read publications. Not only that, I go out and meet people. On both sides, apparently."

"When you left, I went roaming about town, looking into the store windows, listening to people in the cafes talk. You learn a lot that way too." Den-El nodded. "You hear what the general population thinks, not just a faction."

"I'm aware of that, Den-El." Surya squinted at his friend. "You mean to tell me you went out by yourself, acting like an ordinary male human? That can be dangerous in your condition, you know."

Den-El, let out a loud frustrated sigh. "Yes. I wish I didn't have salt rubbed in the emotional wounds all the time. But yes. It's boring staying inside all day. It's not good for you, either. Very bad for the psyche. Humans are inherently wired to be around other people. If they are isolated, they literally go insane. Trust me, you don't want me insane."

"No, definitely not." Surya ate a bite of food. "What did you learn? I haven't heard much from Tujuk and Aleemirin."

"Who?" Den-El paused his glass in front of his lips.

"They are my first friends, and they're part of a group called Law of One."

"Yes. And there's that other group you talked to. There are issues brewing between the two. I'm sensing something big will happen. And no, you don't need to help anyone fight anything. That's not what we do."

Surya looked up at Den-El. "Do you think humans are worthy creatures?"

"Are you kidding me? I never wanted to come here on Earth. I was perfectly fine in my own backyard on Ontarus 9. We were fourth dimension, Surya. That's higher than these brutes."

"You got the shaft, didn't you?"

"Yes. And you walk around free, enjoying the good life." Den-El polished off his glass of wine and poured another.

The words bit at Surya like a pit viper, stinging him with pain. He'd never dreamed of such a punishment for his friend. Something had to lay in store for him when he returned home. The Federation couldn't do anything to him while he stayed on Earth. It was out of their jurisdiction if someone made it without getting caught first.

"You resent me, don't you?" asked Surya, a grim look on his face.

"There will always be a part of me that feels it deep down inside. But I did help you. That makes me a clear accomplice. I love you, though. I know you would never do anything with a harmful intent. You and I simply didn't think this deal out fully enough."

"I'll make it up to you, Den-El. I'll find a way." Surya washed down the last bite of food with some wine.

He helped Den-El with the dishes. When they finished, he said, "Let's go to The Atlan before it closes. We need more than bulletins and talking and listening to a few select group of people we meet or overhear. We need the news."

Several minutes later, Surya and Den-El wandered the inner sidewalks of The Atlan, making their way to Aldalain's.

"What can I help you with, Sir?" The gentleman on the showroom floor strode up to Surya and bowed in greeting. He completely ignored Den-El, who stamped his back hoof in irritation.

Surya swatted Den-El on the rump and showed him an evil-eye glance. "Good evening to you," Surya answered, smiling at the clerk.

"Is there anything in particular you're wanting this evening?"

"My roommate and I are wanting a new picture communicator. We moved here recently and haven't picked one up yet."

The store clerk raised an eyebrow, glancing at Den-El. "Your roommate? I see." He frowned.

"And kind Sir," said Den-El, "we want the most sophisticated device you have. Once we install it, do you recommend any specific channels for obtaining political news and information? That's of great interest to my friend and me." Den-El glared at the man, waiting with clasped hands for an answer.

With wide eyes, the man stared at Den-El and back to Surya. "Well, gentlemen, please follow me."

Den-El shot out a hoof, delivering a sharp kick to Surya's ankle. He trotted off ahead, catching up with the store clerk. Surya groaned and rubbed the sore spot where Den-El had hit.

"We have some various models, as you see here," said the clerk. "Some allow more channels than others."

"Which one do you recommend?" Surya asked.

"I sell more of this one than any of the others. Clear picture, crisp sound." The clerk rubbed his hand over the screen.

Surya read the brand name on the bottom of the console frame. AudioView.

The clerk continued, "If you're not interested in other programs, this one is the best. It receives mostly news channels but does allow for three basic non-news frequencies." He moved a lever, and the screen lit up. At the bottom left hand corner, in small letters, were the words Lomasa News. Two faces filled the screen.

Surya gasped, watching and listening. One of the faces was none other than Rhaneen.

"It's very simple, Khandoor. We think we can improve Atlantean life by encouraging people to not be afraid, live life to the fullest, and pursue their dreams." Rhaneen smiled.

Khandoor asked, "Do you think Law of One followers can be persuaded to grasp that philosophy and embrace it?"

Rhaneen displayed his most ingratiating smiled. "It's a goal we'd like to work on. We don't see how Law of One could not go along with some of our concepts, once they gain a better understanding of what we would like to institute."

Surya and Den-El briefly glanced up and stared at each other.

"Sir," said the clerk. "would you like to take this model home with you? We can select one from our stock supply in the back."

"Does your news also cover the other islands of Atlantis?" Surya looked at the clerk.

"Of course, Sir." He moved his head lightly from side to side, thinking. "Don't get me wrong, each island has its own agenda. Likewise, its own propaganda. But people who report the goings on of the islands try to be fair and show both sides. The people make their decisions when it's time to vote."

"We'll definitely take that model," said Den-El. He pointed to the AudioView.

The clerk's brows furrowed. He looked from Den-El to Surya. "If you'll allow me, I'll tell our men in the back, and we can take care of payment at the counter." He pointed toward the back of the store.

"And the price?" Surya asked.

Den-El interjected. "The price is fine." He pointed to a sign on the bottom of the shelf. "We really want this one." He took the liberty of lightly stepping on Surya's toe.

Surya stifled a groan "Yes, we'll take that one."

"Very well. Follow me." The clerk smiled.

Outside the store, Den-El moved easily while Surya carried the new AudioView under his arm.

"You should be carrying this. Not me." Surya scowled at his friend.

"When you get tired of carrying it, let me know." Den-El trotted faster toward another window. He peeped through the pane and gazed inside. His eyes lit up. "Look." He pointed to the object of his attention.

"No, Den-El. We simply can't." Surya tapped his foot. Impatience kicked in.

"Why not? You get what you want."

"I just bought you an AudioView. What more do you want?"

"This is different." Den-El's shifting hooves tapped out loud indignant clicks against the sidewalk.

"I don't really ask for a lot, Surya. If I'm stuck in some horrid place I never wanted to be, in a body I loathe, could I at least have something that is mine?" Den-El's dark eyes lowered. His lips pulled into a grim straight line.

Surya stared at his friend. "Fine. You win."

Chapter Ten

"I can't believe you got him that." Martaam sat on the park bench next to Surya, her hand resting on his.

"I can't believe I got him that, either." Surya chuckled as he watched the scene in front of him.

Den-El threw a ball. As soon as it hit the ground yards away, a small black dog took off running. In a show of speed, Den-El rushed after it, keeping close time with his new pet.

"I beat you, Da-Ina," said Den-El. He swiped up the ball. Da-Ina barked and growled, jumping up on her new master. "Let's go again."

"What made you give in? You never had pets at home. I remember you telling me." Martaam grinned, laying her head lightly on Surya's shoulder a moment.

"Those eyes of his are too much. He looked so sad."

"He's definitely handsome. No one can deny it." Martaam looked over at Surya. "Is he adapting any better to all this? What a horrible way to start out one's experience on Atlantis." She shook her head and stared off in the distance across the water. The walls of the Temple of Poseidon flashed in the sun. "I can't imagine going through such a time."

"I never dreamed he'd undergo such a punishment, either." He wrapped his arm around her. "Please don't think Lyrans are all cruel and inhumane."

"But why would they subject someone to something like that? Okay, he shouldn't have helped you, but . . ."

"Martaam, what do you do with people here who commit crimes or break the law? Atlantis is a beautiful place, but it surely isn't utopia."

She turned her face downward. "No, it's not. Not like it used to be thousands of years ago. If someone commits a crime now, a team of priests gather around the perpetrator. While the criminal holds a magnetic baton, the priests send positive thoughts and energy toward the person."

Surya nodded. "You elevate the person spiritually, rather than bring them down lower with harsh punishment."

"Yes. Law of One always believes that elevating and uplifting the soul benefits everyone. If the person who committed the crime is executed or severely punished, it creates a certain anger in their soul. When their soul reincarnates into a new body for their next incarnation, the anger is still there. They may not readily remember in that new lifetime, but their soul never forgets."

Surya gazed out across the park lawn, barely noting Den-El and Da-Ina. They had sat on the ground together for a rest period. Den-El cuddled the little dog, whispering words into its ear and stroking her fur.

"On Ontarus 9, we do some similar things like that. Sometimes we do things that may seem more severe to humans, but only when it's necessary and for the betterment of the soul, as you say. Den-El and I should not be here right now. We took a chance. I got away. He got caught."

Martaam shuddered. "Why did you really come to Atlantis, Surya? Uncle Aleemirin said you wanted to help humans." She looked at the alien sitting next to her. One so handsome in his new human skin, the mere thought of him took her breath away. "He and I talk sometimes. He told me that much." She linked her fingers through his. "But I want to hear it directly from you. Are we worth it?"

"I won't lie. Den-El doesn't think so. He's never thought it. But I've thought about that question every day since I decided I wanted to come."

"What do you think?" Martaam's gaze fixed on his.

"I thought so in the beginning. I won't deny I'm questioning it now. But if my people and compatriots on other planets seeded Earth, I think it's their duty to see that all goes well." He looked at Martaam. "Kind of like parents caring for their children."

"I guess, if you look at it that way, we are their children, kind of. At some point, children need to grow up and care for themselves. Parents have to make a decision whether or not to support their child."

Surya let out a short breath. "I believe my people have decided to cut the apron strings themselves."

"Are we that bad?" asked Martaam.

"The things I've seen so far put me in a bit of a different frame of mind that when I first arrived." He grinned at the attractive girl sitting beside him. "I haven't given up all hope, yet."

Should he come clean and tell her? Surya knew he hadn't answered her main question. Everything else had been shared, forced out of him. Why not tell her? His time was limited here. A year would pass quickly, if he and Den-El stayed that long. He turned and faced her head on.

"You asked me a question about why I really came here. What I've told you is a partial truth, but there's something else I need to tell you."

Martaam sat up straight, looking deeply into his eyes. "What's that."

"I came because of you."

Dead silence rested between them. Noises by Den-El and Da-Ina faded. Everyone else in the park seemed to drift away into nothingness. Surya feared she'd run away. Her eyes blazed with alarm. The corners of her mouth pulled taut across her face. She'd slid her hand away from his, leaving him with a sense of cold washing over his body.

She blinked several times and looked around the park a few seconds. "And how did that happen? How would you ever find me, of all people?"

He spent several minutes explaining the fateful day in his father's observation room, and what he saw through the lens.

"I had to come down here. You left me no choice." Surya took a chance and grasped her hand. "I needed to find you, or go mad."

Her face lost its intensity. The sparkle in her eyes danced. Martaam leaned over and whispered in his ear. "I saw you in my dreams."

Surya didn't know what possessed him. A strong human urge to possess her, taste her, like he wanted the first night he slept in his own apartment. He wrapped a hand around the back of her head and pulled her face toward his. When his lips pressed against hers, he slipped his tongue inside her mouth.

She didn't resist, but encouraged him, allowing him to explore with gentle nudges and caresses. His breath invigorated her, sending her heart beating with excitement. Her fingers ran through his hair, tracing around his ear.

Softly, he stopped and pulled away. Her gaze remained locked on his face, eyes searching his. At once, she looked briefly away, as if gathering her sensibilities.

"I care very much for you, Martaam. I did the moment I saw you." He brushed his cheek against hers.

Without a word, she removed her enamel butterfly pendant from around her neck and anchored it in the middle of his headband. "Always remember me when you see this. Together we endure through all changes. Nothing will strike us down. Our souls endure forever."

Surya kissed her again.

***

Several yards away, Den-El watched the bench. A flood of envy filled every fiber of his being. If he had to be here on this dreadful planet called Earth, why couldn't he reap some of the benefits? He glanced down in horror between his legs. His flesh had swollen and inched out from where it had been hidden.

He casually repositioned himself in such a way that his legs and hands kept everything covered. Taking several deep breaths, he closed his eyes and willed himself into a state of calm. Da-Ina's cold nose against his cheek and soft lick of her tongue distracted him from his momentary problem.

When he checked everything again, he had gone back to normal. "That was close," he said to the dog. "I wish you could bark and let me know when something's out of place." He chuckled and nuzzled the dog.

A shadow fell over him. He looked up. The figure before his eyes took him completely off guard.

"New pet?"

Den-El swallowed and licked his lower lip. His mouth had oddly gone dry. Da-Ina sat down next to her master and let out a few high-pitched sounds.

"She's absolutely beautiful."

"So are you," Den-El blurted out. He shook his head. "Um, I mean, yes. She's a little beauty." He gazed at the woman standing over him.

Her skin held the same red-brown tones as other Atlanteans. Raven-black hair spilled down her shoulder. A bright silk green ribbon had been braided into the locks that spiraled down in one neat twist. Her lithe figure bore a red-violet silk top and matching billowy sailor pants. Gold jewelry of every type had found a place on her body.

Her face had been tastefully painted with cosmetics, making her an almost angelic vision.

"Does she bite?"

"I don't think so. You see, I just got her." Den-El sat up carefully. The old bulging sensation had crept up again, and he cursed silently to himself.

The young woman stooped down, holding her folded hand near Da-Ina. The dog gently licked, allowing a few tickles behind her ear.

"I think she likes you," said Den-El.

"Mind if I join you?"

"Please." He motioned for her to sit beside him. Silently he sent a prayer of thanks to the cosmos.

"I'm Cata-Lin. I haven't seen you in this park before."

"I'm Den-El. Just arrived not long ago." His momentary battle with adolescent emotions finally simmered out.

"Who is your master?"

Den-El pointed in Surya's direction.

Her face lit up. "You must be quite special. And to have your own pet? It's unheard of with Things." Cata-Lin's face didn't display disdain, but a sincere interest in knowing.

"I had to earn it. Trust me on that."

"You speak with such lucidity. I detect sharp intelligence in you. Again, not like normal Things."

Cata-Lin tilted her head. Through partially opened lips, Den-El glimpsed a trace of her tongue resting lightly behind a neat row of teeth. The vision sent a rush of lust shooting through him. He grappled with an overwhelming desire to kiss her. She smiled, attempting a bit of modesty.

He recovered composure. "I'm not your normal Thing, but I won't bore you with details about me. Tell me about you."

"Such a gentleman you are." She leaned in closer to Den-El. "I could tell you were by the way you treated your little doggie. So sweet and tender." Cata-Lin ran a slender finger over the grass, tracing an imaginary line to nowhere.

Den-El fought off the fantasy of her fingers coursing all over him. Something about her hinted of a higher vibrational human, someone who could tap into the fourth focus and higher if she worked a little harder at it.

"I never answered your question, did I? I'm a priestess in one of the temples." A seductive smile covered Cata-Lin face.

Den-El nodded. "Anything in particular that is your specialty, your focus?"

"I mostly do energy work." She glanced around. "I have dabbled in some spell casting," she whispered in Den-El's ear. "I don't tell many people about that, but I can trust you."

He arched an eyebrow. The whole expression of his face, with the presence of the horns, must have created a comic effect. Cata-Lin stifled a laugh.

"You're really cute when you look like that." Her face sobered. "Has anyone ever told you how handsome you really are? And I'm not saying that to be flattering or win your favor."

Den-El thought a second. "I believe you're the first who has told me. Thank you." On Ontarus 9, he had no trouble attracting females. Nor did his so-called "master." With Surya a royal prince, he would never have gotten away with some of his recent behaviors. Both he and Surya had broken the rules. On Earth, old rules didn't apply anymore.

"Enough about me. Tell me a little about you." Cata-Lin stretched out, resting back on her hands for support.

"Not a whole lot to tell. My master rescued me from the horrid mines, and the rest is history."

"Does he ever let you go out alone? A Thing smart as you?" Cata-Lin touched Den-El's arm.

"I sneak out sometimes. Mainly I take advantage when he's gone away." He chuckled. "He doesn't like it, though."

"What does your master do? He must have a trade or skill to support the two of you."

"My keeper is self-made, you might say." Den-El sat back a little, gazing at the woman next to him.

"Ah, a man of resource. I like that. You're lucky he found you. But with a wonderful Thing like you, he would have been unwise to pass you up." Her eyes held a provocative look. They contained a thousand fires of pure passion.

Den-El wanted nothing more than to lose himself in them, taste her lips, and feel every part of her. A rustle in the trees distracted him. A bird fluttered its feathers, settling down on a lower branch. Its eyes glinted when they blinked. They stared straight down on him and Cata-Lin. From deep within, a gripping intuition cautioned against sharing too much.

Both sat together in silence several minutes. Da-Ina dozed against Den-El's thigh.

"I need to go. I have a client who scheduled an appointment." Cata-Lin stood up, giving Da-Ina one last ruffle on the ear. "I hope I see you here again sometime, Den-El. I've enjoyed meeting you."

"I'm sure we'll see each other again. I don't live far from here."

"If you ever make it to the land core, come see me. I'm in the temple east of Poseidon's. It's white with a copper dome on top. You can't miss it."

"I'll see if I can talk Master into taking me there sometime." Den-El smiled.

Cata-Lin waved and left.

Den-El watched until she disappeared in the distance. He was smitten by her. Every move, touch, the sound of her voice, the tantalizing eyes. So this is how Surya felt when he first gaze on Martaam. Another rustle in the trees. The bird twittered and flew off. A small uneasiness hit his gut as if someone had delivered a small blow.

On instinct he closed his eyes, tapping into the bird's frequency. All he wanted was a little information. Uneasiness grew by degrees. He probed harder into the ether into the Infinite Hall of Records. Animals also made their imprint into boundless space.

What he learned horrified him. He called upon an ancient sacred word, one highly guarded and used in desperate situations with honorable intent. Den-El believed his use of it made good sense now, even with an animal.

Many yards away young boys played with slingshots, running, laughing, shooting at their targets. One of the boys spied the bird resting briefly on a statue. He adeptly aimed, pulled back, and let go of the band. The bird promptly fell over dead. At the same time, Den-El smiled briefly, but he knew this was only the beginning. His earlier captivation by the strange woman took a soberer turn.

***

Deep inside the Temple of Jhanana, two bodies lay cloistered away in private personal quarters. Khaluj lay amid a rainbow of soft pillows made of the best silks. A coverlet of bright red lay rumpled on the bed. Earlier he'd been back in his apartment, seething when the bird never showed up.

Once he'd learned what happened with Surya's Thing, coupled with his last travel to Aryan, he knew going full force against an alien would end up badly for him. Now the alien had a capable ally from his own planet. Worse, Martaam met him at her door the night after his return and handed him back every trinket he'd given her.

Her refusal to let him inside her apartment humiliated the most. It took every ounce of will not to break into Surya's apartment and finish him off along with his beastly, odorous friend.

"Dear Khaluj, you must put away such low thoughts. Lower vibrations don't become you, precious one."

"You're the only one I have left for help, Cata-Lin. I'm glad I called on you earlier. I underestimated extra-terrestrial power. How could I do that? I know better, at least from studies."

Cata-Lin coursed a painted red nail over Khaluj's lips, delivering at last a tender kiss. "It's difficult to truly know what you don't know. Reality is always mightier than what is taught in books and the records created by man." She lowered her kisses, gently teething and lapping at both his nipples.

Khaluj groaned and slid his hand under the cover, reaching between his legs. "We've known each other for several years, have we not?" he said, trying to keep his breath steady. His flesh had thickened. Days without Martaam had taken its toll.

"We have, my valiant man. Friendships are stronger than lovers. I've always believed it." Cata-Lin smiled down at Khaluj. Her hand joined his under the covers. Unable to contain himself, the priest groaned louder.

"You think you can get any information out of him? That horrid alien beast I was forced to rescue?" Khaluj distracted himself briefly with the memory.

"They may be aliens, dear, but they aren't without their own vulnerability. You just have to find it." Cata-Lin grinned.

"You make it sound so easy."

"You have to think harder with them. Figure out what their soft spots are. Even they cannot maintain cosmic connection continually. It short circuits one's system if overdone." She ran her hand over the priest's flesh, delighting in watching him weaken under her touch.

"He seemed to like you," Khaluj said, managing a grin.

"And that's what I'm banking on," answered Cata-Lin. "Those aliens underestimate the power of humans. Mainly the emotions and hedonism that is sought. Lust is as powerful as hunger or thirst. The desire for power is as strong. It's mainly the lower emotions we tap into to get what we want, for they guide us first."

Khaluj gazed at Cata-Lin, a light smile covering his face.

"Let me have a chance with the alien mutant and see what he reveals," she continued.

"Find out as much as you can, whenever you can. What we discover dictates whether Sons of Belial go on the offense or defense." He shook his head. "I'd love nothing better than to have had the two aliens with me. I don't like it, but that beast seems extremely bright."

"But you're extremely bright, too, my precious friend. Don't forget that you have an army behind you. Law of One people are weak. Push-overs, really. Once they're conquered, you can bend the populace to your rule." Cata-Lin indulged the priest, teasing his flesh with more intensity. "You'll never be forsaken, dear Khaluj."

The priest chuckled and lifted her on top of him. Cata-Lin closed her eyes and opened her mouth with silent ecstasy. He moved with a slow, easy rhythm, hers matching him with each thrust and roll of the hips. Minutes later, he breathed a deep sigh of relief.

"Sometimes I think we should consider a deeper partnership." He kissed her lips.

***

"You've barely touched your food," said Surya. "That's not like you at all." He gazed over at Den-El, who sat moving his fork around on his plate.

Surya, Martaam, and Den-El sat outside the cafe, Fanedahl. Den-El decided on spearing a steamed mushroom, sniffing it, and popping it into his mouth.

"Den-El, tell us about the lovely woman you met. She seemed to like you." Martaam looked over, sipping a quick drink from her tall glass.

"Well, first of all, she's human. I'm not. So I'm not sure that our meeting will go anywhere." Den-El forked up an unidentified vegetable. "She invited me to her temple if I'm ever near there."

"She has a temple?" Surya glanced at Martaam. "Do people own their own temples here? Or are they built and run by the government or organizations?"

"It's a little of both. There are some priestesses who have their own temple in honor of an ancient deity. They do different work, depending on their preferences. Donors contribute to the building. Some groups go in and sponsor a temple and elect the priest or priestess."

"It's east of the Temple of Poseidon. Has a copper dome." Den-El swallowed down a beverage made of fruit. Surya forbade him alcohol this meal.

Martaam thought a minute. "I know where that is." She looked at both Surya and his friend. "The woman must be the priestess of the Temple of Jhanana."

Surya squinted. "Jhanana." He searched his mind for the meaning of the name. He smiled and stated, "Higher knowledge, especially one gained through meditation."

"Exactly." Martaam nodded. "She gains her knowledge through higher spirit connections. Her place is a noteworthy temple sought after by many people who seek advice or energy work." She lowered her voice. "I've also heard that people from the other islands come to see her in secret. She's that good."

Surya looked back at his friend.

Den-El grinned. "I would have no problem gaining a higher knowledge of her, if you know what I mean. She was really pretty." Just as he uttered the last words, a woman walked by, her nose wrinkled in disgust as she passed.

He turned his face toward her, morphing it into a gargoyle of a goat, complete with crossed eyes and a long tongue lolling out of his mouth. The woman let out a shriek and hurried off. Den-El resumed his normal look and continued eating.

"You're atrocious," said Surya, glancing around. People had stopped a moment for a look in their direction.

Martaam said nothing, stifling a laugh.

Den-El reached over and plucked a tiny chunk of meat from Surya's plate and held the piece in front of his dog's nose.

"How much did you tell the woman you were talking to?" asked Surya.

"I kept the information as basic and little as possible."

The energy vibrations Surya picked up from his friend troubled him a bit. He'd watched a little of Den-El's interaction with Cata-Lin. They seemed amiable enough, with the woman appearing genuinely interested. She had treated Den-El as though he were basically human.

From what Surya had gathered from interacting with the people on Poseidia, Things were placed here only for work, not for expanding in any worldly way. Why would a strange woman suddenly sit down and have interest in a Thing, even if he was handsome?

He knew Den-El kept something deep hidden inside. Tonight, when they were alone in their apartment, he and his friend would talk about this issue. The three ate their meals. As a special treat for Den-El, Surya let him order a dessert to his liking, a glazed fruit tart.

Chapter Eleven

"I'm interested in knowing how you plan on defending yourself if you're ever attacked. Do you think about that?" asked Surya.

Tujuk and Aleemirin sat at the table in their apartment looking perplexed. Neither were sure what astounded them most, the question Surya asked the moment they sat down, or the Thing sitting across from them.

Den-El pulled himself close to the table, placing his hands neatly on top. He minimized the view of his lower body, but could do nothing about the goat horns and ears. Wearing a head covering made him appear more preposterous, not that he hadn't tried, just to make sure.

"The truth is, gentlemen," said Den-El, "we've been watching the news. Are you aware of what's happening on Aryan?"

Aleemirin drummed his fingers on the table. "I know they are wanting control of our firestone crystal, our main power source, if that's what you're talking about. They've been asking us for years."

Surya related the brief newscast they saw when purchasing the AudioView.

"There are certain laws of Atlantis that guide the government and people. We don't pass laws unless it benefits all." Tujuk sipped from his mug.

"Like what?" asked Surya.

"You know the power cell in your apartment?" said Tujuk. "That source of power runs everything in your home. Every home has a cell, and people aren't charged for it."

"Healthcare is available for everyone. The healing centers use crystalline energy to run their equipment. Healers use actual crystal forms for all kinds of therapy. Low cost or none for making this happen."

Tujuk continued, "Some healers are so adept, they tap into etheric power, cosmic energy. No cost, either."

"Some surgeries are performed using crystals." Aleemirin added, looking from Surya to Den-El. "No one goes without care. Ever. Healers make payment plans when patients need a different service if crystals don't work."

"What about workers, business owners, or non-healers? How are they paid?" asked Den-El.

"Atlantis government set up the system as follows," said Aleemirin. "All people receive basic needs. Food, clothing, shelter, power for lighting and running appliances. Sewage, trash disposal, and public transportation are provided as well. Little to no cost.

"We enforce a work requirement so our society doesn't shut down completely. Citizens engage in productive jobs. They work at least four hours daily, choosing their own hours.

"People earn money for that time, and can work more if they wish. Each person enjoys at least two days off. If they need more, they work it out with a manager."

Tujuk smiled at Surya and Den-El, stating, "We like our system because people have more time to pursue what they love."

Surya rubbed his chin. "I see. You've created a system containing a balance of work and play."

"Exactly." Tujuk nodded.

"What I'm trying to understand is what Sons of Belial really want. What more could someone ask for if their needs are met, and they can spend most of their time doing whatever they wish?" Den-El narrowed his eyes. "I don't get it."

Tujuk and Aleemirin glanced at each other. Aleemirin spoke up, "Aryan Island and the others, Atalya, Og, and Eyre are run a little differently than Poseidia. The ones in control there want monetization of most everything. We offer public services free. Atlanteans don't focus on material wealth much."

"You sure about that?" asked Surya. "I also saw views of Aryan Island on the news. It looks different from Poseidia. The architecture, the shops, everything."

Tujuk said, "And there you have it. Basically, Sons of Belial want an oppressed majority ruled by a powerful small group. Sure, citizens can still enjoy all the nice products produced, if they can afford them. But they aren't really in control like they're made to believe.

"No Law of One person wants to say it, but I'm calling it out for what it is. Pure greed. Nothing good will come of anything if they are in power. Period."

Surya and Den-El sat back in their chairs, stunned.

Aleemirin broke the silence. "If they grab control of the firestone crystal, they become the main rulers of all the islands of Atlantis, toppling the balance we have now."

A loud knock sounded from the door. Tujuk got up and answered it. Moments later, Khaluj joined them at the table. Den-El avoided looking at the priest. Surya and Khaluj shared knowing glances and an unspoken agreement to keep their last meeting a secret. For now.

"What brings you here today, Khaluj?" Aleemirin motioned the priest to sit in the vacant chair.

"I must say," said Khaluj, smiling, "this is auspicious timing." He pulled out the chair and sat down. Tujuk returned from the kitchen with a steaming mug and placed it before his fellow priest.

"To what do we owe this pleasant encounter," said Tujuk.

Den-El lightly kicked Surya under the table. He telepathed quickly to his friend, "Watch your facial expressions." Surya cleared his throat and licked his lips, recomposing himself.

"I wanted to talk to you gentlemen—and Surya, I'm so glad you're here too—because I've been approached regarding a certain issue."

"By whom?" asked Aleemirin.

"I've had some people from Aryan ask me about shared responsibility for the firestone crystal, tuning it, caring for it."

Frowning, Tujuk took a quick swallow from his mug. "We've had these talks before, Khaluj. Law of One has never agreed to give up control over the main power crystal. Why does this need to change?"

"I understand completely, Tujuk. Law of One has overseen the firestone for thousands of years."

"And there has been no problems as a result," Tujuk said. His face clouded with frustration.

Aleemirin placed his hand on top of Tujuk's. Focusing his eyes on Khaluj, he said, "Why are you talking to Sons of Belial?"

Surya turned his face up towards Aleemirin and Tujuk, watching closely. Den-El delivered another soft kick, keeping his eyes focused on the table.

"Dear friends," said Khaluj, "We must stop this division. Attitudes change over time. Humans evolve. It's the way of things."

Tujuk stated with conviction, "Laws of spirit and nature never change. They are immutable. Some situations warrant constancy."

Khaluj's lips curved into an obligatory smile. "True. But like it or not, we're humans in a constantly turning environment, with changing needs."

Unable to keep quiet, Surya blurted out. "Do you think sharing control of the firestone will merge the divide between Aryan and Poseidia if there are checks and balances in place? For gaining total harmony, there must be equal buy-in and partnership. When one feels left out, the emotion must be remedied, or dissatisfaction grows, festers."

Den-El jerked straight up in his chair, eyes widening. Tujuk and Aleemirin stared at Surya, surprised. Khaluj's face lit up in brief triumph.

"That's exactly what I was thinking, dear Surya," said Khaluj.

Surya added, "Face it. If people of the islands can't get along, there won't be peace. One group will always feel the other has an advantage. Nothing wrong with checks and balances when caring for the firestone."

"May I add, gentlemen," said Khaluj, "that there is a political system in place for passing laws and managing society in general. There should be no problem in co-managment of the main power crystal. If anything, it creates a partnership. Don't you think that's much better?"

"Oh, come on, Khaluj," said Tujuk, irritated, "you know as well as we do that there are very different philosophies within Law of One and Sons of Belial."

"Dearest Tujuk, of course we know this. It's true Sons of Belial tend to lean more toward focus on self rather than the 'all is one' moniker."

"'All is one' is not a moniker. It's a spiritual law." Tujuk shook his head. "What's wrong with you, Khaluj? What's wrong with us for even considering this deal?"

Aleemirin rubbed Tujuk's back, trying desperately to calm his partner.

Den-El spoke up. "Wouldn't partnering with care of the firestone satisfy an 'all is one' ideal while honoring self at the same time? When all work together, individuals still continue their personal journey.

"Happiness in one creates a vibration that ripples out and connects with another who is content, and so on. Right now, that is not happening on Atlantis." He sat back in his chair. His face flushed with pent-up energy.

The three priests stared, slack-jawed at Den-El. Surya rooted his gaze on Tujuk and Aleemirin.

"I must say, you have a point, Den-El," said Aleemirin.

"My point is focusing too much on self pulls one away from spirit. One becomes vain, snobbish, greedy. I'm extremely leery of turning over even a little control to a group of puffed-up, hateful, profit-seeking, money-mongering, power-hungry people like Sons of Belial." Tujuk clenched his fists.

Khaluj's face burned bright scarlet, his eyes nearly bulging from their sockets.

Surya added, "And if Sons of Belial are considered out of balance already by Law of One, bring them back in check. Help them restore a sense of conscience. Partnership with the crystal is a step in the right direction."

Gentleman," said Khaluj, "it has been suggested to me that if we don't do something in the next few weeks, we will have a serious problem on our hands. And yes, you're thinking what I am."

"Give us one week to mull it over, Khaluj," said Aleemirin. "We'll discuss a final answer a week from today."

***

"What got into you?" Surya asked.

He and Den-El settled back into their apartment after the meeting with the priests.

Den-El plopped down on the sofa. "I couldn't keep my mouth shut any longer. The more I think about this, the more they have to move forward in their own mess they've created." He frowned at Surya. "You're the one who started with the suggestion in the first place, so why are you asking me about it?"

Surya sat down next to his friend. "I'm with you." He looked Den-El head on. "Do you think Sons of Belial will behave if this deal goes through?"

"Not a chance," said Den-El, shaking his head. "Every word Tujuk called that other group is exactly the way I feel too." He eyed Surya. "When are you coming clean to Aleemirin and Tujuk about your meeting on Aryan?"

"Don't know. Doesn't matter right now." Surya scratched his head, thinking. "Khaluj came today to push the issue. The fact we were already there sweetened the pot for him, especially when we opened our big mouths."

Den-El patted Surya's shoulder. "Listen, this whole issue was already headed down a certain path long before we came on the scene." He sat back, a philosophical look waxing over his face. "As I see it, we're trying to soften the blow. And things will blow. It's guaranteed."

"What do we do, then?" said Surya.

"I don't know," Den-El, answered. He turned on the AudioView, watching the news until dinner time.

***

Aleemirin and Tujuk led the way toward a stone building in the business district on the third land ring.

"Why are you so intent on talking with our military leaders?" asked Tujuk. "We still have a few days left before we meet with Khaluj."

"You gave me facts and figures, but I want to see for myself." Surya picked up his pace.

The three men stepped off the sidewalk, landing on a set of steps leading to an open plaza. On top of the building, the Atlantean military logo depicting all three branches shone in the sun. Overhead, a swarm of birds fluttered, twittering in shrill tones.

Surya glanced up, smiling to himself.

"Unusual," said Aleemirin. He glanced up, shielding his eyes from the sun. "I've never seen that before."

"Hmm, neither have I. They don't normally come this far inland." Tujuk opened one of the front doors and headed toward a set of carrier lifts. In minutes, they ended up on the top floor, where they walked to the end of a long hall.

All three entered a sizable meeting room. Uniformed men sat around a long oval wooden table. Each wore medals, pins, and color sets according to their military branch and rank.

Tujuk escorted Surya to a vacant captain's chair at the center where he and Aleemirin joined him on either side. Dressed in his usual tunic and slacks of black, Surya cut a regal figure among the earth-tone uniforms. His headband with gems and bearing Martaam's enamel blue butterfly allowed him a suggested air of authority.

"I believe we're all here," said Aleemirin, craning his neck as he looked around the room. All the men murmured in the affirmative, smiling in Surya's direction. "I want to thank all of you for coming to this meeting. We have a royal in our midst, though he's not from this constellation."

Smiles around the table brightened, accompanied by more emphatic nodding.

Aleemirin continued, "Surya, I've informed these gentlemen of your rank and status as denoted by your home planet. Seated here today are the top-ranking leaders in all branches of our military, land, sea, and air. They have all been sworn to secrecy, and this meeting is top secret."

"Thank you for coming, gentlemen," said Surya, nodding in acknowledgment at some of the men. "I know this seems like an unusual meeting, especially with a stranger like myself. I appreciate you humoring me, if you will."

"We're more than happy to do it, Your Highness. I'm Dhaman, General of the Land Troops. We protect all of Poseidia and land ruled by Law of One. Sons of Belial, as you may guess, have their own military." He stopped and looked to the man sitting beside him.

"I'm Kavi, I'm the Admiral of the High Seas. We protect Poseidia by guarding the waters surrounding her. We are a mighty force that can take out marine craft of all kinds." He waited for the next man to speak.

"I'm Tunda, General of the Airways. We patrol the skies. Our forces are swift and fierce."

"Gentlemen, it's a privilege meeting all of you," said Surya, smiling.

Tujuk spoke up. "A most interesting personal meeting took place several days ago. Another of our Law of One said he was approached by the Aryans, who are apparently insisting we at least share control of the firestone crystal."

The men raised their eyebrows.

"It was suggested that if we don't consider this request, there will be consequences," Tujuk continued.

"Why isn't the person who told you here with us now? I would think that he would be a key member in this meeting," said Dhaman. Kavi and Tunda nodded in agreement.

Surya answered, "The person is Khaluj, one of the high priests, and he doesn't know we're having this meeting."

Murmurs filled the room. Many sat in stunned silence.

"A little disconcerting, gentlemen," said Kavi. "There surely must be a good reason, other than scheduling conflicts."

"The problem is," said Aleemirin, "his conversation with the Aryan people at all bothers me and my two colleagues." He motioned toward Tujuk and Surya.

Tunda said, "I don't see it as bad to be approached by the Aryan people. We must communicate freely. If they have concerns, we need to hear them."

"They should have expressed their concerns through their representative, who would have approached our government officials," said Dhaman. "Not through some haphazard meeting with a priest so it could then be discussed at the dinner table." The general wrinkled his brow."

Kavi stated, "I'll agree it was informal, to say the least, but our Law of One high priests are ruling class priests. They are integral to our government." His lips pulled into a light smile. "I have to agree somewhat with Tunda on this."

"You make excellent points," said Surya, exchanging glances with the military leaders. "However, there is something that I'm sharing for the first time. My two esteemed colleagues aren't aware of this, either."

Surya turned quickly from Tujuk to Aleemirin, cringing at the sight of grave concern on their faces.

Tujuk leaned toward Surya's ear, whispering, "Do we need to talk about this in private before sharing whatever it is you have with such a large group?"

"I'm fine, Tujuk." Surya nodded at the priest, reassuring him. "Gentlemen, I have to admit that when I landed on Poseidia, through the portal, Khaluj witnessed my entrance first . . ."

After a brief history on how he met Aleemirin and Tujuk, and thus how he met Khaluj, Surya finished by briefing everyone about his meeting on Aryan. He ended by sharing the one question the Aryan member asked related to fighting.

"And this, gentlemen, distressed me the most. The members of that group didn't hold back. They were demanding, blunt, and wanted answers. I have strong suspicions that they're planning an attack if they don't get their way. At the very least, they will march on this island and force an agreement first, if they can."

"What do you think we should do?" asked Dhaman.

Surya glanced around the table, ending his gaze on the leaders. "I suggest you try working out a deal."

The room grew silent. Surya expected the glum expressions.

"There is one last detail I need to share with all of you." Surya shook his head. "As much as I dislike breaking the news, your dear Law of One high priest, Khaluj, is the leader of Sons of Belial."

Sounds of disbelief filled the room. Aleemirin and Tujuk winced. Seeing broken-hearted looks on their faces cut Surya to the core. Dhaman, Kavi, and Tunda stared down at the table, speechless.

Tunda spoke first. "I'm guessing Khaluj thinks you're the only Law of One associate who knows about his dual loyalties." He looked straight at Surya.

Labeled with a faction name hit Surya as strange. He'd never consciously identified himself as a Law of One follower, but he knew his personal leanings.

"I'm sure there are those who secretly align themselves with him and his group for their own gain, though they reside here on Poseidia. He only took an interest in me because of what I really am." Surya gazed around the room and back to Tunda.

"It doesn't come as a surprise he'd want to get in your good graces," said Kavi. "Extra-terrestrials are powerful, and he knows it." He nodded toward Aleemirin and Tujuk.

"Oof, you can say that again." Aleemirin blinked several times, glancing at Surya.

Surya grinned. "Both of these gentlemen and Khaluj have seen what I can do."

Tujuk spoke up. "Can't speak for the Aryans, but other than all of us in this room, no one else on Poseidia knows we have an alien in our midst. We must keep this secret. Our friend has been emphatic that he is not on a formal mission. He's simply been thrust into political war against his will, and now wants to help."

Surya nodded. "True."

Dhaman said, "All of us will keep your secret. Everyone knows it's the ruling class priests who govern. The elected leaders are a mere mouthpiece. No problem here." He sucked in his breath. "Sometimes keeping secret weapons to yourself yields a better outcome. It's called strategy."

"Won't disagree with that comment," said Surya. He squared up his shoulders and directed his next question to the military leaders. "How do you want to care for the firestone with two differing groups? Who will create the terms and conditions for this change? As you see, there are many things to consider in this venture."

Dhaman said, "I think we'll have to create these terms with them. I don't see any way around it. To push this under our terms or ignore it means we may be in a real fight."

Tujuk held up his hand. "When we meet with Khaluj, we'll go through proper channels. We've tried stalling this in the past, but I agree with Dhaman. We're out of time now."

"Would you three be willing to let me see your troops, some of what you do?" Surya looked at Dhaman, Kavi, and Tunda. "I'd like to see what you're capable of."

"We're a pretty formidable force, Your Highness," said Kavi. "We have a history of fierce warfare, cunning unmatched by any who fight us."

Dhaman grinned. "And then there's that little extra. Magic, they call it. Our foes do. They don't know our secrets with laws of spirit, let alone how to work with them. Some of us are especially skilled in that arena."

"I hate to break it to you, gentlemen," said Surya, "but you'll have nothing on Sons of Belial. They have exactly what you do. If there is a war, it will truly be a match of military prowess. The strongest, fastest, and smartest wins."

Kavi nodded in agreement. "Won't debate you there, Your Highness."

Aleemirin tapped the table lightly. "I can't think of anything else until we talk with Khaluj. If you three want to start drafting some terms, that will be helpful. I'll get members of our group to start, as well." He shook his head. "Gentlemen, we are in for some interesting times, and I must say I'm a little uneasy about it all."

"I have a question," said Kavi, raising his hand. "What do we do about Khaluj? We can't inform him of our approach. But I fear turning him out of Law of One will bring on incredible hostility."

Aleemirin raised his hand. "Simple. We act the same, make him think we don't know any differently. From our side, we hold secret meetings without him when it comes to planning and strategizing. That way, we keep an eye on him, yet make sure he stays in the dark when it comes to more sensitive matters."

"Agree," said the leaders in unison.

When Surya, Aleemirin, and Tujuk stepped outside the building to return home, the swarm of birds, slowed their twittering, slowly drifting off and scattering in all directions in the Atlantean sky.

***

Martaam and Surya walked hand in hand. The balmy night air blew around them, tinged with smells from the ocean. In the distance the lights from the inner core blazed like they always did, brilliant and true.

Surya enjoyed the warmth radiating from Martaam's skin. When they brushed against each other, the touch filled him with a thrilling energy. Her hair swayed when she walked. In the moonlight, her face took on the beauty and glow of a goddess. He wanted to tell her about his meeting in Aryan, what he'd discovered concerning Khaluj, and the meeting with the military leaders.

He couldn't do any of it. Revealing any part of his experience could blow the whole cover being formulated. The only one who knew everything was Den-El. His friend played an integral role, whether out in the open or behind the scenes. Like it or not, Den-El's powers were nearly a little stronger than his.

Like father, like son. Den-El filled the same position in relation to him. It all worked out in a perfect match. No wonder Mal-Ek had chosen Ahtan-Mir as his right-hand man. Den-El would serve as Surya's. The two worked in tandem, one playing off the other.

Other than seeking Martaam, having Den-El share in this adventure had been his other sole desire. He disliked the way it played out, but he had his best friend, nonetheless. And Den-El seemed to be working with the cards dealt him.

"You've gotten quiet, all of a sudden," said Martaam, looking sideways at him. "Something bothering you?"

"No. Maybe a little tired, but nothing a little extra sleep couldn't handle." He smiled, clenching her hand a little tighter. After debating himself a few seconds, Surya decided to ask. "Martaam, do you ever fear a war happening here on Atlantis, on Poseidia?"

"Why do you ask?" She glanced his direction, a slight startled look on her face.

"Do you ever watch the news, listen to what's being said?"

"I do a little, but I don't find myself pulled in by it very much."

"What about your other friends, other people on Poseidia? Do they ever talk about such a fear or concern?" He slowed his pace a little.

"Do you know what I really fear?" said Martaam. "I fear the loss of all Atlantis. I see darkness and water in my dreams."

Surya led her to a vacant park bench facing the land cord. "What does that mean to you?" he asked.

"It's a thread of fear that runs deep in most Atlanteans, regardless of which island you've chosen as your home. Earthquakes, rumblings in the night, tremors during the day. They all serve as a reminder that we may not endure."

Her words shocked him. For some reason, he'd not caught on to such a fear since his arrival. Had he tuned it out? There had not been a tremor or anything else in nature since he came through the portal. Maybe with time he'd see it, feel it.

"Have you or your family ever thought about migrating elsewhere to a more stable continent?" He leaned over, brushing his cheek against hers.

"Easier said than done. We love it here. It has been our home for generations." She looked over at him. "I think we try and squash the fear, hoping by some chance that none of it's true. This land is like no other. We are a race of people like no other on Earth. I know this because too many people far and wide have said it."

"I guess that many people can't be wrong. Right?" A faint smile played on his lips.

"I hope so."

"If you had to go somewhere, which place would you choose?"

Martaam sank back against the bench, thinking. "This will sound strange coming from a human like me, but maybe you'll understand."

"I won't think you're strange." He entwined his fingers around hers.

"I'd like to go where you came from. What is life like on another planet that's completely different than this one? How would it look? What would the people be like?" She gazed at him. "I know you're in a three-dimensional skin so you can survive the vibrations of Earth and life itself here, but what's it like being you?"

The questions and her answers to his sent his mind returning to thoughts of home on Ontarus 9. Though the highly enlightened on both dimensions had some understanding of the other, neither would fully understand until living in the other. He thought back to the day when he first came through the portal. No amount of classes, reading, or meditating would have prepared him for the shock to his system.

He had heard tales of high council members traveling to Earth for short periods of time. The vibrations on Earth and the impact on their bodies placed them in precarious positions. Continued stay could harm their energy levels. They had to return after a short time as a result.

"Will the extra-terrestrials ever come back again, Surya?" Martaam squeezed his hand.

"I don't know." Surya leaned over, kissing her gently on the lips. "Just know that if I could take you safely on a journey to my world, I would do it."

Chapter Twelve

"Get up," said Den-El. He shook his friend awake.

"Mmm." Surya rolled over, sleepy-eyed. "What's wrong?"

"You need to see this." Den-El jerked the covers back. "Hurry. Get dressed." Da-Ina licked Surya's face, barking once in excitement.

"You're up early," said Surya, petting Da-Ina between the ears.

"Couldn't sleep. Woke up with something bothering me. Went out for a warm drink at one of the food stalls, and then I see them." A look of anxiety filled Den-Els' face.

Surya stared at Den-El for a few seconds. Within minutes, he'd shaken himself free from the warmth of his bed and dressed.

Outside, the cool morning air kissed his skin. Laughing, he watched Da-Ina frolick around Den-El, sniff the flowers, and bark at nothing in particular. He stopped a moment, getting a read on the vibrations surrounding him. Den-El was right. Something didn't feel quite normal. Poseidia usually held an air of calm, people going to work, opening their businesses. Today more people huddled in groups, whispering and pointing. Faces appeared more tense.

He gazed down the street looking for the cause.

"Over there," said Den-El, pointing to a window.

Curious, Surya ran over for a closer look.

"Equal share in crystal care."—Sons of Belial

Walking several steps to another window, he saw another poster.

"No equality; No rest."—Sons of Belial

Den-El trotted up behind Surya. "The streets are loaded with these.

Surya wrinkled his brow. He turned up Trident Street. Another sign hung in a window, more chilling than the others.

"We'll fight for what's right."—Sons of Belial

"This isn't good at all." Surya wiped his eyes and groaned.

"They must have come in the middle of the night. I don't think they'd be that brave to come during the day." Den-El shivered a little in the morning breeze.

"I had hoped your circle of birds would have squashed the urge for posting here. At least give us time to talk with the military leaders."

"I did what I could. Their sonic sounds and flying should have scrambled the vibrational imprint from the meeting and made reading it from the ether nearly impossible. It's bigger than we are, Surya." Den-El stamped a hoof. "Are you convinced Poseidia's military forces are strong enough to fight back? It'll be one-on-one when it blows."

"I know. That's what I told them. They've been formidable foes in the past, but there are no secrets if a civil war breaks out."

Den-El turned his gaze toward the pavement. "I never wanted to come here in the first place. I surely never wanted to be in a war on Earth. We'll be pulled into this. No way around it."

Surya shook his head in despair. "I know."

"Are you sure you don't want to take a chance and go through the portal again? It won't be the direct route like you had the first time, but it will get us out of this galaxy."

"I can't leave her."

"Come on, Surya, she's just a woman. A human. You're so much better." His eyes clouded. "You're royalty."

"She may be human, but she's kind and decent. Her fourth-dimension skills can be developed." Surya frowned at his friend. "There are other humans who are good people. The military leaders care about the citizens they defend. Aleemirin and Tujuk care."

"You believe that?" Den-El stood in defiance, hands clasped on either side of what would be considered his waist. "Neither side is all that great, Law of One included."

Surya considered his words.

"Both sides are corrupt. Both want power. Unfortunately, Sons of Belial want it more." Den-El's ears twitched with excitement. "This whole mess could have been dealt with ages ago. One side pushes the other's buttons."

"Darling! How nice to find you this morning." Cata-Lin stepped up from behind, slipping an arm around Den-El's waist.

Surya stepped to the side, startled. He watched with intense interest. Den-El had only shared a brief skepticism of her, but refused additional information. He'd taken the matter a step further by blocking access to any of his personal thoughts about her.

Cata-Lin acknowledged Surya. "And you must be the lucky master. What a brilliant choice in selecting this creature." She stroked between Den-Els's ears, which flicked and twitched under her touch.

A rising lust in Den-El hit Surya in the same region, the sacral chakra. Thoughts of possessing Martaam flooded his mind. He turned them off immediately. A faint grin on Cata-Lin's face as she watched sent a bolt of irritation scattering through him.

Surya bowed his head lightly in her direction. "There's a special bond between us. Unlike any between master and Thing on Poseidia."

"I wouldn't doubt you, Sir." Cata-Lin tilted her head a little, eyeing Surya. "Would you object to my spending time with your precious Thing, Den-El?"

The smile on Surya's face vanished. "You want to what?"

"I know my request is probably the strangest one on Poseidia, but I delight in his company. He's most intelligent, which you already know." Cata-Lin licked her lower lip. "I make it a priority to surround myself with the most enlightened of creatures, human or animal. Their enlightenment is mine as well."

Her seductive smile caught Surya off guard. He viewed Den-El's glassy gaze. Deep in his friend's eyes burned fires of unadulterated desire and intrigue.

"Would you mind if I brought Da-Ina with us when we meet?" Den-El suddenly asked, facing Cata-Lin.

Such a question from a Thing, even with Den-El's strange possession of intelligence, stunned Cata-Lin. She looked over at Surya. "Your call, good Sir."

"Where do you plan on taking him?" asked Surya.

"I'll not take him far, only to the park where we met, or to a local food establishment." She grinned. "People will think he's mine, so no need for alarm."

"Would you mind if I go to her temple?" Den-El directed his question at Surya, blinking his eyes a few times and grinning. He lightly clicked a hoof against the pavement, swaying his body so he brushed against Cata-Lin.

A quick influx of thoughts from Den-El created a greater understanding in Surya. Den-El had needs as a third-dimension human, and animal. As on Ontarus 9, Den-El harbored a purpose for everything he did. Sometimes Surya didn't understand, but considering the posters from Sons of Belial and the little information his friend had shared, Surya acquiesced.

"I'll allow it only if I'm in the know and in the mood to grant such generosity," said Surya.

Cata-Lin bowed her head in acknowledgment. "As you should." She thought a moment. "Would you mind if I spend some time with him next week? I'll have a clearer schedule."

"I don't see a problem right now," said Surya.

"Very well." Cata-Lin kissed Den-El's cheek. "I shall call on you next week, precious Thing."

The young men watched until Cata-Lin disappeared from view. Da-Ina barked several times and sat down beside Den-El.

"I hope you know what you're getting into, Den-El." Surya squinted his eyes. "The most ingratiating being I've ever encountered. She reeks with insincerity."

Den-El smiled. His tail flicked back and forth with excitement. "I'm right there with her every step of the way." He patted Surya's shoulder. "You should know me by now. I'll get to the bottom of whatever it is she's after. I've already disposed of one spy that priest used."

Surya whirled around facing his friend. "What are you talking about?"

For several minutes, Den-El informed Surya about the bird he saw in the park. "Khaluj had been using that bird as a source of information. He knows all about what happened with me, with us, and how we all fit together. I put a stop to it, at least."

"And now he's using Cata-Lin." Surya sucked in his lips and let out a puff of air. "What's your plan with her?"

"We play it cool." Den-El stepped closer to his friend. "I want Da-Ina around for extra protection. If Khaluj can have his bird, I can have my dog."

"What about Khaluj? I informed everyone in the meeting about him."

"You best play it cool with him too. Get Aleemirin, Tujuk, and everyone else to agree." Den-El tapped Surya on the shoulder. "He's playing the same game. Don't forget how he acted when we all met last time."

"I remember." Surya winced.

"He's still trusting you to keep his secret."

"He's a fool if he doesn't think he'll be discovered soon." Surya reached out and plucked one of the hateful posters from a window.

***

Surya surveyed a group of gargantuan men. They remained at attention, eyes straight ahead, arms down by their sides. Their bodies housed fierce determination and cunning. Dhaman stood by his side.

The leader had selected the best of his men, a small sample, upon Surya's request. Today, he would spend his time with the military leaders, seeing what they could do in the event of an attack.

Dhaman said, "These men are fighters like no others. They strike terror in the hearts of their enemies. We have several hundred who fight on the land."

"I can see that." Surya shifted his weight to the other foot. "You've hinted at more than just their use of weapons or military strategy when approaching a foe. What gives them an edge? Why don't their opponents catch on and do just as much when fighting back?"

Dhaman smiled. "Atlanteans have an edge over most everyone on the planet, it seems. We've fought several battles in our history through the ages. It's the special tricks we use."

"Tricks?" Surya turned in surprise, facing Dhaman.

"I think it's best for you to see for yourself." He called out names, and two men stepped forward. "His Highness wishes to see exercises we use in battle. First demonstration, Operation Smoke."

"At your command, Sir," answered the men in unison.

The two men walked several yards away from their group. Starting with their backs to each other, each one walked the same number of paces until they stood about twenty-five feet apart. Slowly, one of the men advanced a few steps. When his partner moved away, he stepped quicker.

A few more steps by the designated opponent, and the man acting defense stopped, holding out his hands. His face showed a set jaw, focused eyes. Surya tapped into the man's mind and discovered his use of a protective word resulting in sheets of heavy smoke gathering in front of the man on the offense.

Smoke billowed forth, spreading several yards. Blinded by the sheer density, the man moving forward couldn't see his team member moving from one side of the smoky wall to the other. The ability to track and follow ended immediately. An acrid smell wafted in the air.

Inside the cloud of smoke, the opponent gasped and sputtered. Surya watched as the other team member spread his hands, waving away the smoke. In an instant, the air cleared. Both men returned to their former positions within the group.

"Very good, men." Dhaman nodded in approval. He motioned one more time, calling out two different names. The men stepped out front. He called out loud and clear, "Operation Venom."

Like their comrades before them, these two men started out their exercise the same way. This time they stood over fifty feet apart. The man taking an offense role ran toward his teammate. Surya smiled when he tapped into the man engaging in defense tactics. Like Khaluj, the troop member could telepath with other animal species.

One by one, snakes appeared from the nearby woods. The ground seemed to take on a life of its own as the reptiles moved forward, slithering with lightning speed and a target in mind. From the structure of their heads, Surya guessed they were poisonous. Before the opponent moved another step, the snakes were nearly on him.

One looked ready to strike. Just as it retracted back for a full lunge, it stopped. All the reptiles stopped moving and retreated to the woods. From what Surya gathered in his read of the etheric printout, the man who called the snakes had used a special word for their exit. He'd also thanked them and sent love and gratitude for their assistance.

The animals who came had agreed to participate in the exercise and cooperated as if human. They also expressed telepathically their appreciation for being called, even in a practice exercise. Both humans and animals maintained bonds of good will when engaging in these exchanges. Surya knew it.

"Very impressive." Surya grinned at Dhaman.

"I thought you would like seeing the exercises. This is exactly what we do in battle, and what our enemies experience. We've maintained connection with divine spirit since humans were placed on Atlantis. As you see, our men are used for their special abilities. We strategize based on this as well."

Dhaman eyed Surya. He wore a look of consideration, as if debating whether to share one other secret.

"Is there anything else you want to show me? You look like you've got something on your mind." Surya angled his head, staring at Dhaman.

"Your Highness, there is one last exercise I would like to show you, because this technique is our pride and joy on Poseidia. Actually, it's an Atlantean use of technology that we've adapted from early teachings. I only hesitate because I'm not sure how you'll react."

"And that is . . .?" Surya arched an eyebrow.

"Let us demonstrate." Dhaman turned toward his troop, and called out to two of the men, who quickly stepped from the front row. "Weapons display. Get your fire ready."

"Yes, Sir," said the men. They ran to the back row of the troop, each returning with a sleek hand gun. A third man accompanied them, holding targets in both hands. As the two men with the weapons stood side by side, the third man ran fifty paces in front of them.

He deposited four targets on the ground and ran to the back of the troop. Dhaman readied himself for giving orders.

"Men, lift your weapons. Steady now. Aim. Fire."

Surya focused on the targets. A bolt of light sailed through the air, landing on the center of one target. It shattered in a million indefinable pieces. Parts appeared to have disintegrated. Another bolt whizzed by, hitting another target. Again, the piece disappeared. Small particles floated to the air and onto the ground. The same followed suit for the remaining targets.

"Fire out. Return weapons," said Dhaman.

The two men returned to the back of the troop, where they handed off their guns to the weapons manager.

"You've turned galactic technology for use against yourselves or others?" Surya whirled around, staring Dhaman head on. His lips set hard in a grim expression.

Dhaman maintained composure. "Again, Your Highness, I questioned whether you needed to be aware of this or not. It was almost my decision to not demonstrate anything, but you're sure to find out."

"Do you have any shield technology for protection if an opponent uses one of these on you? Are you aware how disruptive those ray bolts are to the environment when they hit the ground?" Surya's jaw set in defiance.

"Your Highness, we are aware of the damage it can do. We don't use these unless absolutely necessary."

"Under what conditions do you determine their use as absolutely necessary?"

The General stepped back, his face blanched with concern. "It is our hope that we won't be using them ever again. We haven't warred with anyone in hundreds of years."

"What about Kavi and Tunda, do they use any special techniques like the ones demonstrated, or these guns?" Surya asked.

"They can show you exactly what they do. I'll take you to Kavi next. Tunda will see you afterward." Dhaman turned to his platoon of soldiers and called, "Disband."

The men fell away, dispersing in several directions. A grim-faced Dhaman escorted Surya to the main office where Kavi waited.

"His Highness is yours, Sir."

"I take it you found the special exercises most intriguing?" asked Kavi, bowing his head in greeting to Surya.

"Very much so," answered Surya. It's good to see people using divine gifts at their disposal.

Dhaman displayed a look of gratitude toward Surya. "Yes. It's becoming a lost art. The priests in both factions are still somewhat adept, but the common citizen, not so much."

"What about the healers?" Surya thought of Martaam. From his first session with her, she possessed an ability to tap into information. But could she do more?

"Adept healers are on the same level as the priests," answered Kavi. They undergo rigorous testing before they are allowed to perform in-depth, invasive procedures."

"That would make sense," said Surya. "Where do we go next?"

Kavi nodded toward Dhaman, who bowed and left the office. "Follow me this way, and I'll show you our fleet of ships."

After an air taxi ride to the far side of Poseidia, Surya and Kavi stood on the roof of the High Seas office building. Surya looked out over the ocean, scanning the vast array of ships tied to docks. The smell of salt and fish filled the air. Garish tones of metal on metal sounded harsh in Surya's ear.

Workmen assigned to different ships carried out their maintenance duties, taking orders from those in charge. In the distance, a ship plowed through the water, heading toward shore.

"We have marine craft of all kinds," said Kavi. "Combat ships, aircraft carriers, submarines, and guard ships. I'll take you to our viewing room so you can see some of what happens when we're in battle."

"I would like that," said Surya. He turned around and followed Kavi inside, leaving the outside noise behind.

They walked down a busy hallway, taking a lift ride down to the bottom floor. The area seemed almost deserted. A lonely silence surrounded the two men. A brief sound of someone closing door suggested other humans worked not far away.

"We keep information like what I'm about to show you carefully guarded down here. No prying eyes. This is top secret." Kavi led the way to a room with a table holding a projector. "Please have a seat."

Surya selected a vacant chair, one with an easy view of the screen the opposite end of the room. Kavi walked to a counter. On one corner sat a black square device. He pressed a button and spoke. "Bring box 259 down here immediately. I need someone to work the electronics."

Within minutes, a man entered the room rolling a small cart holding numerous cartridges. He conversed briefly with Kavi and busied himself in pulling the designated information. Kavi seated himself beside Surya.

The media personnel selected a cartridge and slipped it into the projector. When he flipped a switch, an image filled up the screen. He dimmed the lights for easier viewing.

Once the film started playing, Kavi spoke up. "What you'll see now, Your Highness, are maneuvers our ships undergo when deployed. We placed floating targets on the water. Our ships can fire missiles and hit these from quite a distance. Not only can we shoot out projectiles, but watch this."

Surya turned his gaze back toward the screen. A solid stream of fire shot out from the side of one ship, hitting the target a hundred yards away. The target disintegrated from the fire.

"Look at this next shot," said Kavi.

Another ship blasted out a series of large balls, each one landing on different targets, which were nothing more than small empty rowboats. All burst into flames.

"What is special about this ammunition is that the spheres are filled with an oil-based fuel that is not easily extinguished. Salt water, fresh water, nothing will put out the fire. It spreads rapidly, consuming a ship within minutes."

"Impressive," said Surya.

"But here is another handy maneuver that we use quite a bit." Kavi tapped Surya's arm in excitement.

Surya watched as a submarine moved through the water. A ship sailed several yards away. As the submarine sped up, black liquid shot out in jet streams from pipes in the bottom. In seconds the submarine disappeared in inky darkness.

"We got the idea from none other than what an octopus does when it diverts an enemy," said Kavi. "Here is the counter maneuver. You'll see it now."

The following scenes showed the black inky substance disappearing. When Surya viewed the submarine, the liquid streamed from special pipes designed for pulling in fluids away from the submarine's viewing station.

"Our ships have special devices in the control panels that show topographical layouts under water. We know if there are rock beds nearby, so we can dodge them. Likewise, we can detect other underwater craft or the bottom of another floating vessel."

Surya asked, "Do you mark the bottoms of your craft so you don't accidentally hit your own?" He turned and looked at Kavi.

"Absolutely, Your Highness," answered Kavi. He chuckled. "We have created a numbered coding system. Numbers go in specially selected spots. We had accidents in the beginning, so we learned quickly. That's not to say that the enemy can't retaliate and create a situation where we hit our own craft. They do. We do it to them also."

"Part of strategizing," said Surya.

"Absolutely." Kavi turned toward the man behind the projector. "Can you show what some of our submarines can do? Fast forward a little."

The man nodded, moving a lever to the right. The film sped up. He stopped when Kavi ordered him. "I'll show you this last part, and we'll see if Tunda has arrived."

On the screen, an image of a submarine sat submerged. An empty boat target floated yards away. From a launcher on the submarine, a projectile shot forth, cutting through the water in the direction of the boat. When it struck, the boat split into several pieces, metal sections sinking into the water.

"And there you have it," said Kavi. "Those water missiles can travel at high rates of speed, faster than our street vehicles go, and hit their targets miles away. They are designed to travel for several minutes to hit enemy craft."

"Are you prepared to go against your own Atlantean people? Even though they are of a different faction? How do you plan to win?"

"Honestly, Your Highness, we are hoping it doesn't come down to a civil war. I think once we appease them a little, all will be well."

"You trust Sons of Belial that much?" asked Surya.

"Let me answer this way," said Kavi. He shifted in his seat. "I don't like the idea of allowing them any part in sharing care of the crystal. I also know that we are at a time when we have to give in a little. I'd rather they be up front and honest about what they want and what they might do if they don't get their way."

"Fair enough." Surya stared at the screen. The images had paused while the media operator stood waiting.

"Shall I continue, Sir?" asked the man.

Kavi shook his head. "No, I think Your Highness has seen a little of what we can do."

The black box on the counter cracked with the sound of a voice coming through it. Kavi got up and headed toward hit. He pushed a button on top. "Come again." He nodded. "We're on our way up."

Surya rose from his chair and met Kavi at the counter.

"Tunda is here. He'll show you our aircraft fleet. I think you'll be impressed with that as well."

"I'm sure I will."

* * *

Located also on the far side of Poseidia and opposite the High Seas office, the Airways headquarters bustled with activity. Tunda walked Surya to a viewing box on top of the building.

"Welcome to our branch of the Atlantean military. I've arranged a special demonstration for you by five of our best pilots, though all of ours are superior." Tunda opened a door leading to an open area filled with seats.

Surya looked out over the edge of a chest-high wall and viewed rows upon rows of multi-tiered hangar ports to his left. In each hangar rested an aircraft. He made note of the different colors outlining the sections and coinciding shape of the craft inside.

His heart raced. These aircraft were nothing more than spaceships that mimicked many of the ones in his galaxy and others. It appeared that the Atlanteans had taken the teachings from his extra-terrestrial people to heart.

"We have over two thousand fighter planes, and numerous other types. Today you will see five fighters in flight. We will demonstrate how projectiles are deployed and how the guns work. Mock ammunition is used so you can see what maneuvers might look like in a real war situation." Tunda added in a low voice, "The explosive sounds are there for effect."

"Ah, I see," said Surya, nodding. "Is there only one pilot per craft?"

"Two people per craft. One maneuvers; the other mans the weapons. You'll find it enjoyable to watch, especially when there is no actual war."

"Let's just hope a war doesn't occur," said Surya, angling his head for a better look.

"Your Highness, I couldn't hope for more myself. However, we must always be on our guard." Tunda bowed his head lightly in Surya's direction.

The men walked toward a set of ornate, captain-style seats placed in front and center of the first row of the viewing box.

"Let's sit here. The flight commander will begin the demonstration."

The two men sat, waiting. Five minutes later, a whistle sounded from a speaker located outside the viewing box.

Tunda tapped Surya's hand. "They are starting now."

Surya sat back in the chair, enjoying the breeze rush over his skin. The flight demonstration interested him greatly. He wanted to compare what Atlantis had in relation to similar machines on his planet and in other galaxies he'd studied over the years.

A loud high-pitched whirring sound came from left of the viewing station, starting loud and decreasing with each passing second. A neat line of sleek saucer-shaped air ships flew into view. At the top, a dome outlined in a ring of red lights denoted the pilot and weapons control center of the craft.

They sailed through the air, graceful as a bird on water, and veered into their planned lineup spots, hovering next to each other equal yards apart.

A man in uniform walked out, heading to a metal pole. He picked up a speaking device and mumbled a few words for an audio test. His uniform of bright yellow with black trim and a long leather belt displayed an array of gold jeweled pins and striped ribbons.

"That gentleman will be the one directing the flight program. He announces what the fighter air ships will do," said Tunda.

Surya nodded, settling back again.

The flight commander's voice echoed through the viewing station. "Your Highness, on behalf of the Poseidia Airways Squadron, we welcome your presence today."

In acknowledgment, Surya exhibited the royal wave learned on Ontarus 9.

The commander bowed in response and continued, "We will be demonstrating our newest air ships, the F-777 Comet. These air ships are the only ones of their kind on the entire planet. Manned by a pilot and weapons chief, this two-man craft can fly at supersonic speeds, reaching other continents in under thirty minutes or an hour.

"Our pilots are fierce, strategic, and fearless. Our weapons chiefs ensure all ammunition is stocked, ready for loading, and fully charged."

Tunda quickly whispered to Surya, "Every craft you've seen is powered by crystals, including the nautical ships you saw earlier. We may not be able to travel the world in one trip, but we can go pretty far."

"Our demonstrations begin now," said the commander. "Pilots, prepare positions. Break hover now. Engage power now. Lift off."

On the last command, the air ships blasted from their stations, soaring straight up in the air.

"You will now see our pilots fly in chevron formation. They are flying much lower than they would in actual combat." The commander looked up briefly at Surya and Tunda.

The ships had taken on a chevron form, sailing in unison across the sky. In a fluid back and forth manner, they sliced through the sky, maintaining formation with each ship taking up the lead at the right time.

Surya wished Den-El were present. These fighter space ships reminded him so much of home. A pang of homesickness slammed him without warning. For the first time, he wished he could go home for a brief visit, feel the old fourth dimension lightness and changing realities that shifted as easily as the ships sailing through the air.

The commander spoke again, "Our ships move in all directions as needed. Pilots will demonstrate this now, including the whirling dervish maneuver used when ammunition is distributed for greater coverage."

After disbanding the chevron formation, each ship took turns moving up, down, and sideways. The last movement, turning on edge and moving all directions. Whether upright or on edge, the pilots sent their respective ships spinning at dizzying speeds. In the sunlight, the ships looked like swirling discs of silver, topped with ruby.

If Surya had been invited to ride in one of them, he would have done so without hesitation. The graceful gliding motions generated an endorphin high not felt in a while.

"Now for the weapons show," said the commander. "All our guns and ammunition are powered by our wonderful crystals found here on Atlantis. Again, our weaponry is unrivaled. They create terror in the hearts of our enemies. They destroy down to the last blade of grass standing."

Tunda, tapped Surya's arm, smiling. Surya nodded and turned his gaze back on the ships. The pilots had maneuvered their air ships upright again.

"The commander spoke, "On the ground we have automated weapon launchers in place. These machines will hurl clay spheres into the air. Pyrotechnics have been added for effect."

Glancing up briefly where the ships hovered, the commander gave the orders. "Weapons ready now. Air ship one, prepare discharge now.

One of the ground launchers released a target high into the air. The first craft shot out a bright streak of light, blasting the target into numerous pieces.

"Air ship two, prepare discharge now."

Each craft sent out a wave of rays at each target released from the ground, spinning and twirling as it did so.

Tunda informed Surya about the guns. "They are positioned all around the ship. The weapons chief sits in a control panel and can load, aim, and fire in any direction."

Surya asked, "Are these crystal ray guns just like those used by the land troops?"

"They work the same. Their intricacies involve a calculated use of magnetic technology that works in tandem with the crystal power itself."

"Mmm." Surya nodded. He refused to say much more about the crystal ray guns, but their use alarmed him greatly.

"And now we have our grand finale." The commander's voice rang out once more. "Our show ends with a beautiful sequence of movements that shows the full grace of our air ships. Not only does it look pretty, it's functional when we need it."

The commander looked up one last time toward the hovering space ships. "Pilots, Five Braid Ribbon now. In position now."

The ships lined up in numerical order.

"Forward now," said the commander. "One over two and under three. Five over four and under one. Two over three and under five. Four over one and under two." The ships moved as instructed. "Continue pattern times three and end," called out the commander.

Surya smiled. Such coordination and beauty touched him on an inner level. The hateful crystal ray guns, not so much. On the way back to his apartment after meeting with Dhaman, Kavi, and Tunda, he viewed a sight that sent dread radiating throughout him.

On several street corners, groups of people held signs chanting.

"Crystal care is ours."

"Don't give up our power."

A surge of curiosity bolted through him. Surya hopped a ferry and sailed toward the land core. The main government buildings stood on that patch of land. Had people gathered there? Leaders in the area would surely hear them if they had meetings today.

When the ferry landed at the port for the land core, he stepped off and followed signs to where he needed to go. There he saw it. Large groups of people holding signs and chanting similar words he'd heard earlier.

Surya edged closer. The vibrational energy of the crowd hit him with a strong negativity. He quickly turned away, gathering up his own energy to meet the crowd's. The people of Poseidia didn't like the idea of sharing care of the crystal. He wanted so much to ask some questions, talk to the participants, but he checked any impulsivity toward such an action.

He'd already involved himself enough in government affairs. No need to stir up the populace as well. The work he'd done today pleased him. Surya felt more familiar with some of the intimate workings of Atlantis, what drove the people. Dhaman, Kavi, and Tunda all agreed that Khaluj would not be made aware of their meeting today, either.

Surya stepped away from the crowd. The late afternoon blazed its hottest, fierce and blinding. Martaam's healing school shined in the distance. He walked toward the building, leaving the clanging throng behind him. If she didn't have plans, he'd invite her to dinner at his apartment. If she did have other plans, he'd at least have the joy of spending time in her company traveling home together.

***

Mal-Ek and Ahtan-Mir sat together in the royal observation room, watching through the GalXR90 with the audio turned up.

"I don't know whether to be proud or run screaming to the Federation. If I had total power, I'd stop this nightmare." Mal-Ek shook his head.

Ahtan-Mir sat, thoughtful. "On the one hand, Your Majesty, I see two young men showing concern and taking action. Den-El can only do so much, based on his body. His mind, however, is his best asset.

"Your Highness will rule someday. He's learning information, assessing, and acting on his knowledge."

"He and your son are going to find themselves pulled in a war that will end in destruction. The Atlantean people have been heading down the path of annihilating themselves basically ever since Atlantis was populated with humans.

Mal-Ek's agitation grew. Ahtan-Mir found himself briefly at a loss for words.

"What do we do, Ahtan?"

"We keep a close watch. When the time is right, we act."

Chapter Thirteen

"I'm still not sure why Aleemirin and Tujuk didn't go with you to see the military leaders." Den-El made himself comfortable on a colorful pile of pillows Surya had purchased on request. At times, the animal side of himself like resting on the floor. The human side of him enjoyed a certain comfort level.

"They dismissed the invitation, saying they were already aware of Poseidia's military force. That I should meet with the leaders unencumbered."

"Do you think they're making light of this whole thing?"

Surya wrinkled his brow. "Something more along the lines of simply not wanting to deal with it. It's as if they're throwing up their hands at this point and allowing Sons of Belial to share in the care of the firestone."

"Like they're tired from fighting the people on Aryan and the other remaining islands?" Den-El narrowed his eyes.

"It's possible. But there seems to be a naivete surrounding Law of One. Like they refuse to see potential danger staring them in the face."

"What do we do about the crystal ray guns?" asked Den-El.

"We can't do anything about them. But there is technology to guard against them. I know there has to be." Surya adjusted a few of the pillows behind his back as he rested on the sofa.

"I admit this one has me stumped." Den-El scratched an ear. "You've got crystal power coupled with magnetics and other wiring to charge and discharge energy. Fire so hot and powerful, it not only kills, but will turn the ground into a crumbling mess."

A loud knock sounded at the door. Both men bolted upright.

"I'll get it," said Den-El, jumping up and trotting to the door.

At the sound of a woman's voice, Surya craned his neck for a glimpse of the visitor.

"Ah, my dear Den-El," said Cata-Lin. "I was hoping your master would let me spend some time in your company. Perhaps we can talk. Maybe I can buy you a meal."

"Master," said Den-El sidling up to Surya, "may I enjoy an afternoon off so I can bask in the beauty of this divine lady?" He winked at his prince.

Surya pretended to ponder the request a moment in earnest, rubbing his lower lip. "I think I can spare a little time this afternoon." He smiled. "Cata-Lin, please take good care of him. He means the world to me."

"I'll treat him as if he were my own." Her bright smile showed a beautiful set of straight white teeth. The red of her lips created a sultry, exotic effect.

Den-El took a couple deep breaths, zoning out just quickly enough to recover and think with more sense. He knew the flesh between his legs swelled with excitement. The silk lime green dress showed off her assets on top. Her sleek black hair fell over one side of her shoulder. Through it, she'd laced a long lotus-colored ribbon. In her dainty hand, she carried a colorful dainty bag in the style of a beggars purse.

"Da-Ina, come."

The little dog ran to Den-El, who swiped up a leash and fastened it around a red leather collar. "I'll be back in a couple of hours," said Den-El, wrapping an arm around Cata-Lin and leading her outside the door. He turned to her and said, "Now, you're the mistress."

"And I'm a very good one." Her smile nearly got the better of Den-El's self-control.

When the door closed, Surya clapped his hands, laughing as he thought of his friend and Cata-Lin. What a cat and mouse game this whole ordeal could turn into. He switched on the AudioView to watch Lomasa News.

"How do you think Law of One will feel about being invaded by Sons of Belial?" said Khandoor. He sat at a glass table along with the infamous Rhaneen. "I mean, having the nerve to actually go to Poseidia and put threats and demands on their streets?"

Surya jumped off the sofa and turned up the volume on the AudioView.

Rhaneen shook his head. "That's not at all how it is. I'm so disappointed that people of Poseidia are taking it that way."

"How else would they take it? They go to bed thinking they're waking up to a normal day, and then to see their streets lined with posters?"

Rhaneen folded his hands neatly on the table. He looked smart in a professional rust-colored shirt with a black embroidered collar.

"Listen. All we're asking is to be part of the workings that affect all of Atlantis, all the islands. We must have equal representation. Having Law of One and Sons of Belial working together for any reason should promote good will and trust among everyone."

"Why do you think," said Khandoor, "that Law of One will give in to your demands? What will you do if they refuse? They could do that."

"It is our hope and belief, actually, that they won't refuse. I would think that if they truly adhere to the 'all is one' mantra, surely working with us would fit that."

Khandoor frowned. "Just exactly what are you hoping to accomplish with this whole approach? Law of One has controlled the firestone for thousands of years without an issue. Why is it suddenly such a big deal now?"

"By being involved in its care, it allows us a voice in policies and laws that affect all the islands. We can have Aryan and the other islands well represented."

"Aryan and the other islands have done well on their own for thousands of years. You control the next largest main island plus the other small ones. Law of One has never denied you anything regarding its resources, including power from the firestone. What it sounds like to me is purely a wish to fulfill a power-hungry dream."

"Absolutely not." Rhaneen showed a look of exasperation. "I think your comment is so far off-base it's ludicrous."

"Really? Then why else do you want to be involved in the mother of all power crystals? Why can't you be honest and answer that question?" Khandoor's face showed an intensity that irritated Rhaneen.

"We are not after world domination. We are merely asking for equality among the islands that make up what is left of our beloved continent."

"This will be interesting to watch, if not outright frightful. Let's just hope everything truly works out and agreements can be reached. Vice Commander, thank you for joining us."

"It's always a pleasure to be here. Thank you."

Surya turned off the AudioView and reclined back on the sofa, thinking. Once Sons of Belial got their hands on the firestone at any capacity, it would only set the stage for the next set of demands. He still stood by his suggestion to Aleemirin and Tujuk. Law of One needed to resolve issues with Sons of Belial.

The big question was how to do it safely without blowing all of Atlantis right off the map.

***

The Golden Conch overlooked the canal between the third ring and the second land ring. Cata-Lin had suggested a bistro a little farther out from the usual eateries near Vardhase.

Den-El closed his eyes a moment, enjoying the breeze against his face and ears. The fact he'd polished his horns earlier after he woke up gave him no amount of satisfaction. At least he'd been ready to go for any occasion.

"You're a little far from your temple, aren't you?" he said, casting down a bite of meat for Da-Ina. Cata-Lin had kindly ordered a meaty appetizer just for the dog.

"I like getting out and seeing parts of the other land rings. I think most of Poseidia is beautiful. Even the rougher parts have an earthy beauty." Cata-Lin smiled, placing her hand on top of Den-El's.

"What do you think of all the posters we saw that morning?" He looked Cata-Lin squarely in the eyes.

She took a quick sip from her goblet. "I think the tides are changing. I've sensed this for a long time."

"What do you think is going on?"

"I don't know. There's unrest for one side. The other side likes the status quo. It's always one in search of what someone else has." She locked her gaze on Den-El's face. "I find you and your master interesting. How did you two end up here on Poseidia?"

Den-El ate a bite of his vegetable sandwich. "Like I said when we met, my master rescued me from the horrid mines. I owe my life to him."

Cata-Lin listened, angling her head as she studied him with great consideration.

Inside, Den-El cringed. She still wanted to know about Surya. It struck him just now that he'd not worked out a story where it concerned them both. "I really don't know all the personal details of my master. He doesn't discuss such things with me. And I don't go around asking."

She sat back in her chair in silence, blinking a few times. "You two are the most unusual family—I don't know what else to call you. Your master has such an otherworldly beauty about him. And for a Thing, you have not only a wicked beauty, but a brilliant intellect. It's not natural. I don't mean that as an offense." Cata-Lin took Den-El's hand in hers.

"None taken." Den-El smiled his most enchanting one. "We have an unspoken agreement that we don't get too personal in each other's business. You know how that goes. Intellect or not. I do his bidding. He offers me rewards for being good."

Cata-Lin sat back in her chair, Den-El's hand remaining in hers. "I understand."

Den-El knew he'd dodged a bullet, but for perhaps a short time. From the energy swirling around this delectable-looking lady, he knew her questions weren't idle chit-chat. She knew information about him and Surya. Her whole attitude suggested it, and she wanted him to confirm it.

"Getting back to our original subject, what do you think is going to happen between Law of One and Sons of Belial?"

"It's an interesting question, my dear." A matter-of-fact expression covered Cata-Lin's face. "This has long been a source of tension between the two groups. If it doesn't get resolved one way or another, there will be problems. I think the time has come."

Den-El munched a few more bites from his sandwich. She wasn't coming any cleaner with him than he with her. They would play this game all day. For weeks, perhaps. "I have a question for you, Cata-Lin."

"Ask away, my precious one." She wiped her mouth with a napkin, watching him with sharp eyes like a bird of prey.

"I was watching our new AudioView, and I heard about something interesting. Guns that shoot out rays of fire, or something like that. Do you know anything about it?"

"It's an adaptation from ancient technology, from what I've heard. Those rays do serious damage. They set things on fire, incinerate bodies when they hit."

"Other than dodging them, how does one protect themselves from being hit?" Den-El turned the hand-holding where he now held hers. Their eyes locked on each other.

"One must stay out of the way. Period. There is no protection."

"There's protection from everything, Cata-Lin. You as a high priestess, an energy worker, know this." Den-El's stare turned hard, penetrating.

Cata-Lin focused a moment on her food, swallowing down a few bites as she thought. "Darling, my energy work has to do with crystals, their power, and how I can help those in need. At times, I have sufficient power to change vibrational levels or even the DNA structure in the brain, and how it will furthermore process information."

"And with all that, you still can't find a way to protect against ray guns? If they use crystal power, what would counteract that?" Den-El tapped the table with his other hand.

The two sat for a while. Den-El allowed her time for contemplation. He'd tried looking at the issue from several angles and came blank. There should have been an easy answer to the question. Answering the tricky questions used to be his forte.

An inability to work directly with all his gifts while on Earth frustrated him considerably. If he weren't a mutant, he'd most assuredly return to the portal, jump through, and find another place to live. Traveling far from home alone posed enough grave dangers. He couldn't risk it.

Cata-Lin glanced up, her gaze meeting his. "You're still not totally happy, even though your master saved you from disaster. Are you?"

Den-El swore silently to himself. He should have watched his thoughts better, like he did at home. Earth and being in a half human, half animal skin wreaked havoc on that at times. "Would you be happy being like me?"

A smile lit up Cata-Lin's face. "I have a pet project that I've been involved with for quite a while. I want to talk about it with you. About your question regarding the ray guns, give me a little time to explore this more.

"You make a good point. There must be a way to incapacitate those weapons, simply based on their make-up. These guns are much different than most."

"When do we meet again, then?" Den-El's spirits perked up. Getting out of the house always refreshed him.

"I'll come by. I'm not sure how long it will take. It could take a few days, maybe a week or two."

"You know where to find me." Den-El grinned.

When Cata-Lin and Den-El finished their meals, they took a long walk by the water. On the way, they encountered a few pockets of people standing, holding signs. They chanted their disapproval with Sons of Belial.

* * *

Night had fallen on Poseidia. Cata-Lin slipped down the winding steps leading deep into the bowels of the Temple of Jhanana. Servants manned the area with silent, diligent obedience.

Her shoes clicked over the cobblestone floors. No finery here in the black depths. Torches along the wall lit her way. At last she reached a back room curtained off from the others. Cata-Lin made her way to one corner where cages sat. The beasts were sleeping. They had been thoroughly cleansed, disinfected, and fed well.

These selected Things were the best of their kind. Strong in body, less simple than their fellow Things. One feature she adored best, these creatures showed definite human attributes. Their faces, torsos, and arms. All human. Their genitalia. Somewhat human. Enough to successfully breed.

They didn't come near matching Den-El, but if more of the better breed of Things could be replicated, Atlantis would have a hearty work force, allowing humans more time for pleasure.

Cata-Lin walked to the cage nearest the wall. She grabbed a book with all the information and history on the Thing resting inside. It stirred, lifting its human head.

"Not to worry, precious." Cate-Lin's words cooed as they left her mouth. At the sound of her voice, the Thing lay its head back down on a thin stuffed mattress. She read through the material, nodding as she did. "Strong. Well-made. No major defects, even though mutant traits are prominent." She smiled. "Ah, and here we are. Good seed for breeding."

"May I assist you?" A servant stepped up beside Cata-Lin.

"Perfect timing, Aam-Raan. I'll take this one tonight."

"As you wish, my high priestess."

Within minutes after Cata-Lin reached her room and prepared it with the proper sheets on the bed, the Thing entered her room, led expertly by Aam-Raan.

"I'll take care of him from here. When I ring for you, please come and take him back."

"It will be done, my high priestess."

The Thing regarded Cata-Lin with great interest. His eyes darted from the bed to Cata-Lin.

"Yes, dear Thing. It will be you and I tonight." She shed her clothing and led the creature, part horse, part human, to the bed.

This beast was not a full-sized horse, but smaller. Still, he contained a slick black coat at the lower half, and a magnificent tail that swished gracefully as it moved.

"Come, let us get into position."

The priestess helped the Thing onto the bed, placing its hands on either side where she lay. She spent a few minutes fondling the sensitive area of the beast, delighted as he swelled quickly at her touch. With any luck, she'd be fat with the offspring as soon as they were done. If only it were that quick. Her last two attempts had resulted in nothing.

A soft snort and moan erupted from the Thing's mouth. Its eyes glazed with human lust. On instinct, he lowered his lips to hers. Cata-Lin kissed back, allowing its tongue to probe and explore hers. It suckled her breasts. Their eyes met. They were ready.

***

Three weeks later, a group from Sons of Belial sat at a long table. An equal number of men from Law of One joined them, sitting on the opposite side. In a government building situated on the land core, a meeting room had been reserved.

As part of the group, Aleemirin, Tujuk, and Khaluj joined Law of One. Surya watched the three priests, marveling at how the men kept their cool. A pact had been made to keep Khaluj in the dark as long as possible.

He was a skilled priest, but the longer they could play his game the better. Rhaneen sat calmly with his group on the other side, across from the priests. Surya decided to sit at the head of the table, allowing the leaders from each group to hold the seats in the middle of either side.

The factions needed to work this out themselves with little input from him. He'd been invited because Aleemirin and Tujuk wanted him there for support. Khaluj still basked in the pretense and hope that he still might win Surya over yet.

"Let's start the meeting. We're all here." Aleemirin pulled out several sheets of paper and a writing tool.

The others did the same. He nodded to the man at the large board. The ideas and final rules would be written on the board. A scribe had been assigned to create a formal handbook for all the members after the meeting.

"Do we all agree that this mission is to create a co-partnership between Law of One and Sons of Belial in manning the firestone?"

"Aye." Everyone spoke in unison.

"Do we all agree that once the final rules have been selected and agreed upon, that all members will honor them without fail?"

"Aye."

Rhaneen spoke out, "Is our friend, Surya, going to actively participate? I didn't see him agree or disagree." He looked directly at Surya. "If you're in this meeting, don't you think you need to have some input?"

"I'll provide input when I think it's necessary. The bulk of the work needs to come from the citizens of Atlantis, not from someone like me. Honestly, I'm not sure how long I'll be here. And let's not forget. I'm really here unofficially."

The room grew quiet. Rhaneen looked at Surya. Khaluj grimaced. Aleemirin and Tujuk simply wore glum expressions on their faces.

Surya held his ground. No point in being vague or misrepresenting his part in the most important agreement coming to pass on Atlantis. "I'm here to assist when needed. I defied rules of my galaxy and came to help. But dictating the agreement is not helping."

"Have you picked a side?" Rhaneen asked, persistent. He glanced quickly at Khaluj.

"I think Surya seems more in line with Law of One. From what I've seen," said Khaluj. "Isn't that right?" He turned his gaze toward the alien sitting at the end of the table.

"If you want to know the truth, I'm really on both your sides." Surya sat up straighter, clasping his hands neatly together in front of him on the table. "You have differences. Work them out. Choose rules that both agree are fair and can be followed."

Tujuk nodded. "Very well. Let us continue." He motioned toward Aleemirin.

"Who will offer the first rule?" Aleemirin looked around the room.

A Law of One member raised his hand. "I think our faction needs to have more controlling members caring for the crystal than Sons of Belial." The man looked across the table to the others. "No offense, gentlemen, but this is a big step for Law of One, and quite honestly, we're still not totally enthusiastic about this agreement. I won't lie."

Rhaneen nodded and glanced to the right and left at his own faction members. "Anyone disagree?"

Silence.

"I think we allow it," said a Sons of Belial member.

When Aleemirin glanced toward the board, the man standing next to it wrote down the first rule.

"There must be a formal meeting before there are tuning changes to the firestone." Another Law of One Member had raised their hand.

All members of Sons of Belial nodded.

Another Law of One member spoke up. "We set a limit on the maximum tuning level for the firestone. We can discuss this at the same time we talk about tuning changes."

"We only tune upward in a set number of increments. This value is set at the formal meeting noted by my brother." Another member pointed to the man who spoke before him.

At the board, the scribe wrote furiously as each man spoke.

Again, Rhaneen and his members agreed.

Surya sat watching everything in complete dismay. Something about this meeting didn't set well with him. Glances exchanged between Rhaneen and Khaluj didn't help matters at all.

"I need to interject," said Surya. He stood up and strode to the board and stood next to the scribe.

"Well, well. How refreshing to finally have your participation," said Rhaneen. A smirk covered his face. "What would you like to say, Your Highness?" Rhaneen emphasized the title.

In a burst of anger, Surya shot out a raw energy bolt so fast and firm, no one in the room saw it flash from his eyes straight to Rhaneen's hand. In a surge of power, it traveled midway up his arm, surrounding it in a swath of white light. The effect dissipated in an instant.

"Ahh!" Rhaneen cried out, jumping up from his chair. "What was that?" His face contorted in pain and confusion. Everyone in the room turned in his direction.

"I suggest we all address each other in this room with utmost respect, whether or not we agree with the person. I hereby rule that as an ultimate command." Khaluj exchanged glances with Aleemirin and Tujuk. He shook his head quickly in admonition at Rhaneen. All members of both factions sat in their chairs, stunned.

Surya didn't fall for Khaluj's pretense in honoring him or anyone else. The priest simply had engaged himself in a balancing act. The clown would fall at some point. Surya knew it.

"I'm a bit dismayed by this meeting." Surya stood straight, arms crossed.

"And how is that?" Khaluj asked.

"Sons of Belial have all but declared war on Poseidia. They insisted on a meeting, or else. Now we have no member offering terms for the group? I'm shocked."

Khaluj sat back in his chair, considering Surya's words. The room filled with a brief silence.

"True. Many on Poseidia feel like we've received a declaration of war." Khaluj's face held an expression of understanding. "Perhaps this is why Sons of Belial wish for Law of One to lead in setting terms." He eyed Rhaneen and the members across the table.

"To what end?" said Surya. "The intent has been made. Therefore, surely Sons of Belial have terms they desperately want. To have come to this meeting with nothing in mind?"

Aleemirin cleared his throat and shifted in his seat.

Tujuk said, "Sons of Belial are free to disagree with any of our proposals. Being on the defensive, Law of One obviously has an urge to get their terms out first." He winked lightly in Surya's direction.

"Are there any other rules or suggestions from Sons of Belial?" Surya headed back to his chair.

"I propose monthly meetings to discuss firestone care, tuning issues, and placement of more power grids if needed." The suggestion came from a Sons of Belial member. "At our first monthly meeting, we can determine exact numbers on everything."

"Aye." Law of One members spoke in unison.

"If there are suggestions for new businesses models or services, the creation of these may pull more power from our dear crystal. Even so, we need to allow for some of these services or businesses to exist. We need progress at some point, or we stagnate." A younger member of Sons of Belial had spoken up. His eyes flashed with a certain defiance.

"And this is what we were afraid of." A Law of One gentlemen spoke out from near the end of the table. "Overburdening the crystal. It's dangerous and can upset the whole series of power grids." He clenched his fists. "We most certainly cannot allow an overload to occur."

"Could you allow one or two just to start and see how it goes?" Surya surprised himself with how easy the question slipped out. "Could you not find ways to expand the power you have? Perhaps seek other sources for power enhancement?" He made eye contact with each member. "It's just a small suggestion."

"I think our esteemed friend makes a good point." said Khaluj. "It might be time to focus more heavily on our crystal-creation abilities. Maybe we start looking to higher intelligent beings for assistance in problem-solving." The priest directed his triumphant smile Surya's direction.

Surya returned an obligatory smile. Inside he cringed. Pretenses always sapped a bit of his energy. Coming from a world of mostly pure truth, falsities didn't set well with him. He may have sneaked his way onto Earth, but his burning desire to do it never contained insincerity.

Two hours passed, and both groups rounded out their set of terms and conditions. Aleemirin reminded everyone to check their mail for a copy of the final document. Everyone filed out of the meeting room, leaving Aleemirin, Tujuk, Khaluj, and Surya alone. Rhaneen mumbled a few hurried words to Khaluj before leaving, never once looking in Surya's direction.

"How do you think it went?" asked Khaluj.

"Most interesting," answered Tujuk. "We'll have to see how this goes. Give it a trial period. If something breaks down, we'll revisit everything."

"Sure, sure." Khaluj nodded, wearing an almost sincere look.

Surya gazed at the three priests, expressionless, his mind whirling.

"You made some good points today. Thank you for your contribution," Khaluj cocked his head in Surya's direction. Khaluj's attempts at game-playing were met by Surya's stony stare.

The priest let out a sigh and turned to his other two brethren. "I'm heading on out. If you two ever want to get together, go for some dinner, I'd be delighted. It would be nice to do something non-work related. Don't you think?"

"Yes, yes. Call us anytime." A gracious smile covered Tujuk's face.

Surya grinned. He couldn't decide who faked better, Khaluj or Tujuk. Aleemirin remained silent.

When Khaluj left the room, and the three knew he was well out of ear-shot, they relaxed.

"I'm so glad this farce of a meeting is over." Aleemirin showed a sign of exasperation. "I hated every minute of it."

"Aren't you the least bit worried about Sons of Belial?" Surya asked. "Just a little too complacent for my taste."

"Maybe we're worrying a little too much. Now that we have had the meeting, maybe they will calm down a little. It could go better than expected." Tujuk cast his glance toward the door.

"My suggestion is you two pay really close attention. I have a strong uneasy sensation about them." Surya narrowed his eyes.

Aleemirin and Tujuk gazed at each other without a word. Surya knew in an instant they felt it too.

Chapter Fourteen

Khaluj left the meeting room and started toward the ferry. He grumbled to himself. No matter how much he tried to win over the alien, it wasn't going to happen. Respect or not, the fact Surya played cool held a certain draw, almost like a magnet that wouldn't go away. Something else held on to him too. Memories. Or was it pure obsession?

Nudged by a spur-of-the-moment thought, Khaluj whirled around and made his way toward Martaam's healing school. The energy there always put him in a better mood. When caught off guard, the energy inched him to a higher vibratory level where he often wondered why he hadn't gone all in with Law of One.

Though Belial was an ancestor, and he understood hedonism all too well, Khaluj acknowledged the merits of higher divine aspiration. After all, both factions started in that line of thinking when beings first populated Atlantis. Martaam still clung to the older ways.

Law of One discouraged their people mixing with the Aryans. Aryans were considered corrupt, lacking in divinity. They wanted a population with an ideology that would endure through the ages. Martaam had almost succumbed. If everything had gone as planned, he would have been able to tell her the truth about himself and perhaps not have lost her.

Such nonsense Law of One perpetuated. Did they not know that divinity existed in all people, regardless of race, skin color, or culture? Regardless of which island one chose to live? A human may choose evil as their path, may have lost their way, but divinity endured at a soul level.

Khaluj stepped over the sidewalk, nearing the school. The closer he got, a strong hunch indicated Martaam was in her own designated office. He knew the way up there. He'd surprise her. If she ached as hard as he did right now, maybe he'd persuade her over to his way of thinking again. He'd done it once.

He reached down, quickly touching the thickened flesh, bobbing and straining against his clothing. Khaluj left the sidewalk. Hiding behind a large tree trunk, he took a moment to adjust himself. He'd reach Martaam's room in a few minutes. After some moments, he willed a greater control over his body.

Quickening his pace, Khaluj headed toward the building. A blast of cool air hit his skin the moment he opened the door. Echoes of students laughing around the corner of the hallway filled the air. He peeked into the window of a classroom door. A teacher lectured while students stared straight ahead.

He located the stairs and made his ascent. Much to his relief, her door stood ajar. She didn't have her "session in progress" notice out, either. All favorable signs. He gently pushed the door and quietly stepped inside.

"I've missed you," he said, whispering softly in her ear.

Martaam let out a sharp scream when she turned around. Khaluj clapped his hand lightly over her mouth. He took a brief moment and shut the door.

"Shh. It's only me. Surely I don't scare you that badly, do I?" His lips pulled into an indulging smile.

Martaam's face clouded with an intense scowl. "What are you doing here?"

"I want to know why you gave my presents back?"

"Wasn't my explanation of 'I don't want to see you again' not enough?" Martaam focused her attention back on her box of stones.

"But you didn't tell me why. Not really." Khaluj stepped in her direction, sidling up beside her. "Why did I suddenly not please you? I want to understand. Maybe I can do better." He wrapped his arms around her, resting one hand between her legs."

She tensed under his touch. "I don't have anything more to say to you."

"You don't mean it, Martaam. We've loved passionately enough. For you to suddenly pull away, it makes no sense." He cupped one of her breasts, indulging his fingers in fondling the engorged nipple. Khaluj smiled. She still reacted to his touch.

He pulled up her dress, slipping a hand inside her undergarment. Martaam jerked against his anchoring arm, squirming as his fingers reached sensitive areas. "Don't fight me. Just give in." Khaluj tried pinning her to him, grinding the flesh between his legs against her backside.

"Remember how we enjoyed times like these?" He said between breaths. Rubbing himself against her body sent a wave of temporary relief all over him. "We can do it here. Now." His fingers worked with more urgency.

Martaam grew still. The energy in the room changed. The door opened.

"Get away from her, old man."

Khaluj's exuberance slipped away.

Surya strode in, wedging himself between Khaluj and Martaam. "You call yourself a priest, a gentleman?" His voice maintained a firm but calm tone.

Martaam backed herself against the tiny window leading to the crystal-filled pipe. "I called out, and you came." She breathed a sigh of relief. A light smile played across her lips.

"I'll always hear your call, Martaam." Surya spoke, keeping his gaze fixed on Khaluj. "As for you, good Sir, a little gift from me so you'll behave in the future." Surya cast his gaze on the bulge between Khaluj's legs. The erection deflated, leaving a limp, dangling member inside the priest's trousers. "It's time you rule using brain instead of animal instinct." Surya grinned. "Besides, it's so unbecoming of a Sons of Belial leader."

The priest's eyes widened in horror. Heat flashed through him. A sensation of weakness hovered around his lower region. At once, he felt physically drained. Martaam staring at him, maybe mocking him silently to herself became too much.

In a wave of humiliation, Khaluj blurted out, "Too bad you won't be staying long on Poseidia, my dear prince. You said so yourself." He turned and dashed out of the room.

Surya turned to Martaam, disheartened by the sadness on her face. "You needed to know about him, if you hadn't already figured it out yourself."

Martaam walked toward Surya, falling into his open arms. "It doesn't surprise me. He really fooled me at first, though." She gazed up into Surya's eyes. "I hope you decide to stay longer on Poseidia. If you're not entangled with people like Khaluj, it's not so bad."

"If you've finished for the day, I'll go back to the third ring with you. Spend the rest of the day with me."

She smiled, placed her box of cherished crystals back in the cabinet, and left the room. Surya held her hand as they both caught the next ferry off the land core. When they reached Vardhase, he led her back to his apartment. The unit held a strange stillness.

He glanced in each room, spotting no sign of Den-El. "My Thing must have decided he needed a break from being inside."

Martaam laughed. "He's really special, Surya. I bet you two really have fun back on your own planet."

Surya led her into his bedroom. "We have our good times. Fun, you say." He closed the door, locking it in place. His voice softened into a whisper. "Maybe it's time we have our own fun. I've waited a long time for this. I've risked everything for it."

Her eyes blazed with desire. "Your wish is my command."

He answered her with a deep kiss, wrapping his arms around her and drinking in her energy. She exuded hot passion. Immersing himself in it nearly drove him mad. He tasted her lips, ran his tongue over the walls of her mouth and teeth.

She let out a soft moan. The sound from her throat enflamed him more. He led her to the bed. Directing her arms upward, he removed her soft lilac dress. The silver headband she wore found a resting spot on his bedside table. Within seconds, she lay bare before him on the sheets of his bed.

Martaam's eyes glazed with lust, watching as Surya stripped naked. He may have been an alien in mind and soul, but the human body created by Den-El enshrined pure carnal beauty.

Surya slipped into bed next to her. The late afternoon light shimmered through the window. Harsh spots of bright white flashed across the walls. He closed his eyes and concentrated. A light breeze filled the room, sending the curtains ruffling into closed position.

"Better?" He asked.

"Better."

He gazed down at the lithe body next to him, delighting in the soft creamy skin and rosy lips. Her black hair cascaded across the pillow. His excitement mounted.

Martaam reached out and ran her fingers through his hair. Softly she coursed a path with her finger from his throat, over his chest, and down between his thighs. Grasping his hard flesh, she fingered the tip and squeezed lightly around it.

Surya let out a soft groan. He closed his eyes briefly, indulging in the sensations that ricocheted throughout his body. He opened his eyes again and feasted on the sight of her full round breasts.

Surya cupped one of them and gently squeezed. His fingers toyed with the swollen nipple. He flicked the sensitive flesh, watching with eager eyes as it sprang back in place with the slightest touch.

Martaam smiled, wrapping her arms behind her head. Surya responded. He kissed her lips, suckled her breasts, and ran his tongue all the way down to the space between her thighs. The breath hitched in her throat.

Encouraged by her response, he pleasured her with gentle nudges, probing with his tongue. An ache throbbed in his loins. She let out a soft gasp as he explored her tenderly and with reverence.

The sight of her opening like the most beautiful flower sent him into another dimension. Her trust and submission overwhelmed him. He felt power and tenderness all at once, wanting to devour her, yet savor every moment.

The root chakra of Surya's body vibrated with great force. When neither could stand no more, Martaam spread her thighs wider apart. Surya glided into place. The union he'd desired had come to pass.

He thrust his hips, feeling her clench against him. The wet smoothness of her captivated him, yielding yet determined to firmly hold all of him inside her. His hips moved faster at times, slowing when he wanted to heighten his own pleasure.

Martaam's eyes closed. Her face showed as one in the throes of pure ecstasy. Surya moved harder and faster. She moaned. Following carnal instinct encoded in his human body, he switched to quick circular motions with his hips, interchanging with staccato pumping movements.

Her breasts bounced slightly as he moved, filling her, thrusting forward and retracting. Emotions came in a flood, washing over him with passion so raw and love so deep he wondered if he still breathed or existed any longer in the third dimension.

He was now the lover. Holding her tightly next to him, their energies mingled and entwined, one wrapping around the other, flowing into a harmonic synchronicity as he moved in a steady rhythm. Time stilled. The world outside ceased to exist, and nothing mattered except the present moment he and Martaam found themselves.

The dull ache had reached a crescendo. With a few more thrusts, he released himself fully. The climax ignited with such power, Martaam let out a loud moan.

Surya basked in the delight of letting go and floating down, a sensation he felt when energy gently lowered as he came back to pure present consciousness. Exhausted, he lay quietly cradling Martaam in his arms.

Inside the dimly shaded room, a light glow floated all around. Martaam said nothing, but with a quick glance at her expression, Surya grinned. This had been a powerful physical merger. It rivaled ones he'd experienced before on Ontarus 9.

"Spend the night with me," Surya whispered.

"I will," answer Martaam.

***

Khaluj lay in Cata-Lin's arms. "Just look at this. I've tried everything. Nothing works." His face contorted with despair and shame.

Cata-Lin stared down at Khaluj. Her eyebrows arched in surprise and curiosity.

"Let me try," she said. A light grin covered her face. Settling into a comfortable position, she lightly teased the priest, flicking her tongue, pressing and sucking. She tried using her fingers, her hands. Nothing.

She sat up, stunned. "Oh, dear. He really has done it, hasn't he?" Cata-Lin shook her head as she released the limp flesh between Khaluj's legs. "Why would he do something like this to you, dearest?"

The priest frowned. "I don't know. We had a meeting today about terms for the firestone. Maybe it was something I said. I tried being polite and acknowledging his statements."

"Mmm," said Cata-Lin. She knew all too well the alien must have had a reason for brash actions. Aliens weren't fully human, even if they wore a human skin. They took on human characteristics and emotions, for sure, but alien skills and techniques lingered in some form or fashion. Surya and his buddy, Den-El displayed this nicely.

"Well, precious one, perhaps the spell is only temporary. Give it a few days and see if things don't get better for you." She lowered her head, delivering a lick and a kiss to the most sensitive part below his belt line.

"And if it doesn't get better? Then what?" Khaluj winced, turning his gaze away.

"Darling, you may need to divert your focus elsewhere. Concentrate on how you're going to rule all the islands of Atlantis." Cata-Lin kissed his lips. "Don't you think that subject matter is much more deserving of your attention right now?"

Khaluj let out a huff. "Correct. Everything has its time and place, no?"

"Ah, my sweet. Of course. Now you're coming around. That type of focus and thinking will get you far." She whispered in his ear. "Rejecting fear and turning away from negative vibrations breaks the spell, the code of bondage."

"Have you found out anything more from spending time with that abhorrent Thing?" He stared up at Cata-Lin.

"That abhorrent Thing, as you call him, is not one to be trifled with. Don't forget that the Thing and his friend come from the same place. Their loyalty and devotion to each other run deep. It won't be easily broken."

"Very well," said Khaluj, waving his hand with impatience. "What have you learned?"

"I know the Thing is not happy being a Thing. Who would be?" Cata-Lin repositioned herself, lying down beside Khaluj. "But he asked me an interesting question."

"Khaluj raised up lightly, squinting his eyes at Cata-Lin. "What was it?"

"How does one stop the power of crystal ray guns?"

"I don't think there is any way to stop them. They're pure crystal energy teamed with other technology. Those weapons are unmatched on the planet."

"True, darling, but it's not the weapons. Sure, weapons destroy, kill. But always remember it is the strategy of outfoxing your enemy that secures the victory."

"True." Khaluj nodded and sank back down on the silk coverlet. "There have been times Atlanteans have been defeated by primitive tribes who surely didn't have our technology."

"But they had finesse, determination, and strategy," Cata-Lin added. "Their sheer will to conquer drove Atlanteans back. Let's not forget those times so that we may be the next to conquer and be victorious."

"I love the way you talk to me," said Khaluj, blowing a kiss toward Cata-Lin. "Your words alone seduce me." He reached out for her breast, fondling the nipple between his thumb and forefinger. "What did you tell him?"

Cata-Lin answered, closing her eyes briefly at Khaluj's touch, "I didn't. I don't know the answer, either. But there must be a way. It's crystal power we're talking about. Not the usual mechanics in other weapons."

"I say there is no other solution other than to duck, run away, or give Sons of Belial what we want."

The priestess laughed. "I know the last suggestion is one you dream of day and night."

"Are you going to find an answer? You seem pretty intent on it." Khaluj ran his finger down her cheek.

"There is an answer to everything. Nothing is a total mystery. At least not to one who seeks enlightenment and asks a question with utmost sincerity." Cata-Lin turned and faced Khaluj. "And I sincerely want to know an answer. I want the truth revealed." She stroked through the hair covering Khaluj's chest. "Knowing this would save lives. At least on one side."

"When you discover the answer, please let me know."

"I wouldn't do less, my precious one." Cata-Lin showered Khaluj with a stream of kisses all over his body.

"While you're at it, can you please find a solution to my other problem?" Khaluj returned Cata-Lin's affection.

***

In a trance, Den-El gazed into the large quartz crystal sphere resting on an exotic orichalcum stand. He and Da-Ina had come in after Surya and Martaam's love-making session. The light ghostly glow shining out from under Surya's bedroom gave everything away.

Slipping quietly into his bedroom, he had closed the door and reclined on his bed lost in thought. A flash of intuition igniting in his gut instilled a sudden urge to scry. At times he did this on Ontarus 9, especially when his corporeal faculties failed him.

Deep within the crystal, images had shown themselves, flickering into a life of their own. A stream of running scenes with live characters played out before his eyes. The only difference, these did not reflect premonitions. They showed action in real time. A man and woman lay together, conversing.

He'd seen Cata-Lin's futile efforts in re-erecting Khaluj's most precious treasure. As he watched, the man's emotion of distress struck him with great interest. Perplexed, Den-El sank back in his chair and closed his eyes. Within the etheric records, he scanned information, tracing back in time until he located what he wanted.

Every word he read like a stranded sailor begging for a drink of water. He read on as each action of the two shown in the sphere etched itself in the record of endless space for eternity.

Den-El clapped a hand on his mouth. He glanced down at Da-Ina and snickered. The dog wagged her tail. "Our master knows how to set someone straight, dear girl," he barely whispered out loud. He didn't care about Khaluj. The hateful man deserved everything he got.

He did care that Cata-Lin had not yet discovered a way to thwart crystal gun power. Why did this question elude everyone, including himself and Surya? Of all beings on Atlantis, he and his friend should know an answer of some kind, some tidbit of knowledge leading down the path to a correct answer. Den-El turned his gaze back to the crystal ball, watching until the priest finally left. Intrigued, he concentrated on the continuing sequence of images, watching with great interest.

***

Cata-Lin sat in a simple wooden chair in front of a fine polished silver mirror. Two lit candles burned on each side. From a cabinet beneath her altar, she removed a small orichalcum chalice and a crystal decanter filled with a brown liquid. The special elixir was her prized recipe, valued above all the tools in her collection.

Only in desperate times when all traditional means of divination and meditation failed did she resort to using her Mohacana, a concoction she'd created with special rare mushrooms hidden in the deep forests of the Atlantean islands. If none could be secured on Poseidia, she didn't hesitate to seek them from Aryan or the smaller islands of Og, Atalya, and Eyre.

She removed the jeweled stopper and poured a little of the elixir into her chalice. The bitter taste never appealed to her, but solid results is what she wanted. Centering herself, concentrating with all her might, she swallowed down the liquid and waited.

Twenty minutes later, Cata-Lin felt the warm sensation growing in her stomach. Her nerves and mind calmed, though she never lost mental clarity. Over her body, inch by inch, a serene calmness crawled into place and settled in.

Cata-Lin gazed into the mirror, releasing her mind into the depths of the spirit realm. Her consciousness soared, passing from dark to light. When the visions came, she wasn't mentally connected to the third dimension any longer.

Her spirit master appeared, dressed in white robes and a headdress of long pure white feathers. They radiated around him, glowing like the sun. His piercing eyes gazed at her. The beauty and purity he radiated almost frightened her. It always did when she made contact. He'd never harm anyone. This truth she kept reminding herself.

"What is it you desire, beloved Cata-Lin? If you come in truth and humility, I shall answer in truth and strength."

"What aborts the power of crystal rays? Those that burn, destroy, and kill?" She averted her eyes momentarily.

The light and righteousness of the guide had become a bit much to handle. Or was it guilt nipping at her heels? The fact she would only share her secret with one side? Regardless, the knowledge would save lives.

"Such a simple answer, Beloved. You know the sobriety stone. The stone for toxicity." The guide smiled. When he did, Cata-Lin winced in pain, shutting her eyes. "Ah, a fool's question. Many pardon's for calling in ignorance."

"A questioning fool leaves a wise man." The guide bowed graciously. "Such is the path of the querent."

"Your answer to this one question is all I seek. My humble thank you will never be enough."

"Humility, wisdom, and truth are all we ask." The guide bowed again and vanished.

Cata-Lin brought her level of consciousness down by degrees until she grounded herself again in the present moment.

"How could I have missed this?" she said, chiding herself. "Now, what to tell the Thing. He will want to know." She continued speaking her thoughts out loud, as if reaffirming everything to herself.

"If I told him, I'd have to stop him some way after uttering the answer. Or I could say I simply couldn't find the information. The way is closed." She smiled, eyes widening with glee. "Whatever I do, I must quickly tell Khaluj first. He will be pleased." Cata-Lin laughed.

***

Den-El stopped watching and sank back in hi s chair. The ball had more than served its purpose for this scrying session. He wet a cloth with salt water he'd collected from the canal and wiped his prized sphere, placing it back in its special place on a shelf in his bedroom.

The quicker he reached Cata-Lin, the better. How would he approach her? What would he do? Information learned from the spirit guide didn't need sharing with Sons of Belial.

If Cata-Lin wanted to stop him, there would be only one way to succeed in such an endeavor. Kill him. At no other time did Den-El need quick wit and swift action more than now. He would not die here on Atlantis. On Earth. He would not allow Cata-Lin to share her knowledge with the opposing faction that sought to rule all.

He knew one truth. No amount of magic or spiritual help in Cata-Lin's arsenal would match his or Surya's abilities. Killing Cata-Lin directly wasn't the answer, either. If he refused, who would silence her? Who or what would be the executioner?

Den-El lay down on his bed, mind whirling. He looked at the window. The afternoon had moved on. Evening would be rolling in soon. Surya hadn't come out of his bedroom still. Tonight, his beloved master would have to fend for himself regarding dinner.

Pet project. Cata-Lin had mentioned something about a project of hers. Ravaged by curiosity, Den-El settled back on the bed, concentrating on his breathing. He needed another look into the Infinite Hall of Records. For several minutes he scanned the information, traveling as far as the past ninety days. What he found filled him with horror and disgust.

No wonder she'd taken such a keen interest in him. If he had his way about it, the use of Things would be stopped immediately. Thoughts of her copulating, holding animal seed deep inside her, and birthing mutant creatures sickened him to the point of near vomiting.

He sat up, smiling at an idea. It would suit everyone's purpose. Almost, but not quite, depending on which side you were on. The notion of what he considered was diabolical, sickening, and expedient. A perfect plan.

Den-El lay on the bed and clutched his scrotal sac. As he closed his eyes, he visioned the inside workings of his own body. His sperm, which would of course produce another mutant like himself, needed altering. He focused with greater intensity, going deeper into a cellular level, viewing the helical form itself.

On each chromosome, he reworked the codes that created life. He did this on each section, taking great care in choosing what he wanted. He watched on the inside as the former codes faded and the new ones blazed in place. When he finished, his seed held a completely different make-up.

His sac tingled, growing into a dull throb. He squeezed a little, subsiding the pleasure ache. He didn't want to waste anything tonight. And he intended to stop Cata-Lin once and for all. Den-El quietly hid some money in a small leather pouch and left with Da-Ina. Swiftly they moved. He'd hitch a ride on the first boat he could flag down.

Money always worked on Poseidia, regardless where it came from. That's how he managed to roam about and make small purchases of food and drink when Surya wasn't around. Nobody bothered him too much if he sat far enough away, paid a little extra, and kept quiet.

***

Surya and Martaam came out of the bedroom. The afternoon sun hovered at the tip of the horizon. Patches of pink spattered over a dwindling blue sky. Surya went to Den-El's room. Empty. He saw the rumpled top covering of his friend's bed. The most notable sign that caught his eye was the crystal ball. The dragon stand sat more to the right on the shelf than it had before.

"Martaam, how would you like staying in tonight? Perhaps we can cook a meal together?"

She wrapped her arms around Surya's neck, kissing him square on the lips. "Only if you promise me a really special dessert."

Chapter Fifteen

The early night air blew in blustery gusts. Den-El sniffed and looked around as he led Da-Ina by her leash. A storm brewed, threatening to shower down its fury and might any minute. The faster he reached Cata-Lin, the better. Perhaps the impending weather might hold her back, buying him time.

He followed the sidewalks, zig-zagging behind buildings, and staying close to the shadows of the trees. "Da-Ina, let's run." He made a break for the canal, running full force with Da-Ina fast at his side. Having four legs at times had its advantage. He loved the wind in his face, covering ground at speeds he wouldn't be able to do as a two-legged human.

Neither stopped until they reached the edge of the water. He was a long way from the ferry port. Catching a ride on a passing boat would be quicker. Fifteen minutes later his luck kicked in.

A modest craft glided through the water, aiming for one of the many docks lining the canal. Carefully, Den-El picked his way through long grass and reeds until he reached the dock.

A man glanced up from his task of tying off the boat as Den-El approached. When he got a good look at the creature standing before him, his face contorted into a scowl. "Go away." The man motioned frantically. "We don't need you here."

"Good, Sir," said Den-El, "I have some funds with me. I'd be happy to share a little with you, if you are going to the land core."

The man stopped a second, squinting up at Den-El. "You speak properly for a Thing." He finished tying another knot and stood up.

"Ah, I'm one of the luckier ones, I suppose. I've been blessed with a kind and loving master who has nursed me through horrific times."

"A lucky Thing you are." The man relaxed a little, taken in by Den-El's charms and good graces. "And this is yours?" He pointed to Da-Ina, who nuzzled up close, hoping for a scratch on the head.

"She's my pride and joy, fine Sir. I'm hoping your generosity will extend to my beloved pet."

"You must have the most unusual master on all of Poseidia."

"I agree with that statement, as the gods are my witness." Den-El smiled and removed his purse filled with gold and silver coins. "How much will you consider in helping me and my dog reach the land core? I must see the fine Cata-Lin who presides over the Temple of Jhanana."

"You have an appointment with her?" The man's eyes narrowed as he scrutinized Den-El with greater intensity. He rubbed his lip, eyeing the coin purse.

In the lamp light shining from a high post, Den-El detected doubt on the man's face. He couldn't lose out now. "I am as sincere as the finest priest that rules this magnificent island. Cata-Lin sought me first. She has sent me a message and bids that come to her."

"First, let me say, even though you are a Thing, you're most likely better than any of the priests who rule on any Atlantean island. A corrupt bunch they are. All of them."

Den-El grinned. "Should I say thank you?"

The man laughed. "You're still lucky. I am going to the land core to drop off supplies for a night delivery. I'll take you with me."

"Will this coin cover the trip for me and my dog?" Den-El held out a mid-sized gold coin. The metal glinted in the lamp light.

"The coin barely covers the trip. It's still a distance from here to the main canal that leads to the center." He rubbed the back of his neck, thinking. "More like two coins."

The outright lie struck Den-El's senses immediately. What he first offered should have covered a trip to the center of Poseidia and back again, at the very least. A stranger's lingering eye on his coin purse sent a bolt of alarm straight to Den-El's gut.

He took a deep breath. "Two coins it is, fine Sir."

"Since you have an appointment," said the man, "I'll go ahead and begin the trip. I had a delivery to make, but I'll just do it on my way back. Get on."

Den-El's inner alarm fired off again. The man was too helpful. He stepped on the boat, Da-Ina following.

After quickly untying the craft, the man jumped on and headed to the captain's area. He shouted something inaudible to another person. Den-El found a crate and sat on it. Da-Ina settled down at his feet.

"Make yourself comfortable, Thing. My partner is driving us." The man walked away and spent a good amount of time inspecting all the storage areas.

The boat had lurched forward, slicing through the water at a determined speed. Den-El glanced up in time to see lightning split the night sky. A roar of thunder rumbled. In seconds, the rain came bolting down in a merciless, torrential downpour. He didn't care for nasty weather tonight, at least not while he sailed in it.

After mentally inciting two ancient words, he relaxed when the rain stopped as fast as it came. Only on the land core did belting rain soak everything in sight. Den-El smiled, viewing the vision in his mind. Perfect. He continued working out the details on how to deal with Cata-Lin. The wind rushed against his face. The boat rose and fell with the onslaught of waves.

Hurtling through the canal, Den-El enjoyed the rush of it all, an occasional splash of water, the smell of salt and fish. The frantic speed and activity left him with a certain rush of adrenalin he hadn't fully appreciated until now. No wonder sailors fell into the allure of sea life.

His coin purse lay beside him. Da-Ina had sat up, nose twitching, ears standing at attention. At once, she let out a growl and an intense bark. Den-El barely felt a sharp pain in his head before everything went black.

He felt himself spinning into darkness, falling as if he'd never hit bottom. Somewhere in the nothingness, he thought he heard the cry of an animal, a human voice, a yelp, and a few seconds later, nothing.

Den-El woke up. He tried sitting but found himself in cramped quarters. Where was he? Was he in a room or a compartment of some kind? He shook his head, trying to rouse his senses further, but only incited more head pain. A dull throb took over.

In the darkness he blinked, trying to hone in on some kind of light source. At the bottom right hand corner, he spied a small sliver of light spilling through a crack in the bottom of the door. Den-El tried stretching out his arms but met resistance from the sides. He tried standing, nearly knocking himself out again when his horns hit the top of the compartment.

Uneasiness roiled in his gut. Where was Da-Ina? He moved his hands frantically in search of his coin purse. Nothing. Horror set in. Was Da-Ina still alive? There could only be one reason for ending up in his present predicament. The boat owners intended on either disposing of him or using him as their slave.

Neither would occur on Den-El's time. He sat still several moments, thinking of what to do. Get out of his cell. Dispose of the owners. Find Da-Ina, if he could. Get to Cata-Lin. Simple. Maybe?

He closed his eyes and concentrated with every ounce of energy he had left. The door in front of him blew off. Great start. Den-El scrambled out, searching for the men.

"Where do you think you're going?" Footsteps echoed along the floor.

Den-El jerked his gaze to the right, in time to see the same man who knocked him out. He dodged the arm lunging toward him and ran full speed toward the end of the boat.

"You'll never get off here alive, Thing. Give it up." The man laughed.

Den-El quickly looked over the railing, viewing the waters of the canal below. Waves lashed at the boat, piling on in merciless droves. He'd perish in the cold. Would he have the energy to swim to a dock?

The man closed in. "Come on, Thing. Don't make this difficult. We don't mean any harm." He reached out cautiously.

Den-El had gone as far as he could go. Either come up with another plan or jump. He looked over the rail again.

"You won't make it. Land is farther away than it looks."

"I paid you," said Den-El. "We had a deal. Gold for a trip to the land core."

"Things like you have no business running free. Your master is a fool if he doesn't know that." The man smirked.

Rage filled every inch of Den-El's being. "You don't know my master or me. So you best watch your words." He ventured forward a few inches. "You have no idea who you're dealing with."

The man screeched with laughter. "I know something for certain. I've rid myself of one problem, and it's that pesky little dog of yours. Really, Thing? You have a pet?" He roared harder, laughing. "An animal owning another is quite unusual, you know."

Den-El's body moved in auto-pilot fashion. Lowering his head, he aimed his horns straight for the man's ugly bulging gut.

Laughter turned into a shrill scream. The man staggered, nearly reeling over onto his backside.

"Keep talking, you foul, loathsome wretch." Den-El postured himself, ready for another haul at the man.

Skin on the man's belly had begun to bruise, turning a dusty blue. A couple of gored marks oozed droplets of blood. His breaths came in hoarse rasps. "Creatures like you are soulless. You're nothing but a shell with animated parts. When you die, you'll . . ."

Not waiting a second longer, Den-El focused his vision on the man, concentrating on another ancient protective word. His adrenalin rushed as the energy gathered inside. He uttered the word under his breath.

The man screamed and writhed. His body lit up like the lights at night on the land core. Veins with pulsing bolts of energy surrounded him. Within seconds, he morphed into a smoldering pile of ashes.

"One down," said Den-El, quite satisfied with himself. "Now to find Da-Ina." The other sailor piloting the boat obviously had no idea what had just happened. He hadn't left his position when the argument started. As long as he continued managing the helm, there was extra time to find his beloved dog.

Den-El looked up at the sky. He had no idea how long he'd been in that infernal compartment. From the look of the waves, his pet surely had perished. He heard a sharp-pitched noise swirling above his head. Humans wouldn't hear as readily, but his animal ears picked up the sonar vibrations.

A small circle of bats fluttered, round and round. Locking his eyes on them, Den-El concentrated, tapping into their frequency coordinates. One of the bats beelined to him, landing on a narrow railing.

"I need help." Den-El tuned in to the animal. The bat squeaked in affirmation, rotating right and left as it hung. "I'm looking for my dog, and I'm praying she didn't perish."

The bat squeaked a response.

"I think she was thrown overboard. Can you help me find her?" Den-El teared up at the thought of never having Da-Ina with him.

Fluttering its wings, the bat left the railing and soared into the night sky. The swarm took off. Several went one direction. The remaining flew the opposite direction.

***

When the water hit, it penetrated like a million frozen needles stabbing with a killer's intent. Churning waves and biting cold ensured a quick death. Swimming against relentless waves had become fruitless. How long had she been struggling? Land or a dock was nowhere in sight. Was this the price for loving a master too much?

Da-Ina let out a loud wail, trailing off with a whimper. She tried moving her legs harder and faster. A large wave pushed her under, with another thrusting her back to the surface a second later.

She sputtered out excess water before another round of waves threaten to carry her under for good. Her lungs burned and stung inside. Cold, salty water dripped from her eyes.

A firm bite on one of her paws from a sea creature nearly got the better of her. Another loud yelp, and she paddled frantically away. Or was it another swirling round of waves that saved her? One thing Da-Ina knew, she had to get back to her master before ending up as a meal for a shark.

Something grabbed her collar with a grip so fierce, fear became colder than water. Swooshing sounds in her ears mimicked the rhythm of a thousand drums. A large creature had taken hold. It was bad enough to drown, but to be butchered and eaten by a bird of prey was too much.

Da-Ina struggled, barking and wriggling with every ounce of energy left. She tried going under the waves, hoping to free herself.

"Stop!" The eagle screeched. "I come not to kill, but to save." Wrapping its talons tighter around Da-Ina's collar, the bird flew with more determined speed toward land.

The dog's ears perked up. Sound of bats flying above, their rally cry, their guidance and direction trickled into a more coherent message. They had sought the eagle's help, and it had responded with a streak of kindness.

"We see it. Over there. The dock. Put her there. We'll tell the master." Each bat cried out.

"You'll surely choke me, kind eagle." Da-Ina howled. If she were lifted out of the water completely, her neck would snap, it seemed.

"Relax and quit fighting," said the eagle, his shriek pierced the night air.

One of the bats dived down closer to the water, avoiding a near miss with a wave. He fluttered, rose, and swooped until a dolphin came sailing toward Da-Ina and the eagle.

The dolphin let out a series of clicks. Together the eagle and giant fish traveled.

Lights on land showed larger and brighter. Buildings took on more definition. A lamp shined from the top of a pole.

With a shrill call, the eagle announced their arrival as they neared the dock. Da-Ina closed her eyes at the dizzying speed and penetrating lights. Just as they reached the edge, the dolphin slid under Da-Ina, lifting her out of the water and tilting enough so she rolled onto the dock.

Da-Ina lay heaving, soaking wet, shivering. Her back paw burned and ached. She sensed the light warmth of blood seeping between her toes. She telepathed her gratitude to the bats, eagle, and dolphin. Silently she called out in desperation to her master.

"We'll inform the master," said one of the bats. The swarm flew off. The dolphin had already headed out to sea.

"Relax, my friend. I'll keep watch until you're safe." The eagle stood next to Da-Ina, wings spread as a barrier against the wind.

***

Den-El wasted no time heading toward the pilot's cockpit. If he could incinerate one nasty human, he'd do it again to his partner. These men may have done honest jobs, but attempting to kidnap a Thing, steal money, and destroy and innocent dog gained no sympathy from Den-El. Operation Kill.

He stuck his head inside the door, watching briefly as the driver concentrated on the sea in front of him. Lightly he tapped on the door. The driver startled as he looked in Den-El's direction.

"What are you doing out?" His eyes lingered on Den-El, who casually stepped in long enough to swipe his coin purse that had been carelessly tossed on the console.

"I do believe this is mine, kind Sir. My condolences to you and your friend."

"Huh?" The man's eyes narrowed. Without a word he rushed out of the chair, charging with all his energy at Den-El.

"Oops, so sorry about that." Den-El turned and ran onto the upper deck after delivering a cutting blow to the man's ribs with his horns.

"Come back here." The man clambered up the steps, bellowing in between sharp breaths of pain. He let out a string of curse words, sending Den-El into a fit of laughter.

"Ah, is that your best? You can't fight me with words and win." Den-El positioned his body for retaliation.

"You should have been killed the moment you got on here, you nasty Thing. You're all worthless."

"Is anyone else manning this boat, or do I have to do all the work around here?" Den-El crossed his arms and tapped one of his hooves against the floor.

"You . . ." The man came at him, determined.

Den-El worked his magic, thrilling at the site of his opponent lighting up like the last man, only more due to the extra weight on his body. In the end, a pile of ashes lay on the floor, scattering as the winds swept through the boat.

"How I'm going to drive this thing, I'll never know. But time to find out," said Den-El. He scurried back to the pilot's cockpit and seated himself in the chair. "Hmm." He scratched an ear, staring at the controls. "Can't be too hard." As the son of the king's advisor on Ontarus 9, he'd never driven a motorized anything in his life.

Grabbing the wheel, Den-El steered the boat back into position. It had worked its way more toward land. "But land is where I need to go." He mumbled to himself. "That's where Da-Ina would be, if I could find her. If she didn't drown."

The swarm of bats had reached the boat, flying low enough for Den-El to see them. He smiled, listening with perked up ears. "They found her. Praise be to the Creator." He mouthed a prayer of gratitude.

"Follow us," said one of the bats.

In a flash of insight and a rush of knowledge, Den-El placed his hand on the throttle and increased speed, keeping his eyes on both the water and the bats. Two miles down, he spied a bright light shining from a dock.

"She's over there." The bats flew in the direction where Da-Ina lay.

"That's all I need to know, my fine friends. Many thanks and best wishes to each of you."

With great care, Den-El adjusted his speed, slowing down into a position leading him smoothly beside the dock. He bolted out of his chair and sprang for the rope to tie off the boat. The eagle watched, and when he saw the strange Thing taking control, he let out a final piercing cry and flew off.

"And good wishes to you, my friend." Den-El sent his message and smiled. "I'm coming, Da-Ina." He shouted toward the dog. Da-Ina lifted her head and let out a hoarse bark. Otherwise, she didn't move.

If he could get his dog onto the boat and heal her, he'd be fast on his way to the land core, and to Cata-Lin. Den-El jumped from the boat onto the dock, heading fast to his pet. "Easy, sweet girl." He gently scooped up Da-Ina into his arms, carrying her easily back to the boat. "I need to take care of you first before I untie us."

Den-El lay her down on a seat cushion. He opened his mouth and inhaled deeply, filling his lungs to maximum capacity. His light warm breath as he exhaled hit Da-Ina, warming and drying her fur. Holding the injured paw in his hand, he called on ancient words of healing. The blood and wound disappeared until only a normal paw remained.

The dog licked his hand. "Just one more thing, girl, and we'll be off." Den-El kissed the top of her head. He placed his hand on either side of her body and blew once more, this time calling on ancient words for instilling energy and vitality. This act of healing returned Da-Ina to a rested and relaxed state, just like she had been when they left the apartment earlier.

Da-Ina let out a series of barks, jumping off the seat and running around Den-El's legs. He laughed, hugging her. "Let's get out of here."

Several minutes later, the two of them sailed on to the main canal, where they would turn right and head toward the middle of the concentric rings. "Time to tame the storm over there a little, don't you think, girl?" He glanced at Da-Ina. The dog barked, eyes sparkling.

Because no one saw the lower half of him, Den-El looked like any human from a distance. He'd even taken the liberty of wearing a spare hat he saw sticking out from a compartment next to the steering wheel. It was getting darker. He found the light switch and turned on his boat lights.

As he passed others on the water, they held up their hands and waved, nodding in good will. Smiling his widest, Den-El returned the gesture each time. He moved the throttle upward, increasing the speed of the craft. The drone of the engine held a mesmerizing quality as it sent the boat cutting through the water at top speed.

Wind rushed against his face, the spray of water invigorated him. If he didn't have such an important job to do, he would have liked nothing better than spending the night sailing around the rings of Poseidia.

**

Cata-Lin cursed the weather under her breath. She had no intention of going out in a storm like this. But she wanted desperately to talk to Khaluj and tell him what she'd learned. She picked up the receiver to her communication box and input his number. He didn't answer her call. Frowning, she placed the receiver back where it belonged.

Khaluj must be out for the evening. She headed to the window and stared out. First thing in the morning she'd give him another call. Tonight, she could work on prayers and offerings on behalf of the clients who solicited her assistance for various and sundry reasons.

Or she could mate with one of the Things. Nothing had taken hold in her womb lately. It almost seemed like she'd dried up somehow. Maybe if she approached her project with a little more nonchalance, it might work. Focusing too much on failure only created more failure.

Most of the servants had gone for the night. They would return in the morning. Cata-Lin stood in her bedroom at a loss on what to do next. Never had she found herself in such a state of mind before. How odd. Of course, the storm had come out of nowhere. When she'd seen the sky earlier, there was no sign of bad weather brewing anywhere in it. It seemed an unseen force had turned on a faucet and let the water flow and flow.

***

In the middle of dinner, Surya stopped eating a moment. Where did he get the sudden tightness in his gut? Everything had gone so well until now. He sat helpless as a twinge of anxiety became stronger until he felt like he swam in a sea of it.

"Are you all right?" Martaam put her wine glass back on the table. "You seem worried all of a sudden." She placed her hand on his.

"I think I am worried all of a sudden, and I couldn't begin to tell you why." He looked over at her. "Something's happening, and I can't tell you what it is."

"Maybe a panic attack? People get those, you know. I'm working with one client now who has that problem."

"Well, I don't have that problem. Not usually." Surya furrowed his brow and took another bite of food.

"We haven't seen Den-El today at all. Are you worried about that?"

Surya stopped eating again, focusing his attention onto something, a message, a series of events happening in real time. He couldn't get a handle on it. Martaam also put her fork down, watching closely. Surya moved his vibration in line with the sensations he felt.

He opened his mind and tuned into each vision, piecing together reasons for his friend's absence. Intuition heightened, and emotions swirled inside him. They both humored and scared him. Mostly they scared him. What scared him most was that this was only the beginning.

Chapter Sixteen

The land core dripped with rain water. Large puddles reflected buildings lit up by emerald lights shining from the power dome. A good hard rain brightened the crystalline sheaths over each structure, showcasing them in a glorious splendor of shimmering light. On a dock yards away, Den-El had tied off the boat.

He would have liked nothing better than to sit on a bench with Da-Ina and gaze at it all for a while. How could humans create such beauty, learn ancient technology, and yet be so evil and deviant? And how easy had it been for him to obliterate two humans? His only rationale, self-defense.

"Come on, Da-Ina." He tugged gently on the leash. "Don't make a sound, either, but watch everything closely." The dog acknowledged his voice with a small whimper.

He made his way to the Temple of Jhanana, following the signs, dodging puddles as he walked. He tried staying out of sight as much as he could, avoiding eye contact with others. Den-El still had a problem. How would he make it inside Cata-Lin's temple without alerting anyone?

Down a long stretch of sidewalk dotted by lights, he ended at the steps leading up to the temple. He gazed at the massive structure, impressed with the equally massive columns. Under the roof line, he marveled at the details making up carved scenes. Studying these closer, they depicted the history of not only Atlantis, but the temple itself.

He had noted the copper dome earlier. Rain had washed off the surface, leaving it glistening brighter than gold. Stone steps leading up to the front doors seemed to go on forever. Taking a deep breath, he led Da-Ina upward.

When they reached the doors, Den-El gazed in amazement at the inscriptions carved on the orichalcum surface.

From his studies of history on Ontarus 9, he had seen this script before, one so ancient he highly doubted anyone on Atlantis really knew the translation, including the priests and priestesses.

On impulse, he tugged on the broad handle. Locked. He could use the attached door knocker or pull on the heavy silken rope to ring the bell. No doubt people used these to announce their presence. He meandered around the side, looking for other doors. There had to be more than one entrance. Quietly he stole to the rear of the temple, studying the facade. Nothing.

He descended the steep stairs back down, Da-Ina in tow. Den-El found himself on a sidewalk lined with a thick row of hedges. He walked to the right, heading toward the center of the building. A bronze gate had been fashioned in the middle of the hedges.

Curious, he peered through the gate and viewed the scene. Decorative lamplights illuminated four walls of high thick hedges surrounding a magnificent courtyard. Cobblestone pathways wandered in all directions. In the corners he noted different bronze statues. One consisted of a nude male holding out a large orb in his hands. Next to a lit gazing pool a nude female statue held out a large disc. A fountain gurgled nearby.

All species of shrubs and flowers covered the surface. Tall trees stood with stone benches under them. Den-El rattled the gate lightly. Locked. He walked down the sidewalk to the opposite side. Nothing. His ears flicked and twitched with irritation.

"There has to be some other way to get in here," he whispered to Da-Ina. The dog sniffed and wagged her tail.

One main entrance managed people. Any guard could maintain who entered and who left. But every building had its working side, the place where supplies were brought in, where workers and servants came and left undetected. Da-Ina sniffed again, muscles tensing.

She let out a soft bark and tugged at the leash. Den-El decided to follow her lead. They headed back to the gate. Da-Ina pressed her head between two bronze rails, eyes fixed on something in the distance.

"What do you see?" Den-El asked.

Da-Ina pressed with more determination against the gate.

"Let's go." Den-El considered the lock. Concentrating hard, he visioned each mechanical piece inside. With a fixed image in his mind, he trained his thoughts on working the parts so the door swung open with a light squeak. He looked around.

He and his dog were still alone, at least on the back side of the temple. Quickly Den-El led Da-Ina into the garden after he entered. Da-Ina seemed intent on something at the far end. Den-El didn't resist or question, but merely followed his pet to a far corner of the hedges, where he saw another gate, smaller than the first one. It was also locked and didn't have ornate scrollwork like the one they had opened earlier. From what he could discern, the garden backed up to a dense forest. "I think you're onto something, Da-Ina," said Den-El. "Keep working, sweet girl."

The dog sniffed a path away from the gate until she came to a large iron slab on the ground. Ornate scrolled stonework framed the metal piece. On either side, iron rings rested inside indentions, making them less conspicuous. To the casual eye, it resembled nothing more than a carved placard resembling a picture, a monument of some kind.

An inscription read, "The lowliest among us embodies nobility"

Den-El's tail twitched with excitement. He reached out and tapped at the plaque with a hoof. A definite metallic sound echoed back. But he heard more in the sound. Not a dull thud from metal on ground contact, but a distinct clang. He narrowed his eyes. Da-Ina woofed softly and pawed at the plaque's edge.

His pet smelled something he couldn't readily discern, though his ears picked up certain sounds well. He eyed the rings. From his estimation, the plaque was rather large for a decorative piece bearing a simple inscription. He tapped on the surface again. The sound emitted satisfied his first question.

This covering lay over an entrance. Why else would it have been placed on the far side of the garden, tucked away and not far from a gate leading into a forest—or from the forest to a nearly hidden gate. Den-El trotted back to the small gate and studied the surrounding ground.

He smiled. Parts of the grass had been worn, showing mud beneath. Other divots showed up on closer inspection. Overall, it appeared that enough time had passed since the gate had been used. As he angled his head and focused his view, Den-El spied hints of a worn trail from the gate to the iron slab. Da-Ina whimpered with impatience.

"Let's see what we find, girl." Den-El walked back to the plaque, studying each detail. He admired the scrollwork and how the middle of each side showed a floral design. What intrigued him most was the scarab resting within the design he currently faced.

He quickly walked around the plaque. Each floral relief on the sides held a different type of insect, a butterfly, cricket, and a spider. Just as he returned to the scarab, a grinding sound pushed through the ground. He and Da-Ina both startled at the vibrations humming under their feet. The plaque moved.

Den-El tightened his grip on the leash and ran full speed to the nearest tree for cover. As he watched, two hooded figures emerged from where the plaque had rested. His eyes widened. Da-Ina let out a small woof. The two people stopped immediately, glancing around. Den-El clamped a hand on Da-Ina's muzzle, praying they wouldn't be discovered.

When he felt safe to look again, he saw the two people pushing a large box on a cart. A draped had been placed so the contents couldn't be seen. Den-El perked up his ears, listening with every ability he contained.

"How long do you think it will take to get this back?" said one of the men.

"Not long. About twenty minutes." said the other man. "We drop it off, and that's it. They'll take care of the rest."

"I see." The first man who spoke looked at his watch. "I guess we better get moving. Times ticking away."

The other man nodded, and both moved toward the small gate. As Da-Ina started to bolt away, Den-El jerked her back. She let out a bark. Frustrated, Den-El released a quick jolt of energy from his fingers to her backside. Da-Ina sat on her haunches immediately, letting out a yelp.

"Is that a dog? How did it get in here?" The second man spoke up. He let go of the cart and started walking toward the tree shielding Den-El and Da-Ina.

Den-El clenched his fist. If he could put away two humans, two more most likely didn't matter. And why the secrecy in doing work at night? What were they dropping off, and to whom? He remembered what he saw earlier in the crystal ball. Everything started making sense.

"Hey, let's go," said the first man. "If it got in, it will get out. We mess up, we'll both be in trouble."

The second man let out a huff and walked back to his partner. Relieved, Den-El watched with interest as the two men slipped through the gate, locking it securely back in place.

When he thought they were hidden well enough away, he bent down toward Da-Ina. "You give me any more trouble, and I'll let you have it good. Do you understand me?"

Da-Ina whimpered. Dismayed, Den-El watched as the dog stood on trembling legs and let out a stream of urine.

"We don't have time, either, so we have to be quick." Den-El tugged on the leash and ran to the plaque. He wrinkled his brow; his tail and ears flicked in frustration. The entire slab had closed.

He sucked in his breath, thinking a second. How would the two men get back inside? They obviously had a key to the gate, but what about this piece? He shook his head, thinking. Closing his eyes, he mumbled the ancient sacred word for guidance.

An image filled his head. He smiled. Atlanteans were creative, like it or not. They contained capabilities to create something as magnificent as this. Den-El opened his eyes and moved his hand over the scarab, working with it until the wings swiveled away. The mechanism worked smoothly once he knew how it operated.

Just as he hoped, a black button lay hidden beneath. He pushed it. The plaque covering slid away, revealing a set of stairs leading downward into a dark tunnel. Sconces lined the walls, lighting the way.

"Perfect. Let's go, Da-Ina." Den-El took up the leash. At the bottom of the stairs he saw another scarab. He slid the top aside and pressed another black button. The plaque slid in place. Both walked toward the bowels of the temple.

Dampness hung in the air. Firelight from the sconces cast eerie shadows along the dirt floor. Water trickled down the walls in some places. The temple lay yards away, so the walk to get inside would take minutes. Navigating the building presented a challenging enough task. He had no idea how he would reach Cata-Lin unseen.

The tunnel ended with another set of steps going deeper under the temple. Den-El tried looking for a possible hidden entrance to another passage, but didn't readily find anything, nor did he have time to fine one. He stepped down, carefully navigating his way for several more yards. At the end, he reached a door. It stood larger and higher than an average.

He ran his fingers over the middle, noting the cool surface. On closer inspection, the doors apparently slid apart and back together when opened and closed. Den-El's gut wrenched. Such a design wouldn't have troubled him under normal circumstances, except for his previous experience before Surya rescued him.

Doors such as these had been used in the mines, where Things toiled and slaved away for ungodly hours. He tried talking himself into a more logical reason for using freight doors in a temple. Surely the Temple of Jhanana needed supplies. Food, altar offerings, incense, perfumes, tools for healing and energy work.

From his knowledge of history, temples had simpler ways for taking in smaller deliveries. Many of them installed special hidden closets accessed from secret outside and inside entrances. He thought again about the two men pushing a covered box.

Den-El scanned the walls beside the door, hoping to find a mechanism similar to the scarab. Da-Ina sniffed and scuffled to an area of the wall. She stood on her hind legs and pawed, reaching as far upward as possible. Den-El furrowed his brow. In the shadows, he saw it. Another round disc-like object.

He reached for it, moving his fingers over the surface. Not a scarab like before, but a button, nonetheless. Wasting no time, he pressed it. He'd figure everything else as he went along. The doors slid apart, revealing a dimly lit room. Den-El and Da-Ina passed inside, leaving the door to close on its own.

A pungent odor filled the air. Den-El wrinkled his nose. He'd smelled it all before when he worked the mines. Da-Ina had stopped, eyes darting and nose twitching. Voices came from farther away, two people talking. A clear howl of an animal afterward.

Da-Ina pulled harder on the leash. As Den-El and his pet worked their way deeper into the room, which seemed nothing more than a general supply area, the voices became clearer. He stayed close against the wall, moving quietly as possible. Inside the next room, cages sat in neat order. Den-El's stomach lurched.

"Which one do you think she'll want?" said a petite slender woman, pointing to the cages.

"She said to pick one. No preference tonight." The voice belonged to Aam-Raan, the one who always helped with the Things.

"I thought she was going out. Something about seeing a friend," said the woman.

"Weather. Not about to go out on such a bad night. Now it has gotten later."

"Let's go with this one," said the woman. "I really hope he gets the job done. It's a little unnerving being a part of this. It's not allowed."

Den-El watched the two lead a mutant from one of the cages. With a somewhat alert look in his eyes, the creature followed with diligent obedience.

So Cata-Lin decided tonight was a night for love-making, no matter how sordid and despicable. Den-El shuddered but stayed back while the three headed up a flight of stairs. He moved away from the wall and entered the room. Everything looked the same as what he saw in the crystal sphere.

"How did you get out?" A voice whispered.

Den-El whirled around, startled. "What?"

"You're free. Did you see her tonight and no one put you back?" The voice spoke again.

A Thing stood in one of the cages, looking directly at Den-El. It was a conglomeration of part human, part wild game, from the deer species.

"Who are you, and how did all of you get here?" Den-El answered.

"I'm Baldorn. Our masters sent us. It's what she requested." The mutant's tail flicked from side to side.

"Sent here for what reason?"

"Whatever the mistress wants. We do what she bids." Baldorn moved closer to Den-El and stopped short of ramming into the bars of his cage.

"Where were they going?" Den-El pointed to the stairs. He suspected the answer but wanted to hear from one of these unseemly beasts himself.

"To see the mistress. We each get our turn." Baldorn grinned. "It's at least something we can look forward to in our dreary state."

"You're not like the creatures I saw in the mines." Den-El stretched out a hand and patted the Thing, who bowed his head in submission.

"Selected to be here sets us above the others, we're told. But we're really not much better off. At home we move freely. We're better stock, I've heard."

"What happens when she's done with you? I saw two men leaving with a large covered box."

"Ah, that was Elefreed," said Baldorn. "He couldn't give the mistress what she wanted, so it's back to his rightful master's house."

Den-El nodded and stepped away. "I have to go. Best wishes to all of you. May you return home soon." He walked to the steps and made his way to the next floor. "Da-Ina, can you find their scent? Lead me to Cata-Lin," he whispered to his dog.

Da-Ina kept her nose planted firmly to the floor, sniffing like her life depended on it. If she had their scent, Den-El would find his way to the priestess. Da-Ina took the lead, pulling her master up the steps and down a hallway. This area was much better lit, more ornate.

Rooms lined the hall, every door closed. They all had reached the living area of the temple's inhabitants. Hand-fashioned runners lined the floor. Fine marble walls trimmed in silver glistened as light from chandeliers bounced off the surface.

Den-El followed blindly, training his ears in different directions so he could hear if someone else was in the area. Da-Ina stopped in mid step, stiffening. She licked her nose and focused her eyes ahead.

Voices. From the two who had left the room he'd been in earlier. Panic-stricken, Den-El looked all around. He spied an intersecting hallway a few feet down. Quickly he pulled Da-Ina and hid in a recessed area next to a bronze statue. His only hope, no one would come down this hallway for any reason. He waited, impatient.

The shuffling of feet came near. The staff passed by his hallway, minus the mutant. Den-El barely breathed. Da-Ina sat still, not making a sound. When the footsteps died away, Den-El shot out of his hiding place and darted forward. Da-Ina, nose to the ground, picked up a scent and led the way to a set of tall, narrow doors.

A long silken cord hung by the side. He didn't hear a bell echo at any time. Had the staff used it? Markings on the wood signified the entrance to a priestess's quarters.

No mistaking he'd chosen the right room. He pressed his ear against the surface of a door, listening for the slightest sound. With his other ear, he made note of anyone else coming in the area.

Nothing but an occasional rustle sounded behind the doors. Den-El kept his ear in place. Had she gone to another part of her quarters? Was she this quiet when she worked? It was now or never. He twisted the brass knob and pushed slowly. The door opened without a sound, and he peeked inside.

Den-El pulled back, keeping his gaze fixed inside the room. In a far corner, Cata-Lin stood with the Thing. She seemed engrossed in a ritual, open hands held in front of her, head tilted back as she mouthed an incantation or affirmation. Her long black hair cascaded down her back, complete with her fashion statement, a matching ribbon twisted through her locks.

Tonight she wore a bright red see-through caftan. Den-El watched, taking in the subtle curves of her breasts, thighs, and buttocks. His loins ached. He wanted to overpower her, take her over and over. He cursed the power of human lust. It weighed on the body and spirit equal to a hefty sum of gold.

His only consolation, the plan he'd cooked up. He would not forget his purpose coming here, no matter the amount of pleasure he'd get from it. Cata-Lin pulled the mutant Thing closer. Smiling and talking softly, she placed her hands over the intimate part of its body, stroking and squeezing. The mutant let out a soft groan.

From where he stood, Den-El glimpsed the Thing's growing flesh. The beast moved closer to Cata-Lin, nuzzling her ear, flicking out its tongue. Den-El couldn't watch any longer. He stared at the mutant, inciting a sacred mantra. The Thing closed its eyes and went limp, slumping to the floor.

Den-El dropped Da-Ina's leash and bounded toward Cata-Lin. He slipped up from behind and took her in his arms. She let out a sharp scream.

"Shh," said Den-El. His hands had found their way to her breasts, where he cinched each nipple with his fingers. He clamped down with a firm squeeze. "No need for fear, dear Cata-Lin."

The priestess stilled, listening.

"I had to see you." Den-El pressed his cheek against hers, ending with a light bite on her earlobe.

Cata-Lin turned around, facing him, wide-eyed. Den-El didn't know whether he saw happy surprise on her face or horror. They both turned at once and gazed at the Thing lying in a heap on the floor. Its shoulders rose and fell.

"He's only asleep," said Den-El. "But we are more than awake, and I can't contain myself any longer."

"Oh?" Cate-Lin's gaze met his. "Do I consume your thoughts? Is that why you came?" She cupped his face in her hands. "I think of you quite often."

Den-El answered her with a passionate kiss on the lips. His tongue still contained animal traits. Long, thick, powerful. He slid it along the roof of Cata-Lin's mouth and with a little intent visualization, stretched it long enough to reach down her throat a few inches. To his surprise, she held it without so much a batting an eyelash.

He inhaled a rich scent of spicy perfume oil she'd rubbed on her skin not long before his arrival. It still smelled fresh, intoxicating. Den-El ended with another brush of is lips against hers and a small firm bite to her lower lip. She whimpered with pleasure.

"I'm better than any of those beasts you have in the dark rooms of this temple. I love harder and better. Though you surely don't have them for love." He turned his head, quickly glancing at the sleeping Thing on the floor. "Do you love animals, Cata-Lin?"

"I love what they can do. They're strong, powerful. They conquer humans in many ways." Her eyes flashed as she spoke.

Silently, Den-El wrapped his fingers around the ribbon in her hair, unwinding until he held it in his hand. He dangled it in front of Cata-Lin's eyes. A smile played at the corners of her lips. Her eyes glinted.

He pushed her lightly toward the bed, backing her up until she fell back on the silken coverlet. Her breasts heaved with excitement, anticipation. Den-El wound the ribbon around her wrists, securing them firmly in place. "Shh," he said again. He ran to the doors, locking them together.

No one must interrupt us," he whispered when he returned.

"I wouldn't dream of it." She stifled an excited laugh.

"What do you want from me, Cata-Lin? You can tell me. Anything." Den-El leaned in closer, nibbling her ear, licking, kissing. "I want something from you too. Perhaps we can give each other what we want."

"You demand something from me other than myself? Am I alone not enough?" She laughed in a soft, sultry tone.

"Of course, but I tend to be greedy." Den-El smiled. The wild animal body with the face and intellect of a human created an irresistible vision for the woman on the bed.

"I want your seed in me," said Cata-Lin. "I want to create the most magnificent creatures on Earth. Higher than the lowliest animals, and higher than humans. Together we can do it. I know it. I feel it. It can be our secret."

She raised up from the bed, eyes fixed on Den-El. He didn't move, but considered her carefully, listening. "I know what you really are. You're superhuman, super animal. Powerful, brilliant." She smiled and lay back down on the bed with a satisfied smile, letting out a slow audible breath.

Den-El watch with lusty interest as her chest heaved. Cata-Lin ground her back against the bed pretending to get more comfortable, created a more enticing visual effect.

"I want to know an antidote for crystal rays." He whispered in her ear. "I suspect you know the answer." Den-El grasped her sheer caftan, ripping it away. He suckled a breast. Using his tongue, he flicked urgently at the engorged nipple on top. Cata-Lin groaned. "Tell, me," Den-El whispered again.

Cata-Lin lay in silence, eyeing him. She licked her lips and smiled.

"You tease, priestess. It hurts me, you know." Den-El kissed her.

She reached between his legs, grasping a full erection between her hands. Quietly she fondled him, squeezed his sac. Den-El shuddered lightly. His entire groin area tingled and throbbed with a delicious ache. Cata-Lin wasn't giving in easily.

Den-El looped his hands under each of her knees. She let out a light moan as she allowed him to lay her bare and open before him. Their gazes locked for a moment. He let his human instinct kick in full force. This would be the one time he allowed himself the full experience of unbridled human emotion.

Moving his face to her most intimate part, he slipped in his tongue, thrusting with full power, long and hard, swirling and flicking fast. Cata-Lin lay back, eyes closed, mouth open in ecstasy. She let out a sigh.

He continued, relentless, moving faster in all directions. Her face contorted in pain as the sensations changed from pleasant to abrasive. Just when she couldn't tolerate it anymore, Den-El landed his tongue on the most sensitive area at the top of her nether region. He repeated his motions. A look of pure anguish covered her face.

She tried pushing him away, but the ribbon holding her hands made it awkward. Her arms seemed locked in place. "Stop." Cata-Lin gasped for breath, writhing. "I'll tell you. Please stop."

Den-El stopped. "I thought I could convince you." He moved his face close to hers.

"It's amethyst," she said. The stone of toxicity, over-abundance. Crystal rays are the fullest power under the right mechanisms and conditions. Amethyst can absorb it or make the force impotent."

"That simple?" Den-El smiled down at her. "I can't believe neither of us thought of it before."

"The trick will be creating an amethyst shield or a crystalline wall with its energy and essence." Cata-Lin grinned. "It came to me earlier today. I'm so glad you came so I could share it with you and not wait a minute longer."

Without a word, Den-El thrust himself inside her the traditional way. Cata-Lin gasped, writhing beneath him "Now I'll give you what you want."

"Yes," Cata-Lin whispered. "Be gentle."

"I'll give you my best, beautiful priestess." Den-El moved his hips firmer and faster. "Since you know what I am, I'll let you in on a secret."

Cata-Lin opened her eyes, filled with pure lust. Her hands strained against the ribbon "Do tell."

"You'll have offspring beyond anything you could have ever imagined." He pumped his hips, pausing briefly to suckle one of her breasts. "I will multiply everything you've asked of me."

"You're a delight." Cata-Lin lay back, allowing Den-El total control. "Devour me, beautiful creature."

Den-El coordinated his moves with kisses and fondling. The ache and fullness inside himself became unbearable, rendering him powerless to stop it. He didn't want to. His intention, to fill her fully until she overflowed with abundance.

This would be her last reward. He indulged in a series of sure, determined thrusts, grunting after the last few. At once, he pressed against her and let out a soft groan, thrilled at the calmness spreading over his body.

"Time to rest and sleep, dear Cata-Lin. Let the power consume you totally and completely." Den-El said the sacred words and pressed her eyelids shut with his fingers.

Quickly he untied the ribbon, freeing her hands. He gazed at her sleeping figure, deciding he'd leave the woman in her love-making position, legs splayed open like the whore she really was.

Da-Ina got up from her station by the door and headed over to Den-El. Placing her nose on the ground, she sniffed a path to the other side of the room to a bookcase filled with books, statues, and divining tools.

"The oldest trick ever. A secret door," said Den-El. He pushed his way into Cata-Lin's private sanctum area. The room also looked just as it did when he viewed the crystal ball earlier. He gazed all around and walked toward the altar stationed at the end of the room.

Da-Ina protested, growling lightly, and nipping at Den-El's hooves. "What is it? Do you hear something?" He strained his ears. Lower into the temple his animal ears heard snatches of men's voices along with a grating sound as something moved along the floor. Or maybe it was squeaky wheels?

He and the dog stood still for several minutes. As much as he wanted to prowl the sanctum, there wasn't time. If a servant knocked on Cata-Lin's door for any reason, he and Da-Ina risked discovery and capture. He couldn't do it.

Den-El followed Da-Ina as the dog sniffed along the walls. In a corner in the opposite side of the room, she stopped and pawed at the floor. Further inspection revealed another hidden door opening to a secret staircase. The steps wound down to the lower part of the temple.

Together, Den-El and his pet retraced their steps quickly and quietly until they found themselves in the tunnel leading back out. Whatever he heard upstairs had gone. Perhaps the two men must have returned. Staff appeared to have gone to their quarters for the night. A dreary silence followed them until Den-El pushed the button opening the plaque covering the tunnel. He and Da-Ina slipped out of the courtyard and picked their way back to the dock.

When he arrived at his apartment later that night, he crept to his room, silently closing the door. Surya's bedroom door remained closed. Den-El knew Martaam had stayed for the night. He crawled into bed and settled into the sheets. Da-Ina jumped up and joined him, laying close against his legs. All he could do now was watch and wait.

***

Lost in a foggy sleep, Cata-Lin stirred with momentary awakening. Her arms moved more easily with the ribbon untied. She glanced down at her belly and smiled. It had grown full and the weight of it gained her attention. Den-El had worked his magic.

She placed her hands on top, feeling the firmness, the roundness. A strange sensation filled the area. Was it a new super being moving inside her? Having Den-El's offspring, complete with alien DNA overwhelmed her with joy.

The fog of sleep kicked in again, and she closed her eyes for more. Down the hall, no one stirred. Staff slept, deaf and tuned out. Later in the night, Cata-Lin roused from her sleep once again. She let out a blood-curdling scream.

Chapter Seventeen

Surya and Martaam cuddled on the sofa, sipping cups of hot liquid chocolate mixed with ginger and cinnamon. Together they watched Lomasa News on the AudioView.

"This morning we learned that an esteemed high-level priestess in the Temple of Jhanana died last night. The circumstances surrounding her death remain shrouded in mystery. We have our staff there now. Juleena, can you tell us more about what happened?"

"Good morning to you, Andana. We are on site here at the Temple of Jhanana where the popular priestess, Cata-Lin was found dead in her bedroom. Staff awoke early this morning and tried to reach her, but the doors had been locked.

"When they managed to enter, they found her on the floor in a puddle of blood and what has now been identified as amniotic fluid. Rats were found everywhere, and appeared to have attacked the priestess. It is thought that she died from bite injuries and rapid infection."

Andana spoke up. "Can anyone account for rats in her room? When you say amniotic fluid, did she actually give birth to those . . . rats? That sounds rather strange and horrifying."

Juleena answered, "Yes, very horrifying. We must mention that a Thing was also found beside her in the room. It's not clear if he mated with her and she subsequently gave birth, which would be extremely fast, given the biological nature of it all. Doctors have examined her corpse, and it is determined that she was definitely impregnated by something unusual. The Thing was immediately executed for precautionary measures."

"Thank you, Juleena. We'll be sure to stay tuned for any additional information."

"Thank you, Andana. We'll let our viewers know when we find out anything else surrounding these events."

Andana continued her newscast. "Two men have been reported missing. They were delivering supplies for clients yesterday. When the company owner couldn't reach them for delivery updates, it sent up a red flag.

"After hours of no response, he reported them missing. Someone spotted the boat docked and empty on the third ring of Poseidia. No supplies were damaged or missing. The boat appears fine, as well."

Surya placed his mug of chocolate on an end table and scrambled off the sofa. He headed to Den-El's room and pounded on the door. Stepping inside he yelled, "Get up. Get up right now."

Den-El lifted his head, eyes squinted through sleep. "Hmm?" Da-Ina scurried off the bed.

"You have some explaining to do." Surya jerked the covers back. Grabbing Den-El by a horn, he pulled him out of bed.

"Hey, easy. You'll break my neck."

"I will if you don't start talking." Surya's face burned hot with rage.

"Gentlemen, stop it." Martaam ran into the room, pushing Surya lightly away. "Let him wake up. I'm sure he'll talk." She placed an arm on Den-El's shoulder. "Why don't you come into the living room. And no one is attacking the other."

Surya guided Den-El to the dining table. Martaam stopped by the kitchen to make a pot of tea.

"While you were getting your beauty sleep, we watched the news." Surya scowled. "Guess what all of Atlantis knows now?"

"Why do you think I have anything to do with whatever it was you saw on the news?" Den-El slouched in his seat, resting his head in a hand.

Martaam returned and poured everyone a fresh cup of tea. "You were gone all night, Den-El. We were worried about you."

"Correction. I got in late, not out all night." He warmed his hands on the hot cup sitting in front of him.

"What possessed a killing spree and stealing a boat?" Surya glared at his friend. "We're in big trouble if a discovery leads back to us."

"You never answered my question," said Den-El. "Why are you thinking I did anything?" He rapped his fingers on the table. "What if I simply went out last night to have some fun, get out a little?"

"I wish that were true," answered Surya. "But I had visions last night, and you were in them." He leaned forward toward Den-El. "I also saw you used your crystal ball. So why was that, and what did you see in it?"

Den-El grimaced.

Martaam placed her hand on Den-El's wrist. "Just be honest with us. If I know you, there must have been a good reason for what you did, though the killing part bothers me a great deal."

Den-El stared at his cup for several seconds. "Fine. Here's what happened . . ." He reviewed the events of the former evening, ending with, "Do you know what the antidote for crystal rays is?"

"Amethyst?" Martaam's eyes darted between Surya and Den-El. The two men stared at her in amazement.

"You knew that?" Surya asked.

"I actually just thought of it. Came to me in a flash of insight." She shook her head. Maybe I'm channeling you, Den-El. She took a sip of tea. "I'm hurt that neither of you asked me first, just to see if I even knew."

"What surprises me is that no one on the islands have thought about this. Surya and I should have known. I think being here on this planet has warped and slowed our minds," said Den-El. "I don't think as clearly as I did on Ontarus 9."

"We think well enough for what we have to do here, but maybe you're right. The changes from one constellation to another has its effects." Surya wore a glum expression. He looked at Martaam, covering her hand with his. "We have tried to keep political events more private. Some things we don't need to share with everyday citizens. No offense."

Martaam asked, "What's your plan?"

Surya spoke first. "We keep quiet." He looked at her. "Do you think you can do that, even though you don't like what has happened?"

"I don't have a choice, do I?" she stared down at the table.

"Not much," said Den-El. "We wouldn't harm you, but we have the capacity to silence you. And we would do it." He kept his gaze fixed on Martaam.

"Den-El!" Surya scolded his friend.

"Admit it. When it comes to a higher and greater good, we'd simply mute her. You don't have to kill to get results." He contorted his face in a sign of exasperation. "Unless you're about to be killed yourself or taken as a hostage. And if your pet is thrown overboard."

Den-El pounded the table lightly with his fist. "You do it if a whore that mates with Things to perpetuate more Things is intent on telling your adversary information that will be used against you."

"Stop. I get it." Martaam looked at Surya and Den-El. "I sense a war coming on. I just feel it. Do you know that Uncle Aleemirin is saying that the Aryans are already trying to gain more control of our firestone? I know because we had dinner the other night."

Surya and Den-El gazed at Martaam.

"What do you mean?" Surya narrowed his eyes.

"They are already tuning the crystal higher and higher without permission. At some point, it can tax even the strongest energy source. Everything in nature has a limit. It's all about balance."

Den-El chuckled. An expression of sarcasm covered his face. "I knew this would happen. Nothing that group does surprises me. Mark my words, the Aryans will start something. If Law of One would stop being so accommodating and gullible, maybe they might prepare and be ready."

Martaam frowned. "We like to be honorable and concentrate on the best of people."

"That foolish mentality will get you killed. Period." Den-El pointed an accusing finger her direction.

"All right. Enough." Surya interjected, waving his hands for silence. "Law of One was forced to take action. You deal with the hand you're dealt. So we're all in agreement?"

"Aye," said Den-El, turning a pointed gaze at Martaam.

"Yes." Martaam nodded.

All three sat in momentary silence. Out of nowhere, a rumbling sound filled the room. The building shook. A picture fell to the floor, shattering in pieces.

Martaam's eyes widened in fear. "Get out!" She screamed as another wave of shaking rattled the windows.

Surya and Den-El dashed toward the front door, following Martaam out of the building. Tenants who were home had come outside in the courtyard. Frightened looks covered each of their faces. People conversed in panic-stricken tones. Screams ignited when another round of rumbling and shaking sent the ground moving beneath feet.

Poseidia would surely explode and disappear if the earthquake kept up. Surya gazed upward, inciting ancient words for control and safety. At once the rumbling stopped. A little too late, a wing of the complex collapsed with a resounding boom. People screamed and gasped in horror.

"There may be people in there!" Martaam yelled and ran toward the rubble.

"Stop!" Surya ran after her. Den-El beat him to it.

"Don't go there. It's unstable," said Den-El, gasping for breath. In the air, he detected smoke. A volcano must have erupted.

"We need to get people out," said Martaam. Her eyes filled with tears.

Surya came up to her. "Is there a place where we can move these people?" He whispered, "I can probably fix this. I stopped the earthquake."

Her face went blank. She stared at him in shock.

"We have to move fast, Martaam," said Den-El, snapping his fingers in front of her eyes.

"Um, let me round everyone up to the office. I have no idea about the rest of the apartments." She sniffled, stifling the urge to cry.

"I'll help you get everyone together." Den-El wrapped an arm around her. "Surya will fix any damage."

Surya nodded. "You need to do what he says. Honest, I'll take care of everything."

Martaam walked to the center of the courtyard and clapped her hands for attention. "Everyone, I need all of you to follow me to the main office. We need to have engineers check the building for structural damage. We'll help you find places to stay and let you know when you can return to your units."

People mumbled, glancing at each other in fear and dismay. One lady tried running back to her unit to retrieve belongings. Surya stopped her immediately and demanded she go with the group.

He sniffed the air. Smoke from volcanos. The chain of events filled him with grave concern. History had taught him that acts of nature could destroy whole continents as Atlantis had experienced. A large land mass when created, two cataclysms had reduced it to a smattering of islands now.

It wasn't just acts of nature alone, but the corruption and negative vibrations emanating from humans. Their hate and greed and disconnection with spirit played a big part in Atlantis's destruction. No one appeared to notice, anymore. Even Law of One seemed oblivious.

Surya feared he may have spoken to soon. He'd not tried altering anything physical since the day he tried replicating the coins when he first arrived on the island. What made him think he could suddenly fix broken structures like he could back home on his planet? It wasn't dealing with nature in any form or fashion.

It wasn't healing, tapping into coordinates on a vibrational grid, or calling on nature for assistance. A strong desire welled up inside of him, burning strong and heavy in the heart chakra. Earth wasn't a perfect place, by any means.

But humans needed help. Lives and safety were at stake.

The vulnerability and pure fear in their hearts and eyes would haunt him until the day he died. He asked the cosmos for help.

"Sir, can we be of assistance?"

"Excuse me?" Surya broke his spell of concentration and turned around, viewing a man wearing a metal hat. Behind him stood several men in work clothes.

"We're here to fix the damage. Looks like that part really got hit." He pointed to the collapsed unit.

"Who are you?" Surya squinted. The sun had come out again with a blaring light.

The man smiled and whispered in Surya's ear, "Oh prince, son of Mal-Ek, Zedekiel heard your call. He has commanded that we come and right this insult from nature."

Surya smiled. "My gratitude to Zedekiel and his sacred name. My gratitude and highest wishes to you, my friend."

The man acknowledged Surya's words with a pat on the shoulder. "We begin immediately" He called out to his workers, "Check to see if there are people trapped inside." Turning back to Surya, he added, "Take me to the young lady so that I may speak to her."

***

Khaluj's clouded mood had been interrupted momentarily when the earthquake hit Orubis way. A vase and some dishes had broken with the destructive shaking. He righted a tilted painting and reviewed his apartment, checking each room for damage. A long jagged crack sliced across a wall in his bedroom.

He frowned. What an inconvenience. He'd contact the manager to fix it. But the earthquake didn't unsettle him as much as hearing about Cata-Lin's death on the news. He'd cried, cursed, and cried some more. His last ally, it seemed, had been reduced to food for rats.

This knowledge nearly sent his blood to a boiling point. He rubbed his lip and thought. Why had the priestess's death occurred in such a manner? A review of the events ramped up a wave of nausea in his gut. After drinking some cold water, he sat down and thought some more.

Cata-Lin had a Thing in her room. Why? And she wasn't found until the next morning. The Thing was still there. Mating with a mutant wouldn't yield rats, that much he surmised. He immediately got up from his dining room table, dressed, and headed out the door.

***

Aleemirin and Tujuk had slept in late. They had been shaken awake from a deep sleep, cuddled in each other's arms. Together they had thrown on some dressing robes and stepped out of their apartment, joining with others who lived at Sadarma. People looked into the sky, noting the puffs of smoke in the distance.

"I'm telling you, it's the Aryans," whispered Tujuk to Aleemirin.

"What?" Aleemirin frowned as he stared at his lover. "I know we're not fond of the Aryans, but they're not that powerful."

"Our firestone is. I don't like hearing from Law of One workers that Sons of Belial are tweaking the crystal, tuning it up a notch when they think no one is looking. That can have grave consequences due to the energy level produced."

"We're going to have to deal with this, whether we like it or not. It was all in the agreement. I wonder if that nasty Khaluj is telling them to do it." Aleemirin wrapped an arm around Tujuk.

"Are you sure we can't get rid of him? I don't know how long we can keep up pretenses."

Aleemirin looked at his partner, noting the heavy concern filling his eyes. "I thought keeping him in our order would at least let us watch him more closely."

"He's sneaky. I really don't think it will matter by keeping him. He's not going to share anything with us any more than we are with him, now that we know everything." Tujuk tugged on Aleemirin's sleeve. "I say we get him out of our order."

***

Mal-Ek and Ahtan-Mir sat, staring at each other in disbelief. For the past several weeks, watching certain scenes through the GalXR90 had been difficult. When events became too uncomfortable for a father to watch, Mal-Ek and Ahtan-Mir took turns stepping out of the room while the other stayed. They shared information with each other in the end, no matter how sensitive.

"This whole situation has become extremely disheartening," said Ahtan-Mir.

"It will get worse. We've watched both islands." Mal-Ek sipped from a mug, savoring the strong drink.

"The priestess issue has me utterly speechless." Ahtan-Mir grimaced and shook his head. "How could he have come up with such a ruthless idea?"

"It's the human side of him. Indulge lust while exacting revenge. That's why we instituted the Earth Directive to start with. Obviously, humans haven't changed."

Ahtan-Mir drummed his fingers on the table. "We need a plan, Your Majesty."

Mal-Ek glanced up at his advisor from over his mug. "A plan?"

"Yes."

"Write me a detailed proposal."

***

The land core showed visible damage from the earthquake. Some of the healing temples suffered cracks in the facade. A gaping crack split a section of the sidewalk. Khaluj walked six yards out to go around it as he walked to the Temple of Jhanana. A stone statue lay toppled over in pieces.

No matter the challenge, no matter if he had to climb over a wall of rubble, he would reach Cata-Lin's temple. A set of steps leading up to the structure had caved in, rendering them unsafe. Khaluj swore under his breath and walked all the way to the end of the building to use another section of stairs that had remained intact.

Other people ascended to the front door, where they entered the main hall. Inside patrons paid their respects. Several had left bouquets of flowers along the walls. An ornate silver coffin lay between two large orichalcum pots filled with the brightest flowers.

Khaluj knew the coffin had been placed there for show only. He would see her. Surely the body was still secured inside the temple. He pushed past the crowd, showing an obligatory smile as he excused himself to the far side of the main hall. A hidden door behind a burgundy velvet curtain allowed him access to the interior of the temple.

The halls already held an empty feeling to him. The decor, everything, seemed at once dull and almost surreal. Unless he decided he wanted in the good graces of the next priestess, this would most likely be the last time he'd come here.

He scowled as he made his way to Cata-Lin's bedroom. Whatever spell Surya cast on him still hadn't subsided. His member hung lifeless and limp inside his trousers.

"Honorable Khaluj," said a woman's voice.

Khaluj turned around. "Ah, someone at last. It seems everyone has vanished or perhaps are engaged in other tasks."

"Aye, good Sir. It's a day of great sorrow for us all." The woman bowed her head a moment as a sign of respect.

"Where have they placed her? I know the coffin in the main hall doesn't hold her." Khaluj placed his hand lightly on the servant's shoulder and graced her with a kind smile.

The lady glanced around and whispered, "They took her to the death room. Her body has been cleansed the best it can be under the circumstances." Wiping away a few tears, the woman added, "A most gruesome sight. I was the one who found her." She stifled a sob. "Just horrific and dreadful."

Khaluj ran his fingers through the woman's hair. "May I go to her room one last time? Just so I can feel the remnants of her energy before it's erased forever."

The woman nodded. "Shall I escort you there?"

"I know the way, good lady. Just know one thing. Cata-Lin valued everyone who worked for her. She saw goodness and light in everyone, including the darkest of souls."

"She did. We can only hope the next priestess will live up to the fine Cata-Lin's high standards."

The lady curtsied lightly and continued down the hall. Khaluj followed the way to Cata-Lin's room, where he gently opened the tall doors. Inside, the stillness and silence hit him full force. His eyes darted around.

Part of him expected her to greet him as she stepped from behind a curtain. None of it happened, not even a specter to console him. The silk coverlet on the bed had been changed, and a pristine clean one lay on top. Everything in the room seemed in such rigid military order, almost like a museum.

Khaluj jumped with a start. A large rat scurried out from under the bed and across his shoes. He watched in horror as it scrambled out of the room and outside into the hallway, disappearing into the expanse of the temple.

He'd inform the servants that another fumigation was in order. Perhaps an animal specialist who could coax the disgusting rodents out.

Khaluj walked around the room, making his way over to a section of the wall. A picture of what looked like an extra-terrestrial being hung neatly in place. Next to the picture stood the bookcase.

Khaluj studied it closely and gently pushed. The space moved, showing him Cata-Lin's sanctum. Curious, he flipped on a light switch and stepped inside, shutting the bookcase behind him. Khaluj smiled. This was where she performed her work. He knew it. Every item in the room showed signs of it.

A sacred cloth covered the altar. An ankh sat in the middle between two taper candles resting in orichalcum holders. A simple mirror hung over the altar. It all created the perfect atmosphere she needed for doing the best work. In a far corner, a small cabinet sat. Khaluj walked over and opened a drawer.

A collection of healing crystals and a crystal ball for scrying glistened in the light. Another drawer held matches and incense. He inhaled the aroma as it reached his nose. In the last drawer, he spied a small book with some writing implements beside it. What would she have written in a notebook?

Khaluj carefully reach in the drawer and pull it out. He thumbed through the pages until he came to the last entry. Entranced he read the writing and saw the word. Amethyst. The word inscribed seemed to glow a purplish hue as he gazed at it.

His pulsed raced with new excitement. The priest slipped the small notebook into his pocket and closed the drawer. No one would miss it, and he wasn't about to turn it over to a stranger's eyes. Khaluj saw a small door across from the main one in the sanctum. He opened it and found himself on a set of stone stairs leading downward.

Sconces lit up all the way down as far as his eye could see. With caution, he made his descent. These steps led directly to the lower part of the temple, as they didn't seem to branch off anywhere else.

The air turned musty and damp, filling his nose with a moldy, dirt smell the lower he stepped. Why did she have a door leading down to the lower levels? The stairs surely weren't used by servants, from what he could discern. He reached the the last stair and stepped out onto a main floor.

A curtain separated the stairs area from another room. Where was he? Khaluj stood a moment, letting his eyes grow more accustomed to the dimness. The priest wrinkled his nose. He heard something in another adjoining room.

A wild animal sound, almost. He narrowed his eyes, thinking. Khaluj was no stranger to the sounds. Intrigued, he walked through the curtain and found himself in a larger room. There were no windows, and lights glowed from sconces and overhead lamps.

Rows of cages perplexed him to the highest degree. Silently, he walked around, viewing the mutants held captive. It wasn't uncommon for Things to be used in the temples, especially for the lowliest of work. But these somehow looked better than the average mutant.

In one cage, a half deer, half man stirred. When Khaluj saw it, the eyes glinted. A chill shot down his spine, and the priest couldn't understand why. The creature shook himself when he stood up, his antlers waving like one brandishing a trophy after winning a contest.

"Are you looking for someone?" The mutant, Baldorn, stared straight at Khaluj with mild interest.

Chapter Eighteen

Khaluj cleared his throat and forced himself next to Baldorn's cage for a clearer conversation. "Yes, as a matter of fact, I am." With the exception of Den-El, the priest had never heard of a Thing conversing so clearly before.

"Would you be looking for the mistress who commands here?" Baldorn asked.

Khaluj nodded. "That's exactly who I'm looking for. Can you direct me to her from here?"

Baldorn shook his head, warding off a fly, and shuffled his feet. The tip of one of his antlers nearly missed catching on Khaluj's sleeve. The priest stepped back from the cage, irritated. "She's in the room where she always meets us. Upstairs in her grand room."

"Where she meets you? Um, I don't think I understand." As Khaluj considered the beast before him, it dawned on him that any knowledge of Cata-Lin's death hadn't been imparted to it. Not that anyone was obligated to inform the creature what had happened.

"She meets all of us," said Baldorn, lowering his voice.

"In her room?" asked Khaluj. His interest perked up tenfold. "And what work do you do there?"

"Anything she asks."

"Her room looked clean. I just left from there. That's why I ended up here. Did you help get it in order after her death? I heard it was a horrid affair."

Baldorn's eyes went cold. "Something happened to her? I don't understand."

Khaluj blinked several times, staring at the mutant. "Are you and your ilk aware that the mistress, as you call her, is dead?"

"No one has told us." Baldorn lowered his head. "She was very kind, beautiful, and gentle." He motioned for Khaluj to come closer. "We have all mated with her. Did something go wrong?"

The priest grabbed the cage bars for support. Baldorn's confession nearly got the better of his senses. He thought he'd known Cata-Lin and all her secrets, no matter how unorthodox. "Why would you and your kind be called up to her private quarters? And to mate, of all things?" Khaluj swallowed down the bile building in his throat.

"We're good stock. That's all I've been told." Baldorn looked intently at Khaluj. "But I've overheard the humans talking. They don't think we understand what's being said very well."

"I find it difficult to believe, too, if you want to know the truth," said the priest. He suddenly had the urge to cut and run.

"But listen. I've overheard the humans say that she wanted offspring for a special workforce. Strong and smart like me and my friends." Baldorn moved his head around, indicating the others in their cages.

"Let me tell you something," said Khaluj, "you and your kind are not all that smart, even at this level. Though I'll give some credit that you speak with more intellect than others of your kind. Are all of these in here like you?"

"We're all similar, Sir." Baldorn pawed at the floor and shifted his weight to get comfortable.

Khaluj stood thinking. He and Baldorn locked gazes. "Can you tell me who went to her room last?"

"Ah, that was Cre-Dor. No one has returned him." Baldorn paused.

"Is there anything else you can tell me?"

"After Cre-Dor left with the humans, another one like us came to my cage. He was running free." Baldorn shook his head. "I think someone forgot to put him back in his cage. We talked, and then he went up the stairs after them."

"Another Thing?" Khaluj asked stepping closer to the cage.

"Yes. But he was not like the rest of us. He was beautiful. Carried himself like a king. A dog followed him. None of us have pets. And this dog seemed like a pet."

"You've been very helpful, Thing." Khaluj smiled politely at Baldorn. Only one being fit the description he'd just heard. "I'll just find my way out of here." The priest moved toward the opposite end of the room.

"But, Sir, the way out is that way." Baldorn pointed to the same door Den-El had used.

"Yes, I understand. Thank you." Khaluj kept moving, not looking back. Instead of taking the staircase like others had done, he chose the hallway beside it. A man stepped out of a room at the far end. When he saw Khaluj, he walked quickly toward him.

"Honorable Khaluj," said Aam-Raan. "You have come to pay your respects, I see."

"A woeful day for me. She was one of my closest and dearest friends." The priest clasped the man's hand in greeting, only due to the sad circumstances.

Aam-Raan whispered, "You wish to see her, don't you? It was a dishonorable way for her to pass, though. Such sordid secrets. You saw the cages."

"Shh, we must keep this between us," said Khaluj, grasping the man's arm. "All of this will pass. You'll be returning the mutants to their respective owners?"

"We'll do it soon, Sir. None of us who knew approved of this. It was so wrong. It goes against Law of One principles." The man's eyes clouded with emotion.

"Yes, yes. Of course. But now we get those poor creatures back to their owners and concentrate on electing a new priestess." Khaluj would die before admitting it to any Law of One person on Poseidia, but he thought the priestess's plan a rather decent one. If he could get a select group of Aryan women to breed high quality Things, there might be a fine work force created.

"Let me show you where we have placed Cata-Lin, Sir."

Khaluj shut down his personal thoughts for the moment and followed Aam-Raan to a plain door, which led further down into the temple. Could this monstrous building go down any further than where he just left? The air turned cool and damp. A strong scent reached his nostrils, and he paused a moment.

"Did you still wish to come down? Though we've tended to the body as best we could, we've also added lots fragrance to sweeten the air." The man's face showed a sober expression.

"I'll be fine. I think raw emotion is getting the better of me more than anything." Khaluj landed on the next step.

They reached the bottom of the stairs, and the man led the way down another hall. Sconces lined the walls just like those in the tunnel leading to the courtyard. At last they reached a room. Khaluj stepped inside, his heart pounding heavily in his chest. Would he be able to face the ugly truth?

"Sir, we cleaned her up to the best of our ability. Please know that." The man led Khaluj to a table, where an outline of a body showed through a pure white linen sheet. "I'll give you some time alone. Please push this button by the door when you are finished, and I'll escort you out."

"Thank you." Khaluj nodded in gratitude, watching as the man left him alone in the death room.

He concentrated his gaze on the table, noting the lines of the body through the sheet. Nothing emanated from her now. No aura. She'd taken leave of this earth willingly, not even wishing to linger a little while longer. Not even to say goodbye. Not even to disclose what had really happened to her.

The priest already surmised what may have occurred, and the thoughts sickened him to the core. He walked quietly up to the table. Grasping the sheet, he pulled it back inch by inch, in case he needed to stop if the horror of it all became too much.

Once the eyes glimpsed anything, an imprint etched itself into the soul memory. It would only take special spiritual assistance to undo such an insult. Cate-Lin's black hair came into view. It lay loosely around her face. Khaluj let out a deep breath. So far she looked more asleep than dead.

The vision didn't last long. Pulling back the sheet more revealed the horror he'd dreaded seeing. All along her body, huge bite marks and pitted areas where rodents had gouged the skin way from the bone. Bruising had set in. Around the wound edges, body fluids still oozed slightly.

Khaluj sucked in his breath, glancing up at the ceiling for a quick break. When he was ready, he pulled back the sheet some more. Cate-Lin's belly gleamed, swollen and bloated, almost like a woman who'd just borne a child. More wounds, deep, unforgiving.

He studied her thighs and pubic area. All blue from strain and physical attacks. At the top of her nether regions, a broken blistered area shone. It almost appeared as if the rodents bit and clawed their way out once she stopped living long enough to push.

What she must have suffered. The pain, shame, and agony. All because of one bad decision to mate with the wrong one. One who had obviously intended to inflict harm. And for what reason, really? Why would that horrid alien mutant need to go this far? Did he know something?

At this moment, Khaluj couldn't hold back the anger any longer. The more he stared down at Cata-Lin and thought about Den-El, the more he visioned murdering the alien, making him suffer ten-fold. He'd exact revenge or die trying. Poseidia and Law of One would pay for this injustice.

The priest pulled the sheet back over his friend and left the room. He walked back through the temple and exited the building through the same way he'd first entered. Crowds had gathered in larger numbers. Everyone had heard of the death.

When he walked outside, a crowd had gathered near another building several yards away. They chanted and held signs. People still protested the union of Law of One and Sons of Belial sharing care of the firestone. Another group stood in a circle, heads bowed.

A young man recited a prayer, asking that care of the firestone be given back to Law of One. He also requested the restoration of peace and harmony on Poseidia once again. Khaluj restrained himself from marching over to the group and giving them a piece of his mind about how Sons of Belial really had the right idea, and Law of One needed to get with the times.

He wanted to scream, tell all the protesters that their paranoia had gotten the better of them. He wanted to shake sense into each person yelling about how awful Sons of Belial were and how the Isle of Aryan was nothing more than a devil's den.

Ignorant. Narrow-minded. Backwards. That's how the priest saw everyone who stood in a huddle or in a circle. Those people were the enemy, and more like them roamed all over the streets of Poseidia. And then there were the aliens. He took a deep breath and tried clearing his head before rage set in and drove him truly mad.

After taking a ferry ride back to the third ring, Khaluj made it to his apartment. A note hung on his door. He picked it up and read: We need to meet. Please call. Aleemirin had signed his name. Khaluj squinted at the note. He flipped it over. Nothing else was written on it. He opened the apartment door and walked straight to his communication box.

"Ah, Khaluj, you survived the earthquake." Tujuk's voice sounded pleasant enough.

"I did. A little damage in my apartment, but nothing more. You and Aleemirin?"

"We're fine. Very frightful, though."

"Yes." Khaluj had enough of the small-talk. "I'm calling Aleemirin because of his note on my door."

"That. Yes," said Tujuk. "Can you meet with us in the same building where we first had our talk with Sons of Belial? It's an ad-hoc meeting, but very important, just the same."

"I don't see why not. Is everything okay?" An uneasiness settled over Khaluj.

"We'll talk more then. Can't do it now. Next Monday at one o'clock. See you there."

"Fine." Khaluj started to say more, but Tujuk had already ended the call. He grimaced. How strange. And why a meeting next week? The next scheduled one wasn't for another month.

He put the meeting out of his mind. Another matter needed attention, and that was how to deal with Den-El and what he did to Cata-Lin. Khaluj made himself a cup of tea and curled up on his sofa. He removed the tiny notebook from his pocket. His mind ran in a swirl of ideas.

***

Night had set in. Outside Vardhase, Den-El and Surya talked in low voices. Both men held sizable stones of amethyst in their hands.

"I'm wondering where we can practice without anyone seeing us?" Surya glanced around, fearful someone would wander close by. He didn't want to try this experiment in the apartment. Any damage would have to be explained if it occurred.

"Let's go in that grove of trees over there." Den-El pointed in the direction. "It will be more realistic anyway. Not everything will be out in the open when men are shooting at people."

"I'm hoping the day will never come when we have to worry about it." Surya followed his friend to the trees.

"I'm hoping we will go home very soon, and neither of us will have to worry about it. We'll leave it to these wily humans." He turned around a second, staring straight at Surya. "Any chance of that happening? Seriously."

"What's to stop you from sneaking out and going through the portal on your own? You seem to get out a lot."

"I'm not sure how far I'd get. And just for your information, I don't wander that far from home. Only the one time."

The young men reached the tree line and slipped among the branches. The full moon peeked through, lighting up the tiny forest in a soft glow of white.

"Okay," said Surya, "do you want me to go first, or do you?"

"You aim at me first, and we'll see what happens." Den-El walked several paces until he stood by a massive tree.

Neither had a crystal ray gun, but both knew their lightning source would be better. Nothing beat anything man-made like a true force of nature. Surya watched Den-el and held out a hand in his direction. Calling up the sacred word, he shot out a small vein of lightning just to test the effectiveness of the amethyst. He could always go higher in force.

Den-El intercepted the bolt with the stone he held. The amethyst absorbed the ray. "Go a little higher."

Surya shot out another bolt, stronger than the first. Again, his friend warded off the strike. "Seems to work okay so far."

"Stronger. Give it to me good." Den-El widened his stance.

"Your rock holding up?" Surya forgot about the amount of insult a stone could take.

"So far, so good."

"Here I go." Surya sent out a stream of energy surpassing a crystal ray gun.

A large flash of light lit up the area where the men stood. The stone in Den-El's hand shattered in a million pieces. His hand emitted a frying sound followed by a feeling of numbness. He staggered back in shock.

In seconds, Surya stood by his friend's side, holding the damaged hand. Healing words flowed quickly with sincere intent. He visioned the hand losing the throbbing red. Blood vessels worked themselves back together and in working order. Skin returned to its caucasian color. When Den-El breathed a sigh of relief, Surya knew his friend had healed.

"I went really strong on that last one."

"No kidding. I thought you'd blasted me all the way back home." Den-El grinned.

"Not a chance." Surya laughed. "But I think there's something to the amethyst theory."

"What if we tried creating a crystalline shield with the stone you have? I highly doubt our armies are going to be holding rocks in their hand."

"Why not amethyst embedded in their clothing or worn as jewelry. Wouldn't that work just as well?" Surya stared at the formation he held.

Den-El scratched his head. "Maybe? But I like the idea of a shield. The men could make personal ones. That would alleviate carrying anything and having to aim it in the direction of a ray. A shield surrounding the body would be more efficient."

"Good point. Let's give it a try." Surya nodded. He handed his amethyst stone to Den-El. Concentrating his eyes on the stone, he invoked the physical laws of projection and expansion. A violet wall of light burst from the stone, separating him from Den-El.

"I think you did it," said Den-El. "Now go at me again the exact same way you did last time."

Surya walked back several steps, leaving yards of space between him and his friend. He held out his hand and sent out a ray of energy. A light frenetic ripple scatter across the light wall. He went harder the next time. The violet wall briefly turned into a writhing display of pure white streaks.

"Last one," said Den-El.

Taking a deep breath, Surya let out the same force he did before the previous stone broke. The violet wall turned a blinding white, sending waves of energy back a couple of yards and crashing to the ground. The floor of the forest rumbled. Branches shimmied. Leaves fell. The two men stared at each other, stunned.

Den-El ran to Surya. "Did you see that?"

"I'm wondering why the last bolt didn't destroy the wall. Is it because distribution of energy allows the shield to hold up better, as opposed to a concentrated force that blew up your stone?"

"That may be the case." Den-El looked at Surya. "The wall creates a field that absorbs and has a wider space to spread the impact."

"The down side, sending the energy back to the ground creates an unsteady surface, and you know what that could mean."

"It sets up natural disasters like the earthquake we just experienced." Den-El shook his head. "We still need to share this with the leaders."

Surya motioned for them to leave. When they returned to the courtyard again, he pointed in the direction of the land core. "If engineers can create crystalline domes on the buildings where the Temple Of Poseidon stands, I'm sure they can create a shield of amethyst."

"I don't see why they couldn't." Den-El nodded in agreement. "The trick will be getting the leaders to see the value in what we're saying and move fast with it."

"Why wouldn't they?"

"Because Law of One moves like a slug. They tend to downplay everything. Look at how long it took them to finally deal with Sons of Belial."

"True. If they'd taken action ages ago, the problems now may have been avoided." He looked at Den-El. "Can there be a balance between benefit for all and individual contentment and profit?"

"Temperance," said Den-El. "Finding the balance in all we do, all we choose, how we live. It's an archetype that must be embraced, internalized." He stared off in the distance. The light of the moon shone in his eyes. "Until that happens, there will be no discipline or peace."

***

Khaluj sat at the table, scowling as he watched Aleemirin and Tujuk on the opposite side. Surya had joined them, along with Tunda, Kavi, and Dhamon. Managers of every level involved in care of the firestone sat at each side of the table in accordance to their faction association. An aide received the approval that all members were present and closed the door.

Aleemirin spoke. "I want to thank everyone for joining us today, especially on such short notice. We have several pieces of business to go over, the first being care of the firestone power crystal."

Khaluj, placed on the side with Sons of Belial, sensed tension at Aleemirin's words.

The priest from Law of One continued, "It has been brought to our attention that Sons of Belial are tuning the firestone to higher frequencies without permission from Law of One." He removed his glasses and frowned at the members across the table.

One of the managers from Sons of Belial answered. "Sir, as you know, the power needs to be adjusted sometimes due to use. We adjust a little so the people don't have their amenities fail."

"How strange," said Tujuk. "Law of One didn't do all this tuning until your group came along. Citizens didn't have a problem with power shortages, either."

"I don't know what you did before we 'came along,' as you say, but I'm sure there were adjustments made. Perhaps you didn't worry about it then, since your group had control of everything."

A manager from Law of One held up his hand. "Excuse me, it's just as Tujuk stated. We made very little changes to the firestone. Power crystals contain great strength and can handle a lot, but they have their limits."

"Excuse me, then," said the manager who spoke first. "I stand corrected."

"I thought the agreement stated clearly that any adjustments in power level had to be discussed in a proper forum and agreed upon," said Dhaman. "Am I mistaken?"

"You are correct," answer Aleemirin. "At this time Law of One is politely asking that there be no upticks in power without going through the proper channels outlined in the formal agreement we made not long ago."

"And to be fair," said Tujuk, "we also say this to Law of One, as well."

Khaluj's face held an expression of exasperation. "Good heavens. I would think that to do a job properly, there would be minute adjustments to handle the pull on the great crystal. Why can't we set some parameters and not get so nit-picky at everything?"

"Perhaps we can discuss this at the next formal meeting. It wouldn't be proper to do it here." Aleemirin gazed at Khaluj.

"Okay. Fine, let's do it at the next formal meeting. I'm simply not wanting Sons of Belial or anyone to be targeted and attacked for every little thing they do."

Tujuk rebutted. "Well, it was your group that decided to march unannounced on Poseidia making demands or else. I would wager that we Poseidians should worry about being attacked." He narrowed his eyes at the group across the table. "Don't you?"

Khaluj returned Tujuk's hot stare. He lapsed into a round of chuckles. "You know what, I don't intend to fight with anyone today on this matter. We should all want this to work out. But at some point, there has to be some level of trust."

"Then I suggest Sons of Belial behave in a manner that's worthy of trust," said Aleemirin. Khaluj scowled, clenching his fists.

The manager from Law of One spoke up again, "Maybe we the managers can have weekly meetings at our level, talk to the workers and discuss issues before tuning is done. If Law of One sees that there really needs to be adjustments made, we can do it. But I agree that clearer protocols can be added to the agreement at the next meeting."

"Good ideas," said Tujuk, nodding.

"Excellent. I think we've discussed the issue well enough for now. At this time, I would like to dismiss Sons of Belial and Law of One managers. The rest of us will remain."

Khaluj sat up straighter in his chair. A visible look of alarm filled his eyes. The aide closed the door after the last manager exited the room.

Aleemirin looked around. "Good. Now we can get on with the next point of business." He looked straight at Khaluj, who narrowed his eyes. "Khaluj, the true members from Law of One have met in an emergency meeting. We are hereby removing you from our ranks. You may return to your rightful place with Sons of Belial."

Khaluj's face went blank. He glanced at Surya. The alien prince kept his eyes focused straight ahead, avoiding eye contact.

"We have ways of finding things out, Khaluj, so don't spend time worrying about whom or what group exposed you." Tujuk glared at Khaluj.

"Hmm, I have ways of finding out things too. Like who really killed Cata-Lin." Khaluj sat back. He stared at Surya. A smirk covered his face.

Chapter Nineteen

Aleemirin folded his arms across his chest and glared at Khaluj from across the table. "Then why haven't you reported who killed Cata-Lin? Everyone is dying to know that. No pun intended."

"You're disgusting," said Khaluj. His face showed pure animosity toward his former colleague. "I went to the temple myself and did some research."

Tujuk wrinkled his brow. "Why haven't you gone to the authorities, if you know so much?"

"Ask the alien. He knows more than I do. I'm just starting to gather all my facts." Khaluj smiled and landed his gaze on Surya again.

The military leaders, Aleemirin, and Tujuk all turned in Surya's direction, stunned.

Surya kept his composure. "Don't look at me. I surely didn't kill Cata-Lin. Besides, I have a witness who can attest to my whereabouts the night the incident was supposed to have occurred."

Aleemirin smiled. "I see. Well, Khaluj, I think he got you there."

"I never insinuated or implicated Surya. But his Thing that cavorts around Poseidia is a totally different matter. I know because some . . ." Khaluj made eye contact with each man. "I just know."

"Khaluj, you're an Aryan living on a Law of One Island. You've posed as a priest of the highest-ranking order. You are a liar and an imposter, a technical threat to this island. And you want to strut around accusing citizens and their friends of killing a priestess?" Kavi spoke up, outraged.

"His friend?" Khaluj pointed to Surya laughing. "By gods of the stars, that nasty animal he owns has got you fooled."

"Get out. You're done. And get off this island, and don't ever come back." Dhamon answered Khaluj's last comment.

"Fine, I'll pack my little things and be on my way." Khaluj stood up, grabbed his notebook and pen, and left the room.

The door to the room shut with a loud thud. Everyone exchanged glances. Dhamon took a few moments to use the communication box stationed in the room. A few hushed words to an unidentified person on the other end, and he hung up.

"We're sorry about that, Your Highness," said Kavi. "I have no idea why Khaluj would carry on that way."

"Desperation and anger lead to unguarded words." Surya smiled. "He'll not cool off easily. Just know that and be prepared." He got up from his chair. "Do you mind if I have a little break?"

"Let's all break and meet back here in twenty minutes. You have something you want to share with us," said Aleemirin, looking at Surya.

"Yes. It's very important."

Surya left the meeting room and found his way to the men's bathroom down the hall. He slipped into a stall in the bathroom. He needed a few minutes of privacy.

***

An angry Khaluj left the building. His discharge from Law of One would burn in his memory forever. So would his hate. The more he thought about Surya sitting at the table, acting all innocent, the more he fumed. He turned down the sidewalk leading to his apartment.

When he reached his unit, he stared in surprise at the lock. A protective cover had been fastened in place. His key was useless. His pulse raced. Anger flared all over again. This turn of events had to do with the meeting he just left. Indignant, he charged over the sidewalk and bounded into the main office.

A woman looked up in surprise. When she saw him, her face flushed a light pink. She reached for the phone and made a quick call. "He's here."

Khaluj lorded over the apartment manager, hands on her desk. "I demand to know what . . ." His booming voice weakened. He started again. "Why is . . .?"

"Sir, are you okay?" The manager came out from behind her desk. "Do you need some water?" She moved toward a small water station at the opposite end of the office.

The priest grabbed her arm and tried again. Nothing came out of his mouth but an awful hiss. He couldn't even whisper, though he tried.

"Let me get you something to write on." She scrambled through her desk and pulled out a note pad and a writing tool. "Here, tell me what's wrong."

With trembling hands, Khaluj started writing. As the first two words made it to the paper, numbness crept over his fingers, ending at both wrists. Neither hand moved. He glanced up at the manager.

"Sir, are you having a stroke? Do I need to get a doctor?" The concern in her eyes frightened Khaluj. Was he about to die? He tried writing again, but his limp hands dragged the paper and pen off the desk, scattering them on the floor.

Two military men stepped into the office. The manager glanced up quickly, keeping a straight face.

"Excuse me, Sir." said the first man.

Khaluj turned around, horrified when he viewed the men. He moved his lips to speak. No success. His arms dangled by his side, burdened with lifeless hands.

The second man spoke. "Sir, we've been given orders to escort you off Poseidia. A plane will take you to Aryan Island. All personal possessions owned on this island are hereby confiscated and belong to the Poseidian authorities."

Each man took Khaluj by an arm and marched him out of the office. The apartment manager collapsed into her chair. "Close call," she mumbled out loud.

***

Down in the basement of the Temple of Jhanana, the Things conversed among themselves. The only time they truly relaxed is when they had their dank quarters free from servants. All eyes watched the stairs and hallway as the last servant disappeared into the depths of the temple.

Baldorn sidled up to the bars of his cage so he could talk to his friend in the next one. "Did you hear that man say that our . . .?" His voice fell silent.

"What?" The neighboring mutant moved as close to Baldorn as the cages allowed. "Tell me again."

"I was saying that the man who spoke to me . . ." Baldorn shook his head, puzzled. "I don't know what's . . ." He stamped his hooves, more frightened than irritated. Something was wrong.

His friend tried speaking back but didn't get very far. The two Things stood staring at each other in confusion. When either tried talking, nothing came out but a throaty rush of air. Whispering didn't work, either. They glanced around the basement. All eyes were on Baldorn and the mutant in the cage next to his.

From across the room, another mutant tried talking, only to find himself in the same predicament as his friends. Panic swept through the basement. How would they be able to work or talk to their masters or anyone in charge? Pure fright and confusion lit through the room, filling each mutant with utter terror.

In their dismay, they created an uproar of stamping hooves and rattling cage doors with antlers and hands. None stopped until a servant returned.

"What's going on in here?" Aam-Raan looked at the cages.

Each Thing tried talking, but the servant heard nothing, only viewing the frantic movement of mouths.

"You won't talk, eh?" The man moved by each cage, staring each mutant in the eye. "The fairies have your tongues?" Terror in their eyes worried Aam-Raan. Something didn't seem right at all. These creatures had been nothing but cooperative until now. He ran out of the room. The others had to know. How far would the spirit of Cata-Lin go to avenge her untimely death?

***

Inside the bathroom stall, Surya smiled. Done. Calling on the sacred word for silence had etherically sliced the vocal cords once and for all. Neither Khaluj nor the Things would utter a sound again until Surya undid his handiwork. Paralysis for Khaluj sweetened the deal. He remembered that sacred word at the last minute and threw it in for good measure.

Discovering how the priest learned the particulars of Cata-Lin's death took more work. Surya had focused on images of the Temple of Jhanana. He viewed hallways, servants as they walked and talked, crowds gathering to see an empty coffin, Cata-Lin covered with a sheet and resting on the cold hard table.

When he visioned a dark, dreary basement filled with caged animals, it all clicked together in his mind. The horrible truth hit his solar plexus chakra, sending a wave of nausea over him. If Cata-Lin chose higher-level Things as mating partners, these particular creatures contained enough intellect to talk about what they knew.

Loose-cannon statements by the priest had greatly unnerved Surya. With Khaluj unable to speak and write, his leadership ability had all but fallen into the abyss. Since the Things couldn't talk, no one would implicate Den-El. Satisfied for now, Surya returned to the meeting room and waited for everyone else's return.

***

Aleemirin, Tujuk, and the three military leaders convened at one end of the table with Surya at the head position. The aide had been dismissed. Surya requested that no one else be present.

"What do you have to share that is so secretive?" Aleemirin smiled, waiting for Surya to answer.

The alien made eye contact with each man. "Crystal rays can be stopped by amethyst."

The men sat in silence, staring at Surya.

"Where did you learn this?" asked Kavi.

Surya chose his words carefully. "A healer suggested the theory, only because it's a stone of toxicity, sobriety. Crystal rays could be categorized as an overabundance of energy. Amethyst, in theory, should neutralize it."

"But this is just a theory. It has not been tried or proven, right?" Tunda squinted his eyes in thought.

"Glad you asked," said Surya. "I would never have presented this if I hadn't tried it out to see if it really works."

Surya spent several minutes talking about his and Den-El's experiments in the woods. The men sat stunned as he outlined each detail. "I think we may be onto something if we can create crystalline shields of amethyst."

Dhaman said, "I'm really hoping we won't need to go that far. We all know that an all-out war between us and Sons of Belial would be utter destruction of all the islands."

"I'm hoping they won't do anything, either," said Surya, "but I really advise all of you to please think about this. Try it out for yourselves. You're proficient with crystals and what they do. Amethyst isn't necessarily in short abundance. And you can grow them too."

The men sat nodding blankly at Surya. He cocked his from side to side, studying each man's expression.

"Definitely something to think about," said Tunda.

His comment garnered obligatory nods, smiles, and weak affirmations from Kavi and Dhaman.

Surya looked at Aleemirin and Tujuk. "What do you two think?" He sincerely hoped the priests felt differently than what the military leaders did.

Aleemirin said, "I find the whole thing rather unbelievable, except that it's you who are telling us this. We know you would never lie about something so important as military defense."

Tujuk merely nodded in agreement.

"That's all I have to say," said Surya. He drummed his fingers lightly on the table.

"Wonderful. And thank you for your information. We'll discuss it among ourselves, maybe get some of our men to do a test run like you did." Dhaman smiled.

Aleemirin stood up. "I think we're done with the meeting if there is nothing else to discuss." He looked around at the small group.

Everyone shook their heads. Surya stayed still, keeping his gaze fixed on the other side of the room. Like an automaton, he got up with the others and left the building.

***

"I think the new construction looks good," said Martaam. She and Surya stood outside the newly constructed complex affected by the earthquake. "Only two people needed help out of that mess. Luckily, they were alive and taken care of. What a wonderful crew. Every bit of damage was fixed."

"That's why I sent them to you," said Surya. He kissed her on the lips.

Martaam kept her eyes on him. "Something's bothering you. I've noticed it for the past few days."

"Can we go for a walk?" He sniffed the air. The smell of the sea filled his nostrils, and he had an urge to sit near the water.

He and Martaam took a path leading to the shoreline of the canal. They sat on a vacant seat and watched the boats cut up and down the water. Every sailing vessel on Poseidia seemed to have found its way to the seafoam green waves.

"Tell me what's wrong," said Martaam, slipping her hand in his.

"I'm very scared for Poseidia and Law of One." He looked her straight in the eye.

She blinked a few times, letting his words sink in.

He continued, "I told the military leaders and the priests about the use of amethyst. They didn't say much. Didn't act like they cared, from what I could tell." Surya shook his head. "Do they not understand the grave danger they're in?"

"Surya, are you sure you're not just overly worried about everything? Sons of Belial and Law of One know the dangers of a civil war. If they're having problems with the crystal, I'm sure they're smart enough to work it out."

"Have you seen the protesters on the news and out on the island?" Surya didn't like Martaam's answers already.

"That's only a small group of people. They just want to share how they feel. I don't necessarily disagree with them, but I can't think of anything else we could have done, except give Sons of Belial a chance." Martaam cast her gaze to the ground. Her lips turned down in sadness.

"True, but one can still be cautious, can't they? What Den-El and I learned is extremely valuable. Why wouldn't they have jumped at the knowledge, be ready to try it out? Isn't that what the military is supposed to do?" Surya glanced up, embarrassed. A couple passed by, staring at him with interest. He didn't realize how loud his voice had risen.

"You may be getting worked up for nothing. And you don't know that your advice won't be taken." Martaam squeezed his hand. "You know how government works. It takes forever for them to move on anything."

Surya nodded, looking out on the water. Discussing this subject any more would be pointless. Nobody seemed to understand that forever meant sure danger. Only Sons of Belial seemed intent on moving in accordance to their plans. Martaam's way of thinking fell in line with her uncle's and the military heads. After another hour, he and Martaam walked back home.

***

The plane ride back to Aryan Island had been the longest in his life. Khaluj sat in his condo steeped in the darkest despair he'd ever felt. The military of Poseidia had at least done a kindness in requesting that he receive help as soon as possible. Rhaneen was on his way over.

How would he explain all this to his vice commander, who would no doubt end up being the commander? If he couldn't talk or even write, he couldn't lead. Cata-Lin's precious notebook lay locked away in his apartment on Poseidia. What would happen with all his possessions? Out of all he had there, the notebook is what he wanted most of all right now.

"Khaluj?" Rhaneen's voice sounded from the hallway. The door shut. Footsteps sounded from the marble floor. "There you are." The vice commander sat down next to Khaluj, placing a hand on his shoulder. "Can you say anything at all? Write?"

The priest shook his head. He tried uttering a word, but all that came out was the infernal hiss. He lifted an arm, but the hand wouldn't move no matter how hard he tried.

"I simply can't believe this. And you can't tell me anything about it, can you?" Pure dismay covered Rhaneen's face.

Khaluj shook his head, lifting his arms in frustration.

"You're going to need a helper, if you can't move your hands."

The two men sat staring at each other. Khaluj had only one last option. Telepathy. The problem, no one in his inner circle practiced the metaphysical arts to the degree he did. Aryan priests were no match for the likes of Aleemirin and Tujuk. And they were nothing compared to their ancestors.

But some skill would be better than nothing. If he could telepath with Rhaneen, he might stand a chance of at least sharing what he discovered in Cata-Lin's notebook.

He looked at Rhaneen and concentrated with all his might, hoping there might be some mental connection. It would be his last attempt to make a difference. That infernal alien had finally gotten the better of him.

Rhaneen broke the silence. "Did you hurt yourself in any way, become suddenly ill?"

Khaluj shook his head.

"Did this all come on suddenly and with no explanation?"

Khaluj nodded, smiling a little. At least his vice commander was trying to make sense of everything.

Rhaneen's eyes brightened. "Do you think the alien had anything to do with it?"

Khaluj sank back on the sofa, nodding. He tapped on Rhaneen's leg with his arm for more emphasis.

The vice commander continued. "Did you have any meetings at all while you were on Poseidia?"

Khaluj nodded.

"Did the condition you're in now happen after the meeting?"

Khaluj tapped his arm against Rhannen, nodding emphatically.

Rhaneen frowned. "Oh, boy. You know something, and you're being silenced by that hateful alien." He snapped a finger and looked at his colleague. "If you can't write with your hand, you can surely try another way."

He got up from the sofa and walked to Khaluj's office, where he located some paper, a thin stylus, and a bottle of thick colored liquid.

"This will have to do," mumbled Rhaneen. He returned to the living room and motioned for Khaluj to follow him to a table. "I'll put this in your mouth after I've dipped one end in the bottle. At least give me something to go on."

Khaluj nodded and opened his mouth for the stylus. On the paper, he wrote out the word "Amethyst" in dark, awkward letters.

Rhaneen looked down and scratched his head. "I don't understand. What's so special about amethyst?" He dipped the stylus in the bottle once again and gave it back to the priest.

In another set of rumply letters, Khaluj wrote out the words using his mouth. Stop. Crystal. Rays.

Looking down at the words, Rhaneen smiled. "Very clever. Do you know for sure if this really works, or are you being played for a fool?"

Khaluj shook his head.

"Which is it?"

The priest wrote another two words. Try. Experiment.

Rhaneen's smile faded. "We don't have time for that." His face brightened a little. "Besides, I'm not sure it's even necessary to go through all that work. Sons of Belial have a plan." He patted Khaluj on the back.

Kaluj stared up at his vice commander, confused.

"Let me handle this, my friend. Right now we don't tell anyone what's happened. It will make us look weak. I'll get someone to stay with you who can keep a secret."

The priest watched in despair as Rhaneen walked out the door. If he couldn't get his second in command and Sons of Belial to explore what he'd so desperately sought to find out from Cata-Lin, their world could be destroyed. All their ambitions would sink like the land masses during Atlantis's first two destructions.

What did his friend mean by "let me handle it?" A chill shot down his spine. He didn't want any decisions coming to fruition unless he gave the command. But he couldn't speak. He could barely write and looked like an absolute fool doing it.

Khaluj sat down on the sofa. For the first time in years, he cried harder than he'd ever done before.

***

Rhaneen sat with his council members in one of the buildings on Meruvia. A grim expression covered his face. Why did it not totally surprise him that newscasters would tell of the traitorous Law of One priest who was really the leader of Sons of Belial? What happened to loyalty and wanting to protect Aryan leaders and citizens?

He watched the early morning news before the meeting, and much to his chagrin, heard all about Khaluj being ousted out of Law of One, led out of his home on Poseidia, and escorted back to Aryan cloaked in shame and disgrace.

The news had leaked all the way from Poseidia to Aryan. Reporters had snatched up the tidbit like hungry vultures. In Rhaneen's mind, the last thing people on the island needed to hear was morose news involving their top man in charge. Worse, council members in the room with him had jumped on the topic, chattering in animated conversations.

"Let's call the meeting to order, please." Rhaneen pounded his gavel for attention.

All talking stopped. Last-minute stragglers quickly found their assigned places at the table.

"I guess there's no need to explain the empty seat." He nodded toward Khaluj's chair.

Nobody said a word but looked with interest at the vice commander.

One member raised his hand. "I'll go ahead and ask the obvious. Will our esteemed leader continue in his rightful position on Aryan?"

Mumbling filled the room. Men leaned over and whispered among themselves. The pounding of the gavel sounded.

Rhaneen answered. "Right now we want to give our leading commander some breathing room, a little privacy until the dust storm settles." He displayed a fake smile of reassurance. "So let's get on with this meeting."

The talking ceased.

"In case you haven't heard, Law of One is already expressing dissatisfaction with our merger in caring for the firestone. They're making demands, watching everything we do, stifling our work. Basically, they're still in control. There is no true sharing of anything, no discussion of ideas. No partnership of any kind. All we get is grumbling and complaints."

"Are we not able to bring any ideas to the table?" The same man who had asked about Khaluj spoke again.

"No." Rhaneen sat back in his chair, relaxing somewhat. "It was our hope that Law of One would loosen up so there could be dialogue, a discussion about what both sides could do to make the islands better. Nothing is happening. I don't sense there is any opening up where that group is concerned."

Another man raised his hand and asked, "Wouldn't it be better if Sons of Belial focused on our agenda, and Law of One could play it our way, or . . .? You know." He tilted his head from side to side in mock thought. "That's been our goal all along. I don't see why we need to stall and play this silly game anymore."

"My friend, I'm glad you said something. Good point, actually." Rhaneen's lips pulled back into a toothy smile. "We've been prepared a long time for action. Time is not our friend in this instant. Action will be our ally always into perpetuity."

Chapter Twenty

Surya lay in a deep sleep with Martaam spooned against him. After a round of intense, passionate love-making, the two had snuggled together in the after-glow his body emitted each time they finished. Their slumber ended with a series of loud explosions outside. Surya bolted upright, eyes wide. His heart pounded in his chest. Martaam stirred and sat up next to him.

"What was that?" she mumbled.

Another explosion, one with such force and so close the apartment shook.

"It can't be another earthquake, could it?" Martaam threw off the covers and rushed to the window. "I'm not seeing anything."

Outside in the hallway, Da-Ina barked and growled as Den-El's hooves clattered against the wooden floor.

"Let's go," said Surya. He and Martaam threw on some clothes and left the room.

They met up with Den-El at the front door.

"Something's happening, and it's not good. I feel it," said Den-El. His voice sounded off in full-blown panic. With trembling hands, he wiped his brow. "I knew something was going to happen. I felt it in my gut."

"Why didn't you share it, then?" asked Surya, irritated. "Maybe we could have warned somebody."

"Do we even know what it is?" Martaam barely finished her question when another boom rocked the building. She let out a screech and grabbed Surya's arm.

Den-El opened the door and he and Da-Ina stepped outside. "Oh, no," he cried out. "You have to see this."

Surya and Martaam rushed outside to the courtyard where a crowd of tenants had gathered. Everyone pointed to the sky. The sound of plane engines roared above. Another explosion not far from Vardhase.

Den-El tightened his grip on Da-Ina's leash and bolted toward the street. Martaam and Surya followed. In the distance, flames leapt from businesses and homes. As Surya focused his eyes more, it appeared that The Atlan had been hit. Flames roared from that direction, and an acrid smell of smoke and ash floated and wafted their direction.

Voices cried out. Screams echoed through the night air. Ash and smoke gathered in thick clouds, choking people as they ran. Surya squeezed Martaam's hand. The sight of people bleeding unnerved him. Many held broken arms close to their bodies. Others limped as friends, neighbors, and strangers helped them to safety.

Children screamed, crying out for their parents. Men and women tried to stop bleeding from vicious wounds by holding their hands over affected areas. Many asked for help as people passed by.

Families wept in despair at destroyed homes. Business owners ran toward their shops to salvage what was left of their wares or to see if their livelihood still stood. Dogs barked and howled, rounding out human shouts of pain and indignation. Such a sight upset Surya. He blinked back tears and breathed in the best he could.

Den-El strode up to Surya and Martaam. Da-Ina had exhausted herself and plopped down by her master's hooves. "I think Poseidia's being attacked. I've seen tons of planes in the sky. Bombs are being dropped."

A man passed by as Den-El spoke his last comment. He shouted out, "We're being invaded in the streets. The Aryans have those horrid guns." When another explosion blasted two streets over, he took off running fast.

"We need to get back in the apartment," said Martaam. She tugged on Surya's arm and ran. Surya took off with Den-El and Da-Ina following close behind.

"What if we're hit?" asked Den-El. He closed the apartment door when everyone ran inside.

"We'll just have to deal with it," answered Surya. "Being out there isn't any safer, especially if what that man said is true." He walked to the communication box and pressed the numbers for Aleemirin and Tujuk. "I want to know if your uncle is okay."

Martaam watched in silence. Surya tapped his foot, waiting for an answer. He let out a huff and ended the call.

"Maybe they went outside to see what was going on." Martaam's face had grown ashen.

"Or maybe Sadarma was hit," said Den-El.

A loud knock thundered from the door. Den-El ran and jerked it open. "Or maybe they're here." He motioned Aleemirin and Tujuk into the living room.

"Uncle." Martaam ran to Aleemirin and threw her arms around him. "How is it at your place?" She took the trembling Tujuk in her arms and squeezed him close, kissing his cheek.

"We barely got out," said Aleemirin in a cracked voice. "Just as we made it to the main sidewalk, our unit collapsed. We came here to see how you were."

"This whole land ring seems to be nothing but fire and smoke," said Surya. He looked at the AudioView and twisted a knob. Everyone in the room found a seat on the sofa. Martaam dragged chairs from the dining table so her uncle and Tujuk could sit down.

The screen lit up, one side showing the attractive Andana from Lomasa News.

"We are learning that Poseidia has just been hit. The invasion has been blamed on the Aryans, who are confirming the attacks. Juleena, what are you seeing out there on the land rings? Can you tell us more about what is happening?"

The other side of the screen showed Juleena, composed and pretty, though her voice rang out with urgency. "Andana, the sights here are ones you would see in your worst nightmares. Buildings destroyed. Business that once stood are now nothing but rubble and ashes. Homes have been leveled to their foundations."

The bottom of the screen showed areas of the land rings where structures lay in a heap. In the back ground, sirens wailed.

"What about casualties? Are there many people hurt or surviving?" asked Andana. Her face stiffened with concern.

"We don't have an actual count, but I'm hearing that there have been several deaths. There are many more injuries, broken limbs, people hit with debris. There are several medical checkpoints set up or will be set up so the injured can receive attention from our healers and physicians."

A streak of white light lit up behind Juleena, followed by a loud boom. She jumped and looked behind her. "It looks like this could go on and shows no signs of stopping. Worse, Aryan military are running through the streets shooting at our people with crystal ray guns, the fiercest of ammunition."

"Thank you for the update, Juleena. Please be safe out there." Andana focused directly on the camera. "More when we come back."

Surya turned down the AudioView.

Aleemirin scowled. "So those nasty, ruthless Aryans decided to hit first." He ran his fingers through his hair and stared at the ground. "It wasn't enough that we let them help care for the firestone. They wanted more." He looked around at everyone. "They want control of all the islands. You know that, don't you?"

"Can we not contact Dhaman, Kavi, or Tunda?" Surya spoke up.

"They need to be called," said Den-El. "I would think they're mobilizing. Or they should be."

"Let's make a call," said Tujuk.

Martaam jumped up from the sofa and led Aleemirin to the communication box. In seconds the priest had a voice on the other end of the line.

"Aleemirin, Law of One, speaking. I need to talk with the highest in command . . . Dhaman? Are your men ready? We will not go down without a fight. This island and our people are being bludgeoned." He listened for several seconds, nodding as Dhaman spoke. "I see. Good. So Kavi and Tunda are all set. Good to know. Get the ammunition ready. They want war, we'll give it right back to them." Aleemirin ended the call and returned the receiver back in its proper place.

"What's the update?" asked Surya, standing up from the sofa.

"All hands are on deck. Kavi and his fleet are intercepting Aryan ships, blowing them to smithereens. Tunda has his airships already blasting Aryan Island with everything we have." He looked up at Surya. "Sons of Belial are getting a taste of their own medicine."

"Any chance of using amethyst shields? You know. To protect your military. Something like that." Den-El's face held a sarcastic grin His hands moved in exaggerated emphasis as spoke. Surya narrowed his eyes but glanced back at Aleemirin and Tujuk.

The priests stood with blank looks on their faces.

Den-El let out a huff. "Not meaning any disrespect, but it would have been nice for the military to have had that special kind of protection. Crystal rays are brutal. The shields would have given them a better edge."

"Yes," said Tujuk. "But I think everything happened so fast." He cast his gaze to the ground.

Martaam and Surya's eyes met. She subtly shook her head. "Uncle, I have some rooms in the living quarters above the main office. You and Tujuk can stay there until you have your place back in order." She kissed Surya and moved toward her uncle.

"Or we all could stay here," said Surya.

Den-El's face reddened. He pursed his lips together in defiance. Surya shot him a death look.

"We're not that far, and only a call away." Martaam led Aleemirin and Tujuk to the door. I'm hoping they're done for the night."

Surya nodded. His face stiffened with worry. He knew war kept going until the last bullet was fired, the last ship lay on the bottom of the ocean, and the last plane lay crumpled on the ground. The Aryans were getting warmed up.

✳✳✳

Down from Vardhase and Sadarma apartments, Orubis Way lay in ruins. Cata-Lin's notebook ended up as ashes and soot. On the land core, the Temple of Jhanana stood with one side caved in, placing the rest of the structure at great risk of collapsing completely. Tucked down in the basement, away from chaos, staff and the Things quaked in silence. None knew how long anyone or anything would hold out, much less survive. In the marble vaults, Cata-Lin's ashes lay at peace and undisturbed in a golden urn.

✳✳✳

Aryan Island reflected a perfect mirror image of Poseidia. Its once-proud buildings lay scattered from one side to the other. Large sink holes and gashes filled the streets. Glass shards lined the sidewalks. Merchandise lay charred and smoldering on shelves or inside display cases, if they hadn't been incinerated entirely.

People filled the medical facilities. Doctors treated one after the other, switching out with other practitioners after twelve-hour shifts. People who had lost their homes roomed with any family or strangers who would allow it once the hotels and shelters filled up. Those with no resources huddled among the rubbish.

Inside his condo, Khaluj and Rhaneen had holed up. Their prayers for safety had been answered, but neither knew how much longer luck would hold out. Khaluj was half-way through a second bottle of wine. He'd dispensed with a glass and simply drank from the top. Rhaneen had mixed the stiffest drinks he could choke down.

Khaluj balanced his bottle on one knee and glared at his vice commander. He shook his head, scowling more.

"What?" said Rhaneen. He took a quick sip of his drink and let out a mouthful of air. The strong taste hitting his tongue slowly lessened with each gulp. "We had no choice. The game-playing was wearing us out."

The priest contorted his face in frustration.

"You're still not getting your voice and hands back are you?" Rhaneen stared at Khaluj.

Khaluj shook his head. Nothing Surya had taken away returned.

"We'll fix those aliens once and for all." Rhaneen wagged a finger at Khaluj. "Law of One may think they've retaliated and we're all running scared. But those pushovers have another thing coming."

The communication box chimed. Both men sat up, surprised.

"Imagine that," said Rhaneen. He got up from the sofa. "I'm surprised we have service."

The priest sank back on the sofa. Never had he felt so powerless and alone. Decisions were being made without his input. Rhaneen had been too willing to step into the top commanding position. Life had left and continued without him, barely considering his existence.

He wished that Sons of Belial had not attacked Poseidia in the manner they did. A full-on war should have been avoided or at least delayed. Caretakers for the crystal could have toned it down a bit with tuning up the firestone. Negotiations could have been made. Maybe?

Khaluj reflected on history. His faction had started out thousands of years ago bold, determined, full of creativity and ideas bursting forth. Forcing Law of One into a partnership almost seemed like begging, in retrospect. The whole deal was doomed from the outset. But he had no one to blame but himself.

He'd given the okay to march on Poseidia that fateful night. Could he blame Rhaneen for wearing thin on patience and blasting Poseidia to the seventh dimension? Sons of Belial were a resourceful group. They surely could have come up with a power crystal as great as the one standing on Poseidia or grown their own crystals.

But who was he kidding? Poseidia had the best of everything, from a wealth of minerals and stones, to metals and magnetic grids beneath the earth. It's what sustained that island, filling it with unquenchable power. Meanwhile, Aryan seemed to flounder, always a bit behind. Always. Never quite matching up to par.

That knowledge hurt Khaluj's heart. He loved Atlantis and its rich history, but he loved power and wealth more. With a war that had been started, everything would soon lay in ruins, if not perish altogether. He knew it, felt it in his core. The thought frightened him. It saddened him most of all.

The priest closed his eyes. From his knee, the wine bottle toppled to the floor, sloshing out its liquid all over a fine carpet beneath. Khaluj barely heard Rhaneen's voice in his ear or the door shut in the hallway.

***

Den-El slipped out of the apartment, Da-Ina's leash tightly in hand. Together they walked the streets, stepping over debris and chunks of buildings that had crumbled. The streets were almost unrecognizable. He stopped a moment to gather his bearings and find a landmark so he could return home.

He fingered the amethyst stone around his neck. No way would he travel without it. Tugging Da-Ina's leash, he continued down the sidewalk toward The Atlan. To his horror when he arrived, the once beautiful plaza lay collapsed on its foundation. Shop windows lay shattered on the ground.

Some of the business owners who had made it here talked in worried tones as they picked up items and tossed them aside. Several of the women wept as they rummaged through what was once practically their second home. For the first time, something stirred inside Den-El. The human condition.

Emotion, pain, fear, and despair hit him with no mercy. The resulting jolt to the heart chakra nearly bowled him over. Since when did he care about humans? Surya obviously did. That had been a weakness he'd kindly overlooked in his best friend. But his beloved prince had a heart for humans since the day he saw Martaam through the lens.

A monster had been loosened. How would he and Surya stop it? Could they? Whole wars had been fought in other galaxies. Rarely did any of the inhabitants have sufficient means to halt a series of events dead in its tracks. One thought led to an action, leading to another.

That was the law of nature, the cosmos. A set stage, action, reaction. And all over again. Some beings moved through those steps with more foresight and thought than others. Every being had its reason for certain behaviors, from the mighty Arcturians and Pleiadians to the lowliest of the Reptilians and Trantaloids.

Da-Ina tugged on her leash. Den-El walked away from The Atlan and wound his way carefully toward the canal. The boat he drove to see Cata-Lin still remained tied to the dock where he last left it. Da-Ina pulled harder, moving in the direction of the boat.

"Do we go on a ride, girl?" said Den-El.

Da-Ina barked and moved again.

Den-El carefully boarded the boat, taking Da-Ina with him. After untying the craft, he seated himself in the driver's cockpit and sailed out into the canal. Poseidia had been attacked all over, from what he could tell. Navigating the central canal, he sailed to the different land rings.

The sights sickened him. Da-Ina whimpered as she watched, her nose twitching more than usual. Sons of Belial would strike again. Den-El knew this for certain. The first time was a warm-up. He opened the throttle and headed to the land core. Had the healing centers and temples been hit?

The smell of smoke mixed with the salty sea air. Grey covered the island. Den-El, along with other sailors, sped up the main channel, heading to the center. When he reached a spare dock, he turned off the motor and tied down the boat.

"Let's see what's happened, Da-Ina." He placed her on the dock and disembarked the boat.

Den-El's heart sank. Everywhere he looked, spirals of smoke filled the air. Main sidewalks lay in chunks, hindering movement from one place to another. Several of the healing temples appeared mostly intact. Throngs of people surrounded the buildings. Were there enough doctors and healers? He grew worried for the living.

When he looked over at the Temple of Poseidon, his spine chilled. The exterior golden wall stood blackened and cracked. Parts of it had melted and crumpled.

A gate stood ajar. He walked over and gently pushed it open. Inside, much of the silver interior wall had disintegrated. The floor of the courtyard had been blown out. Den-El's mouth went dry as he stepped carefully over the dirt and rubble, side-stepping his way deeper into the temple.

The great golden statue of the god himself lay melted and tilted to one side. While parts of the horses, sea nymphs, and dolphins of the statue remained, the rest had been blasted away. Enormous holes dotted the roof. Sky light poured through, lighting up the room with an eerie glow.

Something moved near the door of the kirtana. Den-El froze. Da-Ina barked and lurched forward, letting out a loud yelp when Den-El jerked her back. He touched the amethyst stone around his neck and uttered a mantra. A crystalline wall of purple wrapped around him and Da-Ina.

"Who's there? Show yourself." Den-El walked toward the door. The shield moved with him.

A figure stepped out from the shadows. From the look of the uniform, an Aryan military man. He held a large gun in his hand.

Den-El stood still. Da-Ina growled. "Shh." He pulled his pet closer. "Who else is with you, soldier?"

The man stepped closer into the light. His height rose to nearly seven feet tall. He grinned as he moved slowly toward Den-El. "It appears no one is with you," said the man. "Who would let a Thing run loose? Or perhaps you're without family?"

"I asked who else is with you?" Den-El called the man's bluff and stepped forward.

"I could kill a lowly Thing such as you, especially for your disrespect," said the man. "But we need more labor to help our armies. We've been hit too." He walked a few more paces.

"And I could kill a beastly Aryan such as you, especially since I'm no ordinary Thing." Den-El's lips pulled into a wide smile.

A red shot flared across the temple space. The soldier had fired off his gun. The rays hit the amethyst crystalline shield and sizzled into oblivion. It was the after-shock that sent a rumble through the building as the remnants of the rays bounced off and hit the ground.

What was left of the golden statue of Poseidon crashed to the ground. More of the roof spilled down. The Aryan backed off, lowering his gun. He stood in silence.

"What was it you said about killing me?" Den-El widened his stance.

In a flood of anger, the Aryan raised his gun. Den-El uttered the sacred word and dissipated his shield. A hot bolt of lightning released from his hand, squarely knocking the gun out of his enemy's. The man's eyes widened with fear. Just as he looked toward his gun, he let out a horrid scream. His other hand burned in hot flames.

"Good enough for you, Sir?" said Den-El. Da-Ina jumped away and ran toward the man, barking.

The soldier positioned himself to strike Da-Ina with his foot. Den-El shot out another bolt, sending his opponent toppling to the ground. He walked over and stared down.

"The less we have of these, the better." Den-El pointed his finger at the crystal ray gun, incinerating it into useless pile of ash. He turned and blew with great force on the man, extinguishing the last flickers of fire.

"I think we've had enough fire and smoke around here. Don't you think, girl?"

Da-Ina growled and turned toward the door of the kirtana.

Den-El walked slowly. The sparring between him and the Aryan soldier wasn't a quiet one. If there were others of his company, they would be hiding out somewhere in this temple. He placed an ear against the door, listening with deep concentration.

Closing his eyes, he tuned in with the ether. An image appeared before him. Dark, quiet. Something sinister filled the space behind the kirtana, the back hallways, and rooms of the temple.

Den-El touched his amethyst stone. It might have some strength left in it. The crystalline shield morphed in place around him.

He threw open the door and stepped inside. His eyes darted around. All clear. Sliding his body against the walls, Den-El stepped his way to the door behind the altar, the one used by priests after a ceremony. A map of the space he was about to enter maintained an imprint in his mind.

Carefully, he pushed the door open and stepped into a long hall. Nobody. He frowned. Something had changed since his impression from the ether. Fast. The hallway matched the length of the kirtana. Enemy soldiers could have accessed other parts of the temple from any number of rooms that he couldn't see readily. It also meant that the enemy could backtrack to his current location.

Da-Ina barked. Den-El stiffened in his tracks. He heard talking in the kirtana. Someone tossed some rubble because he heard cracking sounds when it hit the floor. In his gut, he knew men surrounded him, and they weren't Poseidian military. He had a decision to make. Live or die by it.

Den-El shut off his amethyst shield, burst back through the door from which he came, and unleashed a torrent of white gyrating veins throughout the kirtana. The room lit up like the lights during an ancient solstice celebration. Den-El smiled.

"That should do it," said Den-El. Sadly, the action brought down much of the decor that had made up the room. On the bright side, several Aryan soldiers lay charred to the bone, along with their incinerated ray guns. "At least they won't harm more innocent people."

A loud crash sounded from outside the kirtana. Den-El climbed through ash, bodies, and collapsed benches. He made his way to the room where Poseidon's statue stood. His adrenalin rushed like it never had before. Holding out his hands, he fired off a powerful bolt at the figure backlit from the first bright rays of sun.

The ball of fire crashed against a barrier and sizzled out. Den-El braced himself. At once he knew what had happened. The room shuddered, and one side of the wall fell back in a rough crash.

A faint purple crystalline form moved in his direction. Den-El let out a sigh of relief. Da-Ina broke free from her master and ran toward Surya.

"I didn't even recognize you," said Den-El. He embraced Surya when the prince reached his side.

"Good thing I had my shield up," said Surya with a half-grin spreading across his face. "You would have cooked me into a dusty pile."

"I just roasted some Aryans back there." Den-El angled his head toward the kirtana door.

"And I finished off what I hope is the last one. Here, anyway." He pointed to a body several feet away from the first one Den-El hit. "That group was so close." Surya's eyes darted around. "We're in hot danger. Aryans hiding and attacking everywhere. People with no way of defending themselves. Poseidian soldiers are doing their best."

"Why did you come here?" Den-El asked.

"Why did you?"

Den-El grimaced. "I had to see what was going on, what needed to be done."

"Me too. And I know what needs to be done." Surya wrapped his arm around Den-El's shoulder, and the two picked their way out of the ruins of Poseidon's Temple.

"Where are we going?" Den-El asked.

Surya guided the way toward Martaam's healing school.

"Martaam got the call."

Den-El looked at Surya, confused.

"Her instructors called her and said all healers must report for duty, even students."

"That's pretty bad when you're asking students to help." Den-El Shielded the sun from his eyes.

"I want to protect the healing facilities better."

"How would we even begin to do that?"

"If we could find an amethyst big enough to form a shield over a wide area, that would do it, I think." Surya glanced at Den-El.

"And the problem would be when its capacity is maxed out. Our shields maxed out at some point. Enough ammunition drops, the whole thing will go."

Surya groaned. "We can't win, can we?"

Den-El turned his friend around so they faced each other head on. "In the ideal world, it wouldn't matter. There should be no war, remember?"

"There's always been war, Den-El. Until you eradicate evil out of the entire universe, things like this will happen."

"And there you go." Den-El tapped Surya on the shoulder. "None of this matters. We do the best we can and keep moving." He paused. "Any chance of you and I just getting out of here and let these humans blast themselves away? We cannot help them."

Surya grew quiet as he surveyed the buildings and people surrounding them. He looked at his friend. "Just a little longer."

Den-El's face showed exasperation, and he shook his head. Saying nothing more, he followed Surya to Martaam's building.

It took several minutes pushing through the crowd before Surya and Den-El made it inside. Da-Ina finally had to be carried or risk being stepped on and injured. When people saw her, they patted her on the head. The look of her, the feel of her fur, brought people momentary relief.

Surya led the way up to Martaam's healing room, gently excusing himself as he pushed through the crowd. People who needed less emergent care had lined the hallways, waiting for the next available healer. He used her pass code and entered her space.

He spoke to Den-El. "We'll be doing healing work in here. Between the two of us, I think we can move faster than anyone downstairs.

"Downstairs?" Den-El stood by the healing table.

"According to Martaam, the lecture halls and any other room they can use, have been turned into healing areas. As you can see, our hallway looks like the rest of the floors above us."

Den-El shook his head. "It's going to be a long day. And I don't have a table."

"Use her chair. Some people can sit." Surya pulled out the chair and placed it next to the door of the crystal tunnel. "If we can do two at a time, that will help."

"Okay." Den-El stationed himself by the tiny door. Out of curiosity, he opened it. "That's helpful. I'll leave it open."

"Can't hurt." Surya smiled. "Ready? Oh, you can use any stones from her cabinet. She has all kinds of things in there." He pointed in the direction.

"Good to know." Den-El reached over and opened a drawer. "Ready when you are."

Surya stepped out in the hallway. "I can help two people in here."

Two people, a man and woman entered. Both had their wounds bandaged. Because they weren't on the verge of death, the two had been discharged from the main care areas and sent to this area for the remainder of their treatment.

The woman stared at Den-El, confused.

"Please, have a seat, good lady," said Den-El, wearing his warmest smile. He motioned to the chair.

"But you're a . . ."

Den-El's ears drooped at her comment, and the smile dissipated. In the most reassuring voice he could muster, he said, "I promise you that I and my partner are the best you will ever find on the island."

Da-Ina crept up to the lady and stood, placing her paws on the woman's leg. On impulse, Den-El grasped the lady's good hand and pulled her into the chair. She let out a shout.

"You'll be fine," said Den-El. Without another word, he examined the lady's other hand. It and the whole arm had been bandaged. Blood had seeped through some of the cloth strips. He gently removed all of it, rolling it into a tidy ball and placing it on the floor. He and Surya would need proper receptacles.

Sight of the charred skin and exposed bones and tendons nearly sickened him, and he struggled to keep from vomiting. Healing would have been so much easier on Ontarus 9. If he were home, he wouldn't be engaged in a situation like this. But accidents did happen at times. Even there.

Closing his eyes, he centered himself and uttered the healing mantra as he held his hands over an arm and hand with second and third-degree burns. To his dismay, there were parts he could not heal totally. Where flesh and bone had truly been killed away, there would remain stumps and hollowed areas.

Den-El struggled with having to go with the flow of nature. Even as an alien with extraordinary healing skills, he had to work with laws of nature in the dimension in which he found himself.

Like Surya, he called on the etheric side of himself, using those hands to remove dead bone and flesh, clearing it all away with a strong will of the mind and connection with spirit. Skin quickly regenerated and grew together, covering soft tissue and remaining bones.

The woman would not have to go through the pain of debridement sessions and skin grafting. Den-El took care of all that work in the present moment, leaving her pain free and wounds healed.

"We're done," he whispered.

The woman, who had dozed while he worked, looked up at him and over to her arm. She sat up straight, gazing it, bewildered.

"You've pretty much healed everything. I don't feel any pain, either."

"You're still missing a couple of fingers, and some places were beyond repair. But you're pretty much in working order." Den-El smiled and helped her up.

The man who came in with her waited patiently on the table. Surya had just finished healing a deep gash that had been quickly stitched together. He smiled at the woman. "See, no scars or anything." He shook Surya's hand and left.

"Now for the next two," said Surya.

Down the hall, someone shouted. Surya stepped out. A man had crumpled over, hands over his abdominal area. He gasped in pain.

"Bring him here," shouted Surya. People stepped back while two other men guided the sick man forward. Surya helped them place the man on the healing table. "I've got it from here. Thank you."

Den-El stepped away from the chair. "He's in bad shape. Sir, can you tell us what's wrong?"

The man's eyes started glassing over. "I was hit in the stomach. Had some internal injuries. They operated. I think something has happened. Don't know what." He gasped and sank back on the table, taking short shallow breaths.

Surya trained his focus on the man's etheric coordinates. Using the eyes of spirit, he found his way into the man's body. A lacerated liver and lower part of the stomach. Body contents had leaked out where it didn't belong. The man was about to die.

With higher dimension hands, Surya reached in, sealing the stomach with one hand while closing off the liver with the other. As he concentrated and guided each step with tuned-in will, flesh knitted back together; blood vessels joined and settled in place.

With the leaking stopped, Surya absorbed all the fluid in the man's abdominal cavity, getting rid of every drop that didn't belong there. The last step, he reduced the swelling, using etheric hands to pull heat away from tissue. Organs settled back to normal.

Den-El stood close by, sending light and strength to the man so his spirit would not slip away. The man's breathing gradually returned to normal. He opened his eyes, showing a former spark of life.

"Feel better?" Surya spoke softly.

"I think so. I don't feel like I'm about to die. I guess that's a good thing," said the man, smiling.

"Can you make it back home?" Surya helped his patient up.

The man took a deep breath. Color had returned to his face. "I think so. Thank you so much." He shook Surya and Den-El's hands and left the room.

"Oh, creator almighty." Den-El sank into the chair. "That was a close call."

"If we hadn't been here to help that man, he would have died," said Surya. A grim look spread across his face.

"Ready for another round?" said Den-El grinning. "I honestly don't think it can get much worse than what we just dealt with."

"I think you're right." Surya smiled and stepped out in the hall. "I'll take two people in here."

Chapter Twenty One

Twenty-four hours later Surya and Den-El climbed into the boat docked on the land core. Martaam, leading Da-Ina, joined them. She had worked in the main care centers downstairs. She slumped into a seat, watching Den-El untie the boat.

"I still can't believe he stole this," said Surya. He shook his head and sat down beside Martaam.

"I can't believe someone hasn't confiscated it yet." She rested her head against Surya's shoulder and closed her eyes, only to open them up again.

"What's wrong?" asked Surya.

Martaam didn't say anything but rushed to the side of the boat. In one big heave, she vomited. Surya watched in distress. He rushed from the seat and ran to her side.

"You're sick. Did all this work and seeing everyone upset you?" He wrapped an arm around her, hugging her close.

"Maybe?" she stared at the ground, catching her breath. "I've been going non-stop, so maybe that's it."

Surya nodded. We'll be home soon. He led her back to the seat. Den-El turned on the engine and guided the boat into the open canal. Several yards away a large ship sailed into view. From the style and flag flying, Surya determined it was an Aryan ship. Here in the middle of the concentric rings?

Alarmed, he ran to the cockpit. "Do you see that?"

"Yes, and I don't like it. Now they're taking control of the waterways." Den-El stopped the boat. "I don't want to go any closer." He looked up at Surya. "The problem is, even if I can get us out of the main canal and into the open sea, we're not equipped to stay out there long."

"And staying here, we'll simply be going in circles, literally, no matter which ring we take." Surya grimaced.

"Does Kavi have his ships patrolling the canals?"

Surya shaded his eyes from the sun. "I would think so, but we tend to forget about them. There's only one way in."

"Well, our friends over there found it." Den-El's face and voice displayed his sarcasm.

An explosion echoed through the air. Surya and Den-El watch in horror, as they saw buildings on the land ring burst into a dusty cloud. Three seconds later, more buildings fell, reduced to rubble. All water craft sailing the canal stopped. A strange silence filled the air, with nothing but the rush of water and wind.

"Guide us closer," said Surya, tapping Den-El on the shoulder.

Den-El did as instructed, stopping when Surya gave the order.

Martaam stood in the doorway. "What are we going to do?"

"Taking care of it right now." Surya slipped past Martaam and headed to the upper deck. "Where is Kavi's team?" he mumbled out loud to himself.

Surya eyed the Aryan ship, scrutinizing the size. Definitely smaller than the bigger ones that most likely surrounded Poseidia. If one could slip into the concentric rings, others could too. How was the Poseidian fleet holding up? The prospects frightened him.

He reached out both hands, focused his thoughts, and moved his lips for the words. Two huge bolts sailed across the water, hitting the Aryan ship in separate places. Displaced chunks of metal flew up in the air, followed by more. Surya had let loose another round of bolts.

The ship immediately listed to one side, toppling over into the water. Within minutes, the ship sank to the bottom of the canal. "There, that should stall them a little," said Surya. He returned to Den-El. "Take us to the main entrance."

"To do what?" Den-El stared up at his friend with an incredulous look. "We can't fight all of Aryan."

"Just do it," said Surya in a commanding tone.

Disgusted, Den-El steered the boat to the main canal line and headed straight. Behind them sped a boat of similar size. As Den-El guided his craft toward the entrance to the rings, Surya viewed a fleet of ships belonging to Poseidia.

"They've finally arrived," said Surya. He sat down in the seat next to Den-El.

"Little slow, aren't they?" Den-El frowned. "I would have guarded that entrance much better, long before any war."

Surya shook his head. "There is no difference there than any other part of the island. All of Poseidia should be patrolled, since anyone can enter here at any time."

"I doubt they have ever done a great job at that." Den-El wrinkled his nose and kept on driving. Out of the corner of his eye, he spotted a red flashing light on top of a boat that had sped along side of his. The driver of the craft seemed intent on keeping pace. "Look." He pointed.

Surya stood up and walked behind Den-El to the opposite side of the boat. He gazed at the craft for a few seconds, ending by waving both hands to the occupants. "Cut the engine, Den-El."

"What are you doing?" Den-El's voice reached a high pitch.

"Your Highness," said Kavi. He motioned for his driver to steer the craft closer to Surya's. "We invite you to come aboard."

"I'll come aboard." Surya looked at Den-El. "Do we have a walkway we can lower onto their boat?"

"I don't know."

In seconds, Kavi's boat let down a walkway that allowed Surya to disembark and make his way over.

"Question answered." Den-El sat back in his chair and watched. Martaam stepped into the cockpit and sat in the spare seat.

Surya stepped onto the military boat and shook Kavi's hand.

"Out sinking Aryan ships, I see." Kavi chuckled.

"You saw that?"

"Every bit. We were on the opposite side ready to fire at them, but you beat us to it."

"Looks like you've got troops coming into the rings now."

"We started the moment Aryan fired the first shots. It's bitter fighting out there, and we can't get all of them like they can't get all of us." Kavi turned around briefly, eyeing the water.

"Can you tell me anything about Dhamon and Tunda? I've been wanting to know what everyone is doing, but everything happened so fast."

"Both men have their troops divided. We're crawling all over Aryan and Poseidia. The remaining smaller isles of Og, Atalya, and Eyre, not so much."

"Is there anything I can do?" Surya asked.

"Your Highness, I really think it would be best for you to be careful. Someone such as yourself getting hurt or killed could really be a problem for us." Kavi looked over at Surya's boat. "I also checked the license for that craft. It doesn't belong to you. Are you borrowing it from the company that owns it?"

"Sir, my friend over there knows the men. They kindly offered us their boat so we could work in the healing centers. We've been busy since yesterday morning. Just finished in time to sink an Aryan ship." Surya grinned.

Kavi laughed. "Good answer, Your Highness." He extended his hand for one last handshake.

Surya returned the gesture and walked back to Den-El and Martaam. Kavi's boat roared off down the waterway.

"Take us back home, Den-El. I think we're entitled to some food and rest."

"Aye, Captain." Den-El saluted his prince and turned the boat back toward Vardhase.

Surya led a green-faced Martaam to her apartment, tucking her into bed and kissing her before leaving.

Aleemirin and Tujuk were nowhere in sight. A note on the table stated they had gone to the healing temples.

***

After a few hours of sleep, Surya slipped out into the living room and turned on the AudioView. Khandoor and Rhaneen showed on the screen.

"Thank you for joining us under such precarious conditions."

"I'm thankful I can do so, Khandoor."

"I'll get right to the point. Any reason your military decided to strike Poseidia? And for what reason?"

"We're tired of being attacked and accused by Law of One for not treating the firestone crystal according to their ridiculous standards."

Khandoor squinted his eyes slightly. "Ridiculous standards? You mean to say Aryans have no regard for nature and don't care if they . . . oh, I'll just say it . . . blow up or destroy the main power source that is the life blood of this island and the others."

"No, I'm not saying that. What I'm saying is that there is a lot of finger-pointing by Law of One. Look, power usage varies. Some days or months are heavier than others. It's not uncommon or unreasonable to tune up or tune down so we serve the citizens."

"Sounds good on the surface. But I'm not buying it because Law of One has always kept a steady and stable pace when working with the firestone."

"Oh, please, Khandoor. Anyone with half a brain would know full well that nothing is static. There are fluctuations in nature, in man. You name it."

"While I appreciate your attempt to smooth things over, I find it interesting that there is now a discovered correlation between tuning up our firestone and business growth on Aryan. How do you explain that?"

Rhaneen chuckled. "Of course there's new growth. But that's always been the case on Aryan. Not as much or very little on Poseidia. Maybe you people should look to us as an example."

Khandoor frowned. "You're skirting the issue. Please answer my question. Is Aryan not increasing business and growth at a much higher rate now that Sons of Belial help care for the firestone?"

"Not at the rate that Law of One should be so fidgety and disturbed."

The screen flickered, and the side showing Rhaneen went black. His microphone and picture came back on within seconds.

"Looks like there is some difficulty on your end?" said Khandoor.

"I may lose you. I'll keep on as long as I can." Rhaneen looked a little ashen but smiled anyway.

Surya sat up, watching intently. That technical glitch only meant one thing. Dhamon and Tunda were doing a number on Aryan.

Khandoor continued his interview. "Will Sons of Belial end this war quickly?"

Rhaneen laughed. "Until Law of One . . ."

A blast bled through the sound and Rhaneen's screen went blank for good.

"It looks like we've lost connection. While we lament any loss of life on Aryan, we also lament loss of life on Poseidia. We welcome any dialogue to end this war before we're all destroyed and Atlantis is lost for good. More when we come back."

Surya turned off the AudioView. The apartment shook so hard he toppled onto the sofa with a thud. A statue in one corner fell to the floor, shattering in pieces. Den-El's bedroom door opened. Da-Ina barked until Den-El met Surya in the living room.

"That was too close," he said, catching his breath.

Both men ran to the door and flung it open. To their dismay, the newly repaired apartments, including the ones beside it had collapsed. Their wing was barely missed.

Den-El bolted for the front of Vardhase, Da-Ina taking off after him. Surya followed suit. Homes across the street had been hit dead on, and the reverberation affected parts of Vardhase. Surya looked toward the main office. He ran at break-neck speed, calling Martaam's name.

She opened the front door just as Surya arrived. "It's starting again." Tears welled up in her eyes. "I'm so scared. Everything my family has worked for is falling apart. I've lost friends, classmates, teachers. I don't think I have a future anymore. It wasn't supposed to be this way." She sat on the steps and wept.

Surya said nothing but held her close and let her cry. Den-El and Da-Ina trotted up. Da-Ina licked Martaam's cheek. Den-El prayed in silence.

Later that night, Aryan fighters bore down on Poseidia, firing off more bombs. In the street enemy military attacked anything and everything walking, many times bursting through homes and shooting the people inside with their horrific crystal ray guns.

Cries echoed in the streets again. Blood lined the walkways. Taking up the call of duty, Martaam, Surya, Den-El, and Da-Ina traveled the dangerous waterway to reach the healing temples. Poseidian troops did their best to protect, but it always seemed Aryan was one step ahead.

***

Khaluj lay in a hospital bed, bandaged on the right side. His beloved condo had seen its last when Poseidian military dropped their ammunition in a raining torrent over the city. With burns and a broken arm, he managed to get out, only to be bitten by two venomous serpents slithering through the streets.

He cursed the Poseidian army. They would resort to low down dirty tricks, using poor animals to do their nasty work. Fighting his way through smoke and soot hindered him more.

He'd arrived at the nearest care center, bruised, aching all over, and swollen. Trying to communicate with the staff in his broken ignominious way had been the final straw.

"So here we are," said Rhaneen, looking over at his former leader. Once he learned that his friend had been injured and had reached the facility, he insisted they share a room.

Khaluj shook his head and fell back on the pillows.

"Hey," said Rhaneen, "I just want you to know we've had a good run, you and I."

Khaluj popped his head back up and scowled at his friend. His face twisted into a look of one asking a question.

"My best friend, my pal, my confidante, just know that I've always loved you and had the greatest respect for your sharp wit and cunning mind." Rhaneen took another swallow of the alcoholic beverage in his glass. At this point in time, nothing was refused to anyone who wanted anything, especially leaders.

Khaluj sighed with exasperation but ended up chuckling silently. He nodded in Rhaneen's direction.

"I honestly don't know if we'll get out of here alive, but I wanted to tell you. If those are the last words you hear, they will be mine. Just know that they are sincere and from the depths of my heart."

A rumbling sound filled the room, shaking the walls into a series of cracks. The shaking beneath the men didn't feel like ammunition had been dropped.

Rhaneen reached out and grabbed Khaluj's hand. "Good night, my friend. We'll see each other in another life."

***

The same shaking that jolted the Aryan leaders also shook Poseidia. The Temple of Poseidon came crashing down, sending crowds into a scattering screaming frenzy. Inside Martaam's healing school, screams rang out as the building wobbled. Others shouted news that the ocean waters were cracking through the ground on the land core.

Huddled in Martaam's office, Surya and Den-El had paused healing treatments until the confusion subsided.

Den-El shivered in fear. Da-Ina crept to his side, tail tucked between her legs. "I'm not getting a good feeling about this," said Den-El.

"I'm not, either." Surya's mouth went dry. "We need to do something."

"I'm all ears. No pun intended." Den-El stared wide-eyed at his friend.

"Grab stones we use for an invocation," said Surya.

Den-El did as instructed. Surya set up the different stones in a circle large enough to contain him and his friend.

"Time to call home." Surya held both of Den-El's hands in his and both traversed the quantum pathways that reached far distances in the universe.

***

Mal-Ek and Ahtan-Mir sat staring at each other from across a table in the royal observatory.

"Let's go," said Mal-Ek.

***

Surya and Den-El managed to heal several more people before the dreadful thundering sound occurred again.

"That's it. We must try and stop this. Appeal to the cosmos, the Creator, something," said Surya.

He grabbed Den-El and pulled him out of the room. Den-El followed his friend outside the building and into the courtyard. The air smelled of burning earth. In the distance he glimpsed the higher volcanos spewing out their anger in the form of molten lava. From what could be seen, flooding had hit the land rings. Most likely it had set in on other parts of the island too.

"Are you two okay?" Aleemirin came up behind Surya and Den-El. Tujuk stood beside his lover. Fear had set in the man's eyes.

Surya whirled around, grasping each man's hand. "You two need to get off the island. There's not much time. Do it now."

Both priests stared at Surya, speechless.

"And how do you suppose we do that?" said Tujuk.

Surya thought a moment. He was interrupted by a frantic creature pushing its way between himself and Tujuk. A mutant leapt straight for Den-El and grabbed his hand. In a sign of urgency, he shook his head, pointing to his own throat.

At once, Surya remembered his visions the day he ordered silence for Khaluj and the mutants inside the Temple of Jhanana. He uttered the sacred words, undoing the silence inflicted on the scared creature in front of him.

"Good, Sir. King of Things. Do you remember me?" Baldorn blurted out the words. Relief flooded his face.

Den-El threw his arms around Baldorn and kissed his cheek. "You've escaped." He smiled at his fellow creature.

"I got lucky. I want to save the others, but everyone has left. We were turned out of our cages. The servants had that one compassion."

The idea hit Surya full force. "How about you and the priests leave this island immediately. Go to Oz the land of the dark-skinned, or to Portugal. Just get off Poseidia."

"I'll gladly do all I can," answered Baldorn to Surya.

Surya turned to Aleemirin and Tujuk. Khaluj has an Ultra Marine Pod parked on the far side of the island near the portal. It's well hidden and I'm sure no one has found it. Get in and get out of here."

Den-El turned to Baldorn. "You're a good being. I want you saved too. Would you go with these nice priests and help save yourself and them? I'll give you the same powers I have."

Baldorn stepped back, hand clutched at his heart. "You'd do that for me?"

"I most certainly will if it means preserving a higher good, and you and my friends here are a higher good." Den-El smiled. He looked over at Surya.

With Baldorn between them, both Surya and Den-El placed their hands on the mutant and bowed their heads. Aleemirin and Tujuk watched in awe as a transformation occurred. A white light surrounded the Thing, and he morphed into a creature similar to Den-El. The priests delighted in seeing the indigo and white auras surround the top of Baldorn's head.

"You're ready. Go in peace and safety," said Den-El. He handed Aleemirin the keys to the boat. "Take these. Go to dock number 144. You can take the craft to the Ultra Marine Pod. Baldorn can help figure everything out. If you can reach Kavi, tell him to inform his ships so you don't get mistaken for the enemy."

Aleemirin and Tujuk hugged Surya.

"We love you like a son," said Aleemirin. Tujuk nodded, wiping away a tear.

"You two are the best of what humans should be." Surya smiled. "Now go."

Baldorn and the priests rushed off toward the dock.

"We have to get Martaam out of there," said Surya pointing toward the building.

"And just where do you propose we go?" said Den-El. He glared at the prince.

"I honestly don't know."

Both Surya and Den-El nearly fell over. Another round of shaking gripped the land core. Sounds of cracking and explosions ricocheted in the distance.

"Poseidia is breaking up." Surya barely heard his own words.

Den-El stood rooted in place. Da-Ina did nothing but tremble and whimper.

The sky grew dark. Smoke grew stronger. A sharp chill seared the air. People ran, coughing and shielding their faces. In fear they shouted for their friends and family. Husbands for their wives. Brothers for their sisters. Friends for each other.

Another quake and the ground tore open in multiple places, water from the Atlantic seeped over the land core. Martaam's building would be swallowed up. Fear grabbed Surya. He took a deep breath and bolted toward the healing school.

"Wait," Den-El screamed, grabbing for Surya. "We need to try and stop this."

Surya halted in his tracks. He looked up heavenward and closed his eyes, uttering every mantra with all the sincerity he could muster. The guardians of Earth had closed their ears. The spirits on high stood with a finger to their mouths. They would not listen.

Frantic, Surya gave up. Just as ran, water rushed in, splitting him off from the school. There was no way to reach the building without drowning in the sea. Den-El chased after him, meeting him at the edge. He gasped, pulling himself and Surya back.

Another quake came, splitting Poseidia apart. The tsunami effect didn't play favorites among the islands. One was as doomed as the other. The smaller isles of Og, Atalya, and Eyre had already sunk. Aryan was ripped apart the same time as her sister. Rhaneen and Khaluj held each other as water came pouring into their room, swallowing them up like a greedy, hungry monster.

Baldorn and the priests had dodged cracks in the land until they reached the dock. They fought their way through nasty currents that threatened to sink their boat. Between them, their prayers and powers were sufficient enough to get them to the Ultra Marine Pod and out to sea. The ride was already a rocky one at best.

In fright and anger, Surya stood and defied the gods, shouting his indignation and anger. He held up his hands in retaliation and shot out the strongest bolts of lightning he'd ever set off. The cosmos rebuffed. The streaks returned, hitting the ground with full impact. The earth crumbled into more pieces.

"Stop," screamed Den-El. "You'll get us all killed."

"I have to save her," cried Surya. "I love her with all my heart."

"Maybe she was never yours to begin with. You interfered when you weren't supposed to."

"And you helped." Surya yelled back. He ignored Den-El's protests and prepared to jump into the water.

Den-El's screams were silenced. Surya never made it to Martaam.

Two blinding lights shone from above. Two tractor beams. One for Den-El. One for Surya.

Chapter Twenty Two

Surya opened his eyes. The energy he felt was different, yet it was familiar. He wasn't where he'd awakened recently. He instinctively knew this. His father gazed down at him.

"Welcome home, son," said Mal-Ek.

Surya's heart pounded. But why? He was home, where he belonged. Or was home . . .?

"You're okay." Mal-Ek rested his hand on Surya's chest. "We got you out just in time." He smiled. "And I'm so glad you're back. I've missed you so much. There wasn't a day that I didn't spend all my free time watching you, wishing you only the best."

Surya swallowed hard. The memories flooded back in snatches of images. People, voices, places. Most were good. Some were not as pleasant. Some were beautiful. Others terrifying. "I'm in big trouble, aren't I?"

Mal-Ek squeezed his son's hand. "You will have to explain yourself to the Galactic Federation of Planets. They know you're here, and they've set up a time for a council meeting."

"They will be so angry. I just know it," said Surya. A certain sadness spilled over him.

"Stop," said Mal-Ek. "You'll send yourself into a bad place. You're back on Ontarus 9, fourth dimension. Emotions rule and realities change as a result."

"I really didn't mean to hurt anyone." Surya looked up at his father. He'd almost forgotten how handsome and strong he was.

"We know that. It was the Federation's command that we save you and Den-El."

"Is he okay? He's my best friend." Surya tried sitting up, but Mal-Ek gently pushed him back down on the bed.

"We had to take some extra steps in getting him back to his same physical form before we left. Our genetic creators are outstanding, but an Arcturian specialist helped." Mal-Ek smiled. "They are truly the best when it comes to delicate situations like this."

Surya looked at his arm. It had the same look as before he left Ontarus 9.

"Shall I let you see yourself?" Mal-Ek asked smiling. He handed his son a reflection device.

Hesitant, Surya took it from his father and stared into the screen. An image of his face lit up. It looked like the human form Den-El had made for him.

"We all were so impressed with the work that we decided you should keep it, but more reasons on that later." He took the device from Surya's hands. "Are you happy about it?"

"I don't see a problem with it. I was getting used to it, honestly." Surya smiled. "But wasn't I okay enough the first time?"

"My son," said Mal-Ek, stroking his son's cheek, "you were always a handsome one. You're more so in this form. It's still you."

"When is the council meeting? Is there a way to prepare for it?" Surya reached for his father's hand.

Mal-Ek considered his son. "They said to only be your full self."

***

The Galactic Federation of Planets congregated in a special meeting room in the X49 galaxy of the Virgo constellation. The centrally located area suited all ambassadors.

Surya sat next to Den-El. "Good to see your old self."

"You can't even begin to imagine how happy I am. I'm just glad they recreated my former body."

"Apparently they loved the one you made for me. They insisted I keep it."

"I'm good. How much do I have to keep telling you that?" Den-El chuckled softly, delivering a light punch on Surya's arm.

Mal-Ek and Ahtan-Mir sat together in seats placed to the right of the head council command station. The Pleiadean, King Mahataan, would be presiding over this meeting, since Lyra fell under the Pleiadean Star Council.

"Are you nervous?" asked Den-El.

"I'd be lying if I said I wasn't. I wonder if we couldn't be executed or exiled for this." Surya turned his gaze on the council members.

Sirians, Orians, Andromedans, Lyrans, Pleiadeans, Cassiopeians, and Arcturians were a few of the members representing the full council. This would be the first time he'd seen so many races from different planets and constellations this close.

When every member found a seat, the court announcer called out, "All rise. Hail to King Mahataan."

"Hail to the King." Everyone spoke in unison, including Surya and Den-El.

King Mahataan stepped up to his station and addressed the court. "Greetings all ambassadors who have joined us today. Greetings to the ones who sit in judgement. We gather to address a situation that was brought to our attention the moment it occurred. While we wish to honor the rules and directives that have been established, we also wish to consider what is presented today.

"May we open our hearts and raise our vibration for the higher and greater good and for the benefit of all in the universe. May we continue our path of enlightenment. May all decisions enhance the light work we continually seek to maintain.

"We have before us this day two entities who decided to visit the planet we call Earth, specifically to explore Atlantis, or the remaining islands, to be more correct. As we all know, this was in direct violation of the Earth Directive. When one of the esteemed rulers of Ontarus 9 notified us of what happened, we suggested he merely observe and report back to us."

King Mahataan, looked directly and Surya and Den-El. "We have been appraised of all your activities on Atlantis and all behavior. It was also our decision to bring you back to your rightful star system. We will be offering questions. It is our sincere hope that you will answer them honestly and from the heart so that we may better decide on the most appropriate outcome."

The king sat down, and the court announcer spoke. "As is our custom, we will allow questions from each ambassador who wishes to ask one. The ambassador will press a button on their panel. This system orders the question based on when the button was pushed, allowing everyone a chance to speak.

"The king will always be allowed to ask questions or clarify as needed, after an ambassador has spoken and their question answered. Ambassadors may take notes for their own reference." He looked around the room. "Let the questions commence." A bell chimed.

Surya sat up straight. Inside his chest, he thought his heart would explode. He glanced quickly at Den-El, who also seemed tense. The gravity of what he and his friend had done weighed down on him. What was worse, perishing in the sea when Atlantis went down for the last time or face every galactic creature in this room?

"Can you tell us why you chose to visit Atlantis? I'd like to hear from both," said the Sirian ambassador.

King Mahataan sat erect on his chair and stared down at the two young men before him. A light smile played across his lips. Surya didn't let that fool him. Not that the king would be unkind, but no matter how benevolent everyone seemed, the outcome could be negative for him and Den-El.

Surya answered, "I found human emotions and behaviors interesting. I'd been watching them for a while before I made the decision to go down there. The pull on me was difficult to overcome. The only way I could remedy the curiosity was to go down and see it for myself.

"But it was more than casual interest. When my father told me about why humans were left alone on Earth, I rebelled against it. I still firmly believe that if you have created sentient beings in our likeness, it is irresponsible to turn your backs on them. They need us more than ever."

Surya looked at Den-El.

Den-El gathered up his courage and spoke. "I can attest to that. Though I disagreed with his sentiment toward humans, he talked non-stop about them. I finally thought it would be best to let him pursue his desire and put the matter to rest."

The Orian ambassador spoke. "Were you aware that it was forbidden to meddle in affairs of any kind related to Earth, especially if you were not assigned to do so?"

Surya answered, "I suspected there must have been some reason the Infinite Hall of Records had locked out certain information, but I couldn't ascertain much because of the lock-out."

"I told him that the information was forbidden," said Den-El, "but neither of us fully understood how powerful the Earth Directive was."

King Mahataan raised his hand. "Did you ever discuss any of this with your father? I would imagine he would have been more than happy to enlighten you on the history of what transpired."

Surya's cheeks flushed red. "We discussed the history briefly. I didn't wish to pursue the subject more as he had other business. He didn't need to be bothered."

"Your Majesty, is this true?" King Mahataan looked at Mal-Ek.

Mal-Ek answered, "I must be honest with the Council. I also told my son that Earth was a forbidden place. I also asked for certain information to be locked down. Perhaps it was a foolish decision, but I loved my son. I didn't wish for him to pursue the subject any longer.

"I had been aware of his watching Atlantis through our lens in the observatory. I hoped that our conversations about it was enough. Clearly I erred in this appraisal."

The king considered Mal-Ek's answer. "It's understandable that we wish to protect those we love. Unfortunately, lack of conversation only drove your son's desire more. Alas, we learn, don't we?" When he smiled, the Council members did the same.

The court announcer continued. "Who will ask the next question?"

A voice belonging to the Andromedan ambassador filled the room. "I wish to ask this question to Your Highness's friend. You killed humans during your time on Poseidia. What you did to the priestess was abominable. You understand how we feel about taking such actions. Why did you resort to such barbaric behavior?"

Den-El licked his lips and took a deep breath. Surya reached out and placed his hand on Den-El's for support.

"Honorable Council, I am aware that such actions are frowned upon, but please be reminded that I was not only part human, but part animal. I felt emotions of humans and animals. Fear, excitement. Even lust." Den-El's face colored.

"I only ridded myself of those men for self-preservation. I had already been enslaved as the lowliest foul creature on the islands. There were countless others like me. I would have done anything to save myself. And I did.

"The priestess took part in a project focused on creating a slave force using helpless, defenseless creatures. That was most abominable in my mind, having the body of those beings myself and being horribly treated. It was by the good grace and ability of my prince that I was able to enjoy most of my power.

"Her experience will always leave a mark on her soul, and it is my sincere hope that in future lives, she will regard those less powerful with more compassion.

"Though I made grim choices, I understand how humans and animals feel when threatened. You have been in that frightful place yourself. You have defended yourself. I claim that right as my own and hope judgement of me is not so harsh."

The Arcturian ambassador asked, "I also ask this question to the friend. You also showed extraordinary healing abilities that were quite noble, given your condition. This exemplifies caring. It was clear to us that you were not fond of humans at the outset. It's not clear to us that those sentiments have changed. Can you please tell us more about that?"

Den-El shifted in his seat. "Honorable Council, it is true that my zeal for humans doesn't match that of my prince. Humans can be despicable, conniving, liars, and untrustworthy. There were many others who meant well. They tried to do what was right, and uplifted their fellow beings with healing powers similar to ours.

"When I saw humans hurt, damaged, sick at heart, it sent up an emotion of great pity in me. They hurt, they rejoice, they feel. They have dreams and desires such as we do. To heal and make them feel better filled me with a sense of satisfaction and accomplishment."

The Lyran ambassador nodded when it was her turn to speak. "Greetings fellow Lyrans. It is an honor to speak to ones of your rank. Your Highness, you also exhibited extraordinary healing powers. You showed a willingness to lead and to make decisions.

"You stepped up and took action when necessary. You experienced full emotions of love, hate, and physical desire. Can you tell us more about that?"

Surya nodded, smiling lightly. "When I made the decision to visit Atlantis, I promised myself I would not discriminate when situations arose. I took the bitter with the sweet. How else would I have learned and gained information? I too killed in the name of self-defense and mostly for the protection of others. Evil forces needed containing and to be stopped.

"Otherwise, I chose alternative measures to achieve a desired outcome. Both Den-El and I never lost sight of our connection with spirit and called upon those powers when needed.

"You asked about love and desire. It is the most intoxicating emotion. It's powerful and consumes every thought, every action. To save one I truly loved was something I would have died for."

The ambassador from Cassiopeia spoke. "Are humans worth our time? Did we fail in our experiment? Should we abolish it with harsher means? Your Highness, I want to hear your answer, please."

Surya looked directly at the ambassador. "Humans are very much worth our time. Please remember that they carry our DNA. Would you abolish us? Granted, some peculiar traits have been bred into this race, and I'm not sure how that happened. But even with the evil ones, they also held a certain connection with spirit. They had many similar powers if they chose to use them.

"They are willing to learn. They have great capacity for overcoming evil. It is my thought that if you concentrate on those bred for the light, they will do great things."

King Mahataan raised his hand. "You broke a directive, Your Highness. Do you think you're fit to rule when your father's time comes to an end?"

Den-El shot a glance at Surya and focused his gaze back on the floor.

"Your Majesty, I broke a directive not knowing full information, so I did the best I could. In retrospect, it would have been wise to consult with those in greater power. However, I strongly believe there are times we must go veiled into the unknown, to experience and gain knowledge from that we seek.

"I also considered my place in the hierarchy of the rulers of Poseidia and Aryan. Since I was not on an official mission, I gave my input only as mere suggestions. It was up to the rulers of those lands to accept or reject. They did not take all of my advice.

"May I add that they long for us to return. They long for our guidance and support. They know they have lost their way, and they want to rectify that and be part of us, taking their rightful place with us.

"We should heed their call and consider their request. For all I did on Atlantis, I believe I'm quite fit to rule."

The Pleiadian King turned his focus on Den-El. "Would you serve under this prince if he were to rule as king? Is he fit to take his father's place when the time comes?"

Den-El sat straight up. "I'd die a thousand deaths for my prince, my king. He is a worthy leader and ruler. He has compassion for all. He does not accept evil. He uses only the right amount of force necessary.

"He gained the respect of those in a strange land. They included him in their meetings. They showed him the ways of their military. They treated him mostly like an equal. He didn't abuse his power, human or Lyran. Though I detested my physical form on Earth, it was a privilege standing alongside my future ruler."

"Would you choose the son of your father's advisor as yours? King Mahataan directed the question at Surya.

"I would have no other person serve beside me. Den-El is powerful, brilliant, loyal. We have our disagreements, but we move through them. Never at any time do I fear he'll fail me. We take care of each other. Going to Atlantis was an unforgettable experience, and I had my best friend—and future advisor—by my side."

"Your Majesty," said the court announcer, "There are no more questions."

King Mahataan said, "Let us break for deliberation. We will meet back here to discuss the outcome of this meeting."

Surya and Den-El watched as the ambassadors left their seats. All had taken notes with zeal. King Mahataan stepped out from his station and whispered to Mal-Ek and Ahtan-Mir, who smiled and nodded. They got up from their seats and followed the king to another room.

"Gentlemen," said the court announcer, "you may follow me. We have food and drink this way." He escorted Surya and Den-El to another room. "I will inform you when the meeting starts again."

"Did you mean everything you said?" asked Den-El.

"I meant every word of it. When I first reached Atlantis, I thought of you all the time. We shared an adventure, didn't we?"

"I would have liked to have worn your human skin," said Den-El. "But who am I kidding? I'm so relieved to be home."

"Did we learn anything?" Surya looked at his friend.

"We learned more going down there than we ever would have learned from records and books. Humans are an evolving race. They still have far to go."

Two hours passed before the court announcer returned. "The meeting has started. I'll escort you to your seats."

Surya and Den-El returned to the meeting room and sat down. An onslaught of nerves hit Surya, and he struggled to keep his emotions in check. Den-El grasped his hand and squeezed.

Den-El whispered, "We're in this together."

The court announcer's voice rang out, "The Council Meeting for the Galactic Federation will commence. All rise. Hail to King Mahataan."

"Hail to the King." Everyone stood and spoke.

"Greetings to all once again. We have heard the testimonies from these two gentlemen. Compelling information, I might add. We now have Council consensus on the issue of breaking the Earth Directive.

"I will share the report. We the Galactic Federation of Planets find great interest in the testimony provided by our young Lyran colleagues. While it is not our intent to scold the ruler of these men, we acknowledge that more intense dialogue would have spared us much concern.

"Their information has proved valuable. It is our thought that the Earth Directive needs more attention and consideration. Instead of leaving humans to their own demise, it is our wish to stand with them and offer guidance and support in measured increments as they slowly awaken to their own divinity and connection to spirit.

"We have selected the year 2012 A.D. as the date when the Earth Directive will be rescinded in full, and planetary emissaries will meet with people of Earth as their calls reach our ears. Though our presence will be discreet at first, we will eventually show ourselves to humans fully uncloaked."

Surya and Den-El stared at each other, wide-eyed.

King Mahataan continued, "Your Highness showed true strength of character and judgment in a foreign land, on a foreign planet. We the Council have deemed it appropriate for Your Highness to take his rightful place as ruler when his father's time has ended. It is also our strong recommendation that he choose his closest ally and friend, the one who stood by him on Atlantis, to serve as top advisor.

"We the Council believe that this will ensure strong continuity in leadership and rule of their country. This decision is rendered with great care, with love and light, and for the highest and greatest good of all the universe. So speaks the Council."

The King put the paper down and gazed at Surya and Den-El. "Gentlemen, the Council has spoken. I surely have no objections of my own, nor do I choose to override anything recommended by our esteemed members.

"There is, however, some remaining business I wish to discuss while all are present." The King looked squarely at Surya. "You said you would die for the human lady who won your heart. Does that still stand?"

"Yes, Your Majesty," said Surya. "She's imprinted upon my soul. I gave up and risked everything to find her. My only regret is that I could not save her when the islands sank." Surya blinked back tears. He cleared his throat and repositioned himself in his chair.

"We don't normally do this, because it goes against laws of reincarnation. We obtained permission from the guardians of souls on high. Your Highness, we have saved your chosen one.

"Her soul has been placed in a new fourth dimension form that looks like the physical one she had on Atlantis. This is also the reason you have a fourth-dimension likeness of the physical form created by your friend.

"We believed taking these steps would maintain continuity of a memory and relationship that was started. It will ensure the beginning of a new Lyran-Human hybrid race."

Surya wrinkled his brow. Den-El looked at his friend, confused.

"You see, Your Highness," said King Mahataan, "the entity last known as Martaam carries your child. We preserved both souls."

The room erupted in a hum of murmurs. Many entered notes into their information devices. Den-El laughed and slapped Surya on the back. Mal-Ek and Ahtan-Mir sat looking on with sober looks on their faces.

"Would you like to see her?" asked King Mahataan.

Surya tried standing but fell back down in his chair. "I would love nothing better, Your Majesty. She's a fine human."

"Of course. Your Highness would pick nothing other than the finest." King Mahataan gave the signal and the court announcer led in Martaam.

She looked as stunning as ever. Being fourth dimension heightened her vibration so that an an etherial light surrounded her. Martaam smiled and fell into Surya's arms.

"You remember?" he asked her.

"I remember. They preserved everything so there is no time loss. Another kind concession they made for me. And you. Us." She smiled.

"Den-El," said King Mahataan, "we know you understand the power of lust and engaged in the human way. We also understand that human females are not your choice, and that you prefer one of your own race and dimension. However, you did love while you were on Poseidia.

"We would like for you to have a personal reminder of Earth." King Mahataan paused and chuckled. The ambassadors sat smiling, but Surya noticed the look of expectancy in their eyes.

The court announcer smiled and opened a door to one of the rooms. Out bounded Da-Ina, barking and running straight to Den-El.

Everyone in the room laughed. A round of clapping ensued for several seconds. When Da-Ina broke away and checked out the group, many patted her on the head.

"We also would like to inform our young gentlemen that the two priests and the mutant made it safely to Portugal. They will always remember the kindness you showed them. Their lives and future lives will be better for having known the two of you.

"I think this covers it," said King Mahataan. "Our meeting is adjourned. May all your travels home and elsewhere be filled with light, life, and love." A bell chimed, and the king stepped out from his station.

***

Back on Ontarus 9, Surya sat a table with Martaam and Den-El, enjoying the sun. Da-Ina sat dozing by Den-El's feet.

"I'm glad we're all here together. But part of me misses Poseidia. Just a little." Surya sighed and sipped a hot tea from his cup.

"Atlantis went through a lot. Hopefully not all is lost," said Martaam. "Earthly things may decay and perish, but wisdom endures for eons."

"In its utopian days, Atlantis was like no other," said Den-El. "But everything is a cycle and returns back to us. I don't think that world is totally lost forever."

Surya grinned and squeezed Martaam's hand. "From what I hear, Atlantis will rise again."

END

Acknowledgements:

I'd like to extend warm thanks of appreciation to those who helped me with this book: My spouse for beta reading; Jay Aheer for creating an amazing cover and allowing readers to enjoy her artistic talent. My proofreader, Monica-Marie Vincent, who has hawk eyes and helped improve this manuscript significantly. I also want to extend a special thank you to Jeff Radcliff whose humor kept me laughing. His expertise as a metaphysical minister placed him in a unique position to beta read and critique this book.

About the Author:

Scarlet Darkwood wields a mighty pen, or at the very least, delivers mighty punches to the computer keys when she's typing furiously on a story. She likes dark and twisted, and the weirder, the better.

Always preferring Avant Garde themes, her stories take the reader on unusual adventures, exploring the darker parts of the human psyche as she whips out cunning prose wrapped in provocative themes. Sometimes she veers from her beaten path and takes a happy-go-lucky romp in the brighter sides of life, kicking up her style into sharp, snappy dialogue and clever descriptions.

Writing in several genres unleashes her imagination so she never grows bored. From a young age, she's enjoyed writing and keeping diaries, but didn't start creating novels until 2012. She's a Southern girl who lives in Tennessee and enjoys the beauty of the mountains. She lives in Nashville with her spouse and two rambunctious kitties.

For more information about the latest concerning Scarlet and her work, you can do the following:

Visit her BLOG at: www.scarletdarkwood.com

Follow her on Google+ at:
http://google.com/+ScarletDarkwood

Follow her on Twitter at: http://twitter.com/ScarletDarkwood

Follow her on Facebook:
http://www.facebook.com/scarletdarkwoodauthor

Check out Scarlet's other works:
Romance:
Escape from Purgatory
Words We Never Speak

Crime:
Death by Design

Erotic Romance:
Pleasure House
Dance of Desire
Taming Bad
Master of The House
Mistress of The House

Short Stories:
Hard Way In
Fun with Dick and Peter
Naughty and Nice
Tech Support
An Enchanting Hideaway
Three Card Spread
Castus Vindicta
Sweet Secrets